REG
Desire

Margaret McPhee

First Published in Great Britain 2016
By Mills & Boon, an imprint of HarperCollins*Publishers*
1 London Bridge Street, London, SE1 9GF

REGENCY DESIRE © 2016 Harlequin Books S.A.

Mistress to the Marquis © 2013 Margaret McPhee
Dicing with the Dangerous Lord © 2013 Margaret McPhee

ISBN: 978-0-263-92375-9

52-1216

Our policy is to use papers that are natural, renewable and recyclable products and made from wood grown in sustainable forests. The logging and manufacturing processes conform to the legal environmental regulations of the country of origin.

Printed and bound by
CPI Group (UK) Ltd, Croydon, CR0 4YY

A REGENCY

Collection

Mistress to the Marquis

Margaret McPhee loves to use her imagination—an essential requirement for a scientist. However, when she realised that her imagination was inspired more by the historical romances she loves to read rather than by her experiments, she decided to put the stories down on paper. She has since left her scientific life behind and enjoys cycling in the Scottish countryside, tea and cakes.

Chapter One

London, England—April 1811

'Razeby, you surprise me! I wasn't expecting you until later.' *Much, much later.* Miss Alice Sweetly's fingers were flustered as she shoved the sheet of paper she had been writing upon into the drawer and rammed it shut, but her sudden anxiety had nothing to do with not being ready for her protector. Within seconds she was on her feet and hurrying towards the Marquis of Razeby to distract his interest from the desk. 'You've caught me unawares.'

'Forgive me, Alice. I did not mean to startle you when you were so absorbed.' Razeby said in his rich, aristocratic voice.

'Hardly absorbed. I was just writing a letter to a friend.' In her nervousness her natural soft Irish lilt grew stronger than ever and she felt her face burn with traitorous colour at the lie.

'Lucky friend.' Razeby smiled with his usual good nature.

She tensed in case he meant to quiz her on the fictitious letter and friend. But, true to form, Razeby trusted her and did no such thing. He did not even glance over at the little bureau.

'Finish your letter. I will fetch myself a brandy while I wait.'

'I'll do no such thing.' Embarrassment rippled through her, making her face grow hotter just at the thought of sitting back down at the desk with him watching. With a glance down at her shabby moth-nibbled woollen shawl and the morning dress beneath it, with its old-fashioned style, the pretty muslin faded and worn, she changed the subject. 'Look at the state of me! I'm only wearing this old thing to keep my fine clothes good.' It was a habit she found hard to break, having grown up with nothing. 'And I've a lovely silk ready to wear tonight. I best get up the stairs and change into something decent.' She made to pass him.

But Razeby swept an arm around her waist, stilling her panic and pulling her against him. 'Relax, Alice. You look beautiful just as you are. As ever.' His eyes, deep brown and true, met hers as he stroked an escaped strand of hair away from her cheek. 'And have I not told you, it is not the clothes that are important, but the woman beneath?'

'Flatterer,' she accused, but she smiled and his tall, masculine body in such proximity sent waves of attraction and excitement crashing through her.

'It is the truth as well you know it.' Razeby could charm the birds down from the trees. He was still smiling as he pulled her closer. 'But if you have a wish for a new wardrobe, then you shall have one.'

'I've no wish for a new wardrobe. I've enough dresses up those stairs to clothe half the women in London!'

'I like buying you things—it makes you happy.' He gathered her right hand in his left. 'And I want you to be happy, Alice.'

Alice tried to curl her fingers to hide the black ink-stains that marred her fingers, but Razeby did not let her. He slid his thumb to rub against the marks on her skin.

'Mmm...' His eyes lingered over the inkstains before moving teasingly to hers. 'I do believe a new pen is a requirement.'

'No.' She laughed, but her face flamed anew at the mention of writing and of the precious silver pen that was so dear to her. 'I don't want another pen. I like the one I've got just fine.'

'I am very glad of that,' Razeby murmured huskily and pressed her inkstained fingers to the warmth of his lips.

'You know I'm happy. Very happy...' She paused before adding softly, 'And not because of the things you buy for me.' It was the truth.

He smiled a strange, almost poignant, smile, stroked his fingers against her cheek and stared into her eyes.

And it did not matter that she had been his mistress for six months, sleeping with him nearly every one of those nights. When he looked at her with that look in his eyes she felt that same flare of desire that had sparked between them the very first moment they met in the Green Room of the Theatre Royal in Covent Garden. Indeed, familiarity had not diminished the passion, or all that had grown alongside, between them, only sharpened and heated it. Her stomach turned cartwheels, her skin tingled all over and her thighs seemed to burn. He glanced away, over towards the window, a pensive, sombre expression upon his face. 'Alice…'

But whatever he meant to say was lost as she gently took hold of his face, turned it to hers and kissed away the worry that she saw there.

Razeby retaliated in kind, his mouth passionate and warm and irresistible as the night he had first kissed her in the moonlight outside the theatre stage door.

Breaking the kiss, she watched him as she smiled, a mischievous smile this time, and let her hand stroke lightly over the hard bulge in his breeches. He swallowed and she felt the shiver that rippled through his body, felt the way it strained to meet her and heard the slight catch of the breath in his throat.

He caught her hand in his own and moved it away from temptation, his eyes darkening to that familiar smoulder that made the fire of desire twist and curl and dance all the more, low in her belly. 'Alice, you are a wicked woman,' he breathed in a velvet voice that tickled against her ear and sent a shiver tingling across her skin.

'Very wicked, indeed, Razeby.' Her top teeth caught at her bottom lip. 'So wicked that you might need to put me across your knee and spank me.'

'I would be remiss in my duty to you if I did not do so.' She could hear the low stroke of desire beneath his words.

'And the one thing about you, Razeby, is that you're never remiss in your duty.' Again she thought she saw the shift of a shadow in his eyes so she teased her skirts higher to flash him a glimpse of a stockinged ankle, wanting to make him forget whatever was troubling him. And it worked.

'Be careful, Miss Alice Sweetly,' he cautioned.

'I prefer to be reckless, James Brundell, Marquis of Razeby. But isn't that the truth of why you like me?' She arched an eyebrow and playfully unfastened the buttons at the top of her bodice, allowing the dress to gape and reveal the bulge of her breasts over the transparent linen of her shift.

Razeby's eyes darkened. His focus narrowed and sharpened upon her. He swallowed, then wetted his lips. 'Alice, you are a temptation I cannot resist.'

'I hope so.' She laughed, and one by one she plucked the pins from her hair, until the neatly coiled length of fair hair loosened and tumbled long and wanton over her shoulders.

Razeby discarded the neatly fitted dark tailcoat on the sofa behind him. His fingers moved to the buttons of his pale waistcoat, unfastening it and shrugging it off. Around his neck his white cravat was still neatly tied in a fashionable knot. She reached and tugged an end of it, pulling it free and draping it over the back of the sofa. Through the fine white lawn of his shirt she could see a hint of his flesh and the dark peppering of hair that covered it. Her eyes swept lower to the tight buckskin of his breeches that did little to disguise the extent of his arousal or the long muscular thighs beneath. And lower still to the glossy black riding boots that were coated with dust from his having ridden from his own town house in Leicester Square to the one he kept for her here in Hart Street.

She knew the body beneath those clothes, intimately, every inch of honey-coloured skin, every hard taut muscle. She knew the sweep of his tight buttocks and the breadth of his chest, the feel of his skin beneath her fin-

gertips and the way his heart beat fast and hard after
he had loved her. She knew the scent of him, the feel
of him, the taste of him and the way he made her heart
blossom with such warm tenderness. It just made her
want him all the more.

She turned round and, sticking out her bottom, wig-
gled it to taunt him.

'You are playing dangerously, Alice.'

'Are you close to yielding?' she asked over her shoulder.

He stepped towards her.

She skirted around the other side of the sofa so that
they faced one another as opponents across that bar-
ricade.

'When I catch you, Alice...'

'*If* you catch me...' She smiled and arched an eyebrow. 'What are you going to do to me?' she asked, as
excited by the game she had instigated as he was.

'I am going to pull up your skirts.'

'Yes...' she breathed.

'And bend you over my knee.'

'And then...?' She felt breathless at the thought.

He stepped closer to the sofa, lowering his voice to
little more than a husky whisper as he did so. 'You know
there is only one way this can end, Alice.'

'Really? How might that be, my lord?'

He lunged over the sofa for her.

Alice dodged clear, making a run for the door of
the drawing room. 'You'll have to be faster than that,
Razeby!'

She made it to the first landing of the staircase before he caught her, his arm fastening around her waist
and pulling her to him.

She gave a yelp and a giggle.

'Minx,' he whispered in her ear as he kissed the side of her neck, where the blood pulsed strong and wild.

He scooped her up as if she weighed nothing at all. Her breathing was loud and ragged while Razeby's was barely changed at all. For all her squeals he threw her over his shoulder like some marauder from olden times abducting his woman and strode up the rest of the stairs.

'Razeby!' she protested and gave a wriggle, but all she got in return was a slap on the bottom before he kicked open the door to their bedchamber and threw her down upon the bed.

'Now, woman of mine,' he said. 'We have a score to settle—a matter of some spanking, I believe.'

'Oh, you think so?' She laughed and, rolling on to her stomach, began to quickly crawl across the bed to evade him.

'I will not let you escape me,' he said in a strict voice as his fingers fastened around her ankle and hauled her back across the bed towards him, catching her skirts on the bedcovers and hitching them up her legs in the process. She was still lying on her stomach, her stockings revealed. He pushed her skirts higher to expose her naked thighs and bottom in full.

'Now there is a sight to behold,' he murmured and she caught her breath as his fingers traced down the curve of her hip.

The mattress dipped as he sat down upon it and she gasped as she felt herself hauled to lie across his thighs, her skirts twisted high around her hips, her buttocks bared for whatever he chose to inflict upon them.

'Mercy, my lord Razeby, I beg of you,' she pleaded,

but she was smiling and the words were breathless with anticipation.

'I swear, my love, that when it comes to you I have no mercy...or resistance.' His hand stroked against the fullness of her buttocks, then he spanked her bare bottom, several small light slaps that were little more than cupped caresses.

She laughed again, as did he, as he turned her in his arms, cradling her to him and kissing her mouth. She wound her arms around his neck, kissing him with all the passion that was burning within her. He rolled her flat on to the mattress and she pulled him down on top of her, stroking his face, threading her fingers through his hair.

'Alice,' he whispered, and caressed her cheek. His eyes were a dark liquid brown, so filled with both tenderness and desire as they stared into hers.

'Razeby,' she said softly.

Their eyes held as he plucked a single deep intimate kiss from her lips.

He rose, long enough to divest himself of his shirt over his head and unfasten his breeches and drawers. Her fingers were still working upon the buttons of her bodice when he returned.

'Allow me to assist,' he offered, and then in a move that would have done justice to any Viking warrior in the midst of some rape and pillage Razeby took hold of the neckline and tore the length of the bodice open.

'Such impatience, my lord,' she chided.

'It is the state you push me to, wench.'

'You'll be tying me to the bed next.'

He glanced up at the lengths of black silken cord that

dangled from the headboard of the bed. 'Let us save that game for later.'

'If you insist, Lord Razeby.'

'I do, Miss Sweetly.'

She smiled at that and felt the place between her thighs grow hotter at the thought.

He gave a growl as he pushed the flimsy torn linen and sprig muslin aside, exposing her nakedness to the hunger of his gaze.

'Do you know what you do to me?' She could hear the strain in his voice, see it in his face. He touched her lightly, trailing his fingers across her breasts, making their tips harden and grow unbearably sensitive.

'I could hazard a guess,' she murmured as he lowered his face, all the while keeping his gaze locked with hers, and flicked his tongue to taste her.

The gasp escaped her, loud and needful, and in response his torture grew only more exquisite.

She groaned her need of him, arching her back to thrust her breasts all the more into his mouth so that he suckled her in earnest. Her fingers threaded through the dark feathers of his hair, clutching him to her, wanting him never to stop, wanting this, and more, so much more. He laved her, worked each rosy nipple in full until it was bullet hard and so sensitive that she was in danger of finding the fullness of her pleasure before he had even touched between her legs. She tried to hold back, tried to resist, but, seeing how close she was teetering to the edge, he smiled.

'No mercy, Alice,' he said in his low, sexy velvet voice and then did something so clever with his tongue that rendered all resistance futile. She let go and exploded in a bliss that was blinding and overwhelming, making her body ripple and shimmer as the pleasure, absolute and all consuming, filled her from head to toe and she was gasping aloud with the wonder of it.

She was still pulsing inside as his face came up to hers. 'Razeby,' she whispered.

'Naughty girl,' he said and he was smiling.

She let her hands glide over the pale honey-coloured contours of his shoulders, over the muscles at the top of his arms. He was strong and lean from all the fencing and horse riding and pugilism, his body so different from hers, so much bigger, so masculine.

'It's all your fault,' she said.

'Guilty as charged,' he admitted, and his eyes smouldered all the darker. He kissed all the way up the column of her neck, kissed the line of her jaw, kissed her chin.

Already she could feel the desire stoke again within her. Her woman's place between her legs ached for him.

She scraped her teeth against the naked skin of his shoulder, licked him there, sucked him there while one hand slipped lower to caress the long hard length of him.

She felt the involuntary contraction of his muscles, heard the sharp intake of his breath as she stroked him.

'Alice…'

She smiled and bit his shoulder.

Razeby took her mouth with masterful possession, plunging his tongue into its depths as she wrapped her legs around him and welcomed him home.

They moved in a dance as old as time itself. A man and his woman, mating, bonding, sharing all that was possible to share on this journey that could have only one destination for them both. Striving together until she was gasping and crying out his name as he spilled his seed within her and she pulsed around him and shattered into a myriad of stardust and magic that transcended all else.

And afterwards, as ever, he held her safe in his strong arms, curving his body around hers as if he would protect her from all the world. She could feel the stir of his warm breath against her hair and the possessiveness of his hand around her breast, the warmth of his hard masculine body preventing the cooling of her own lover's rosy glow. His lips brushed against the top of her head and her heart gave a little dance of utter happiness and joy. She snuggled in closer and basked in the aftermath of their lovemaking.

But when she opened her eyes to look into his she glimpsed again something of that same pensive undercurrent that she had seen in the drawing room. She stroked her fingers against the faint blue stubble of his cheek. 'What's wrong, Razeby?' He was not his usual self. He had not been entirely himself for the last weeks. 'You've something on your mind.' Please God, don't let it be what she had been writing upon the desk. If he asked about that, she was not sure what she was going to tell him.

He looked into her eyes, studied them, and just for a moment she thought he was going to tell her. Then it was gone, replaced by that smile of his that made her melt inside.

'Nothing that cannot wait a little longer.' He caught her fingers from his cheek and pressed them to his lips.

But she was not so easily reassured. A little whisper of unease stroked down her spine. 'Razeby,' she began, but he rolled her on to her back and followed to cover her, staring down into her face all the while.

'Please not yet,' he said, and it sounded almost like a prayer; then he silenced any further protestations with a kiss. The kiss led to another, and another, until the passion that consumed them made all else fade away.

Chapter Two

Razeby stood by the window of his study in his town house in Leicester Square, observing all of normality go on in the street outside. A carriage rolled by, the Earl of Misbourne's crest painted upon its door. A coal cart rattled slowly out of the nearby mews, its load lessened following its delivery. Two gentlemen upon horseback had pulled over by the gardens to greet each other. Servants hurried along the pavements on errands for their masters. A nursemaid was taking a baby for a walk in a child's pushchair. He turned away from the window at that last sight.

The brandy decanter was sitting on his desk. The heavyweight crystal engraved with the Razeby coat of arms and motto—The Name of Razeby Shall Prevail—was a taunting irony. Regardless of the earliness of the hour he lifted the decanter, filled one of the matching engraved glasses, and took a sip.

The heat of the brandy hit the back of his throat, the smooth warmth tracing all the way down to his stomach. He took a deep breath and set the glass down upon the letter that lay open upon his desk. A bead of the rich tawny liquid trickled down from the glass's rim, slipping slowly, inexorably, down the stem to the base, where it finally crept upon the paper beneath to blur the inky words his cousin Atholl had written there— Atholl, who had defied all advice to buy a commission in the cavalry and taken himself off to fight against Napoleon. Yet another reminder. Everywhere Razeby looked there were reminders.

There was not a sound within the house. Only the slow steady tick of the tall clock in the corner, marking how quickly time was slipping away. He had left it so late, almost too late. He could leave it no longer.

He thought of Alice, his Alice, with her beautiful dark blue eyes and her passion and her warmth of heart and spirit, of how much she had been looking forward to the fireworks tonight. He thought of Alice and all that had been between them these past months, and felt an ache in his chest. His eyes strayed to the long, slim brown-velvet box that lay beside his pen holder. Just a momentary pause, as he steeled himself to the task. Then he slipped the box into the pocket of his tailcoat.

Razeby downed the remaining brandy in one go, but it did not settle the sourness or dread in his stomach.

The night sky was a canopy of clear midnight-blue velvet sewn with a smattering of diamonds that twinkled and glittered. The moon was a thin crescent hanging high in their midst. Although the winter had passed, the spring night air was cold, turning Alice and Razeby's breaths to smoke as they climbed from the little boat and walked hand in hand across the grass to Vauxhall Gardens.

Alice wrapped the cloak around her more tightly and felt Razeby's arm pull her closer.

'You are cold.'

'Only a little.' She smiled up at him. And he stared down into at her face with a curiously tender expression, as if he were branding her image upon his memory never to be forgotten. 'Why so serious? Hmm?' she asked, still smiling, and cupped his beard-scraped cheek.

He moved his lips to kiss the palm of her hand. 'It has been an unpleasant day.'

'Then we'd better make sure we enjoy tonight.'

'Every last precious minute.' The words were so softly murmured she had to strain to catch them. Then he seemed to shake off his megrims, and, taking her hand in his, led her to watch a host of entertainers: jugglers and knife throwers, dancers and musicians. A hurdy-gurdy man with a little monkey upon his shoulder, its tiny furry body all dressed up smartly in a fine coat and matching hat, was drawing quite the crowd. They could smell the food from the banqueting tables beyond, but the night seemed too chill for the wafer-thin cold ham and champagne that was being served to the guests.

'I'm glad we ate at home,' she said.

'Me, too.' Razeby pulled a bottle of champagne from his pocket. 'No glasses. I am afraid we will have to slum it. Even if it is the best bottle from your cellar.'

'*Your* cellar,' she said and laughed, as he timed the popping of the cork to merge with the explosion of the fireworks in the sky.

The froth exploded over the top of the bottle, cascading down the bottle's neck as Razeby offered it to her.

Alice took a swig from the bottle and spluttered at the furious fizz of bubbles.

Razeby's swig gave not the slightest hint of choking.

Then she leaned back against his chest as his arms wrapped around her waist, and together they looked up and watched the magnificent explosion of coloured lights and flashes fill the sky. All around them the crowd was 'oohing' and 'aahing' with amazement and appreciation at the spectacle. She could smell the sulphurous stench of the fireworks and catch the drift of the scent of smoke from the braziers not so very far away.

Razeby leaned down to kiss her and he tasted of the green grass and of strawberries and champagne, and of Razeby and all that was wonderful in life. They watched the fireworks and they drank the champagne and they kissed, not caring who saw them, because it was dark and because this was the slightly *risqué* Vauxhall Pleasure Gardens, and because it would have been too much to keep their lips from one another. As the fireworks began to wane Razeby took her hand, not even waiting until they had finished in full, and led her back towards the boats so that they would not have to wait in the crush that would follow.

Within their bedchamber at Hart Street the glow of the firelight burnished the dark blonde of her hair a red-gold. He reached out and caught a vibrant strand that had loosened from her pins, running it between his fingers before tucking it behind her ear. His thumb stroked against the softness of her cheek. She closed her eyes and angled her face into his hand for the breath of a moment before stepping away beyond his reach.

He shrugged off the midnight-blue tailcoat he was wearing, throwing it to land on a nearby armchair. But as he did so the slim brown-velvet box fell from the pocket to land upon the rug beneath their feet.

Alice smiled when she saw it. 'You bought me another gift. What did I tell you the other day?' she demanded.

He picked up the box, kept his eyes on it and could not rise to her teasing.

'Honestly, Razeby, you shouldn't have.'

He gave a small tight smile and passed the brown-velvet box to her.

'I'm mystified as to what it can be.' She stared at the jeweller's box, stroked her fingers once against its velvet, hesitating for a moment before finally opening the lid. The radiance of the diamond bracelet, lying within on its cream-velvet cushion, caught the firelight to glitter and sparkle and illuminate the room around them.

She gave a soft gasp. 'Oh, Razeby! It's beautiful!' She pressed a kiss to his cheek. 'It must have cost you a fortune.'

'You are worth every penny, and more.'

'I love it.' Her hands came to caress his face, her eyes scanning his. 'Thank you.'

His heart squeezed tight.

Slowly she touched her lips to his.

'Alice,' he murmured and, pulling her into his arms, he kissed her.

He kissed her and he could not stop. He kissed her and lost himself in her, as ever he did. She made him forget everything else, all of his responsibility that weighed upon his shoulders, all of the darkness that was coming. Her eyes were filled with a passion and need that matched his own.

'Make love to me, Razeby.'

He could not deny her. He could not deny himself, or all that he felt for her.

He undressed her in silence, their eyes clinging together all the while, and laid her down gently on the bed. He never took his eyes from hers even while he stripped off his waistcoat and shirt and cravat. Nor while he unfastened the fall of his breeches and freed himself from his drawers.

He took her tenderly, with reverence, with meaning, all of which seemed to make the force between them only stronger and rawer. Claiming her as his own, gifting her all he could, so neither of them would ever forget. And she rose to meet him. He opened himself to her entirely, gave all, held nothing back. And in Alice's reply he felt her do the same, this woman for whom he would pluck both the sun and moon from the sky and give them to her if he could.

Their bodies had been made to be together. To merge. To be as one. She was his complement, and he hers. Together they found another place distinct from the world. But the lovemaking between them tonight took them further than he had ever known. It was poignant, special, a bonding between them like no other. As if she touched an even deeper part of him he had not known existed. They clung together, strove together, looking into one another's eyes as their bodies reached a new nirvana, and together stepped over the edge to tumble into a shared climax the force of which made them capture each other's merging cries. And afterwards, he could feel her heart and his beat in time, as they lay entwined together watching the flicker of the firelight dance upon each other's naked skin.

Her fingers gently caressed the muscle at the top of his arm.

'Alice...' he said, and there was a terrible pressing tightness in his chest.

'Did you get the tickets for tomorrow night's show?'

'I have the tickets.'

'Well, that's a relief.' She smiled but Razeby could not reciprocate. 'We'll have a grand time. Ellen says the horses are amazing. That a body wouldn't believe they could be trained to do such tricks.'

He closed his eyes, took a breath, forced himself to say the words aloud before he could not. 'I cannot accompany you to the show tomorrow night.'

'I thought you said you had the tickets.'

'I do, but there is...another occasion...which I am obliged to attend.'

'What occasion?'

The small silence hissed loud.

'A ball at Almack's.'

'Almack's is not usually one of your haunts.' She gave a little laugh. 'All those débutantes and fierce matrons intent on landing eligible husbands for their daughters. Is Devlin finally on the hunt for a bride?'

'I am not going with Devlin, but with Linwood.' Viscount Linwood, who almost six months ago had married Alice's best friend and London's most celebrated actress, Venetia Fox.

And he felt the withdrawal of her body and saw in her face that she realised the truth even before he said the words he did not want to say, 'We need to talk, Alice. There is something I have to tell you.'

Chapter Three

Razeby fixed his drawers and breeches into place before sitting up in the bed. Leaning his spine against the massive carved-oak headboard, he stretched his long still-booted legs out before him over the counterpane.

Alice felt the rush of cold air fill the space where he had been. She shivered at its icy touch as she pulled the sheet to cover her nakedness and sat up next to him, leaning back to rest against the headboard in the same manner.

And even though he moved his hand to cover hers, threading their fingers together, her stomach dipped and a cold draught moved across her heart. She waited, knowing what Razeby was going to say and willing with all her heart and mind and soul that it would turn out to be something different, that later she would laugh over this foolish pound of her heart and tight fear in her throat.

'You best get on and tell me then.' She smiled as if dread were not trickling like ice through her veins.

'I have a duty, Alice, to my title, to my estates and the people upon them. A duty to safeguard them for future generations. And part of that duty is to marry and produce an heir. I was raised for that purpose. I must produce a son who will do the same. I must marry.'

'Of course you must.' She had always known it, they both had. But he would marry at some distant time in the future, not now, not when what they had together was still so fresh and vital. 'But you're young enough yet. Surely you don't need to step upon that path right now?'

'I'll be thirty in six months' time.' He glanced away and raked a hand through his hair.

'What's the significance of thirty? Is there some kind of stipulation that you have to be married and breeding an heir by then?'

A shadow moved in his eyes as he glanced away. 'Something like that,' he said. 'Atholl will be coming home on a stretcher. It could too easily have been a coffin.'

'Your cousin who got shot in battle.'

'As it stands he is my heir, Alice.'

'I thought he was on the mend.'

'He is. Now. He very nearly was not. What happened to Atholl…it has forced me to reconsider things. I have deferred my duty for too long. I can defer it no longer. I have to find a bride for Razeby.'

Their fingers still lay entwined together. Neither of them had moved, both just sat leaning back against the headboard of their bed, as if this was just an ordinary conversation, one of the thousands they had had before, when it was anything other. She sat motionless, feigning relaxation, pretending that she was not shocked and reeling from his words.

'So is this you giving me my *congé?*' She smiled

with the incredulity of it, half-expecting him to deny it, to tell her they could still go on as before. On the ivory of the bedcover she could see where the dust of his riding boots had smudged dark.

But he made no denial. 'I am sorry, Alice.'

She slipped her fingers from his. Looked round at him, but he stared straight ahead, as if seeing into the distance, and did not meet her eyes.

Not five minutes ago they had been making love, their breaths and bodies and hearts merged as one in that ultimate act of intimacy. Now he was sitting there dismissing her. It felt like she had just been punched in the stomach.

She glanced down at the diamond bracelet that glittered as beautiful as a night sky full of stars. 'That's why you bought me the bracelet!' She laughed a mirthless laugh. 'As a pay off.'

The silence hissed.

Her fingers unfastened the latch and slipped it from her wrist. The diamonds sparkled and cast shimmering lights against the shadowed walls as she let it fall on to the pale counterpane.

She could not think straight. Her thoughts swayed and staggered as she struggled to understand. 'You were going to tell me the other day, weren't you? That's why you came round unexpectedly.'

Again he did not deny it.

She gave an ironic laugh and shook her head.

His eyes were dark and serious.

The tide of emotion threatened to engulf her. She turned her face away, barely able to conceal her anger and incredulity, and the splintering unbelievable hurt. How could she have been so blind? Six months of thinking that everything was happy and good and wonderful. And believing that he had felt the same. She could barely take it in that he was telling her it was over.

'You can stay here as long it takes to find other lodgings. There is no rush to leave.'

'How kind of you.'

He ignored the irony. 'I will, of course, make a settlement of money on you.'

'I don't want your money, Razeby.'

'It is part of our contract.'

'Oh, so it is.' She thought of the piece of paper with its fancy black writing, secure and tied neat within its green ribbon. 'How could I have forgotten?'

The silence seemed to pulsate between them. There were so many thoughts running through her head, so many words crowding for release upon her tongue. She closed her mouth firmly to prevent their escape.

Climbing from the bed, she grabbed an old dressing gown from where it hung over the back of a chair, pulling it on and tying the belt around her waist as she walked to stand by the window and stare down on to the lamp-lit street below. In the continuing silence she watched the occasional group walking along the pavements. Theatre goers who had gone elsewhere after a late show. Women who, despite the quality of their dress, were ladies of the night, plying their trade; Alice could pick them out with an expert eye—like could always recognise like. A carriage passed and then a gentleman on a horse.

She heard him move and glanced round to see him get to his feet, all six feet of him, with his tight dark breeches and his naked chest, and that ruggedly handsome face. And, despite what he had just told her, her traitorous body reacted with the usual rush of desire for him.

'Arrangements like ours are not meant to last, Alice.'

'They're not,' she agreed.

'I have to do my duty, Alice.' His mouth, which had always been so warm and smiling, was unhappy and determined, the expression in his eyes unreadable.

Her heart was beating harder than a horse at full gallop. 'Maybe you should have considered your duty six months ago.' When he had pursued her while the play in which she and Venetia had starred together took London by storm. When he had wooed her and swept her off her feet and made her his mistress within weeks of their meeting.

'Maybe I should have,' he said.

His quiet admission stripped her raw.

They stared at one another. He was grim-faced, serious in a way she had never seen him before.

'For what it is worth, I really am sorry, Alice.'

'So you said.'

He swallowed. 'Thank you for everything.' His eyes clung to hers. He took a step towards her, reached a hand as if he meant to touch her.

Alice recoiled, sweeping her eyes over his extended hand with its long manly fingers and its lightly tanned skin. It was a hand that had caressed her lips and stroked against her naked skin, a hand that had touched her in the most intimate of places. It was all she could do to stop herself from striking it away with every ounce of strength in her body.

She raised her gaze to meet his with fierceness.

He swallowed, glanced away, let his hand drop to rest by his side. 'If there is anything more you need—'

'There isn't. You should go now,' she said with feigned calmness before turning away again to the window. Clutching her dressing gown all the tighter around her, she stared down at the gas-lit street, seeing nothing of it, waiting only for him to leave.

But he did not leave.

She heard him come up behind her. He did not touch her, but she could feel the heat of his proximity scorch the length of her spine.

'Alice…' there was a straining pause '…I hope I have not…hurt you.'

She turned to him, held her head up to look him defiantly in the face. 'Hurt me? Don't flatter yourself, Razeby. It was nice while it lasted, but…' She gave a shrug as if she did not care and bit hard at her bottom lip to stop the threat of the betraying tremor.

She saw the bob of his Adam's apple in his throat, the way his dark eyes studied hers.

'That at least is something.' He gave a nod. 'Goodbye, Alice.'

'Goodbye, Razeby.' The words were tight. She forced a smile and turned away to the window again as if she were more interested in the dark view.

He turned and walked away, but she could see the reflection of his leaving in the glass of the window pane and her own face watching, pale and haunting as a ghost.

The bedchamber door closed with a quiet click that seemed louder than an almighty slam.

She stood there and listened to the stride of his booted footsteps along the corridor and down the stairs. Her breath caught in ragged gasps, but she caught her hand to her mouth to silence them. Five minutes later the front door shut. Only then did she let herself sag back to lean against the wall and allow the sob to escape.

For what remained of that night Alice sat in the little blue armchair by the fireplace and stared into the flames. They licked high around the fresh coal she had thrown on to it, devouring the black rocks with a ferocity that matched the force of emotion whirling and tumbling through her. It did not matter how much heat they threw out, it did not warm the chill from her bones. Nor did the dressing gown or the woollen shawl clutched tight around her shoulders. It was the shock, she thought to herself. And the anger. And that feeling that she had drunk ten cups of coffee and that it did not matter if she lay on the bed and closed her eyes; her thoughts were running so wild she would never sleep again.

Don't you dare shed a single tear for him!

But her eyes were swimming and she felt she could have wept a waterfall. She swallowed down the lump in her throat, but no amount of swallowing could shift the boulder from her chest that felt like it was crushing her.

It was just sex. It had always been just sex. And the way she was feeling now, so scraped and raw and bleeding, was down to the shock of it; that was all. Razeby's words had come out of nowhere, catching her with her guard down.

She breathed, calmed herself. Stared into the flames. She had survived worse things than this. She thought of her family back in Ireland, of her coming to London to find a job that she might help them, of the hunger and the desperation. She thought of playing the role of the masked Miss Rouge in Mrs Silver's high-class brothel, her identity hidden from the world. So few people knew. But Razeby did. God only knew why she had told him. She was regretting that now.

Her eyes glanced across at the bed with its sheets still rumpled from their lovemaking. Amidst them she could see the sparkle of the diamond bracelet, so brilliant and beautiful and expensive. She gave a shaky laugh and shook her head at what a fool she had been.

Never let them see how much they hurt you. Her mother's words, drummed into her across a lifetime, played in her head. *The bastards can't take your pride away from you unless you let them. Look life straight in the face, Alice, and always, always keep smiling.*

Alice was not clever. She was not smart. But she was practical and hard-working and determined. And she still had her pride, every damn inch of it.

She turned her face away from the bed and, staring into the low golden flickers amongst the red glowing coals, made her plans.

Chapter Four

Within the hallowed grounds of Almack's ballroom, the chandeliers sparkled beneath the flames of a thousand candles. The walls were painted a soft cream and outlined in antique gold. The ceiling had recently been reworked in an array of white plasterwork. In its centre was a line of three elaborate roses, from each of which hung an enormous crystal chandelier. There was a three-piece matching peering glass set above the fireplace, with candles fitted to the fronts and a series of matching mirrored wall sconces positioned at regular intervals around the room. Small chairs and tables were seeded around the periphery. The musicians played from the balcony above, the music floating sweet and melodic to fill the ballroom and haunt Razeby.

'I was not sure they were going to let you in,' he said to Linwood standing by his side.

'I did have to call in a few favours.'

'I am glad you did,' he admitted.

There was a small silence as the two men let their eyes wander to the other side of the dance floor and the crowd of white-dressed débutantes there that posed and giggled and chattered amongst themselves while their stern-faced turban-wearing chaperones looked on.

'Does Alice know you are here?' Linwood asked.

'It is over between me and Alice.' Razeby felt the weight of Linwood's gaze, but he did not shift his own, just kept his face impassive and remained staring straight ahead so that nothing of his feelings showed.

'I am sorry about that.'

'So am I.'

There was the music and the droning hum of surrounding conversations and the tinkle of women's laughter.

'You could have kept her on at least until you found—'

'No.' Razeby did not let him finish. 'A clean severance is for the best.' He met his friend's eyes.

Linwood raised an eyebrow. 'I was under the impression that you and she dealt very well together.'

'We do.' He glanced away and corrected himself. 'We did.' He swallowed to ease the sudden tightness in his throat. 'But she was my mistress, Linwood. And now it is time to find myself a wife.'

Linwood looked at him with that too-perceptive gaze of his, as if he could see the way that Razeby's stomach clenched at just the mention of her name. He was doing the right thing, the thing that had to be done. The thing he should have been doing six months ago, before Alice Sweetly came into his life and changed his best-laid plan. Six months and he could regret not one day of it. Six months and... He changed the subject, pretending something of his usual lightness of spirit when what he felt was anything but.

'See what you missed out on by not playing the marriage mart?'

Linwood smiled, which was a sight that was a deal more

common since his recent marriage. 'I would rather be tried for murder and catch a wife in the process,' he said, referring to exactly what he had done just a few months ago. 'Scandalous and dangerous—but more than satisfying in its end result.' He smiled again and there was a softening of his expression so that Razeby could tell he was thinking of his wife, the former star of the Covent Garden stage, Venetia Fox. Venetia, who was Alice's best friend.

A vision of Alice swam in his mind. Alice, with her mischief and her heart and her laughter. Alice standing in their bedchamber looking at him with that expression of shock in her eyes as he told her it was over. Something churned in Razeby's stomach. He forced that last image away and turned his gaze to the hordes of white-frocked débutantes across the floor, one of whom by the end of the Season would be his wife, in his bed and carrying his child. He felt numb at the thought, but it had to be this way. He had had his fun and Alice had been more than he had ever anticipated, but now it was time to bite the bullet and do his duty…before it was too late. He turned his mind from all other distractions and summoned a cold determination.

'So which lucky débutante are you going to ask to dance?' asked Linwood.

'The first one I come to,' replied Razeby with a smile that did not touch his eyes and, setting his champagne glass down on the silver salver of a passing footman, he made his way across the room.

The day had been a long one, following a night in which she had not slept, but Alice was not tired.

It had been a mammoth effort and one which had seen her travel round half of London. But it had been worth it.

The large travelling bag lay open at her feet.

'Shall I help you, ma'am?' The maid hovered awkwardly in the doorway as if afraid to enter the bedchamber. The girl's cheeks were flushed with embarrassment, her manner awkward. Alice saw the way her eyes dropped to take in the travelling bag before meeting her face.

All of the servants knew, even though she was sure that Razeby would have told them nothing of it. Alice had two sisters in service in Dublin. She knew that servants always knew these things.

'No, thank you, Mary. I'll see to myself. But if you could have Heston see that a hackney carriage is summoned for me.'

'Yes, ma'am.' The girl bobbed a curtsy and hurried off to update the rest of the staff.

Alice went through the wardrobe, pulling out a minimal selection of clothes, all of which she had brought with her when she had come to this house, and ignoring the expensive silk dresses and accessories that Razeby had paid for.

She made short work of gathering up the rest of her possessions. There were not many. Alice travelled light. She preferred it that way.

It was when she moved to close the wardrobe doors that she stopped, her eyes drawn, as if not of their own volition, to the dress hanging on its own at the very end of the row. She hesitated, bit her lip, knowing that she should shut the door upon it just like all the rest, but unable to do so. Before she could think better of it, she slipped the emerald-silk evening dress from the hanger and folded it into her bag.

Of all the gifts that Razeby had given her, she took only one, opening the lid of the long thin cherrywood box just long enough to check that the engraved silver pen was inside. But she did not look at it. She did not touch it, just snapped the lid shut and stuffed it into the travelling bag with a tortoiseshell comb and the rest of her toiletries before buckling the bag closed. Then she swept the black-velvet cloak over her shoulders and lifted the travelling bag.

One final glance around the bedchamber, at the dressing table and its peering glass, at the wardrobe and the armchairs and the pretty little table with its ivory vase of deep-pink roses that had had their day. The heads were blown, the petals starting to fall. But their perfume was still sweet and lingering in the room. She moved her gaze to the bed, which she and Razeby had shared, let her eyes rest there for only a moment. Then, with her bag in hand, she walked away, down the stairs and out into the waiting hackney carriage.

The driver flicked the reins and the carriage drove off into the sunset. Alice kept her focus on the glorious rosy-streaked sky. She clutched her hands tight around the travelling bag and kept her mouth set firm with determination.

And not once did she look back at the house.

Razeby lost track of the number of women he danced with. They all seemed much the same. He made conversation. He went through the motions. But all the while he could not get last night's scene with Alice out of his head.

She knew more than most how the games between men and women played out. She had been under no illusions. Neither of them had. And yet…

I don't want your money, Razeby.

The words whispered again in his ear. It was that one phrase more than any other that worried him.

Last night had been about a clean, quick break. It was the only way. The best way for them both. Just as he had told Linwood. The theory of it had been easy, the practice anything but. He had handled it badly. More than badly. He wondered if he could have handled it worse.

Alice had been good to him, good for him. She was like no one he had ever known. It explained the gnawing feeling he had felt since telling her. Guilt. He should make sure she was all right, now and for the future. He should up the sum of her severance payment from that which his lawyer had specified in the contract, regardless of what she said.

He delivered Miss Thomson back to her mother. And bowed.

Hurt me? Don't flatter yourself, Razeby. He was not sure he believed her. The thought niggled him. He felt the guilt gnaw harder, even though he had spoken the truth to her. Arrangements like theirs were not meant to last. But he could not stop wondering how she was.

'Leaving so early?' Linwood raised an eyebrow. 'The night is still young, Razeby.'

'Breaking myself in gently, Linwood,' he lied. 'There are only so many débutantes a man can endure in one evening.'

'Do you want to go to White's to recover?'

'Another night,' said Razeby.

* * *

The lights glowed through the blind-shuttered windows. The house in Hart Street looked as welcoming as ever it had done. He wondered if he had made a mistake in coming here. But he needed to reassure himself that she was all right.

'What do you mean she is gone?' It had been the early hours of this morning when he had left her here alone. Not even twenty-four hours had elapsed since that botched confrontation.

He saw the awkwardness of the butler's expression before the man remembered his professional decorum and schooled his face to the usual attentive impassivity.

'Miss Sweetly was out all day, my lord, returning earlier this evening to pack a travelling bag.'

Something twisted in his chest. 'Did she leave a note?'

'There is no note, my lord.' There was something in the way the old man's eyes looked at him that made him feel even more of a bastard. He paused before adding, 'She gave instructions that she would not be returning.'

'And did Miss Sweetly say where she was going? Or leave a forwarding direction?' Razeby knew in his heart what the answer to those questions would be, but he asked them in the hope that he was wrong.

'No, my lord, she did not.'

'But she must have given a direction to John Coachman?'

'Miss Sweetly did not travel by your lordship's coach when she left.'

He understood the significance of that very clearly. She did not want him to find her, and, in truth, he could not blame her.

Razeby dismissed the butler and climbed the stairs

to the bedchamber they had shared. Everything looked just the same as it always did, as if last night had been just some bad dream. The wall sconces on either side of the fireplace were lit, the flames of their candles reflecting soft and subdued in their adjoining looking glasses. The roses he had brought her not a week ago were still in their vase. A small fire burned on the hearth, making the room cosy and warm. The scent of her was in the air, the sense of her entwined in the very fibres of the place.

Her jewel casket still sat upon her dressing table, beneath the lid all of what he had given her lying neat in their own little compartments.

He walked to her wardrobe, opened up the door. There were only a few spaces where garments no longer hung. The myriad of coloured dresses that he had paid for from Madame Boisseron's were still there. Their matching slippers and shoes sat in neat pairs at the bottom of the wardrobe. On an impulse he opened his own matching wardrobe and saw all of his clothes just as he had left them.

He closed the doors over, letting his eyes survey the rest of the room. Nothing was out of place...except... His gaze stilled when it came to the ivory bedcovers, neat and smooth upon the mattress, for laid carefully upon them, in their very centre, was the brown-velvet box opened to reveal the cream-velvet cushion and the diamond bracelet that lay sparkling upon it.

He felt his jaw clamp tight and a cold realisation seep through his blood. Alice had gone. He did not know where. Without her severance payment. Without a single thing he had bought for her. And there could be nothing for the best about that.

* * *

'I came as soon as I got your message.' Alice's best friend and mentor, the woman who had saved her from her life in Mrs Silver's bawdy house and set her up as an actress, Venetia Fox, or Viscountess Linwood as she was now, handed her cloak to Alice's new maid and followed Alice through to the drawing room of her new home in Mercer Street.

'You must have dropped what you were doing and come straight away. I only sent the boy half an hour ago.'

'You are my friend, Alice. What else did you expect I would do?' There was a concern in Venetia's face that made Alice feel guilty.

'I didn't mean to worry you, Venetia. I was just letting you know where I was.'

'I am glad that you did. I really have been worried.' Venetia sat down next to her on the sofa and took her hands in hers. 'What happened?'

Alice smiled as if the words were easy to say. 'He gave me my *congé*. Said it's time he found himself a bride.'

'Oh, Alice, I am so sorry.'

'Don't be. It had to happen one day. I'm an actress. He's a marquis. How else was it going to end?' She shrugged and gave a little laugh. 'Besides, I was tired of him. I fancied a bit of a change, myself.' The joking words tripped easily from her lips.

Venetia did not look convinced. 'Neither of you could have anticipated what happened to Atholl. I suppose it made Razeby see things differently.'

'Atholl was a grand excuse for the both of us.' An excuse for Razeby, more like. She knew now what had been bothering him all those weeks and months leading up to it and she was more fool for being worried over him. 'Our time was on the wane.'

'You left Hart Street very quickly.'

'Striking while the iron's hot.' She smiled. 'I've got myself sorted out. What do you think of the new rooms? I've had my eye on them for a little while.' The smile broadened to become a grin. 'Nice and handy for the theatre. And not too high a rent.'

'They are very nice. But I did not come to see the rooms, Alice,' Venetia said carefully.

'You did warn me not to become his mistress. Do you remember?'

Venetia gave no reply, only held her gaze with eyes that were filled with compassion.

Alice hated to see it. It made her feel angry and even more determined. She did not want anyone's pity, not even Venetia's. 'You told me it was better to earn your own money than put yourself in any man's power.'

'And did you put yourself in his power, Alice?' Venetia asked softly.

'Of course not! I'm not that daft. I knew the score with him. Just as he did with me. With my background, how could I not?' The secret of her scandalous past whispered between them. She smiled again as if it meant nothing. 'I kept my hand in at the theatre, didn't I? Doing the odd appearance. Which is why Kemble's agreed to take me back full time.'

'I am glad of that.' But whether Venetia's gladness was due to Kemble taking her back full time or her attitude over Razeby was not clear. 'But there is more to power than money, Alice.' Venetia looked at her. 'I do understand something of how it has been between you and Razeby. How it was even in the very beginning.'

'You're imagining things, Venetia.' Alice gave a dismissive laugh. 'What was between Razeby and me was a kind of mutually beneficial business arrangement, nothing more. Great sex and a good time, and money, of course, lots of money.'

'It seemed as if there was a lot more than that.'

'I'm a good actress. What can I say? You trained me well.' She smiled again.

'You are,' said Venetia, 'a very good actress.' There was no edge to the words. Alice did not know why they brought a blush to heat her cheeks.

The little clock on the mantel ticked, reassuring and steady.

Alice busied herself in pouring tea into the pretty bone-china cups that came with the fine furniture and everything else in these rented rooms. She added a lump of sugar to each and a few drops of cream before passing one small cup and saucer to Venetia.

'You seem as if you have everything in hand, Alice.'

'I have, indeed.'

'If there is anything I can do to help...'

Alice glanced across the room to the side table, where the folded cream paper lay with its red ribbon tied around it. 'Actually, there is one thing you could do for me, Venetia, as you're here. Kemble's given me the contract for the theatre. I was going to come and see you. But I was waiting for a quiet time.' She fetched the document over and set it down next to the coffee tray.

'You can come round any time, you know that.' But that was not true. They both knew it.

'We move in different worlds now, Venetia. You're

no longer an actress, but a viscountess. If I'm seen visiting, it wouldn't look good for you. Reputation is everything in the *ton*. They're starting to accept you. It's going well. I don't want to ruin it.'

'You will not ruin it. You are the very height of discretion.'

'I try.' She laughed. 'Well, only where you're concerned, if I'm honest.'

'I am glad you are keeping your spirits up.' Venetia smiled.

'Why wouldn't I? Razeby's in the past. Ahead there's only the future. And the future looks good for me.' She smiled again. 'I'm planning to throw myself into the theatre life. Make a real go of it. You have to get on with life, don't you?' Another of her mother's teachings. Very easy to say, not so easy to do. But Alice would do it. She was very determined of that.

'You do,' Venetia agreed. Then she lifted the document Alice had set before her and slipped off the red ribbon that bound it.

A small companionable silence opened up as they sipped their coffee and Venetia read the wording of the theatre contract.

'Is it all in order?'

'It seems to be. You are in a strong position, Alice. Your return to the stage full time will fill the theatre. You could push Kemble to pay you more.'

But Alice shook her head. 'I'm happy with what he's offered me. I just want to get on with it. Get started.'

'If you are sure?'

'I am. Although I must confess to being a little nervous at playing so many leading roles.'

'You will be fine upon that stage, Alice. More than fine. You will be great. I know you will.'

'I hope so.' Alice bit at her lip and her cheeks turned pink at the compliment.

'Kemble has told you the plays that are scheduled?'

'Right up to the summer. There's nothing new, nothing I haven't done before, thank the Lord.'

Venetia met her gaze. 'If something new does come up…any new part to be read, come to me.'

Alice gave a nod. 'I will.'

The two women looked at one another, bound by more than this secret that they shared. By sensitivity and friendship and past histories that were too much alike.

Alice took a deep breath. 'Go ahead, sign it,' she said.

Venetia gave a nod and then, moving the tray aside, she lifted the plain black pen, another one of the house's possessions, from its holder and dipped the tip into the ink well. Very carefully she signed at the end of the contract, *Alice Sweetly,* then sprinkled some fine sand upon the still-wet ink of the signature.

'It is done, Alice,' she said.

They both knew that it was more than the signing of the contract Venetia was referring to. This commitment to going back to the theatre full time was the drawing of a line under all that had gone before with Razeby. It marked the end of that chapter in Alice's life and the beginning of a new one. She was fortunate to have such an option, and more fortunate still to have such a friend as Venetia who had helped her. Alice knew that, so she smiled and held her head up. 'It is,' she agreed. 'Thank you, Venetia.'

'I will come and see you in your first performance.'

'You do that. I'll be looking out for you.' Alice smiled.

They walked towards the front door.

The thought was pounding in Alice's mind, and the words whispering in her ear, and Alice tried not to say them. But once Venetia walked out that door it would be too late and Alice had to be sure.

Just as Venetia was about to leave, Alice placed her hand on her friend's arm and said quietly, 'If Razeby should enquire, which I'm sure he won't, you won't tell him the direction of my new rooms, will you?'

There was the tiniest of hesitations in which Venetia looked into her eyes in a way that made Alice regret speaking the words.

'Rest assured I will tell him nothing, Alice.'

There were no accusations. No denials or admissions. Just a hug of understanding. And a farewell.

Chapter Five

~~~~~~~~~~~~~~~

Within the study of Razeby's town house in Leicester Square, Collins answered the question he had just been asked. 'Two maidservants, no menservants. Apart from that, no one.'

'Thank you, Mr Collins.' Razeby slid a neat pile of folded bank notes across the gleam of the mahogany desk top.

The wiry, sharp-eyed man pocketed the money without counting it. It was not first time the Bow Street Runner had undertaken a little work on the side for Razeby. Although it was in all probability the last, thought Razeby with a macabre sense of humour.

'All in a day's work, Lord Razeby.' Collins made no comment as to the information he had just given Razeby, although he could not have been unaware of its significance. The Bow Street Runner was too smart for that. It was why Razeby had used him. 'I will bid you good day, my lord.' Collins gave a small bow and left, closing the study door silently behind him.

Razeby sat where he was, staring at the panels of the door without seeing them. A man had his duty and his fate. And honour. None of which he could escape, no matter how much he willed it. That knowledge was ever present in his mind these days.

A few thousand pounds and his duty to Alice would be discharged, all monies owed paid. The severance between them finalised. And after that maybe then he would be able to stop thinking of her, maybe then he would be able to focus on the task in hand. Finding a bride. Breeding an heir.

His gaze lowered to the desk, to the scrap of paper that Collins had given him. He looked at it again, his eyes lingering on it even though the words written there were already imprinted on his memory. There could be no room in his life for sentimentality or faltering. Only getting the job done. He knew that, but he still folded the paper carefully and stowed it safely in the pocket of his waistcoat before ringing the bell for his valet and moving to ready himself for tonight's dance.

In the days since Venetia's visit Alice had done just as she had said and thrown herself into the theatre. She was working hard in preparation for her opening night at Covent Garden's Theatre Royal. The enormity of the challenge before her left little time for that. She rose early and tumbled into bed late, exhausted. She loved the smell of the theatre, that dusty polished scent unique to the grand stage. The way it gave her a purpose on which to focus.

Every day brought new challenges, refreshing herself as to the plays and the roles, running through lines last heard a year past. She took home scripts at night and returned them the next morning, pretending she had read them, as if she could, but Alice had no need to read a single line. She only had to hear something once to remember it for ever. It was her special gift. And she was truly thankful for it.

All day, every day was spent at the theatre, with Mr Kemble and the other actors and actresses, rehearsing. Everything that she feared she might have forgotten of the art of playacting came back to her as easily as if she had last stepped upon a stage in a leading role only yesterday. Even the feeling of fear but also of excitement, like walking a knife edge. It made her concentrate, made her focus. It took away the luxury of time during which she might dwell upon Razeby.

Alice was about to leave for rehearsals one morning when the maid brought her a letter.

'A footman has just delivered this, ma'am.'

She lifted the letter from the maid's small silver salver, wondering who had written. So far, only Kemble and Venetia knew the address of her new rooms. Kemble she saw in person each day and Venetia knew better than to write. But as soon as she turned the letter over in her hands she knew without opening it, without needing to be able to read a single word of it, the identity of the sender.

'Have him wait, Meg,' she instructed.

The thick red-wax seal impressed upon the back was a crest she recognised too well. One that made her pulse thrum uncomfortably hard and her heart beat too fast with anger and too many other emotions she would rather not name. She swallowed, torn between not wanting to open it and the need to know what lay beneath that seal. Wetting her lips, she swallowed again and cracked the wax. The letter unfolded. Inside was a cheque with Razeby's name signed against a sum she could not read. The letter itself was blank other than signed with his name. That familiar bold black scrawl—Razeby.

It was her severance pay, a common enough negotiation between mistresses and the men in whose keeping they had been. A lump sum to tide them over until they found their next protector. Or to keep them for life. But for Alice there would be no new protector. And she would keep herself, earn her own money. Venetia had been right in that. Too late she realised just what her friend had been warning her against.

She stared at the cheque. She might not know the figure written there, but she knew it was high. Common sense and practicality told her she should accept it. Take it to the bank this very day. You had to be careful with money. Save it. Look after it. The future was never certain and life without money could be very hard indeed. Who better than Alice knew that? But when she looked at the cheque, Razeby's money, and all that it meant, she could not bring herself to do it.

Folding the cheque within the letter just as it had been, she heated a blob of rich red wax and let it drip to cover and melt away Razeby's crest. Within a few moments it had cooled and the letter was sealed once more, the wax disc smooth and even.

She took it out to the footman who waited in the hallway. A footman she recognised from Razeby's town house in Leicester Square. He recognised her, too, although he said nothing. If he knew the contents of the letter, he gave no sign.

'If you would be so kind as to return this to Lord Razeby.'

'Certainly, Miss Sweetly. Is there a message you wish relayed?' he enquired.

'None other than what is within the letter.' She smiled at him.

'Very good, miss.' He bowed and left.

Alice watched him go.

It had taken Razeby less than a week to find her. Just for a minute she wondered if Venetia had told him. But she knew in her heart her friend would never have broken her word. Razeby was a marquis, a man of power and money and contacts, all of which he had clearly used.

But he could keep his money. She would not touch a damn penny of it.

Chapter Six

Razeby had checked every entry in the estate account books. The task kept his mind from wandering to other thoughts he had no wish to think. Thoughts of the future. And even more thoughts of the past…with Alice.

Lifting the pen, he made to enter the figure in the column at the bottom of the open page and found the inkwell dry. He opened the top drawer of his desk to find a fresh bottle of ink and saw, lying there, the cheque he had written to her.

He stilled, his eyes fixed upon it. Four thousand pounds, twice what was specified in their contract, and she had sent it back as if it were some kind of insult. Some men might have construed it as a means of angling for more money, but Razeby knew in his gut that it was not. There was a finality about it, a closure rather than an opening of negotiation, and it made him uncomfortable. Had she asked for three times the sum he would have felt happier. Maybe then he would not be worrying over her.

The memory came again of the expensive dresses still hanging in the wardrobe at Hart Street, all the jewellery still in its casket, the diamond bracelet abandoned upon the bed. And the same uneasiness rippled through him, the gnawing feeling that it was all wrong, the unmistakable essence that there were layers between the two of them that he dare not explore. He quelled the feelings, reassured himself that he had done everything he could. He could no longer be a part of Alice's life, nor she a part of his. What she chose to do was no longer his concern. Lifting out the bottle of ink, he turned his eyes from the cheque and shut the drawer.

He had just blotted the entry and closed the books when the butler announced that Linwood had come to call.

'Were we supposed to be riding this morning?' Razeby asked.

Linwood shook his head. 'Not this morning. I came to ask if you are attending the Lords this afternoon.

'I am.'

'It is the debate on Wellesley-Pole's circular letter.'

'The Irish issue.' Razeby could almost hear the whisper of Alice's Irish accent, so soft against his ear.

'I heard that there are plans to bring up the fact that you are biased on the matter.'

Because of Alice. The words went unspoken between them.

'Do they not know she is no longer my mistress?' he asked.

'I am sure they are well aware, but they will still use the association against you. Feelings are running high on the subject. Better be prepared, Razeby.'

'I will,' he murmured. 'Sit down. You'll take a brandy?'

'A trifle early in the day, Razeby.' It was, but he needed it.

'Coffee, then?'

Linwood gave a nod.

They spoke about horses and other inconsequential things while waiting for the coffee. He waited until they were sipping their coffee, bitter and strong, before he asked what he could no longer stop himself from asking. It was natural, he justified. Any reasonable, fair-minded gentleman would do the same, although the words perhaps would not have clamoured so desperately for release.

'Have you heard anything of Alice?' He did not meet Linwood's eye.

'She opens tonight in Covent Garden's Theatre Royal, playing Lady Macbeth,' said Linwood. 'Kemble has made quite a fanfare. It has sold out. There is not a seat to be had in the house.'

'So I saw in the newspapers.' He paused. 'Has Venetia seen her?'

'I believe so.' Linwood sipped at his coffee. 'They are as much friends as we two.'

The silence was loud between them

Razeby swallowed, wondering how far he dare go without raising his friend's suspicions. 'How is she?'

'I understand that she is well.'

Razeby gave a nod and cleared his throat. There was another awkward pause. 'If you should ever hear otherwise…'

'Do not worry, Razeby,' Linwood said quietly. 'Should that be the case, I would let you know.'

'Thank you, Linwood.' He breathed a little easier.

* * *

There was a rap on the dressing room door. The same dressing room she had shared with Venetia all those months ago, before Venetia had married Linwood and Alice had become Razeby's mistress.

'Five minutes to curtain up, Miss Sweetly.'

'Thank you.'

It was Alice's opening night, her grand return to the Theatre Royal as a full-time actress.

Her palms were clammy with nerves, her stomach turning somersaults at the prospect of walking out on that stage alone before a packed house. It had always been this way. But it had not been as bad when Venetia was here as the leading lady and Alice just sharing the spotlight. And thereafter, during her occasional appearances, there had been Razeby. Just his presence, with his easygoing manner and his smile, with his utter belief in her and the way he could rub that little spot at the back of her head that, no matter what, relaxed her tension and made all of her nerves and worries fade away.

There was no Razeby tonight. She sat alone and looked at her painted face in the peering glass, lit bright with candles. She looked strong and capable and determined, even if she said so herself.

She inhaled slowly and deeply. She could do this. She would do this. Pour all of everything she did not feel over Razeby into the part. It was a simple strategy.

Another deep breath and Alice rose and walked out of the little dressing room, along the corridor and through the wings.

'Miss Sweetly on stage in five, four, three, two…' They counted her down with every step she took.

'One.' She walked out on that stage before a packed Theatre Royal.

Her eyes slipped unbidden to Razeby's box.

It was empty. And she was glad of it.

She shifted her eyes to Linwood's box. And there, beside Linwood, was Venetia. Just as she had promised.

Alice smiled, and when she opened her mouth to speak she was not Alice any more but Lady Macbeth.

The clock ticked on the mantel. The sunlight streamed into the study, catching on the crystal drops of the wall sconces on either side of the fireplace and making them shimmer and sparkle with a rainbow of colours. From somewhere in the house there was the quiet opening and closing of a door.

Razeby noticed nothing of it. He stood, rather than sat, at his desk, his focus trained on the newspaper spread open on his desk before him, more specifically on the article about the woman whose return to the stage had taken Covent Garden by storm. London was in awe, as it regaled the delights of the previous night's play with Alice in the role of the leading lady. His eyes followed down the printed column, reading each and every word.

Since her separation from a certain Lord R., Miss Sweetly's acting talent has blossomed and taken on a new and vibrant dimension. She has a passion and realism that quite transfixed the audience and left them shouting, nay, begging, for more.

He had always known she had such wonderful talent upon the stage and he was truly gladdened by her success. But beneath his happiness for her was also an ache.

A subtle rap of knuckles against his study door and then his butler was there, showing his lawyer in.

'Mr Ernst of Ernst, Spottiswoode and Farmer, my lord.'

Razeby's eyes lingered on the words for only a second longer. Then he closed the newspaper and set it aside.

'You sent for me, Lord Razeby, to undertake an audit of the Razeby estate and monies.'

Razeby did not allow himself to think of Alice, but only of what lay ahead.

He took his seat at his desk. 'Please sit down, Mr Ernst.'

Alice was in the middle of removing her stage make-up after her fifth evening of performing when Sara, her fellow actress and mistress to Viscount Fallingham, popped her head round the door of Alice's dressing room.

'Hawick asked if you'll be coming with us tomorrow. There's a little outing arranged to Hyde Park, a promenade at the fashionable hour. I've already run it past Kemble and he's all for it. There's me and a couple of the other actresses, Hawick, Monteith, Frew, and Fallingham of course, not that he doesn't trust me.' She smirked.

Alice thought of her theatre contract. Being seen with the top gentlemen of the *ton* was all part of the promotion she was required to undertake. And now that the performances had started there was no longer any reason to avoid this side of it.

'You don't need to worry, Alice. Razeby won't be there. I checked for you.'

Alice felt her blood run cold. 'You checked?' she said softly.

'I didn't think you would want to bump into him any time soon.'

It was the truth, but she knew she could not let the comment go unchallenged. 'Why not?'

'Because it's only been a couple of weeks since…' Sara glanced away awkwardly.

'He gave me my *congé*,' Alice finished for her with a smile. 'You can say the words. I'm perfectly fine with it.' She knew whatever she said to Sara would be all round the theatre by this time tomorrow.

'I thought that you and he…the way the two of you were together…that maybe you were loved up on him.'

Alice dreaded that was what they were all thinking. She gave a scornful laugh. 'Don't be daft. It was an arrangement, nothing more.' She still had her pride.

'But the way you looked at one another. If Fallingham looked at me like that…' Sara fanned a hand before her face as if just the thought brought her out in a scorching flush.

'We had a good time.' Alice gave a shrug of her shoulders as if it was nothing so very special. 'But these things aren't meant to last.' A parody of the words Razeby had said to her, standing there in that bedchamber.

'Was it an amicable separation?' Sara's curiosity was getting the better of her. She looked surprised, making Alice wonder just what the gossipmongers had been saying, given that they had so little to go on. Maybe she needed to give them a little grist for their mill.

'Sorry to disappoint the girls, but, yes, it was.'

'We thought you were upset, you've not been seen out anywhere on the town.'

'I've been busy. Give me a chance. I've not even finished my first opening week!'

'I suppose so,' said Sara.

'And I'm not upset in the slightest.' Alice smiled to prove it.

Sara gave a grin and looked like she believed her. 'So you'll come tomorrow?'

'I'm looking forward to it already.'

The door closed behind Sara.

Alice took a deep breath. There could be nothing of avoidance. Avoidance was tantamount to admitting that she cared, that she was hurt, that she could not bear to face him. And none of that was the case, as London would see soon enough.

She was getting on with her life. And if Razeby happened to cross her path, then so be it.

It would make not one jot of difference to her. *He* would make not one jot of difference to her.

Within Hyde Park Miss Pritchard was strolling by Razeby's side, her concentration more on the people in the park who were looking at them than anything else. Behind them, Mrs Pritchard, her younger daughter by her side, was espousing on the merits of good breeding and outlining a detailed Pritchard family lineage in the process.

The Pritchards were wealthy and well connected. A suitable alliance for Razeby. But Razeby did not know if he could suffer Mrs Pritchard's incessant boasting. Or, indeed, Miss Pritchard herself. All he had to do was marry her and bed her. It should be simple enough, especially for a man like him who had bedded no shortage of women in his life. But the prospect left him cold.

He stared into the hazy afternoon distance and tried to not to think about it.

The last time he had been here in Hyde Park was with Alice. She had shunned the use of his curricle and insisted they walk. She did not care about being seen on his arm or not. What she had cared about were simple things—the glory of the sunshine, the freshness of the air, the birdsong and the furls of new green buds on the trees; riches for the eyes, as she called nature or art or anything that she liked to look at. He had been unable to prevent his fingers from curling in hers. And she had smiled and not given a damn about who was watching them.

The memory made his heart swell.

He felt Miss Pritchard's hand upon his arm stiffen. Mrs Pritchard was still talking, but he could hear the increased arrogance and volume of her tone, that sudden slight edge of superiority and distaste.

And then he saw the reason why. Ahead, rounding the corner was a small party of men and women, out taking the air and being seen at this most fashionable of hours in the park. But not just any men and women. The men were some of the highest in the *ton*. Of the women, Razeby only noticed one. A woman who stood out from the others because she was golden and beautiful and she just seemed to glow with life and with happiness. He could hear the playful banter within the little party, the laughter, the teasing, flirtatious air.

Alice, clad in her plain pale-yellow walking dress and contrasting cream spencer and gloves, was walking by Hawick's side, listening to something the duke was saying to her. Perched at a jaunty angle on her head was a small stylish hat he had not seen her wear before.

Beneath it her fair hair, so haphazardly pinned up, had allowed pale golden strands to escape and waft art-lessly around her neck. It was fresh and simple. He had watched her so many times twist her hair up and pin it all within a minute, only to have him unpin it and slip his fingers through those long silken skeins and take her into his arms and kiss her.

She looked comfortable, confident and yet with that same slight shyness that had always intrigued him. Her eyes were lowered as she listened to something that Ha-wick was saying, but she was smiling. The sight of her made Razeby feel things he did not want to feel. Not now that it was over and he had set his mind to doing what must be done. There was the hard thud of his heart. The fast rush of his blood.

And the awful sinking sensation of his predicament.

Miss Pritchard was by his side, her mother and sister walking behind. Razeby realised what he was going to have to do. What any gentleman in his position would have to do. And the prospect of it sent a chill all the way through him.

Alice had been his mistress. The woman walking by his side could be his wife.

Duty. The word seemed to resonate with every beat of his heart.

Du-ty.

Du-ty.

Du-ty.

He had no choice.

He turned his eyes away from Alice. Kept his focus steadfastly elsewhere. Cutting her, as the rules of po-lite society dictated. As if she were some stranger. As if she were not the woman he had loved every night of the past six months.

But he could see her in his peripheral vision, that blur of yellow and cream and blonde, slight beside the tall loom of Hawick's darkness. And he could hear the rustle of the silk of her skirts, hear the distinctive lilt of her softly spoken words, smell the faint scent of her perfume.

His heart beat faster.

He could sense her, feel her, the awareness as sharp as if his eyes were studying her every detail.

He measured every step that brought them ever closer on this path, knowing that they must pass one another, that it was far too late for retreat. Neither of them could turn away from this.

He knew that Alice's attention was all fixed on Hawick. As if she had not even noticed Razeby. As if she were cutting him every bit as much as he were cutting her. And he should be glad of it. Truly he should. But it was not gladness that he felt as the little group strolled towards him and his party through the sunshine.

Every step brought her nearer.

Five feet... She was so close now that he could hear the soft breathiness of her laughter at Hawick's joke.

Four feet... Everything sharpened. Everything focused. The hushed ripple of grass blades in the breeze. The sweep of her eyelashes, soft as a butterfly's wing.

Three feet... The sound of his breath. *Alice.*

Two feet... The beat of his heart...and of hers. *Alice.*

One foot... Razeby turned his gaze to Alice. And in that very last moment, that second in which all of time seemed to slow and stop, she raised her eyes to meet his.

The jolt hit his stomach and rippled right through his

body. It was as if they were the only two people in the park. As if all of the past six months flashed between them in stark vivid clarity. As if the dark blue depths of her eyes swallowed him up and submersed the whole of him in this moment and this woman and all that was beating through him.

Their gazes locked and held. And he could not look away, not if all of the future depended on it, which in a way it did.

And then the moment was past.

She was past.

Walking on with Hawick and the others. Walking away from him.

His steps never faltered. He kept on walking. As if nothing had just happened.

No one else noticed. Everything else went on just the same. Miss Pritchard's fingers still lay upon his arm. Mrs Pritchard was still selling the family pedigree behind him, her younger daughter chipping in smart little comments here and there.

But Razeby was not the same.

Something had just happened and the force of it shook him more than he wanted to admit. Something had just happened, something which Razeby did not understand.

Alice did not hear what it was that Hawick had been saying to her, all she could hear was the rush of her own blood too loud in her ears and all she could feel was the tremor that vibrated through her body. She deliberately kept her gaze low as if playing coy with Hawick, when in truth, it was to hide the storm of emotion suddenly raging within her.

She had seen Razeby and his party, the rich, beautiful young woman clinging so possessively to his arm, and the women who could only be her mother and sister walking so proudly behind, the minute she had rounded the corner. And she had prepared herself. Knowing that he had no choice but to cut her. Knowing she had no choice but to not give a damn. To cut him right back.

And she had almost done it. Would have done it, despite the pound and throb of her heart, and the raw rush of air that rasped in her lungs, and the tight knot that worked itself ever tighter in her stomach, except for that last moment, when it felt like his voice had whispered her name, calling her. The sound of it stroking right down her spine. Tingling against her skin. And she had answered without pausing to think. Yielded to it instinctively.

And when she looked, those liquid brown eyes had been on hers, not looking away, not cutting her, only holding her as intensely as they ever had done, perhaps even more so. As if all that had gone between them had not ended, but grown only stronger. Her heart was still beating nineteen to the dozen.

By her side Hawick shifted infinitesimally closer.

'So you will come, Miss Sweetly?' he was saying.

She calmed herself, hid the shock of what had just passed between her and Razeby. By the time she raised her eyes to meet Hawick's she had herself under control again.

She smiled at him, although she had not the slightest idea of what he had just invited her to. 'If I'm free,' she said. 'I'll need to check my diary.' Truly the consummate professional. Venetia, her teacher, would have been proud of her.

Hawick smiled, too, with a particular interest in his eyes that made her want to shiver in the warmth of the spring sunshine. She hid the urge, along with all the others.

The party walked on through the park.

Hawick began another story, but Alice was not listening to Hawick or his story. She was thinking of Razeby and why, despite everything, it felt just like it had done when she had seen him for the very first time.

Chapter Seven

Razeby dreamed that night that Alice was with him in the bed, that they were still together and all was as it had been.

'Razeby,' she had whispered in her soft Celtic lilt and stroked her fingers against his cheek. 'Razeby.'

Alice. In the dream he had whispered her name through the darkness. 'Alice,' the word murmured aloud on his lips as he held her to him, so glad she had found him, to save him from the terrible thing that was coming, although in the dream he could not remember the nature of the dawning threat, no matter how hard he tried.

The early morning sunlight danced across his eyes, waking him from sleep, dragging him back from his dream world to reality. His body was primed and hard, his erection throbbing for release, but Alice was not in his arms.

He was alone.

And he knew the terrible dark thing that was coming.

The warm comfort of the dream world fell away, leaving in its place the hard coldness of reality and a sinking feeling in his gut. His arousal deflated.

The sunlight that had crept through the crack in his curtains dimmed behind the greyness of cloud. Razeby threw aside the covers and sat up, swinging his legs round to sit on the edge of the bed, relishing the sting of the cool morning air against the nakedness of his skin. It helped clear his mind of Alice and the bittersweet echo of the dream.

The clock chimed nine just before his valet knocked on the door and entered, followed by a maid bearing a pitcher of hot water and his secretary carrying a diary that Razeby knew was crammed full of appointments. He pushed aside the dream as surely as he had pushed aside what had happened yesterday in Hyde Park. Guilt, lust, desire—whatever it was. He could not name it otherwise. He would not name it otherwise.

Not Miss Pritchard, he thought. But tonight there was dinner at Mrs Padstow's at which twenty young respectable women would be present. And tomorrow afternoon, a débutante picnic organised by Lady Jersey. Then there was Almack's, and Lady Routledge's matchmaking ball. And he would find a wife at one of those.

He raked a hand through his hair and, taking a deep breath, rose to face the day.

Alice came offstage to rapturous applause that night. Three curtain calls and still the audience were whistling and calling for more. Her dressing room was so crammed with flowers there was scarcely room for the rail of costumes and table of face paints with its peering glass. Their perfume filled the air of the little room: roses, lilies, sprays of blooms she did not recognise. All with letters and cards attached. All sealed with red wax which displayed the crests or monograms of their senders so prominently. Her eyes scanned over the seals, searching for one in particular. She could not help herself. He had been too much in her mind since yesterday and Hyde Park. Although heaven only knew why. She caught what she was doing and, with a harsh sigh of annoyance, averted her eyes and got on with wiping the make-up from her face. Then she slipped into the fawn-silk evening dress that was hanging over the dressing screen.

A knock sounded on the dressing-room door. The stage hand's voice shouted through the wood.

'Five minutes to the Green Room, Miss Sweetly. Mr Kemble says to tell you that both the Duke of Hawick and the Duke of Monteith are in again tonight.'

'Right you are, Billy. I'll be right there.' She checked her appearance in the peering glass. The woman that looked back from the glass was pale without the thick grease and colour of the stage make-up. And she thought again of that moment in Hyde Park.

'Don't be such a damned fool, Alice Flannigan, you're imagining things,' she whispered to herself, using the name with which she had been born, rather than that she had taken for the stage. 'You put a smile on your face and get through there, girl. Life goes on— if you're lucky. And he isn't worth it.' She rubbed a little rouge on to her cheeks, added a spot to her lips and tucked an errant strand of hair into place.

Taking a deep breath, she held her head high, fixed a smile on her face and went to sparkle and entice the gentlemen of the Green Room, just as her contract required.

* * *

'Razeby,' Viscount Bullford exclaimed, wandering over to where Razeby stood filling a plate with choice selections at the débutante picnic. 'Thought Aunt Harriet would have lampooned you into coming this afternoon.'

'Bullford.' Razeby gave a nod.

The weather was sunny and dry, although a slight chill still sat about the fine spring day. The trees surrounding this corner of the park lent a level of protection against the breeze, but not enough to stop the gentle flutter of bonnet ribbons and muslin skirts amongst the ladies milling all around.

Bullford lifted a small, perfectly formed pork pie from one of the serving dishes on the nearby table and took a bite. 'Couldn't get out of it myself. Pater had m'arm up my back. Insisted I had to bring m'friends with me. Apparently too many ladies and not enough gentlemen.'

'You managed to persuade the others to come?' Razeby raised an eyebrow in surprise.

'Not an easy task, I can tell you, old man.' Bullford took a deep breath as if the memory of what that had entailed was difficult to bear. 'Will be years till I can clear the favours owed over this one.'

Razeby smiled.

Fallingham, Devlin, Monteith and a few others wandered up, glasses of champagne and large chunks of food in hand.

'How goes the bride search, Razeby?' Devlin asked.

'Well enough.' He felt himself tense just at the question.

'Found one yet?' Fallingham enquired.

'Not yet.' He kept his face impassive, his manner cool.

'Don't seem quite yourself of late, Razeby,' Monteith observed.

He smiled at the irony of Monteith's remark. Would any man be the same were he to stand in Razeby's shoes? 'Can't imagine why,' he said drolly.

'Losing one's freedom, weddings, wives and nurseries,' Devlin supplied and gave a shudder.

The rest of the group chuckled as if that was the reason.

'Not regretting giving up the delightful Miss Sweetly, are you?' Monteith asked as he helped himself to a bottle of champagne from a passing footman and topped up all their glasses.

Nonchalantly uttered words, yet they cut through everything to touch some raw inner part of Razeby. It was all he could do not to suck in his breath at the sensation.

'Not at all,' he said smoothly and held Monteith's gaze, denying the suggestion all the more.

'Do not know why.' Monteith smirked. 'The common consensus is that you have run mad. Dismissing such a little gem when all of London is panting after her.'

It took every bit of willpower to keep his jaw from hardening and the basilisk stare from his eyes, and to prevent the curl of his fingers into a fist.

'You could have kept her on,' said Devlin. 'I would have, had it been me.'

'We all would have,' said Monteith.

'I am not you.' And Alice deserved a damn sight more respect than that.

'Why exactly didn't you keep her on?' asked Fallingham and stopped sipping his champagne to hear the answer.

The rest of the group looked at Razeby expectantly, a speculation in their eyes that had not been there before.

'Do you really have to ask?' he drawled with a deliberate ambiguity that did nothing to answer the question.

'What you need is to get her back in your bed,' said Fallingham.

'What I need is to get myself a wife.' He gritted his teeth.

'The two need not be mutually exclusive,' Monteith commented.

'For me they are,' Razeby said it with nothing of his usual jest or charm. He smiled, but the smile was hard and his eyes cool. He saw the look that was exchanged between his friends. And he did not care.

The awkwardness of the moment was alleviated by Bullford's mother, the formidable Lady Willaston, who appeared amidst their circle. 'Sorry to interrupt your little chat, gentlemen, but, Lord Razeby, Miss Frome is nigh on ready to swoon with hunger from waiting for the plate of food you went to fetch her some considerable time ago.'

'My humble apologies, ma'am.' Razeby gave a nod. 'If you will excuse me, gentlemen...' Picking up the plate from the table next to him, he made his way back to Miss Frome and her friends.

On the day after the débutante picnic Alice's visitors sat in her new little drawing room while she poured tea into the three china cups set on their saucers on the table before her.

Ellen and Tilly were old friends—they worked secretly as Miss Vert and Miss Rose at the blot in Alice's past, London's infamous high class brothel, Mrs Silver's

House of Rainbow Pleasures, in which the courtesans each dressed in a different colour and hid their identities behind feathered Venetian masks.

'You ain't half landed on your feet, Alice,' said Tilly, glancing wide eyed round at the warm yellow decor of the drawing room with its gilt-and-crystal chandelier and peering glasses. 'Razeby must have seen you all right in his severance settlement.'

Alice smiled and passed the teacups to each of her friends in turn. 'Of course he did.'

'What did you manage to wangle from him? A suitably large sum and a nice piece of expensive jewellery, I hope,' Ellen said.

Alice thought of the diamond bracelet and felt that same chill ripple through her. 'I couldn't possibly comment,' she said, still smiling. She could not tell them the truth. Everyone knew the deal in relationships like hers and Razeby's. Everyone knew she would have taken everything she could from him. It was what any mistress would have done to her protector.

'You held him to the letter of the contract between you?' Ellen asked.

'Absolutely.' But Alice had no idea what was written within the legal contract that had defined her and Razeby's arrangement. The document had never been unfolded; it still lay, tied in its green ribbon, in the drawer of the desk in Hart Street. She remembered the day that Razeby had presented her with it and how she had refused to accept it until the red ribbon that was used to secure all such legal documents was changed. Razeby had sent out immediately for a green ribbon and tied it in place himself as she stood and watched.

'Don't let the bastard wriggle out of it.' Ellen grinned.

But Razeby had not tried to wriggle out of anything. Quite the reverse. It made her feel angrier, both at him and herself.

She stretched her smile wider, pushing the feeling away. 'I've a good head on my shoulders when it comes to money.' It was true. She thought of the money that Razeby had given her through the months they had been together, little of it spent on frivolities. A regular sum had been sent to her mother in Ireland, the rest she had saved.

'And a good head when it comes to men.' Tilly grinned. 'You did all right out of Razeby.'

'I did,' she admitted and turned her mind away from why the knowledge made her feel queasy.

'You're a clever girl, Alice.' Tilly poured her tea from her cup into her saucer and sipped it as daintily as any lady.

'Aren't I just?' she exclaimed in a voice that made them all laugh.

'Thank you, Mr Brompton. We will continue our discussions later, when you return.' Razeby dismissed his steward from his study and turned to where Linwood was standing by the fireplace, examining the portrait of Razeby's father that hung on the wall above.

'I would have come back another time when you were not busy,' said Linwood, turning to him. 'I did not realise you had summoned Brompton down from the Razeby estate.'

'One has to get one's affairs in order...' he glanced away '...before one's marriage.' The ticking of the clock punctuated the silence.

'You do not seem yourself, Razeby.'

He did not feel himself. 'Prospect of parson's trap does that to a man.' He attempted a light-hearted response. 'You should know.'

Linwood's dark eyes met his and there was not a trace of humour in them. 'I do not,' he said, admitting the truth outright of what lay between him and Venetia. 'But then you are already aware of that.'

Razeby turned away and poured them both a brandy, handing one to Linwood.

'It is not that. There is something more. There is a change in you,' said Linwood, still holding him under scrutiny.

Razeby gave a laugh and turned his gaze away from those shrewd black eyes. 'You grow both fanciful and poetic in your old age, Linwood. Have you been in Byron's company?'

'No.' Linwood was to the point.

Silence.

Razeby gave a shrug, but made no more denials. 'Maybe it is time for a change. A man must face his fate, sooner or later.' The inescapable fate that they all would face in the end.

'He must indeed. But it does not need to be like this.'

'Believe me, it does,' said Razeby with a grim smile.

'There is a rumour circulating about you and Hart Street.'

'There is always some rumour or other circulating,' he said curtly, not wanting to discuss anything of that.

'And Alice?'

'I have already told you, it is over with Alice.' His voice sounded too harsh and defensive.

Linwood knew better than to probe further.

* * *

Before heading to the Green Room within the Theatre Royal that night, Alice called in at the dressing room that Sara shared with two other actresses.

'Oh, Alice, I'm not ready yet! I just can't get my hair to sit right. All the curls have fallen out because of that damn wig! Look at the state of it!' Sara wailed.

'Just leave it as it is, Sara!' one of the other actresses said. 'Or we're all going to be late for the Green Room and Kemble will have something to say about that.'

'You two go on ahead and keep Kemble happy. I'll help Sara with her hair,' Alice said.

'If you're sure, Alice?' They did not look certain.

'Go! The pair of you!' Alice ordered with a grin.

The two younger women smiled and hurried away, while Alice, elbows akimbo, hands on hips, turned to where Sara sat before a peering glass, her hair lying limp and straight from three hours of compression beneath a hot heavy wig.

'Lucky for you I'm a dab hand with hair that'll not take a curl. Now, missus.' Using just her fingers she scraped Sara's hair back into a ponytail, twisted it round, gave it a flick and secured it in place with just three pins.

'Alice, you're a wonder!'

'I am, indeed,' Alice teased. 'Now, come on, get yourself moving, girl.' She turned to leave.

'Just before we go through...' Sara put a hand on her arm. 'The gaming evening at Dryden's, the one I told you about last week.'

'It is still on, isn't it?'

'Yes.' Sara smiled and gave a nod, but there was a slight look of unease in her eyes. 'It's just...well...I was talking to Fallingham about it last night and it seems that he's invited Razeby.'

Razeby. Just his name made Alice's heart skip a beat.

Sara screwed up her face in an expression of awkward apology. 'Sorry!'

'What's to be sorry about?' Alice gave a smile. 'It doesn't matter to me whether Razeby's there or not. I've already told you, it's fine between us.'

'Really?'

'Really,' Alice reassured her.

'I hope so, or it's going to be an awfully uncomfortable evening.'

'You don't have to worry about that, honestly.' Such confidence. Truly worthy of her best performance upon the stage.

Sara smiled her relief.

'Now come on.' Alice slipped her arm through Sara's. 'Kemble will be wondering where on earth we've got to. Better make sure you dazzle him with that new hairstyle of yours.'

Sara gave a giggle as the two of them hurried from the dressing room towards the Green Room, to dazzle and sparkle, to tease and entice. But beneath all of Alice's air of glamour and charm was the constant knowledge that tomorrow would bring Dryden's and a night spent gaming with Razeby.

Chapter Eight

Dryden's Gambling Palace was busy. It was a luxurious affair that rivalled Watier's, with tables to cater to every taste and every pocket. The top room had a chandelier reputed to have real diamonds amongst its glass. Entry was by invitation only and the stakes could stretch to match the highest in all of London.

The room was spacious, airy, the walls papered in plum-coloured paper embellished with real gold patterning. The floor was tiled in marble imported from Italy, black and gold to match that of the blinds that masked the windows. There were no footmen, only the prettiest girls dressed up in footmen's livery who served free drinks to the men who came here to game.

Along the full length of one wall was a bar that housed any drink a man might desire, whatever the time of day. On the opposite side was an enormous Palladian-style fireplace of black marble. The walls themselves were hung with expensive works of art depicting Rubenesque women and wondrous exotic landscapes. But no clocks. Not a single one.

A champagne fountain flowed in the centre of the

room, the filled glasses from which were being served and replenished all around. There was a faro table in one corner, casino in another, and tables for *vingt-et-un,* hazard and piquet in between. In the furthest corner a whist table catered for the more elderly gentlemen or the few ladies who ever dared enter this hallowed place. Women of the *demi-monde* were a different story.

Alice stood with Sara looking over the men seated round the *vingt-et-un* table. Razeby was not here and Alice felt a curious mix of both relief and disappointment at his absence.

'Do you play tonight, ladies?' drawled Monteith.

'I'm here only as Fallingham's good-luck charm,' said Sara, stepping up close behind the chair at which Fallingham was already seated and resting her hands upon his shoulders in an intimate fashion. Alice watched while the viscount lifted one of her hands to his mouth and kissed it. The display of charm and affection reminded her too much of Razeby, making her feel awkward. The smile felt stiff upon her mouth.

'Somehow, gentlemen, I feel my luck is in tonight whatever chances to happen upon this table,' Fallingham said in a playful tone.

Sara's smiled deepened and Monteith and several of the men smiled in that knowing way.

Alice swallowed her discomfort and glanced away.

'And what about you, Miss Sweetly?' Monteith raised an eyebrow. 'Which one of us lucky gentlemen will be fortunate enough to have you act as our charm this evening?' There was speculation and interest in his eyes, in Frew's, and too many of the other men's. She knew what playing the part of any of their lucky charms in this place would entail and she would be damned if she would do that, no matter that she wanted to prove that Razeby meant nothing to her. Flirtation was one thing, an illusion of sparkling enticement, but an illusion just the same. She could not go so far as to let any of them actually touch her.

'Oh, I'm my own lucky charm,' she said smoothly. 'I play tonight, Your Grace.'

She saw the stir of interest around the table, the way they liked that idea.

Monteith smiled, as if amused by both the double meaning of her words and her challenge. 'Do you need anyone to…refresh your memory as to the rules?' He put it so delicately, but she knew what he was thinking, that she had no idea how to play a serious game of cards.

'No, thank you, Your Grace. I think I can remember them.'

They smiled at her indulgently.

As if she could ever forget. Razeby had taught her the trick behind stacking the odds in your favour of winning in *vingt-et-un*—the way to count and memorise the cards. It was a game that they had liked to play often. A game that they had played not for money, but for the removal of their clothes. Razeby always said that the excellence of her memory made her a natural at it—either that or a desire to have him stripped naked before her.

The last time they had played it had been only three weeks ago and they had ended up making love on the dining-room table on top of the forgotten scattered cards. The memory made her heart skip a beat and brought a slight blush both of anger and embarrassment to her cheeks. She thrust it away and took her seat beside Fallingham.

The *vingt-et-un* dealer, dressed in the smart black-

and-gold livery of the gaming house, sat in the middle of the other side of the table. There were empty chairs on either side of him, one of which would not have been empty had Razeby been here. She felt a slight sense of pique at his absence, part of her wanting him to see this proof of how little he had affected her.

'The house rules apply. Are you ready to begin, gentlemen...and Miss Sweetly?' The dealer smiled politely at her.

There was common agreement.

'Then we shall commence.'

Alice kept her eyes on his hands as he dealt a card to each of them and himself last of all, before dealing a second card in a repeat of the process.

'Not too late, am I, gentlemen?'

The smooth velvet voice stroked all the way down her spine. A voice she knew too well, which the mere memory of could set her skin a-tingle and her heart racing. Alice froze in that moment, her heart skipping a beat before setting off at a thunderous tilt. She forced herself to breathe, to stay calm, to focus. And only then did she raise her eyes to look at Razeby, at the very same minute his eyes met hers.

There was the tiniest of moments—that catch of time, that ripple of tension. And then he bowed smoothly. 'Miss Sweetly.'

'Lord Razeby,' she replied politely, as if all of the previous six months had never been. Round the table every pair of eyes looked not at the cards upon the table but at Alice and Razeby.

She had prepared herself for seeing him this time, she reminded herself. And she *was* a very good actress. She breathed, calmed herself, smiled.

'Miss Sweetly decided to play tonight,' Monteith said, the unnecessary explanation a subtle message to Razeby, as if Alice would not understand.

Her eyes met Razeby's, a silent comment upon Monteith's transparent and wasted subtlety passing between them. She remembered what she had come here to do and she smiled at him, a smile that only he would understand.

He knew her challenge. Accepted it by selecting the chair directly opposite her to take his seat.

'I hope you have deep pockets tonight, Razeby,' she said.

All the men laughed, not appreciating the full depth of her tease.

But Razeby did. 'Perhaps not deep enough,' he said. She could see it in his eyes as they met hers, knew it for certain with his next words. 'Maybe we should lower the minimum stake on account of Miss Sweetly's playing.'

There were murmurs of assent as the men around the table mistook his meaning. They all thought it was because, otherwise, she would be out after the first few hands.

'Afraid, Razeby?' She arched an eyebrow, and held his gaze boldly, all the while letting the small smile still play around her mouth.

'My concern is all for you, Miss Sweetly.'

She smiled at that, a smile of genuine amusement, and only then released his gaze, so that she could place a counter onto the green baize.

Bullford looked at the size of her stake, then leaned to her, a look of concern on his face. 'I say, Miss Sweetly, you have played before?'

'Once or twice. But, I admit, not usually for money,'

she said carelessly, and could not resist flitting a glance at Razeby. His eyes were on hers, deep and intent. He was remembering all the times they had played when it had not been for money.

Bullford lowered his voice a little. 'Razeby is considered something of a shark when it comes to *vingt-et-un*. Perhaps he did not tell you.'

She smiled at Bullford in a wickedly flirtatious way, knowing that Razeby was watching, then leaned in closer to him as if they were two conspirators. 'I thank you for the warning, my lord.' Then to Razeby, 'I hear you have something of a reputation when it comes to *vingt-et-un*.'

'I make no such claim.' His voice was soft, his manner subdued, his eyes sharply watchful.

'If you do not wish to play, Razeby…' The same words with which she had teased him on a hundred nights before.

'I do want to play, Miss Sweetly.' His eyes darkened ever so slightly as he gave the same reply he always had done.

Like two players in a script full of secret meanings to which only Razeby and Alice held the key.

She felt the tension tighten between them.

His eyes flicked to the dealer. 'Deal me in.'

Two cards came his way.

His eyes held Alice's. 'I hope you know what you are doing, Miss Sweetly.'

'Oh, I know all right, Lord Razeby,' she said softly. 'You needn't worry about that.'

'In that case…let us play.' He smiled.

And she returned the smile. A real smile. It was impossible not to. Despite everything.

* * *

After fifteen rounds, only four of them remained in the game—Monteith, Devlin, Razeby and herself. Monteith and Devlin were almost out of counters. The pile of counters in front of Alice was only marginally larger than that in front of Razeby. Men had wandered over from the other tables to watch the play so that a small crowd now surrounded them.

The sixteenth hand was dealt.

For all her laughter and sparkle and feigned joviality, all evening Alice had been watching the cards very carefully, memorising who held what, the cards that had gone from the pack and therefore, by default, those that remained. It was an easy enough task when she could hold the whereabouts of three packs in her head at any given time.

Razeby was rolling a counter within his hand. 'Fifty pounds.' He threw a pile of ten counters into the centre of the table.

She swallowed at the enormity of the bet.

Monteith glanced down at his three remaining counters and shook his head. 'Too high. Out.'

All eyes moved to Alice. She stayed calm, relaxed, still. Leaned back in her chair and met Razeby's warm brown eyes.

His gaze seemed to stroke against hers as he waited with everyone else for what she would do.

She smiled. 'Fifty pounds.' She matched the stake with ten counters of her own.

Monteith gave a chuckle. 'You do not frighten her, Razeby.'

She did not let herself think of the sums of money with which they were playing. Enough to last a poor man a lifetime. If her mother knew just how much money was on that table being gambled away…! Alice pushed the thought away, focused her mind. Money or clothes, in the end the game was just the same, if she kept her nerve.

Razeby did not so much as raise an eyebrow. He stayed cool, impassive. Just the hint of a smile upon his face.

Devlin met the stake. But when they turned over their cards Devlin lost his counters and was forced to bow out of the game, leaving only Alice, Razeby and the dealer to play the seventeenth hand.

The dealer dealt each of them their two cards.

It was Alice who was to set the stake this time. She met Razeby's gaze. Their eyes held, each knowing the other's strengths and weaknesses in this game. A test of nerve, a test of so much more.

Never let them see how much they've hurt you.

She smiled, hearing the words from so long ago in her head. Hurt just made you stronger. She did not let her gaze drop from his, held it as boldly as she had done that first night in the Green Room before he had been hers, and she, his. Held it and did not let it go.

'All in, two hundred pounds,' she said, and pushed all of her counters forwards.

The gasp rippled round the table.

'Good Lord,' she heard Fallingham mutter.

Beside her, Bullford produced a handkerchief and mopped at his brow.

The whole room was tense, poised for the next step. They stared at Razeby to see what he would do.

His eyes met hers again.

The attraction, the affinity that had always been between them was still there, stronger than ever. Power-ful. Dangerous. Beguiling.

'As you will, Miss Sweetly,' he murmured, and pushed all of his counters in to match hers.

Not a single voice spoke, not a glass sounded. Even the serving maids stopped where they were and stared to see what would happen.

The dealer's voice broke the silence. 'Lord Razeby…'

Razeby looked his cards. 'Stick.' He smiled at her.

'Miss Sweetly?' the dealer prompted.

She lifted her own, glanced down at them. 'Twist.'

The dealer dealt her a third card.

'Twist again.'

A fourth card came her way.

'And again if you'd be so kind, sir.'

There was a murmur of voices all around.

The dealer looked at Razeby. 'Please show, Lord Razeby.'

There was a craning of necks to see as Razeby laid his cards down on the table.

'Queen of hearts, king of hearts. Twenty,' the deal-er's voice intoned.

There was an irony in both cards. She wondered if Razeby realised it, too. That deep dark look in his eyes was so full of meanings that she could not tell.

'Please show, Miss Sweetly.'

Everyone looked at Alice as she laid the five cards down on the green baize: ace of hearts, two of hearts, three of spades, five of diamonds, queen of diamonds.

'Five-card trick,' said the dealer.

The buzz of excited voices spread throughout the room around them, followed by a silence as the dealer turned over his own cards. A ten and a seven. He added another from the pile—the six of clubs. 'Bust.' He cleared the cards with one smooth movement of his hand. 'Miss Sweetly wins.'

'Congratulations, Miss Sweetly.' Razeby was magnanimous in defeat, his dark gaze lingering on hers.

'Thank you, Lord Razeby,' she said with an innocence that belied the look in her eye.

'Alice, I cannot believe your luck tonight!' Sara exclaimed and hugged her, and the gentlemen clamoured excitedly all around.

'I say, Miss Sweetly!' Bullford was beaming by her side.

'Congratulations, Miss Sweetly.' Devlin was shaking her hand.

'Well done!' Frew took her hand next. 'You have a lucky streak to rival Razeby's.'

She smiled. Both Alice and Razeby knew that when it came to winning *vingt-et-un,* there was a great deal more to it than luck.

'I think you have played this more than a few times, Miss Sweetly.' Hawick was by her shoulder.

'Maybe,' she conceded. Her eyes flickered to Razeby's, resting there only for the briefest of moments. 'But never before in public.'

'We must have a game together some time,' said Hawick.

She saw the tiny telltale narrowing of Razeby's eyes, the slight flicker of tension in his jaw at Hawick's words, and she smiled a mischievous smile.

'Indeed, we must, Your Grace,' she said, and wandered away from the table with Hawick.

Chapter Nine

The early morning was bright, the air in Hyde Park fresh and filled with spring and all the promise that came with it. Razeby could smell the scent of leather and of horse, mixed with the freshness of earth and dew-laden grass, and feel the warmth of the early morning sun on his face.

'You seem in better temperament this morning, Razeby.'

Razeby smiled. 'It is a fine morning and I am out riding with my friend.'

Linwood kept his gaze forward facing. 'I heard that Alice was at Dryden's last night.'

'News travels fast.'

'It *is* London, Razeby.'

Razeby gave a laugh.

'Indeed, the news is that she was in your party and that she fleeced all of the table.'

'She did,' Razeby admitted.

'With a skill that matched your own.'

Alice's skill far exceeded his own. She had been a most ardent pupil. Razeby remembered how too many of those long dark winter nights had started between him and Alice, of him sharing his secrets, of her sharing hers....

'Strange, that,' commented Linwood.

'Is it?' said Razeby, all innocence.

'Who would have known she was so skilled at *vingt-et-un?*'

'Who indeed?' Razeby answered, revealing nothing of it.

'There is nothing of...awkwardness...between the two of you?'

'Nothing.' Awkwardness was not what lay between them. There was as much desire, tension and excitement as ever there had been. She had been flirting with him, flirting with the others. Light-hearted, teasing, mischievous. Just as she had done before. But there was a difference this time. There were other layers there that had not been present then and a subtle sense that she had removed herself from his reach—that he might look, but not touch. He could not get her out of his head.

'It was an enjoyable evening.' He told that part of the truth. Enjoyable, and exciting, in a way nothing had been since the last time he had glimpsed her in Hyde Park. He could still feel the thrill of it running through his blood. The thrill of her. Right up until Hawick and that naughty little jibe about playing cards with him. Razeby did not like the thought of that one little bit. That had not been enjoyable. That had been something else altogether.

'I am glad that the separation seems to have been an amicable one.'

But what things seemed and what they were in truth were not always the same thing. Razeby gave no reply.

He did not fully understand what was between him and Alice. But he knew that it was anything but amicable. It was raw and powerful and hungry. There were complexities to it that he did not understand, depths that were downright dangerous.

'It makes no difference whether it is amicable or not.' He needed to stay away from her and keep his mind focused on the marriage mart. But last night and this morning the marriage mart had never been further from his mind.

'In that case, you will not have an interest in which of your events Miss Sweetly is booked to be present.'

'I did not say that,' said Razeby quietly and looked over at him.

Linwood glanced up, the look exchanged between them saying much their words could not. 'She will be at White's next week. For the awards.'

'You are sure?' Razeby felt his heart beat quicker at just the prospect of seeing her there.

'My father is on the committee. Alice is the new darling of Covent Garden. The theatre has gone from barely making ends meet to being practically sold out every time she steps on stage. White's know she will go down a storm with its members. They have offered Kemble, the theatre and Alice a substantial amount of money for her presence.'

Razeby gave a nod. 'Thank you for the warning, my friend.'

Alice stood in the small anteroom that adjoined the main banqueting room in White's Gentleman's Club in St James's Street.

A nervousness ran through her, making her palms

clammy and her stomach turn a few cartwheels, and she knew it was not down to presenting a few awards to some stuffy, rich old gentlemen. She knew Razeby was in there. She knew, too, that he would be in receipt of one of the awards. Kemble had warned her. And the fact that Kemble had felt the need to do so was all the more reason that she could not refuse the invitation to be here tonight.

Had she and Razeby never been, she would have accepted this opportunity without hesitation. It promoted both herself and the theatre, and it paid well. So she accepted it just the same now. Not letting Razeby dictate her actions. She was getting on. Making a success of herself. Refusing to avoid him. And maybe there were a few other reasons, too.

It gave her another opportunity to show him how much she was over him. And maybe even to rub his nose in what he had given up just a little more. She smiled at that thought.

She was a successful actress. She earned her own money. And she really was over Razeby.

Alice took a deep breath and smiled.

The men were seated around the table in the banqueting room of White's Gentlemen's Club.

The dinner had been eaten. Their glasses were filled with port, cigarillos were being smoked, snuff boxes being opened and offered.

Mr Raggett, the proprietor of the club, had come in person to host the dinner and awards.

'And now, gentlemen, we come to the purpose of this, our annual awards ceremony. The giving of awards for services we, within our little club, consider outstanding in the past year. Services to our gentlemen's community, to the general well-being of the city of London, those in support of charities, and of the arts. And those a little less serious in nature...' He smiled and everyone in the room smiled, too, at what was coming. 'The member who has won the most entries in the betting book, and the least. The member who consumed the most bottles of port and still left standing, and he who holds the record for sleeping the longest in the drawing room.' Everybody looked at old Lord Soames.

'Speak up, young man,' Soames said in a loud voice. 'Can't hear a word you are saying.'

A chuckle rippled round the table, all the more so given that Raggett was sixty if he was a day.

'Every year we invite someone special to present the awards to each of our gentlemen and this present year is no exception. I guarantee you will not be disappointed. Gentlemen, please put your hands together and welcome straight from the stage of Covent Garden's Theatre Royal...'

Razeby knew what was coming yet he felt the anticipation of just hearing her name spear through his blood.

'...the delightful Miss Alice Sweetly,' finished Raggett.

Every man at the table got to his feet and applauded as Alice swept into the room.

She was dressed in the same pale-green silk evening dress as he had seen her wear a hundred times. A dress that complimented her fair colouring. The bodice was low, but not indecently so, fastened in the centre with a line of pearl buttons that he was most adept at unfastening.

The light from the overhead chandelier cast golden

tones in the dark blonde of her hair. She had not followed the fashion, trying to curl her hair and wear it up in a mass of flowing ringlets. She had told him so many times that her hair defied all attempts to hold a curl, no matter how tightly she tied the rags in it or how long she left them in place. She wore it in its usual simple style, caught back in a simple chignon. And tonight she would pluck those pins from it and uncoil it to hang loose and free down her back in long silky straight lengths. With deliberate control he turned his mind away from that image.

Raggett announced each award in turn, then read the name of the winner from the list, before passing the appropriate small silver cup to Alice. It was Alice who presented the cup to each winner, brushing a light kiss against each man's cheek.

He felt his stomach curl with anticipation. He tried not to think of it. It was just an award. Alice had been his mistress, nothing more. The sex had been amazing. She had been amazing. But that was over, done with. Or so he told himself. And he was taking Miss Longley out in his curricle in the morning. Doing what had to be done. He should just propose, move things on faster.

'The Marquis of Razeby.' Raggett's voice brought him back to himself.

He got to his feet, walked the length of the table to where she stood. And he couldn't take his eyes from her. She was so self-contained, so radiant and golden, exuding that same strange paradoxical play of shyness and confidence that had enticed him right from the very start. And as he walked towards her, her eyes watched him with that same calm which did not quite cover the teasing playfulness he knew lurked beneath.

'Congratulations, Lord Razeby,' she said in that sweet, soft, sexy voice. It stroked against his ear, rippled down the length of his spine, straight down into his breeches.

'Miss Sweetly,' he said in a voice that was nothing more than polite, but the hint of a smile played about his lips as much as it played about hers.

She knew what she was doing to him. Her smile broadened as she passed the silver cup into his hands, the tips of her fingers so close to his that his own tingled as if she had stroked against them, when in truth they did not touch. He could smell her perfume, the familiar clean scent of her, making his heart beat faster and stoking the heat all the hotter in his blood. Triggering memories he could not stop: Alice in his arms, Alice naked beneath him on the bed.

She had kissed all of the others. Her eyes held his with that hint of mischief and he knew that she was going to kiss him. And, God help him, he wanted it so much, even standing there while half the members of White's looked on.

She leaned closer, tilting her face up to his, her eyes holding his all the while. And he could feel the speed of his heart and the driving urge to move his mouth and take hers with all the force of what was crackling between them. She smiled as if she knew exactly what he was thinking.

Her breath was warm against his cheek, the brush of her lips soft and hinting at so much more. All of which he knew, all of which he longed for.

His fingers tightened around the cup. 'Miss Sweetly,' he said in a low husky voice.

He saw the way her smile deepened and he smiled,

too. Sharing this moment. Like so many they had shared before. As if there were only the two of them in the room. As if nothing else mattered. As if there were only light in his life.

It was with a supreme effort of willpower that he managed to turn away and give his thanks to those assembled in the room before resuming his seat. But after it was done he kept his eyes on her for every last moment, until she walked from the room with that sexy little wiggle he knew too well.

Alice Sweetly, you minx! And he smiled again and felt a glow in his heart.

'Razeby was at Almack's again last night.' Within Alice's little parlour two days later, Sara announced the fact without so much as a glance in Alice's direction.

Alice should have been glad of it because it meant that she really was fine over Razeby and all of them knew it. But the words did not engender gladness. Rather it felt like a hand had tightened around her heart.

'Was he?' She concentrated on pouring the tea. Part of her did not want to hear how Razeby was getting on in his search for a woman to marry and part longed to know every damn detail. She did not ask the question but Sara told her the answer any way.

'He danced with Miss Penny, Miss Lewis, Lady Persephone Hollingsworth.' She counted the names on her fingers as she rhymed them off. 'Miss Jamison, and twice with...' she paused for effect '...Admiral Faversham's daughter, who is quite considered the catch of the Season.'

'Was Fallingham there,' Ellen asked, all sweetness, 'making a list of Razeby's partners for you?' She sipped at her tea, a picture of innocence, but Alice was not fooled. It both gladdened and worried her.

'Only because his crowd were all there. It's not as if he's bride hunting. He'll not be looking to settle down for ages yet.' Sara could not quite keep the defensive tone from her voice.

'You hope,' murmured Tilly beneath her breath.

'What was that?' Sara snapped. 'I didn't quite catch what you said.'

'I didn't say nothing, it was just a bit of wind. Tea don't half make me burp.' Tilly shot a smile at Alice.

Alice shook her head and barely suppressed the grin.

'They're saying that Miss Faversham has quite set her mind on him.'

'She ain't got a chance in hell,' said Tilly.

'She's an heiress,' retorted Sara.

'She'd have to be,' said Ellen. 'She's got a backside on her the size of a horse and a face to match.'

Tilly sniggered.

'He'd have to be blind to go for her,' Ellen said.

'It's about breeding and money,' protested Sara.

'Just like a horse,' said Tilly with a giggle.

'Enough, girls,' Alice said with a chuckle.

But when her friends finally left and the maids came in to remove the used tea tray, the image of Razeby dancing with all of those women, one of whom would be his wife, lingered.

For all the teasing and the jest, she knew what Ellen and Tilly had been doing—trying to protect her. As if she needed protecting! As if she were hurting from the split with Razeby! She felt mortified just at the thought, and a determination to prove to them otherwise, that it was just as she said, Razeby had never meant anything serious to her.

A vision of him sneaked into her mind. Standing before her at White's, with those smouldering brown eyes that sent spirals darting through her body. And it was as if she felt again the rasp of his cheek beneath her lips and smelled the scent of him in her nose. And felt that sense of heady power. And despite everything, she smiled at the memory. She could not help herself.

It was a very dangerous line she was walking. A knife edge, just like being on stage at the theatre. Avoiding avoidance. Temptation—for him and maybe even for her. Showing him what he could not have. But she could not turn back from it. Not when there was still clearly work to be done.

Chapter Ten

Within Lady Hadley's stifling ballroom a few days later, Razeby and Linwood were standing by the glass doors that led out into the back garden, breathing in the draft of cool air.

'How goes your search?' Linwood asked.

'Well enough.'

'Almack's, matchmaking, picnics and balls… You have been busy.' Linwood paused. 'And yet you do not appear to have narrowed down the field.'

'Keeping my options open.' Razeby took a sip of champagne.

Linwood gave a nod of understanding. 'White's betting book has Miss Faversham as the favourite.'

Razeby said nothing.

'With Lady Esme Fraser as a close second.'

'There are better alliances for Razeby out there.'

'Maybe, but it seems you find a reason to reject every suitable woman who comes your way.' Linwood held his glass up to the light and examined it.

Razeby felt the slight tension in his jaw. 'Nonsense.'

'Indeed, one might almost think that your heart was not in it, Razeby.'

His heart…? Razeby thought of Alice at White's. Of the mischievous look in her eyes, of the caress of her breath and the warm tease of her lips. He thought of her in Dryden's and of that heart-stopping moment in Hyde Park. All the tension that rippled between them. And the way he felt when he saw her, when he was with her, when he touched her. He pushed the memories away, crushed the feelings that were coursing through his mind and body, knowing they were something he could not allow.

'What has heart to do with it?' he said grimly. 'It is about consolidating positions, about power and money, and safeguarding the future. Duty, my friend, nothing else. We all know that.'

'And Alice?'

'Alice has nothing to do with it.' He said it too quickly. 'It is over between us.' If he said it enough times maybe he would come to believe it.

'So you keep saying,' said Linwood. 'But from where I was sitting in White's the other night, it looked any-thing but over.'

'You are mistaken.'

Linwood said nothing, just looked at him.

'We are both adults. We both understand how these things work. '

Still Linwood said nothing.

'Hell, Linwood! We still move in the same circles. What do you expect? That we should snub one another? Alice is not like that. I am not like that.'

'So it would seem.' Linwood raised his eyebrows by

the tiniest degree. 'And you do get to forgo Almack's tomorrow.'

'I am the charity's patron, for heaven's sake! I can hardly miss their benefit ball. It is just unfortunate that it happens to coincide with Almack's.'

'Most unfortunate,' agreed Linwood with his usual deadpan expression, but Razeby knew exactly what his friend was thinking.

And the problem was Linwood was not far wrong.

'Are you sure about this, Alice?' Venetia set the fan back down upon the dressing table in Alice's bedchamber.

'Frew has invited me and it's for a very good cause.' Alice pushed the last hairpin into place and turned away from the peering glass to look at her friend. 'The Benevolent Society for the Assistance of the Unfortunate and Homeless of London.'

'You do know that Razeby is their patron.'

'Of course I know.'

'And that as such he will be there tonight.'

'I can't let that stop me. If I avoided every place I thought he'd be, I'd never set foot outside the door.'

'Alice…'

'What?' She tried to look all innocent. 'It's the truth!' And it was, just not all of it.

'You do not have to do this.'

Alice met her friend's eyes directly. 'Yes,' she said firmly. 'I do, Venetia. If I avoid him, what message does it send all of London? I'll not turn away from a single situation.'

'Proving to the world that he did not hurt you?'

Proving to herself. Proving to him. That was what this was about.

'Or punishing him by showing him just what he has lost?' Venetia asked.

'Maybe a bit of both. I'm not afraid to face him, Venetia.'

'You are not afraid of much, Alice Flannigan.' Venetia's eyes held hers. 'I heard you beat him at Dryden's.'

'I beat them all,' Alice said carefully.

'At *vingt-et-un,*' pointed out Venetia. 'Razeby's game.'

'So?' Alice gave a shrug, but she knew Venetia understood something of the game's significance between them.

'You are playing dangerously with him.'

'We always played dangerously, me and Razeby.'

'Such games do not always turn out the way we think.' Venetia's warning, though veiled, was unmistakable.

'Maybe not, but sometimes for the sake of our pride we have to play them,' Alice said and met Venetia's gaze. 'I'm getting on with my life, Venetia. I'll not let Razeby get in the way of that. And if, along the way, he's made to feel just a tiny bit of regret, is that such a very bad thing?'

'As long as you know what you are doing, Alice.'

'I do, trust me. I'll flirt with him just the same as the others. But it doesn't mean anything. Honest.' She gave a grin. 'Well, maybe I'll flirt with the others just that bit more to annoy him!' She pressed a swift kiss to Venetia's cheek.

'Alice Flannigan, you are an incorrigible woman.'

Alice laughed. 'I'll say it now because I can't say

it once we're at the ball. Enjoy the evening. Dance with Linwood until your head's dizzy. It really is for a good cause. Had there been a similar charity in Dublin years ago, it would have saved my mam a lot of trouble. Being homeless with thirteen mouths to feed isn't much fun.'

'I hope you enjoy yourself, too, Alice.'

'Oh, I'll be doing that, all right. You needn't worry on that account.'

'Will you be all right with Frew?'

'I know how to deal with Frew. He'll be getting a few dances and not a thing more.'

The two of them laughed, knowing that Alice could more than handle herself.

The ballroom was crowded. Alice caught sight of Venetia and Linwood standing talking with Linwood's parents, Lord and Lady Misbourne, and Venetia saw her, but they could not give any acknowledgement, or even appear to notice one another. *Ton* and *demi-monde*. Two different worlds indeed, even if they were standing only a few yards apart in the same room.

Alice was wearing a new dress from Madame Boisseron. It had cost a small fortune, much more than Alice would ever normally have paid for a dress, but she had bought it, and a few others, with the winnings from her card game. The skirt was plain ivory silk, the bodice was gold silk, suggestively cut and fitted, but without even a hint of cleavage on display. The dressmaker had said that it would make every man that looked at it unable to take his eyes from her, which, judging from Frew's reaction, seemed to have been an accurate prediction.

It had small gold sleeves that were really just two bands of silk framing her fully exposed, naked shoulders. She wore not so much as a ribbon or a necklace, neither a bracelet nor a ring, and yet Madame Boisseron had been right to say the dress was designed to be worn this way, without a single item of adornment. Alice had known it the moment she looked at herself in the peering glass. And she knew it now from the way every gentleman in the room was looking at her. And the way Venetia raised her eyebrows and sent her a secret smile.

Razeby was dancing with some respectable young lady across the dance floor. Alice told herself it did not matter. Every man in Razeby's position had to do the same, eventually. It was just as he had said—he had a duty to marry and provide an heir. She ignored the stab of jealousy and moved her mind to more pleasant thoughts.

She glanced across at Frew, and the fact that he so clearly thought himself so handsome and a gift to all of womankind made her want to chuckle; he set not a single firework alight in Alice's arsenal.

'You are looking especially beautiful tonight, Miss Sweetly,' he said.

'You're too kind, Mr Frew.'

'My given name is Edward.' His eyes stared deeply into hers, affecting a smoulder that at best appeared contrived, and at worst as if he had contracted an ocular complaint.

'How interesting, Mr Frew.' She smiled.

Razeby would have laughed at the response. Frew just looked slightly aggrieved.

She refrained from teasing him further and resigned

herself to a very dull evening in his company. 'So what was that poem you recited in the Green Room the other night?'

'I wrote it just for you, Miss Sweetly.' Frew began to recite the flowery words again, but Wordsworth had nothing to worry about. After two verses she knew that if Frew made one more reference to long thrusting swords and softly dewed maidens she would not be able to keep a straight face.

Halfway through the dance his hand took hers and their steps led them to exchange places. It was the point she had been waiting for. She glanced again towards Razeby, whispering his name in her mind as if to call him.

Razeby's eyes moved to meet hers, as if answering her call. She watched his gaze drop to her dress and sweep over it before coming back up to her face. She held his gaze, gave him a small teasing smile. *Nice?* it asked.

Very nice, indeed! His eyes answered with an unmistakable interest.

She gave him a naughty arch of her eyebrows, knowing full well what it would do to him, before she turned back to Frew.

She leaned her mouth closer towards Frew's ear, let him hold her that little bit closer than respectability decreed. 'Tell me that last line again, Mr Frew. You do have such a way with words.'

Frew positively puffed out his chest, and, looking like a man that thought his luck was in, he obliged.

By the next time she could glance in Razeby's direction she saw he was watching Frew with a distinctive glower.

She drew Razeby an admonishing look.

He put on his innocent face.

She gave that smile that told him she was not fooled for a minute by his protested innocence.

He grinned an admission.

The dance took them away from one another. She did not see him again, only Frew. And she could not help feeling a little deflated at that. But not as disappointed as Frew at only being allowed a chaste kiss of her hand when he delivered her home.

When she lay in bed that night it was not Frew she was thinking of or his terrible poetry, but Razeby.

No one could accuse her of avoiding him. Not after Dryden's. Not after White's. And not after tonight. She smiled because it felt like her plan was coming together. And she smiled just because she had enjoyed the little exchange with him and it made her feel warm and dangerous and excited. In the back of her mind she heard again the whisper of Venetia's warning. There was a truth to it, she acknowledged, because as surely as Alice dangled an enticement before Razeby, she felt the pull of him. There was a rapport and an attraction that existed only with him. And that was a very dangerous thing. Venetia was right; she should have a little more care in her dealings with Razeby.

'You know you are more than welcome to come, Razeby, but do you really think it is a good idea?' Linwood asked his friend as they sat together in the drawing room of Linwood's home a few nights later. He got up and poured two glasses of brandy from the decanter that sat on the nearby desk, passing one of them to Razeby.

'A man is entitled to one night off.' Razeby accepted the brandy with a murmured 'thank you'. He knew what Linwood was saying was true. Going to watch Alice in one of her plays in the company of Linwood and his wife was the worst idea in the world. He knew it and yet here he was sitting in Linwood's drawing room, suggesting the idea. 'Besides, I have a wish to see the play.'

Linwood raised a single, dark, sceptical eyebrow. 'Or a wish to see Miss Alice Sweetly.'

'Maybe,' he conceded. 'She *is* the most talked-about actress in all London. Her reputation as a serious actress on stage challenges both Venetia's and Mrs Siddons's. Maybe I just want to see how her performance has developed.' And part of that was true. But only part.

Linwood did not look convinced. 'Your presence will not go without comment.'

'Because Alice was once my mistress? Am I never to set foot in the Theatre Royal again?'

'No one is saying that.' Linwood met his gaze. 'But what happened to the clean severance?'

'The severance was clean. Alice understands the situation as well as I do. There is nothing between us save for civility.' But he was lying. There was something very much more than civility between them. Something that was driving this compulsion he felt to see her.

'It is not as if I have lost sight of what I am doing. I will be at Almack's tomorrow.' There was no harm in just seeing her. He drank the brandy down and glanced away towards the window. It changed nothing, save made him feel better. 'I will have myself a wife before the Season is done, Linwood. I have to. There can be no two ways about it.'

'I understand that it is "over" between you and Alice,

but have you considered that when it comes to finding a wife there is always next Season?' asked Linwood.

Razeby smiled and met Linwood's eyes. 'No, my friend, there is not,' he said quietly. It was as close to telling him the truth as he could come.

Linwood's eyes searched his as if seeking to glean the answer that was there. But Razeby held his gaze, steadfastly refusing to give away anything more, until at last Linwood, with a tiny incline of his head, acknowledged defeat and dropped the challenge.

Linwood topped up their brandy glasses. 'Well, in that case, Razeby, you had better spend this evening in the company of an old friend at the theatre.'

Alice stepped out on to the stage that night. It was another full house. The part came naturally to her. She closed off her mind to all of real life and just let herself be this other woman. She acted. And it was almost as exhilarating as teasing Razeby across a room, but nowhere near as dangerous.

His box was empty, just as it was empty every night. But her eye caught a glimpse of figures in Venetia's box. Alice slipped her gaze to her friend and saw not only Venetia and Linwood. Her heart skipped a beat at the sight of Razeby sitting there with them. She turned her eyes away, careful not to allow herself to be distracted.

It meant nothing, she told herself, but her heart quickened all the same. He had just come for an evening at the theatre. But following on from Dryden's and White's and the benefit ball, she knew that was not the case, that really his presence here did mean something. Alice just did not want to think precisely what.

* * *

He would not be in the Green Room. He would not dare. She knew it, yet the first thing she did when she walked in there was to look for him.

But Razeby dared.

'Miss Sweetly.' He bowed.

'Lord Razeby.' She curtsied. Her heart leapt at the sight at the sight of him, her nerves shimmered in delight. She could not stop herself from smiling.

All attention in the room was upon them for all it feigned otherwise. Every conversation was conducted with half an ear on theirs.

She could not avoid him. Could do nothing other than treat him as if he were any other man.

'I trust you enjoyed the play, my lord.'

'More than I could have imagined,' he replied.

'Then perhaps your imagination is a little lacking.'

'On the contrary, Miss Sweetly, my imagination is most excellent. I have often been complimented upon it.' She saw the message in his eyes.

She was the one who had complimented him on it… when they were making love.

Something exciting and bold and deliciously dangerous whispered between them.

'Your acting talent has blossomed and taken on a new and vibrant dimension.' He smiled.

'Mmm,' she said, sharing the smile. 'I think I've heard that somewhere else. And there's you laying claim to a most excellent imagination.'

'You wish for originality in the compliments to be paid you?' He raised an eyebrow.

'I'd settle for truth,' she returned.

He leaned closer, lowered his voice slightly. 'Then the truth is, Miss Sweetly, that you were wonderful.'

The same words he used in this same Green Room a lifetime ago. The same words he had whispered in their bedchamber every time he had come to take her home after those occasional stage appearances. The world seemed to shift and detach around them.

'And you're as much a flatterer as ever,' she said softly, her eyes tracing his.

'Never that, Alice,' more softly still. He was smiling that smile of old, making everything seem so right.

Their eyes held, stretching time, making the Green Room and its people disappear. She could feel the beat of her heart and sense his beat in time. Between them was that same connection there had always been.

'Ah, Razeby.' Hawick's voice interrupted. 'How goes the bride search?'

The words crushed the moment, dragging them both back to the reality of what could not be.

'Well enough, thank you,' said Razeby. He smiled politely at Hawick, but there was nothing of a smile in his eyes when he looked at the duke.

'You were supreme as ever, Miss Sweetly,' said Hawick, lifting her hand and pressing a kiss to the back of it.

'You're too kind, Your Grace,' she replied, easily enough, but she was acting. And beneath that bright surface it felt like the dark hidden depths of a pool had been disturbed.

'If you will excuse me. Your servant, Miss Sweetly.' Razeby bowed and walked away.

Such perilous, glittering allure. Alice knew she was playing with fire. But she could not turn away from the path she had chosen to walk, as if there had ever really been anything of choice in it. She could not turn away

from Razeby, for the sake of her pride and her live-
lihood. And more than that she could not turn away
from Razeby because, even knowing what she did, she
wanted to see him. It was a disquieting realisation. And
one which she sought to distract herself from with a
shopping expedition in the company of her friends the
next day.

The four of them sauntered along Bond Street laden
with parcels and boxes. Alice had allowed herself to be
persuaded into buying too many fripperies, but she had
to admit, it did make her feel good, even if the parcels
were cumbersome to carry and her feet were aching
from too much walking in shoes that were stylish and
new, but less than comfortable.

They had just left the milliners when Sara asked
the question.

'You did say you cleared out everything you could
from Hart Street, didn't you, Alice?'

'What do you mean?' Alice glanced across at her,
a sudden panic drumming in her breast that Razeby
might have revealed something of just how much she
had walked away from.

Ellen drew Sara a look of daggers.

'I saw that look, Ellen Devizes,' Alice chided.

'Lord, Sara, but you have some size of mouth on
you.'

'What do you mean?' Sara looked hurt. 'She's fine
about Razeby.'

'Even so,' countered Ellen.

'What aren't you telling me?' Alice asked.

There was a resounding silence.

'Out with it,' she said.

'Razeby's kept the house on,' said Ellen at last.

'That can't be right,' Alice murmured before she could stop herself.

'It is,' insisted Sara. 'He's been seen there.'

'Why on earth would Razeby do that?' Alice asked, her pace subconsciously slowing.

Sara raised her brows, widened her eyes and gave her that look that brought a blush of embarrassment to Alice's cheeks.

It was Tilly who finally told her. 'The rumour is it ain't just a bride he's looking for, Alice, but a new mistress. We thought you knew.'

Alice felt the words hit her hard. She glanced away to hide her shock. 'Rumours aren't always true.'

They all looked at her in a way that made her regret saying the words aloud.

'Going in there late at night. Leaving early in the morning. A girl doesn't have to be a bluestocking to work it out,' said Sara.

'You know what men are like.' Tilly patted her arm as if to console her.

'I do.' And yet she thought Razeby different. Even now. Even after all that had happened. It could not be true. She knew Razeby. And what he was doing was about duty, no matter how much she disliked the way he had gone about doing it.

'It's always about what's in their breeches,' said Ellen.

'It is,' agreed Alice with a smile to mask how much she was still reeling from the revelation.

'But you didn't leave anything behind, did you?' Sara persisted.

Alice's smile broadened. 'I didn't leave one thing.'

But, in truth, she had left a lot more than a diamond bracelet and some expensive dresses.

'You don't want some other woman getting her hands on anything that's rightfully yours.'

Tilly and Ellen nodded in agreement with Sara's words.

Alice laughed. 'I don't think there's any danger of that.'

'Glad to hear it, girl.' Tilly slipped her arm through hers.

'Come on—' Ellen gave a smile '—I need some new stockings and Benjamin Preece has been advertising ladies' white silk hose made of real China silk for only 7s 6d a pair.'

'I could do with some stockings myself,' said Alice, denying the disquiet she was feeling. 'And then we'll go and have tea.'

'Like ladies.' Ellen raised her eyebrows and affected a posh accent.

They giggled like girls.

'Preece's it is,' said Alice and, with her arm still linked in Tilly's, the group made their way towards Preece's warehouse.

In all of the days that followed the shopping trip Alice could not stop thinking about Razeby keeping on the house in Hart Street. It worried at her, like a dog at a bone. She tried to push the thought out of her head, throwing herself all the more into her parts on the stage over those next few nights, and afterwards, in the Green Room, working the room with a charm and a control that would have done all of Venetia's best teachings proud. But none of it stopped her thinking. At night, in bed, the thought was there just the same.

She looked at herself in the peering glass. There were much prettier women out there. Women who put her ordinary looks in the shade. She sucked in her tummy, examined her teeth and scrubbed a finger against the faint freckles that marred the bridge of her nose. Maybe he really had just grown tired of her. Maybe he had lied and misled her because he did not have the courage to tell her the truth.

She shook her head, unable to believe it. Razeby had more integrity in his little finger than the whole of any other man she had known. And rumours were just that, she told herself. A fire of gossip over nothing.

But all rumours started with a grain of truth, the little sharp thought countered.

And then pricked away at her relentlessly. Even if it was true, what difference did it make? she demanded.

But it did make a difference. Alice knew that, no matter how hard she tried to pretend otherwise. And because of that she knew she was going to have to discover the truth for herself.

She rose much earlier than normal the next day.

'Shall I fetch you a hackney carriage, Miss Sweetly?' the youngest maid, Rosie, asked.

Alice shook her head. 'It's a fine morning. I've a mind to walk and take the air.'

'I'll just fetch my cloak, ma'am. At this hour of the day it's still a bit chilly out there.'

'Don't bother yourself, Rosie. I've some lines to think through, it's best if I walk alone.'

'Very good, ma'am.' The maid bobbed a curtsy and opened the door for her.

The hour was still early enough that the streets were quiet. The ground was damp with rain that no longer fell, and, as the maid had warned, the morning was still cool with the night's chill. But the sun was out and the air was bright and clear, just the way she liked.

She walked slowly, breathing in the damp freshness of the air, while all around her London stirred. Carts with animals and vegetables come up from the country for the market rolled by. Milk maids leading cows by a rope, a gaggle of geese still wearing the little shoes to save their feet from all the miles they had walked. Alice walked, too, down Mercer Street and along Long Acre, crossing over to walk down Banbury Court. And, finally, onto Hart Street.

She strolled as if it were just a street like any other. Pretended not to even look at the house in which she had lived with Razeby. She deliberately stayed on the other side of the road. But her feet trod slower and her heart beat faster, and as she came closer her eyes fixed upon the building that had been her home for half a year.

It looked just the same as when she had left it. As if she could walk back in there right now and turn back time to be what it had been not so long ago. But then the fittings and furniture came with the house when Razeby had rented it, just as hers had come with the new rooms in Mercer Street. It did not mean that the house was not in other hands. It was just a damn rumour and she was a fool for even being here.

But at the very moment she chided herself with that thought, the black glossy front door opened. And Alice's heart jumped at the prospect of being caught here spying. She ducked out of sight behind a tree. Her fingers held hard on to the wide gnarled trunk as she watched while a tall, dark-haired handsome man she recognised too well emerged.

The breath caught in her throat. Her stomach gave a somersault before her heart stampeded off at full tilt.

The expression on his face was serious. He was not smiling. Indeed, there was nothing of his usual good-natured manner with which she always thought of him. He walked off at a brisk pace in the opposite direction, not glancing back at the house once.

Her heart was thundering and she felt shocked, and all she could hear in her head were Tilly's words: *The rumour is it ain't just a bride he's looking for, Alice, but a new mistress.*

And he must have himself a new girl, or why else would he have spent the night there? She stared at the windows. All the blinds and curtains were opened, but there was no movement, no hint of a woman's face watching him leave.

She waited until he was almost out of sight before stepping out from behind the tree and making her way back to Mercer Street.

Chapter Eleven

Razeby was at Almack's again. So many times, going through the same motions. All with one purpose that was contrary to that which he desired. It was bad enough being here without his friends turning up to witness it. Linwood was different, because, despite all of Razeby's denials, Linwood knew something of the truth and he understood, in part.

'Came to give you a bit of support, old chap, in the old bride hunt.' Bullford beamed.

'How considerate of you all,' said Razeby with an irony that sailed right over Bullford's head.

'Well, we couldn't abandon a brother in need. You seem to be struggling, so we thought we'd better step in and help.' Fallingham sipped at his champagne.

'Struggling?' Razeby raised an eyebrow.

'Dragging it out,' Devlin explained.

Razeby smiled because the barb was dangerously close to the truth. 'I am merely being selective in my choice.'

'Selective? That's a good one,' quipped Monteith. 'I

must remember "selective" when it comes to deferring putting my head in parson's trap.'

'What's to select?' asked Fallingham. 'There's only three criteria to be considered: how well connected they are, how much money they bring to the deal, and how far they can open their legs.'

The men laughed at Fallingham's crudity. All except Razeby and Linwood.

Razeby glanced round at his friends—the group of society's most disreputable gentlemen. 'One glance at the company I'm keeping and the duennas won't let me near their charges.'

'We could always take care of the duennas for you, Razeby,' Monteith said. 'There's much to be said for the older, more experienced lady.'

'There's a truth in that and no mistake,' agreed Devlin. 'I heard a story about the widowed Mrs Alcock—'

'We've all heard the story of Mrs Alcock and if you repeat it in here you'll have us all thrown out, and then where will Razeby be?' said Bullford.

'Push off, the lot of you,' said Razeby as if in jest, but meaning it. 'Before Lady Jersey sees you.'

'There's gratitude for you,' drawled Monteith.

Razeby gave an ironic smile.

'You know where we'll be.' Fallingham finished the contents of his glass in one gulp and waved a farewell.

His friends moved off, all except Devlin and Linwood.

Razeby met Devlin's eye. 'I really have heard the story of Mrs Alcock, Devlin.'

'Wanted to speak to you,' said Devlin. 'Slightly sensitive subject.'

Razeby felt a sudden uncomfortable premonition of just what that 'slightly sensitive subject' might be.

'Not like you to be bashful,' he said and waited to see what Devlin would say.

'I just wanted to ascertain the situation. Regarding you and Miss Sweetly.'

Razeby's heart beat harder. 'I am looking for a bride, Devlin. Does not that say it all?' He forced his muscles to stay relaxed.

'I thought perhaps you and Miss Sweetly might still have something going.'

'We do not.' The words were curt. He kept control.

'I am glad to hear it.'

Razeby's gaze sharpened on Devlin. But Devlin did not seem to notice.

'The thing is, Razeby...' Devlin cleared his throat. 'There's something I've been meaning to ask you. Now that you and Alice are no longer together I thought I might ask her out. You wouldn't have any objection to that, would you?'

'Why would I possibly object?' he said drily. But inside he could feel the thud of his heart too loud and hard in his chest and the cold prickle of his skin, and something primitive and menacing snake through his blood.

'Thank you, Razeby.' Devlin gave him a nod. 'I had better catch up with the others.'

'You had better,' said Razeby in a voice that barely concealed the warning. He stood there and watched Devlin leave with a jaw clenched so tight it was painful, only shifting his gaze to Linwood once Devlin had disappeared through the door.

The two friends exchanged a glance.

'You are over her, remember,' Linwood said quietly.

'I remember,' Razeby replied grimly. 'Remembering is all I do.'

Alice slipped the cloak hood from her head as the Linwood butler ushered her into the hallway of Venetia's rooms.

'Alice.' Venetia came hurrying out of the drawing room to see her.

'You don't have anyone in, do you?' Alice asked, darting a cautious look over at the drawing room.

'No one. I am just writing some letters while Linwood is out this evening.' She made no mention of exactly where Linwood had gone. She did not need to. Both women knew that there was a matchmaking ball at Almack's tonight and that Linwood would be there with Razeby.

'Is something wrong?' There was a look of concern on Venetia's face that made Alice feel guilty.

'Nothing,' Alice lied. 'I just fancied a chat, that's all.'

'Come on through. A chat sounds much more inviting than dealing with a pile of business letters.' Venetia ordered a tray of tea with crumpets and jam.

The drawing room was cosy, the curtains drawn against the darkness outside. They drank the tea and ate the crumpets, even though Alice was not one bit hungry. The scene reminded her too much of the dark winter nights when she and Razeby had toasted crumpets by the fire and spread thick butter on them to melt and drip down their chins and all over their fingers as they snuggled together beneath a blanket. She pushed the memory away.

They talked of the theatre, of how much Venetia

missed it, of the current plays, of Kemble and people they knew in common—indulging in a little gossip and laughing together.

'Talking of gossip,' Alice said and it sounded a little contrived even to her own ears, 'I was wondering...' She hesitated, then, taking a breath, asked the question that she had come here to ask. 'Have you heard any rumours concerning Razeby?'

'What kind of rumours?'

'About Hart Street.' Alice swallowed. 'It seems he's kept the house on.'

'I had not heard.'

Alice looked at her friend, wondering if she was telling the truth, or just sparing her feelings.

'I am sure if it is true there is a perfectly good explanation behind it.'

'It's true all right,' Alice muttered and then blushed when she realised just how much that reply revealed.

Venetia did not question her on it. 'Whatever Razeby's reasons, I doubt very much they stretch to what the gossipmongers are saying.'

'I thought you hadn't heard the gossipmongers saying anything about him.'

'And neither I have, Alice. But I can well imagine.' Venetia raised an eyebrow. 'I know what you are thinking.'

'Do you?' Alice looked into her eyes.

'Do you really think he is interested in another woman as his mistress?' Venetia asked quietly.

'No. Maybe.' Alice closed her eyes and shook her head. 'I don't know what to think any more, Venetia.'

'Whatever is going on with Razeby, I think you may rest assured it is not that.'

'You're probably right.' Alice gave a sigh. 'It shouldn't matter a toss, even if he's taking a different woman back there every night of the week. But a woman has her pride.' But pride was only part of Alice's problem.

Venetia gave a nod of understanding.

'I best be away.'

'You will not stay for some more tea?'

Alice shook her head. 'Thank you, Venetia.'

They both knew it was not the tea Alice was thanking her for.

Alice tried to put Razeby out of her mind and get on with her life. The prospect of seeing him worried her, because she felt like something had changed in her and she knew it was more important than ever that she maintain a façade of normality. But she had to see him again, and she did, only two days after speaking to Venetia.

The musicale in Mr Forbes's drawing room was in full swing, the formally arranged rows of chairs filled completely. Some gentlemen were standing against the walls at the back of the room and some at the sides. Forbes was a personal friend of Kemble's. He was a wealthy man, but not exceptionally so. Precisely how he had managed to secure the talent of Angelica Catalani to sing for them tonight was a coup that had everyone asking the question. The soprano was famously difficult in temperament and her fee was reputed to be beyond the reach of all but the richest in the land. But when she opened her mouth and sang, it was the most beautiful sound in the world. She had a voice with true clear clarity, a voice that made Alice think of crystal and purity and perfection.

Alice was here with Kemble and his sister, the famous tragedy actress Sarah Siddons. Their seats in the middle row meant they had a good view of Madame Catalani, and were the optimal distance to appreciate the music. Alice was trying very hard to focus herself entirely on the singer. Trying to block out the knowledge that Razeby was sitting at the back of the room with Miss Althrope, who accompanied him this night.

The programme for the evening, neat and nicely printed, was lying open on her lap. Before the music had started she had pretended to read it, and chatted with Kemble and Mrs Siddons. As she had suspected, Kemble could not help himself running through the scheduled music and discussing each one. Alice had smiled and listened and added in her tuppence, conscious that Razeby could see her and her every reaction. It was important that she look as if she were having the best time in the world. Without him.

It should have been easier once Madame Catalani started singing. All Alice had to do was sit there, looking serenely engrossed in the music. But it grew strangely more difficult.

Madame Catalani's voice was so haunting and melodic that it made Alice feel emotional. Emotions were dangerous. Especially emotions of the sort that were seeping into her chest. She glanced away from the soprano, seeking to distract herself, but all she could see were the fashionable red-painted walls around her. Red—pray God that they had been any other colour!

The applause sounded. Kemble glanced at her, applauding for all he was worth, nodding at her and smiling his enjoyment. She made herself smile back and clap all the harder. But then Madame Catalani began to sing again, a piece so devastatingly haunting that it had the power to pierce through all the armour Alice had donned. It moved her. It made her think of things of which she did not want to think. The truth of feelings and pretences.

It made her think of Razeby.

She dropped her gaze to rest on the programme lying on her lap. But the beautiful voice sang on and inside of Alice all of her emotions seemed to be twisting and turning and welling dangerously high. And there, ever present, was that burning awareness of Razeby sitting behind her with another woman. It was like a burr, cutting into her. Or maybe it was just the haunting voice and that music, and those red, red walls. All of it pressing in on her. Suffocating her, until she did not think she could bear it for another minute.

She leaned closer to Kemble, whispered near his ear, 'If you'd excuse me for a few minutes, Mr Kemble. I'll be right back.'

Kemble gave a nod, barely taking his eyes from Madame Catalani.

Alice made her way from the row as inconspicuously as she could.

Razeby was not focused upon Madame Catalani like everybody else in the room. Rather, he was watching Alice leave alone, and a few moments later the sleazy figure of Quigley slip out after her. No one noticed. Madame Catalani sang on. The whole audience was transfixed.

Razeby whispered his excuse to Miss Althrope. And went out after them.

The hallway was empty. Not a footman or a maid

was in sight. Madame Catalani's voice was softer, more muted in volume out here. Beneath it Razeby heard the quiet footsteps on the staircase. He moved silently to follow, reaching the top of the stairs just in time to see Quigley's black-jacketed back at the end of the passageway disappear through a door signed as the ladies' withdrawing room. Razeby's eyes narrowed.

He made his way along the passageway.

Alice had no need to avail herself of the withdrawing room's facilities behind the modesty screens. She could still hear Madame Catalani's voice, even up here, but at least she was alone. And the walls were a cool pale grey rather than red. She could breathe. The sky was a clear blue through the windows, the afternoon sunshine lighting it brightly, but the sun was at the front of the house, and this room at the rear. It was cool in here, the fire unlit. And Alice was glad of it. It was just that aria, she told herself, and those red walls and the heat of the room downstairs. A few moments in here and she would be in command of herself once more. She took another breath just as the footsteps sounded outside the door.

Alice pretended to be smoothing down the skirt of her dress as the door opened behind her. She did not look at the reflection in the full-length looking glass, just lowered her eyes and turned to leave.

'Why, Miss Sweetly. There is no need to rush off, my dear.'

She stopped dead in her tracks, the sight of the lecherous Mr Quigley standing there making her stomach tighten in shock. 'Mr Quigley! What on earth do you think you're doing in here? This is the ladies' with-drawing room!'

'Yes. I am well aware of what room this is. But I wanted to have a little word with you, in private. And it is so very difficult to get you alone.'

'You'll understand if I don't oblige. Mr Kemble and Mrs Siddons are waiting down the stairs for me.'

'Now, you cannot expect me to believe that Mr Kemble and Mrs Siddons, or indeed any person in that drawing room, are not so engrossed in Madame Catalani's singing that they will miss you for a little while. And with you, I do only need a little while.' He licked a tongue against his lips as if he could taste her upon them and she could not suppress the shudder of revulsion that went through her.

She made to pass him by, but he caught hold of her wrist lightly with his little claw-like fingers.

'Now, my dear Miss Sweetly,' he began. He smiled in a leering sort of way, leaning in close so that she could smell the stench of stale wine upon his breath. 'I have had my eye on you for a long time. And now that Razeby is off the scene and you are left alone, without a protector, I thought I would do the chivalric thing and take you under my wing.'

'Honoured though I am by your offer, sir, I'm afraid I must decline it.' She said it politely but firmly.

'Come now, Miss Sweetly.' He put on a cajoling voice.

She looked pointedly at where his hand was fixed. 'If you'd be kind enough to unhand me, Mr Quigley.'

'Now, don't be like that, little Miss Sweetly. Such a stern tone does not suit.' His fingers tightened around her wrist and he dragged her close to him, sliding his

hand round her hip and over her buttock to fasten there.
'Just one little kiss for an old man.'

'No!' She tried to push him off, but he was surpris-
ingly strong for a man of his age.

Her eyes met his and she saw the lust that had always
been in them when he looked at her and the new intent
that lurked there. And the panic rose in her.

It happened so fast she was not sure what had actually taken place until she saw Quigley, face pressed
against the wall, his arm up his back, held there by a
tall dark figure she knew too well.

Quigley gave a little whimper of fear.

'What the hell do you think you are doing, Quigley?'
Razeby's voice was quiet, but it cut through the sudden
silence of the room like a whip.

She stared, unable to believe that Razeby was really here.

'I thought you were done with her, that she was
avail—' Quigley gave a yelp as Razeby inched the older
man's arm higher. 'I made a mistake. I'm sorry. Won't
touch her again.'

'It is to Miss Sweetly you should be addressing your
apology.' Razeby's face was like flint. She had never
seen him like this.

'Apologies, Miss Sweetly.' Quigley's words were
strained and urgent.

She nodded her acceptance, her eyes darting from
Quigley's contorted face to the dark, dangerous expression on Razeby's.

Quigley gave another moan of pain.

'Let him go, Razeby. I think he's drunk.'

She saw the snarl on Razeby's lip. 'Stay away from
her, Quigley,' he hissed.

Quigley nodded, his face powder white. 'Message understood, my lord.'

Only then did Razeby release his grip on the man.

Quigley picked up his hat, which had been knocked off in the process of being slammed face first into the wall, and disappeared through the door.

Alice did not move and neither did Razeby. They stared across the few feet that separated them. Her heart was thudding hard enough to break free of her ribcage. Her blood was rushing so fast she thought she might faint. But neither were because of Quigley.

'Are you all right, Alice?' His voice was quiet, but intense and loaded.

She nodded, not trusting herself to speak.

He moved slowly to stand in front of her, his eyes raking hers. 'He did not hurt you?'

'No.' She shook her head.

And all of the tension that was roaring between them had nothing to do with Quigley.

Their gazes were locked, unable to look away. Inside she was trembling so much she feared it would show.

'I am glad of that.' He reached his hand to hers and took hold of it, his fingers surrounding hers with warmth and strength and gentleness. 'You are shaking.'

'It's cold in here,' she lied.

He slipped off his tailcoat and wrapped it around her shoulders.

The scent of him enveloped her, bringing with it too many memories, too many conflicting emotions that warred and struggled within her chest.

'No!' She pulled his coat from her shoulders and thrust it back into his hands.

The silence hissed between them, the tension winding tighter.

And still she could not look away. And neither could he.

Their eyes held, conveying so many words, none of which could be spoken.

Her heart was thudding so hard she could feel each beat reverberate through her body. A shiver rippled down her spine and tingled across her skin. She was breathing faster now, more shallow, not knowing how much longer she could keep herself together.

He looked at her for a moment longer. Then he drew her a small incline of his head and walked away.

Through the open door she watched him pass the two young ladies who were poised on the brink of entering the withdrawing room.

'Ladies,' she heard him say politely as he calmly walked past them.

The two girls were giggling and gaping as they entered the withdrawing room. But they fell silent when they saw her standing there, their eyes growing wide with shock and speculation.

Alice held her head up, flicked some imaginary dust from her skirt, then sauntered out with all the dignity of a duchess, as if she did not give a damn that she had just been caught with Razeby in the ladies' withdrawing room.

When Razeby came back into the drawing room Quigley's chair was empty. Razeby returned to take his seat by Miss Althrope's side, who was far too well bred to comment upon a gentleman's absence. Whether she had noticed Alice leave he neither knew nor cared.

His blood was still pounding from the sight of her, his mind still focused and intent—with lethality towards Quigley and something else altogether for Alice. He could feel her in every beat of his heart.

It was not supposed to be like this. He was not supposed to feel like this. He knew that, but sitting there with Miss Althrope by his side, his eyes half on Madame Catalani, half on the door waiting for Alice to return, he did, and there was not a damn thing he could do to change it.

At last Alice slipped into the room, resuming her place beside Kemble once more. She did not so much as glance his way. Just sat there seemingly quietly intent upon Madame Catalani's performance. But she did not need to look at him. He was so damned aware of her that Madame Catalani could have missed every single note and he would not have noticed. He could feel the sense of Alice thudding through his chest, feel the knowledge of what was between them in his blood and in his bones. He stared straight ahead, as if watching the soprano, but he was watching Alice for every minute of that concert. And he could not look away.

Chapter Twelve

Alice did not know how she got through the rest of that musicale. Her hands were still trembling when she got home. She told herself it was because of Quigley, but she knew it was not.

It was wrong on so many levels. Razeby had rid himself of her without the slightest regard for her feelings. What had been between them was nothing more than sex. He was actively searching for a woman to marry. And yet this afternoon in that ladies' room made her think she had got it all wrong. It was preposterous. Downright ridiculous. But that look in his eyes, filled with meaning, piercing, as if he could see right through to her very soul. As if he felt, really felt, the same as her. The whole experience had shaken her more than she wanted to admit, stripping all her denials away for the flimsy pretences they were.

And that realisation made her feel weak and out of control and afraid. Afraid that the mask was in danger of slipping, the threat of all that lay beneath exposed to the world.

Never let them see how much they hurt you.

The mantra came easily to her lips. She knew it by heart and had said it to herself a thousand times since that night with Razeby. And yet now she was panicking, gathering her armour around her all the tighter. Telling herself that she had been mistaken in what she felt and what she thought she had seen in his eyes.

He had taken all she had to give, used it and discarded it. She could never allow herself to forget. All she had left was her pride. She would not let him take that. She could not let him take that. She had no choice but to carry on.

'So, how was Madame Catalani the other day?' Venetia took a small sip of coffee and glanced across to where Alice sat on the sofa in Mercer Street.

'She's got a wonderful voice on her. Magical almost.' So magical that it could make a woman betray herself and imagine things.

'I heard Razeby was there, too.'

'Was he?' She tried to sound vague, but she could not meet Venetia's eye.

'Alice,' Venetia said softly, 'there is a rumour going around, about you and Razeby, at the musicale.'

'There are always rumours,' Alice said flippantly.

Venetia said nothing, just held her eyes, looking at her, knowing she was lying.

Alice closed her eyes and gave a sigh. 'It wasn't like that.'

'What was it like?'

'It was Quigley. He followed me into the ladies'. You know what he's like.'

'A lecherous old toad.'

'He made a pass at me. He's got a strength in him

that you wouldn't credit, Venetia. I thought he was just an old man. I never thought that he'd actually use force.'

Venetia paled. There was a look of horror in her pale eyes, even though she was trying to hide it and her voice when she spoke was calm. 'Did he...hurt...you, Alice?'

'No. He tried to kiss me. I don't know how far he really meant to go, but he got nowhere. Razeby stopped him.'

'And how did Razeby come to be in the ladies' withdrawing room?'

Alice glanced away. 'He was just passing.'

Venetia raised her eyebrows and Alice could see the scepticism in her friend's expression. 'Are the two of you back together?'

'No.' Alice closed her eyes with a weariness. The confusion milling in her brain since that day seemed like it was sapping the very life from her. 'How could we ever be back together? After all he di—' She caught back what she had been about to say and stopped herself. 'He's searching for a bride. He was there with Miss Althrope.'

'You still have feelings for him, don't you, Alice?'

'Yes. No.' She glanced away. 'How could I?'

'We feel what we feel, Alice, regardless of sense or logic.' Venetia paused. 'I know you have no wish to avoid him, but maybe you should, just for a little while.'

'No. I can't.' She shook her head, feeling more afraid than ever. 'I won't, Venetia.' Because to do so would be to admit the truth. *Never turn your face from the thing you fear. Be bold and brave. And never, never let them see how much they hurt you.* 'In fact, what I need to do is the very opposite.'

'Alice...' Venetia cautioned softly.

'He saved me from Quigley. But it doesn't change anything,' Alice said. 'I mean, I'm grateful for his intervention, of course I am. But—' Her heart was beating faster even at the memory of his eyes staring down into hers, of all that had strained and trembled between them. And the dreams and nightmares that had made sleep impossible. And the thoughts that jibed at her all night and whispered in her ear every day. 'It changes nothing,' she said again, more firmly. 'I have to get on with my life. I have to show them all Razeby doesn't matter to me. I have to show *him* he doesn't matter to me.'

There was a small silence.

'Then be very careful, Alice.'

'I will,' she replied softly.

The doors of her wardrobe were wide open. Alice stood before them, looking in at the line of new silk evening dresses hanging there. They were both beautiful and expensive. They were her fresh start, bought with the money she had won at Dryden's that night.

Her eyes moved to the emerald silk dress at the very end of the wardrobe, hanging slightly separate from all the others. The one dress that she had taken from the house in Hart Street. The dress she had had made with Razeby in mind. The dress that he always swore he could not resist her in.

She reached out and lightly touched her fingers to the long flowing green silk of the skirt and the images flashed in her mind—vivid and real enough to make her gasp: Razeby's mouth on hers, his hands peeling off the bodice to expose her breasts naked and aching for his touch. Her rucking up the skirt and straddling

Razeby in his town coach because they could not wait until they got home. Making love across the desk in his study, on the sofa in the drawing room, on the Turkish rug before the drawing-room fireplace. And the time on the staircase and then again on its window seat before they had made it into the bedchamber. The razing intensity of the memories had her shivering. She snatched her hand back as if the cool silk had burned her.

She forced herself to breathe, to still the tremor that was racing all through her body and deny those feelings that were threatening to escape from the dark place in which she had locked them, grasping at anything to shore up the cracks in the walls of her defences.

It was just sex. It had always been just sex, and nothing more, for Razeby. And for her. She needed to prove that to herself, once and for all. And she knew the very way she could do it...if she was brave enough.

Alice took another breath and turned her eyes to the emerald-green silk once more.

Wearing the emerald-green evening dress had seemed such a good idea at the time, but standing here on the threshold of the Brewer Street Rooms, with Devlin looking at her with desire so blatant in his eyes, Alice was not so sure.

'That dress, Miss Sweetly...' Devlin's eyes dropped lower to the pale swell of her breasts over the tight green silk of her bodice. He leaned a little closer and lowered his voice for her ears only. 'You look positively irresistible.'

Irresistible. The same word Razeby always used. She did not want to hear it on Devlin's lips. It felt wrong. As wrong as wearing this dress in any man other than

Razeby's company. But that was all the more reason to wear it. To take away its power. To take away *his* power over her. To prove once and for all there was nothing left between them, that there never had been, no matter how he looked at her.

'You certainly know how to make a woman blush, Lord Devlin.' She smiled.

He held out his elbow to her in invitation.

She ignored the unease that stroked like a feather against her skin, closed her ears to the doubts and the discomfort, and the nervousness that was jittering in her stomach. It might feel wrong but it was the right thing to do, she reassured herself. Besides, it was too late to change her mind. She had better just get on with it. Everything would be fine. This was not the place a marquis came to find a bride. With a smile she rested her fingers lightly against his arm and, holding her head up high, let Devlin lead her into the room from which the music was playing loud. Everything would be fine, she told herself again.

But the minute she walked through those doors she knew it was not.

On the opposite side of the dance floor stood Razeby.

Alice felt a sudden panic well up and threaten to spill over. The urge to turn around and run right back out that door almost overwhelmed her. She swallowed, forced herself to breathe, reined herself back under control.

It should not matter if he was here. It should not make the slightest difference. Indeed, maybe it was even for the best. That he would witness this ultimate show of denial. Denying her feelings. Denying him. Maybe he even deserved it, that taunt of what he had so thoughtlessly cast aside. She had almost convinced herself of it by the time Devlin led her over to him.

'Razeby.' Devlin bowed. 'Did not think you would be here.'

'Change of plan,' Razeby replied and there was a coolness to his voice that stroked a warning down her spine.

Too many women, young, old and in between, were eyeing Razeby with a barely concealed interest. But Razeby seemed unaware and, notably, Miss Althrope was not by his side this evening. Indeed, there was no sign of a woman. Only Linwood.

Devlin's smile was slightly stilted. 'Not your usual scene.'

'Nor yours,' replied Razeby. He smiled, but there was something in the way he looked at Devlin, something almost threatening.

Devlin's smile faded. 'Miss Sweetly and I can certainly vouch for the quality of the champagne.' He took a sip from his glass.

Alice said nothing. Her glass was still brimful, not one drop had passed her lips, even though her mouth was as dry as a bone and her pulse was thrumming in her throat.

It was just a dress, she told herself. But it was not. She knew that.

And so did Razeby.

There was nothing of Razeby's charm this evening, only a veneer of politeness so thin as to barely conceal a darkness and an intensity that made Linwood look positively light in comparison. She could feel the strain of the atmosphere between Razeby and Devlin, heavy with things that had nothing to do with friendship.

Devlin slid an arm around her waist, making her jump at his touch. 'Does not Miss Sweetly look charming tonight?' Spoken so politely, and yet there was that sense that he was deliberately baiting Razeby.

Razeby finally moved his gaze to her, letting his eyes wander from the green sparkle of her slippers, slowly up the silky green skirt, over her bodice and her breasts, until it finally met her own. Her heart was hammering harder than a blacksmith's hammer against an anvil, her pulse pounding so fast in her throat that she felt sick.

His gaze was long and cool, his mouth unsmiling. 'Charming indeed. But it is not the word I would use.'

Irresistible. The word whispered between them, and all that had passed between them while she was wearing this dress was there in the room, making the nerves flutter all the more wildly in her stomach.

She tore her gaze away. Swallowed. *Oh, Lord!* She quailed at the challenge, longed only to walk away. But she knew she could not do that. So, instead, she breathed and she stood there.

'Shall we dance, Miss Sweetly?' Devlin smiled.

'I thought you'd never ask,' she said and she meant it. Anything to get her away from Razeby and that terrible sense of something brewing, and the feeling that she could not have got this more wrong. She forced a tight smile and let Devlin lead her onto the floor.

Devlin did not return them to Razeby and Linwood. And she did not look at Razeby again, just got on with the evening. Danced two dances with Devlin. Drank half a glass of champagne. Smiled. Pretended she was interested in what Devlin was saying, that she was not conscious for every second of Razeby and the fact that he did not once dance.

* * *

Razeby saw Alice the minute she came into the room. He saw the evening dress she was wearing—the emerald silk—and he understood her message too well.

By his side he knew Linwood was watching her, too. Every man and woman in the room was. How could they fail to? She was the celebrated Miss Sweetly and looked golden and radiant and downright irresistible.

He thought of the rows of fine silks and satins she had left hanging in her wardrobe in Hart Street, and of the diamond bracelet and cheque that she had turned her back on. He had not understood it at the time. But now he did. She had chosen her weapon well. Saved it. And now she wielded it, pointed and sharp as a stiletto blade.

Linwood murmured something, but his friend's voice went as unheard as the music that played.

He watched Devlin lead her out on the floor. He knew he should go and claim a woman to dance with. Any woman. It would not matter. But he did not. He just stood there and watched Devlin handle her upon the dance floor, wearing that dress.

He could hear the beat of his own heart, the rhythmic thump so hard that it seemed to reverberate in his throat, through his bones, deafening in his ears.

She did not look at him. She did not need to.

And all of the past was whispering through him, taunting him as surely as she was.

Something inside of him felt dangerously close to snapping.

Alice sipped her champagne and let herself relax a little. They were halfway through the evening. She had got this far. She could manage the rest of it. Just about.

The notes of the next piece of music began, just those first few notes and her stomach sank and her blood turned to ice. And she was gripping the glass so tight that her knuckles shone white.

Fate could not be so cruel. *Please God, let her be mistaken.*

But the notes played on, blossoming into music, and there could be no mistake. She knew that music, knew that dance. The *Volse.* Their dance. Hers and Razeby's.

Her heart faltered, stumbling over its beats.

'Shall we dance, Miss Sweetly?' Devlin's voice was warm and close.

She felt frozen with horror. *No!* she wanted to say, categorically, unreservedly. *No!* It wasn't supposed to be like this. 'I'm only halfway through my champagne, Lord Devlin. We'll dance the next one.' She forced the smile to her lips.

'Come, Miss Sweetly,' he chided in a teasing tone. 'Leave the champagne. I'll buy you a bottle of the stuff when we come off the floor.' And then to her horror he held his hand out in a gesture that was an obvious invitation on to the dance floor. Anyone that was looking would have known that he was asking her to dance.

Her heart felt like it was about to give way. She swallowed. Wetted her suddenly dry lips. Maybe he was not watching. Maybe he had not seen. She glanced over at Razeby.

But Razeby's dark watchful gaze was fixed upon her. And so were too many other eyes.

Her blood was rushing so fast, twisting and turning in such a torrent that she felt dizzy. Beneath her arms prickled with sweat, but her fingers felt chilled through to their bones.

She knew what she was going to have to do. Knew there was no way out without losing face, without admitting the truth—that this music, this dance meant something to her. That Razeby meant something to her.

She turned her face from Razeby's. Laid her fingers on Devlin's waiting hand. And let him lead her on to the dance floor.

Her steps in the dance were perfect. The dance she had been so nervous about, the dance Razeby had taught her, the dance they had practised together so many times alone in the drawing room of the house in Hart Street. Their very first public dance as a couple. When Alice had worn this dress just for him. Their dance, their music, their dress.

She brazened it out the best she could. But there was a cold sick feeling in the pit of her stomach. And the smile she wore felt like it was tearing her face apart. She could not look at Razeby. Not at all through the dance. Until the very end, when it was finally over. And then she could not stop herself. Her eyes moved to the spot where he had stood. But Linwood was standing there alone.

She scanned the room for him, her eyes raking the crowd to find him. But Razeby had gone.

'Now for that champagne.' Devlin smiled as he led her from the floor and she felt the small intimate stroke of his fingers against her wrist.

It was done. She had done it. Worn the dress. Danced the dance. Denied him.

'Are you all right, Miss Sweetly?' Devlin sat her down in her chair. 'You do not seem to be your usual self. Your cheeks have gone quite pale.'

'If you would be so kind as to take me home, Lord Devlin.' She swallowed. 'I'm feeling a little unwell.'

'Of course. I will summon my carriage at once.'

Devlin's coach rolled away along the road.

Alice was walking up the steps to her front door when Razeby stepped out of the shadows.

'Razeby,' she whispered his name through the darkness. 'What are you doing here?'

She saw his gaze lower pointedly to the green silk of her skirt that peeped, so vibrant and taunting, from beneath her cloak, even in the yellow glow of the nearby street lamp, before coming back up to her face.

'Are you deliberately trying to torture me? Because if so, it is working.'

The breath was shaky in her throat. She opened her mouth to speak, but the look in his eyes made her rapidly close it again.

'Does that knowledge make you happy?' he demanded.

She stopped in her tracks, glanced round at him, told him the truth. 'No, Razeby. It doesn't.' She turned away, moving towards the steps that would take her up to her front door.

'Damn it, Alice! Do you think that you can just walk away from me?'

'Like you did to me?' She swung round to face him. 'What did you expect, Razeby?' She had spent all these weeks denying it, everything she had done had been to hide it—from the world, from Razeby, and most of all from herself. But his words, his being here, the whole night... All of the walls she had spent these weeks building, higher and wider and deeper, exploded apart.

The anger, the hurt, the pain—all of it surged up in a great wave to rush through her.

'That you would understand.' His expression was one of torment.

'Understand?' She walked right up to him and stared into his face. 'Oh, I understand too well! You cast me aside like I was a piece of clothing that you were done with. Quickly, easily, without a single consideration for my feelings.'

'It was not like that!' All denial and shock.

'No? One minute we were in bed making love. The next minute you were coolly dismissing me. Am I making that up?'

'Alice...' He raked a hand through his hair.

'Don't you *Alice* me! You could have said something before. You could have had the decency to give me some sort of warning. All that time you were planning it. And not one word did you utter.'

'You are wrong. I never planned any of it. That is part of the damn problem. Atholl—'

'Atholl was an excuse!' She shouted it.

'No!'

'Do you think I didn't know that you were brooding on something all those weeks and months? When you thought that no one could see you.'

He glanced away.

'Oh, yes, Razeby, I saw. And do you know something? I was worried about you. Not about us—I thought we were happy together. About you.' She poked her finger hard into his chest. 'When all along you were planning to be rid of me. Bastard!' She was breathing hard, shaking with the force of emotion rolling through her.

'I have already told you there was nothing of planning with you.'

'I don't believe you.'

'I have a duty to do. I cannot walk away from it, Alice. No matter how much I might want to!' There was an agony in his voice.

'Yes, you do. I never denied that. But there's a way of doing it, Razeby. A man might do his duty and retain something of a heart in doing so.'

'I am not without a heart, Alice.'

'Aren't you?'

'Hell, Alice. I did what I had to do.'

'In a cruel and callous way. You hurt me, Razeby!' she shouted. The words were out and there was nothing she could do to call them back. The echo of them resonated in the silence between them.

He stared down into her face, a look of horror in his eyes. 'Alice...'

'You hurt me,' she said again, more softly this time. 'I just wanted—'

'To hurt me back,' he finished quietly.

'No.' She glanced down at the small puddles that glistened on the darkness of the pavement beneath their feet. She had never meant for it to be like this. It was not supposed to be about hurting him, but denying that he had hurt her. About salvaging her pride and protecting herself. But there was an element of truth in what he said. 'I suppose I did, a little bit.' She swallowed and her throat felt dry and tight. She looked directly into his eyes. 'But you deserved it. You made me believe there was something more than sex between us. It doesn't come much more callous than that.' She turned to walk away.

He moved so fast. One minute he was standing there, the next he had her in the shadows and backed against the wall, his body so close she could feel his heat, smell the heartachingly familiar scent of him.

'You think I do not have feelings for you, Alice?' His voice was so harsh with passion that she trembled to hear it. 'You think that being apart from you is not tearing me apart?'

Her breath was as ragged as his. All she could see in the darkness was the glitter of his eyes, but she could feel the razing intensity of his stare.

'There are other factors at play, Alice. Things I could not tell you. Things I still cannot.'

'Things like you were tired of me and that it was time to move on. I saw you leaving Hart Street the other morning, Razeby.'

His eyes narrowed with both incredulity and anger. 'And you think I am keeping another woman?'

'It's what they're saying.'

'Then it must be true.' His tone was cold.

'Why else would you have stayed there overnight?'

'Why else, indeed?'

He leaned his face so close that she felt the caress of his breath against her cheek, so close that she thought he was going to kiss her.

His whisper was low and intimate, and dangerous. 'If you honestly think that, then you do not know me at all.' He looked at her for only a moment longer, then he released her and walked away into the darkness of the night.

Alice was shaking so badly that it did not matter how hard she bit upon her lip, she could not stop it. She watched him go and could not move. She stood there alone in the darkness, feeling the light patter of the rain against her hair, feeling its dampness mingle with the tears that wetted her face, as the chill of the night air seeped through her bones.

All of her defences lay in ruins around her. There could be no more denials. No more lying. Alice finally admitted the truth to herself. And with the truth came a pain that was hard to bear.

She loved Razeby.

She loved Razeby and he had broken her heart.

Chapter Thirteen

Alice was sitting exactly where Razeby had thought
to find her. On the marble bench positioned in the furthest corner of the room, staring at the painting opposite. Three days had passed since that night outside her
rooms, and he had come here to the Royal Academy's
Exhibition Room on every one of the mornings since
to look for her.

The Exhibition Room was quiet, only one or two
more committed visitors having risen so early to come
and study the artworks without the press of the usual
crowd. The night's rain had given way to sunshine,
but little of it reached in here. The light from the softly
arched ceiling windows was soft and muted, illumi-
nating only the central portion of the floor so that the
richness of the paintings hanging upon the surrounding walls would not fade.

His footsteps were quiet against the wooden floor
as he made his way across the gallery and sat down
at the end of the bench, as if he too were studying the
Canaletto's painting of Venice's Grand Canal.

She glanced round at him briefly before returning
her gaze to the painting.

'How are you, Alice?' He spoke quietly, for her ears only.

'Grand.'

A pause.

'It has gone far beyond the stage of pretence, Alice. How are you really?'

'Bearing up.' She met his eyes. 'And you?'

'I have been better.'

She smiled at that, but it was a sad smile. She took a breath and returned her gaze to the painting.

'I have been sleeping alone at Hart Street because I can still smell you on the sheets and still feel your presence in the rooms.'

He heard the way she caught her breath. 'Razeby...'

'You did not really believe otherwise?'

She shook her head, but did not look round at him. 'Not in my heart.'

'I am sorry that I hurt you. I am sorry for the way I told you and for the suddenness of the parting. But clean and quick is supposed to be the best way of severing something that one has no wish to let go. I thought it was the best way for us both. I see now that it was not.'

'I'm sorry, too. I never meant to hurt you that night, Razeby. With the dress, and the music and the dance.'

'And Devlin,' he said.

'You looked as if you might be about to lynch him.'

'I came seriously close.'

She was still looking at the painting, but she smiled another smile tinged with sorrow. 'It was all as much a torture to myself.'

There was a small peaceful silence.

'How did you know I would be here?' she asked.

'Just a gut feeling.' He let his eyes sweep along the yawning turquoise of the Venetian sky upon the canvas. 'You always said this painting took you to another world. I thought we could both do with another world just now.'

Her hand lay flat upon the bench they shared. He rested his own beside it, feeling the marble of the bench cool beneath his palm. The edge of his little finger just touched against hers.

'If only.' Her expression was composed, relaxed even as her eyes rested upon the painting. 'It looks so beautiful, doesn't it? The detail of the architecture. The colour of the sky. The way the light shimmers on the water. I've never seen a sky that colour.'

'Riches for the eyes,' he said.

She gave a little laugh, but there was an unbearable sadness beneath it. 'Is Miss Althrope the one?' she asked softly.

'Not Miss Althrope. I found the one over half a year ago. I just cannot marry her.'

She closed her eyes. 'Don't.'

'Why not? It is the truth, even if it has taken me this long to realise it.'

'It'll only make it harder.'

'It could not get any harder.'

'You shouldn't be here with me, Razeby.'

'No, I should not.'

They sat in silence, their eyes fixed only on the Canaletto and another world.

And then he got to his feet and walked quietly away.

Alice kept on going. One day at a time. Acting upon the stage most evenings. Rehearsing most afternoons. Sparkling and enticing within the Green Room because that was part of her job as much as the acting, the promotions, and all the other little things that had to be done. She kept on smiling, kept her chin up. But inside she felt hollow, as if everything of any worth had been emptied from her. She kept on going, because she had to, and because she did not know any other way to be. But when no one was looking, when she was alone, it was difficult to bear.

It had been four days since he had come to the Exhibition Room. And she had taken care to avoid him on each and every one of them. Only four days and already it felt like a lifetime. She wanted to see him so much, to hear the sound of his voice, just to look into his eyes, and to see his smile. But it was better this way, she told herself, for them both. She no longer cared if the world knew she was avoiding him.

The letter arrived the following week.

Lots of men sent her letters. Alice never opened a single one, just burned them as they were. But she did not burn this one. She recognised the rich black scrawl of pen on the front before she even turned it over to see the impress of Razeby's crest in the seal. Her heart was beating too fast, her hands trembling as she cracked the thick red wax and unfolded the letter, trembling as she traced her index finger along each line of patterned ink. But it did not matter how long she stared at them, or how hard her eyes strained, there were only two words upon the page that she could read, one at the start of the letter, and the other at the end—*Alice* and *Razeby*.

She wished she had told him now. She had told him everything else. About her secret life in Mrs Silver's. About her family in Ireland. Truth and conversation had always flowed easy between them, even from the very start. And yet she had not been able to admit that

Miss Alice Sweetly, star of the stage, whom all of London thought could read and write, could do neither; that she had learned her parts only through Venetia. Being an actress was the only proper good thing Alice had ever done in her life. She could not bear to have that one achievement stripped away and be exposed as a liar, not before Razeby of all people. But standing here with Razeby's letter in her hand, she would have done just that to know what it said.

She could hardly ask a stranger to read it to her. Nor could she take it to Venetia—the letter felt too intimate, too private for that. So Alice refolded the letter very carefully and hid it in the bottom of her travelling bag next to the most precious of her possessions, the engraved pen that he had given to her. Maybe not today, but one day, in the future, she would be able to read it.

Another week passed and it felt like a month to Alice. She sat alone in the fine, gleaming new black carriage that Kemble had sent to take her to the charity auction, wearing the new dress she had collected only the day before from Madame Boisseron. Using up yet more of the money from her savings, but she knew this was something she needed to do. The neckline, high as a débutante's, would have them all talking, but Alice did not care.

The carriage rolled to a stop and the door opened. She took a deep breath, summoned up a smile and the protection of her persona, and, taking the footman's hand, let him help her down to step outside.

A crowd had gathered to watch society's richest and most famous turn out in force. Newspaper artists were sketching in a frenzy. Reporters were scribbling notes.

Voices in the crowd were shouting her name. 'Miss Sweetly!'

'Is it true that a dance with yourself is to be auctioned, Miss Sweetly?'

'Now that would be telling.' She smiled. 'You'll have to wait and see, gentlemen.'

'I'd pay me last farthing for a dance with you, Miss Sweetly,' an old man at the front of the crowd shouted. He looked poor, his face lined from a hard life.

'Then you're a very generous man, sir.'

The crowd laughed.

She walked right up to him. 'And I like a generous man.' She smiled and kissed his cheek.

The old man beamed. 'God bless you, Miss Sweetly.'

The crowd erupted in a roar of astonishment and delight, then took up the old man's chant. 'God bless you, Miss Sweetly.'

She smiled and made her way up the red carpet that lined the stone stairs up into the fine mansion house.

The light of a thousand candles magnified through the crystal drops of the chandeliers and wall scones blazed as bright as daylight dazzling her eyes. She paused for just a moment on the threshold of the ballroom, collecting herself and letting her gaze drop down to the skirt of her dress, the silk of which was newly imported from India. Its colour was a highly unusual pale-green aqua that reminded her of Canaletto's sky. It made her remember the words Razeby had uttered so quietly at the Royal Academy.

Alice took a deep breath, and Miss Sweetly, with her head held high, walked into the ballroom.

Within the charity auction ballroom, Razeby was standing with Linwood and Venetia. He had heard the crowd outside chanting Alice's name. When she walked through the door, the sight of her took his breath away. The dress she was wearing was pure, innocent almost, and yet sensually beguiling in every sense of the word. The colour made it a secret message that only he would understand.

He had thought it hard seeing her when he knew that he could not have her, hard being tortured by watching her dance with Devlin. But these past days of not seeing her were worse.

She smiled and sparkled as if nothing was different. But everything was different. It was so palpable that he wondered that everyone else could not feel it, too. She moved around, circulated, talked to those who had only bought their tickets to come here and see her. But she was very careful to keep her distance and more than careful not to look at him, not once. And by that small tell he knew that she was aware of his presence.

There was a little dancing, and then a light supper before the auction.

He drank champagne and chatted with Linwood and with Venetia, and he watched Alice. On the surface she seemed as she always did, that quiet contentment, that glow of slight innocence. But he could see beneath the façade to the real Alice and it was not happiness that he saw, but a pain and longing that mirrored his own.

On every other occasion she had danced. Tonight Alice stayed away from the dance floor. For the sake of the auction and the dance she was selling, so the whisper of explanation went.

Razeby should have been asking Miss Althrope or Lady Esme Fraser up on to the floor, but he made no move.

When it came to supper, Alice's plate held a selection from the dishes spread out within the supper room, but she ate not one single bite.

Razeby did not bother to go through the pretence of the supper.

He willed her to look at him.

But she stubbornly refused.

And then, at last, it was time for the auction to begin.

The Foundation for the Support and Education of Orphans had engaged John Philip Kemble himself to play the part of auctioneer for the evening. Kemble's noble bearing and great acting experience meant he knew exactly how to drum up interest, to create drama and effect and play a crowd. The Foundation wanted as much money wrung from the audience and Kemble was the man to do just that. He auctioned a glass of champagne with Prinny, a promenade around the room with Sally Brooke, a session of secrets and advice from the lady patronesses of Almack's on how to land your desired catch from the marriage mart—his mother had told him to bid on that one—a personal poetry recital by Lord Byron, and, at last, the one that had generated the most interest, the one for which almost every man in the room had been waiting for—a dance with Miss Alice Sweetly, the sweetheart of Covent Garden.

Kemble introduced her and Alice, clad in the Canaletto silk, walked out to stand before them all. She smiled in that slightly shy way of hers. She was not sophisticated or polished. There was nothing contrived about her in the slightest. She was uncomplicated, beautiful, honest and the warmth in her heart and her soul showed in every glance from her eyes, in her every aspect. She did not think herself some beauty, even though she was. She did not pose or pout. But that indefinable quality shone out of her brilliant as a flame in the darkness. And Razeby knew that every man standing there was helpless as a moth before its pull.

'Gentlemen, the dance for which you are bidding is...' Kemble paused for effect '...the *Volse*.'

Razeby felt the muscle of his jaw tighten.

He saw the way Alice's eyes widened ever so slightly, the hint of frozenness in her expression before she covered it with a smile. She had not known.

The hum of excitement moved through the room. The *Volse*. It was a dance of courtship and of wooing, for them at least. A scandalous dance that allowed something of an intimacy of both touching and conversation. It was a dance that belonged to Razeby and Alice.

The bidding opened up and there was so many tipping of programmes, so many nods of heads and raised hands that Razeby lost count. Like the rutting of stags, there was an undertone of competition and of pursuit. And all the while Razeby stood there and watched it, until the mêlée faded, brought low by the fierceness of the bidding and the enormity of the sums offered. Until it came down to two of the richest men in the room— Hawick and Monteith.

'Two thousand pounds,' Monteith offered.

'Two thousand one hundred,' Hawick came back.

'Two thousand, three hundred.'

Quick as a flash, Hawick replied. 'Two thousand, four hundred.'

'Two thousand, five hundred?' Kemble enquired of Monteith. But Monteith shook his head with the graciousness of the defeated.

'Two thousand, five hundred anywhere in the room?'

Razeby saw the smile that slid across Hawick's face, the certainty that he had won.

'Going,' said Kemble.

Hawick's eyes turned to claim Alice, as if she was already his.

'Going.'

Those surrounding Hawick were already shaking his hand.

'Five thousand pounds,' Razeby said in a lazy tone.

The gasp that went round the room was audible.

He saw the way both Linwood and Venetia stared at him, even their usual composure ruffled.

'Your Grace?' Kemble enquired of Hawick.

Razeby could feel the beat of his heart and hear the hiss of the collective silence within the room. It was the longest few seconds of his life.

'My congratulations to Lord Razeby,' Hawick said, but the look that he shot Razeby was a deal less friendly.

'Going.'

'Going.'

'Gone.'

Only then did Alice look at him.

'The dance is sold to Lord Razeby for the most generous sum of five thousand pounds.' Kemble was still talking, but Razeby's focus was fixed on Alice.

Chapter Fourteen

Alice's hand was in Razeby's and it did not matter that all of London was watching them, the sole couple on the dance floor—it made everything feel right. It warmed the coldness. It filled the void. It lit the light within her heart, just to be with him for these few moments.

Their steps were perfect, their bodies moving in perfect time, each a perfect complement to the other. It was their dance. And as the music, so sweet and melodic, played on she knew that she would never dance this dance with anyone else.

She looked up into his so-beloved face. 'You have created a scandal,' she said, but she could not stop herself from smiling.

'All for a good cause.' He smiled, too, that same smile of old.

And that attraction, that same connection that had existed between them from the very start, bound them stronger than ever.

'You have been avoiding me, Alice.'

'It is for the best, Razeby.' Their eyes held and the

dark liquid warmth and tenderness that she saw in his sent a thrill right through her body to her heart.

'You admit it, then?'

'I admit nothing.'

'You did not answer my letter.'

'What letter?' she said teasingly, but her heart missed a beat and her stomach gave a little somersault.

'You know very well, Miss Sweetly.'

'You must be mistaken, Lord Razeby.'

He smiled. 'Over many things, but not this.'

'I get so many letters.'

'I am sure you do.'

'Refresh my memory. What did the letter say?' She bit her lip while she waited to hear.

He lowered his voice so that it was soft and dark and smooth as black velvet. 'Do you really want me to say it aloud, Alice? Here?' The smoulder of sensuality in his eyes stroked a shiver down her spine.

She felt a faint blush warm her cheeks. 'Maybe not here,' she conceded.

They danced on.

'I know why you did not take the dresses from your wardrobe.'

Her heart skipped a beat at his words. 'Because I wanted a new wardrobe,' she replied smoothly.

'Really?' He arched an eyebrow.

'Now that I'm a famous actress I've got to be keeping up with the fashion.'

'And the diamond bracelet?'

'Diamonds are so passé. Didn't you know?' she teased.

'And the cheque?'

'Such an inadequate amount.'

'Why don't I believe you?'

'Because you've a mind that runs to suspicion.'

He smiled. 'I have another theory.'

'That I knew that you had taken to wearing ladies' dresses?'

He laughed. 'You did tell me that I looked good in your old polishing apron and nothing else.'

She couldn't help herself. She laughed, too.

And when the laughter died away and their eyes held, both were filled with the simple joy of just being together.

'No, my theory is a little different to that,' he said quietly.

Her smile faded. She swallowed, suddenly afraid. Her eyes clung to his.

'Do you not want to know what it is, Alice?'

'Not here, Razeby. Please.'

'Not here,' he said, soft as a breath against her ear.

They danced on together as all of London looked on.

Venetia sat beside Alice on the sofa of the little drawing room in Mercer Street.

'Last night, you and Razeby…' Venetia let her words drop away, but not her gaze.

Alice shook her head. 'We're not back together, if that's what you're asking.'

'It is what all of London is asking, Alice.'

She swallowed. 'Creating a bit of scandal is just a part of the job, isn't it?' But when Razeby had taken her hand in his, nothing of it had been about the job. 'And it was for charity.'

'It was. And that means that you can get away with it. But you only get to play that card once.'

Alice did not meet her eyes. She knew the truth in what Venetia was saying. They had got away with it this once. They would not get away with it again.

'Are you still playing your dangerous game with him?'

Alice shook her head. 'I never really was.'

'You have feelings for one another.'

Venetia's words were not a question but Alice nodded her admission, glancing down at her tea, knowing she could no longer pretend a denial.

'Oh, Alice,' Venetia said softly. 'What are you going to do?'

'Keep on going. Me in the theatre. Him finding a wife. There's nothing else we can do, is there?'

'No, I suppose there is not,' agreed Venetia, and gave her a little hug.

They drank their tea in silence.

Razeby was not faring any better.

His mother had come to call upon him at his house in Leicester Square with a rather obvious purpose in mind.

'You look tired, darling. Did you have a late night?' His mother touched a hand to his cheek as she scrutinised his face.

'No.' He did not elaborate.

She took her seat on the sofa and turned her attention to the tea tray. 'I took tea with Teresa Darrington yesterday.' Her focus was seemingly all on her tea-making ritual, but Razeby was not fooled.

'Did you?' He stood by the mantel, watching her measure out two rounded dessert spoons of tea leaves into the tea pot before carefully locking the caddy and pocketing the key. Alice refused to lock away the tea from her servants. *What harm does it do if they take a little to make a bit of extra money for themselves, as long as they aren't greedy?* she always said. It was typical of her attitude to life.

'The family are somewhat parochial—they come from trade—but a good alliance nevertheless,' said the Dowager Lady Razeby.

'Because Darrington is minted?' He wondered whether his mother had read the newspaper reports over him and Alice at the auction.

'There is no need to be so vulgar, James. But yes, if you wish to put it in such a fashion. He owns half the mills in Yorkshire and has vast investments overseas. And his lands...' She lifted the kettle from its small lagged box and poured the hot water into the tea pot.

'Run concurrent with Razeby,' he finished.

'Miss Darrington, his only child and heiress to the entirety of his fortune, is making her come out this Season. Perhaps you have already met her?'

'I do not recall.'

She gave the tea in the pot a stir and replaced the lid before turning over the small timer that still sat upon the tea tray to time the brew. His mother was very precise in the way she liked her tea. 'I thought to invite Miss Darrington and her mother to accompany us on our little outing next weekend.'

His eyes focused the grains of sand rushing too fast through the narrow glass of the timer. Rushing like all of life around him, when the only haven within it was Alice.

The ticking of the clock was loud within the quietness of the room. The timer was almost done.

He gave a nod, but it felt like there was an iron band around his chest that was growing only tighter.

'Splendid,' his mother pronounced. 'I thought you would agree. I will send a note round to Mrs Darrington today.' She smiled and, as the last grains of sand slipped through the timer, lifted the teapot to pour the tea.

Alice kept on going, just as she had told Venetia she would. Every afternoon she rehearsed on stage. And every evening she performed before a packed theatre. And just as ever, all the emotions that she was trying to hide were channelled into the parts she played. But it was growing more difficult. There was a sense that the boundaries between the roles and reality were beginning to blur.

She cut back on the promotions she accepted. She was afraid of seeing Razeby again and even more afraid of not seeing him. Afraid that he had guessed the truth in full. *I know why you did not take the dresses from your wardrobe.* The words haunted her.

He was searching for a bride. This could not be. She had to avoid him, to stay as far away from as she could, she told herself determinedly again and again. But what she felt in her heart was something else altogether.

She yearned to see him, longed to hear the sound of his voice, needed to feel the warmth of his eyes, the touch of his hand. It felt like part of herself was missing.

She filled every minute of every day with activity, filled her mind with lines and acting and everything she could, but none of it made any difference. Amidst all of the activity and the people who surrounded her she was lonely. Amidst all she tried to cram into her head he was still there in her thoughts. Always. As if he were a part of herself that she could not deny.

At night she could not sleep. In the mornings she could not wake. And in between she still put a smile on her face. With dogged determination she still kept going. She still sparkled in the Green Room. But it was becoming harder with every day that passed. In her ear was the whisper of his name. And in her heart was the beat of his. And she had the sense that something bigger than either of them had been set in motion that they were powerless to stop.

Time was running out as surely as the grains of sand in his mother's tea timer.

Razeby knew that every accusation about prevaricating, about making excuses and stalling for time over finding a woman to marry was true. When he stood in that ballroom at Almack's all he could think about was Alice. The dance at the auction had buoyed him, elated him almost, but now, as the days passed without a sign of her at a single function, the feeling had faded to be replaced instead with a sense of bleakness.

He needed to marry. Before his thinking had been so clear. Black and white. Now he saw only shades of grey. And what he thought about, what he dreamed about, what he could not get out of his head was not the future of Razeby, not the days that were ticking down to his thirtieth birthday, but Alice Sweetly.

'A little water clears us of this deed.' Within the empty Covent Garden theatre came the prompt for the fourth time that afternoon.

'A little water clears us of this deed,' Alice said.

'Everyone take a break. We will reconvene in half an hour,' Kemble ordered.

The stage cleared of everyone except Alice and Kemble. He walked over to her.

'I'm sorry for fluffing the line.' She smiled and gave a little shake of her head, trying to clear the thick cotton wool feeling from it. 'I must be a bit tired today.' She could not remember the last time she had slept the night through.

Kemble was both an acclaimed actor and a manager. And as such he had high standards, he pushed hard, expected much. The slip was not her first. There had been too many of late. All those lines she was holding in her head were becoming confused and slow to recall—Alice, whose memory had never been anything other than perfect. It was how she had managed to fool people for so long over her inability to read. She expected him to harangue her, but Kemble did not look angry, only worried.

'You look pale, Alice.'

'I always look pale when I've no make-up on my face.'

'You've been working too hard of late.'

'Not hard enough.' Razeby was still there in her head and in her heart.

'You need some time off. Some early nights. A rest.'

'I don't need a rest.' If she rested, she would start thinking more and she did not want to think, could not bear to think as it was.

'In my opinion, you do,' Kemble countered.

'No, I—'

He placed a fatherly hand on hers. 'I need you at

your best, Alice. I need Miss Sweetly to sparkle and be happy. We all do.'

'I am sparkling, aren't I?' she asked, suddenly afraid.

'You will be again, after a rest. Sort out whatever is going on in your life and come back in a week.'

She kneaded her fingers against the tight spot on her forehead.

'They will want you all the more for the absence. And I do not want to risk losing you.'

She took a breath.

'Will you get through tonight's performance all right, Alice?

'Of course I will. I'm fine, really I am.' But she was not fine. She knew that. And so did he.

He nodded and called over to a stage hand, 'Have a cup of tea taken to Miss Sweetly's dressing room.' Then, to Alice, 'Go and take your break. And then we will rehearse a little more before tonight.'

Razeby stood by the unlit fireplace in his study as Linwood took his seat in one of the nearby winged leather chairs. The morning light seemed harsher than normal, the ticking of the clock too loud.

Linwood's eyes moved to the empty brandy glass that sat upon the mantelpiece, although he made no comment upon it.

'Bad night, Razeby?'

Razeby glanced away. More an impossible night in which all that was happening haunted him and made sleep impossible.

'You did not go to Almack's.'

'No.'

The clock ticked louder.

'This is to do with you and Alice, is it not?' Linwood asked quietly.

Razeby raked a hand through his hair and did not deny it.

'You still want her.' Not a question, just a statement.

'I have never stopped wanting her.' Although want was not the right word. It was too petty and inadequate to describe what he felt about Alice. He gave a dry laugh and shook his head. 'I have never felt like this before, Linwood. Never felt what I feel for her for any other woman.'

Linwood gave a slight nod, as if he understood. 'It is hard when it happens.'

'I did not think it would be like this.'

'Does Alice feel the same?'

'We are stepping round it, Linwood, and I cannot blame her. She will admit nothing, but I believe the feeling is reciprocated.'

'You know that what is between the two of you—it is not going to go away, Razeby.'

'I know.' Razeby lifted the decanter and poured some brandy into his empty glass, before offering it to Linwood, who declined. He swallowed his own measure down in one go, but the burn and the strength of the alcohol did nothing to numb what he was feeling.

There was a small silence.

'Have you considered the unthinkable solution?'

'Were it that easy, I would make Alice my wife and all of society be damned.' He gave a bitter laugh. 'Just now she is their golden Miss Sweetly, but you, more than most, Linwood, know what they would do to her—what they did to Venetia, who is the daughter of a duke no less. And your family closed around her to ease her way. Alice has no such link to either nobility or gentility. You and I both know her past.'

'Few enough others do.'

'Even so.' He shook his head. 'Do you think my mother would take her to her bosom and protect her as Lady Misbourne does with Venetia?'

Linwood gave no reply, so Razeby told him the answer. 'I care for my mother, Linwood, but I am under no illusion as to her prejudices. She would feed Alice to the lions rather than have her in our family. Just now Alice is the *ton's* darling, but it would not be so were I to make her my wife. She would be ostracised, cast out, treated like a leper.' He rubbed a hand against his forehead. 'And I will not always be here to protect her.'

'You will be here long enough to—'

But Razeby held up his hand to stop him. 'I cannot marry her, Linwood.'

The silence hissed between them.

'The question is, feeling the way that you do, can you marry another?'

'I have to.' Every time he closed his eyes he saw the grains of sand slipping through that tea timer. 'There must be an heir for Razeby.'

'Then you had better stay away from Alice.'

'I know.' Razeby gave a smile that held nothing of happiness. 'It should be easy enough done. She is avoiding me.'

'Then it sounds as if she is doing the best that she can for you both.'

Razeby knew that. He knew he had to stay away from her.

He knew that he had to marry.

He knew what was coming.

And none of it made any difference. He still craved to see Alice with all of his heart.

Chapter Fifteen

Alice cancelled her engagements and stayed in her rooms for the next few days. She was no longer confident that if she were to see Razeby she would be able to hide from the world what she felt for him. Her sensibilities were running so wild that she felt like she was going mad. She needed to step back from it, to take charge of herself. Maybe Kemble was right, maybe she was just working too hard. Maybe she just needed to get some sleep. And then she would be able to don her mask once more, hiding the truth from the world, and from Razeby himself.

She did everything she could to make that happen. And she polished, polished for hours, polished for days. Polished until every inch of wood in those rooms gleamed and the air was sweet with lavender and beeswax. But none of it helped.

In the end she surrendered to the one thing that made her feel closest to him. She ran her fingers over the engraving on the barrel of the silver pen he had given to her, smiling a bittersweet smile at the message.

She took Razeby's letter from its hiding place at the bottom of her travelling bag and tried so many times to read the words he had written. It was useless, of course. There was no magical wand that made sense of the letters and words. And at the end of the day it did not really matter what he had written, for it did not change anything of the situation.

At night she dreamed that Razeby was making love to her. It felt so real that she could smell the scent of him, feel the warmth of his skin against hers, hear his voice calling her name and her body was welcoming his as she woke.

'Razeby,' she whispered his name as the dream slipped away and, in realising that it was just a dream, she felt the loss stronger than ever.

And so it went on, until her friends came to call.

'Where have you been hiding yourself, girl?' Tilly asked. 'We ain't seen you in an age and it's all over the newspapers that Miss Bolton is in your part at the Theatre Royal.'

'Kemble's just trying to stir a bit extra interest in the place. Making a mystery out of nothing to intrigue them.'

'He tell you to lie low, did he?' Tilly asked.

Alice gave a nod. 'Just for the week.' It wasn't exactly a lie, just slightly misleading.

'We were worried about you,' said Ellen, her gaze too shrewd as she studied Alice's face.

'I appreciate the sentiment, but there's nothing to worry about. Honest.'

'What you been up to then?' Tilly sat down beside her. 'Bet you don't know what to be doing with your time.'

'Catching up with some long-overdue sleep and letting my skin breathe; that stage paint doesn't half play havoc with my face.' It was an excuse for the shadows beneath her eyes and the pallor of her cheeks.

'We didn't like to say,' teased Ellen.

Alice smiled. It was the first time she had smiled in days. Already she felt better with her friends' presence.

'You're not being entirely honest with us, Miss sneaky Sweetly.' Ellen drew her a look.

Alice kept the smile on her face, but her heart skipped a beat. 'I'm sure I don't know what you mean.' She said it teasingly, but there was a sudden tension in her stomach.

Ellen gave a sniff of the air.

Tilly giggled. 'Your secret's out, Alice. The place is stinking of lavender and beeswax.'

Alice held her hands up. 'I admit it. I did have a quick little polish.'

All three women laughed.

'We've organised a night out at the theatre tomorrow with a few of the girls,' said Tilly. 'Hired a posh box at the side, with a good view of the stage. We know visiting the theatre's nothing special for you, I mean you're there nearly every day. But it'd be an experience to see it from the other side. To be one of the audience. And you'll be with us. It'll be a laugh. Say you'll come.'

'I shouldn't really.' But Alice was tempted.

'Staying in these four walls all day and all night until the end of the week will drive you mad, Alice,' said Ellen.

'Maybe you're right,' she admitted. Staying within them the last few days had not exactly helped.

Ellen smiled. 'You know we are.'

'All right then. Tomorrow night it is.' Alice smiled. Maybe a night with her friends was just what she needed.

Razeby knew he was being a fool, that still staying here alone in Hart Street was just torturing himself unnecessarily. But he had a perverse sense of needing to be here. Every room in the house held some lingering echo of Alice's presence. Within the bedchamber they had shared he stood by the window and watched the sun set, sipping his brandy and trying not to think of the night ahead with Miss Darrington and his mother.

Tilly had been right. It was a novelty for Alice to see the theatre from the audience's side. For too long she had only stood up there on that stage she knew so well. Tonight was different.

She had taken care with the rice powder and rouge to repair the shadows and the pallor that betrayed the truth upon her face. She wore the green silk, not to prove that she did not care, but to prove that she did. It made her feel connected to him. And she had been safe in the knowledge that he would not be at the theatre. But she had been wrong.

She sat in the box along with Tilly and Ellen and four other women, watching the players on the stage without seeing a thing of it. It was the dress that had brought him here, she thought. It had a magic all of its own. And she did not know whether to weep or to rejoice over it, because both those urges were vying in her breast.

'I'm glad we persuaded you into accompanying us.' Tilly slipped her arm through Alice's. 'We couldn't leave you in your rooms all alone, on a Saturday night, polishing furniture. I don't know why you don't get them maids of yours to do it.'

'I like wood polishing. It gives me a sense of satisfaction.' Alice did not tell them that she only polished when she was feeling anxious.

'I like polishing wood, too,' said Ellen. 'Just not the kind you're talking of.' She raised her eyebrows suggestively. Everyone laughed. Including Alice.

She was strong and resolute for such a long time, keeping her gaze fixed firmly on the stage below. Not once did she turn her head to look over towards Razeby's private box. But she knew he was there by the way Ellen's eyes turned too often towards it and the looks the women exchanged when they thought she would not see.

Tilly leaned closer to her and lowered her voice. 'We didn't know that he'd be here and with Miss Darrington, honest, we didn't.'

'Who's here?' she asked, as if there could be any other man in the world.

Tilly smiled. 'That's the spirit, girl. Sod him!'

Alice forced a smile. 'I hope not.'

They all laughed at the rude joke.

Then they all settled to watch the play—*All's Well That Ends Well*. A woman of low birth who was in love with a nobleman who was both beyond her and had no wish to be married to her. And then the low-born woman, Helena, spoke the words, 'T'were all one that I should love a bright particular star, and think to wed it.'

It was as if Alice could have spoken them herself of Razeby. They just seemed to reach inside her and touch the nub of all that was between them. It took so much effort not to flinch, not to tremble, not to show a single sign of it.

She dare not look away from the stage lest her eye found Razeby and Miss Darrington. And yet there was a lump in her throat that she could not swallow and the dangerous prickle of tears in her eyes. She managed through all of the first act and most of the second, before she knew that if she did not get out of this auditorium at that very moment she, who never wept, would disgrace herself by weeping in public.

'Please excuse me a moment, won't you? I'm away to the ladies',' she whispered to Ellen.

'Do you want me to come with you?' Ellen asked.

Alice shook her head. 'I'll only be few minutes.'

She escaped from the box and hurried out into the foyer, desperate for some small place to be alone. Just a few minutes in which to compose herself. Just a moment's relief from this torture of emotions. She could not hide from him for ever. It would get easier with time. It had to get easier with time, for she did not think she could keep going like this.

The foyer was quiet, not another soul present. Floating through from the auditorium she could hear the faint voices from the stage and, more loudly, the audience's reactions. She leaned back against the wall and closed her eyes, trying to find the strength to get through the rest of the evening.

'Alice.' At first she thought she was imagining his voice. Her heart missed a beat and then began to thunder. She opened her eyes to find Razeby standing before her.

'I saw you leave your box. Are you unwell?'

'I'm fine,' she said and tried to smile, but her lips would not curve to her will. 'I just needed a breath of air, that's all.'

They stared at one another. The faint noises from the auditorium and stage seemed very far away. Out here, standing with him, they might have been the only two people in the world.

'You have not been on stage for the past few days.'

'It's Kemble's idea of stirring more interest in the theatre.' She used the same excuse.

'When there's not a seat to be had at your every appearance?' He raised his eyebrows ever so slightly.

The silence hissed between them.

'Nor have you attended any of the dances or events.'

'I've just been taking a bit of a rest.'

'I know you are avoiding me, Alice.'

She shook her head, but her eyes never left his and she saw the shadows beneath them where before there had been none. 'You look tired, Razeby.'

'So everyone keeps telling me.'

'I'm sorry,' she said.

'So am I,' he said and she knew it was not the fatigue on his face that they were talking about.

'I should go back in. The girls will be wondering where I've got to.' But she made no move to leave.

'About those dresses in your wardrobe…'

'Don't, Razeby…please.'

'Not here, either?' He raised his eyebrows again but he was smiling and there was a gentle teasing in his voice.

'Definitely not here.' She smiled.

They looked at one another and there was such a depth of emotion between them that their smiles faded.

'I do know the reason, Alice.'

She closed her eyes. 'No,' she whispered and shook her head.

'I thought that seeing you and not being able to have you was a torture. But not seeing you is even worse.'

'I feel the same.' She clutched a hand to her forehead. 'But we can't be doing this, Razeby.

'I cannot stop, Alice.'

She stared at him. There was no teasing between them now. There was no smile, no laughter. Only dark intensity and brutal honesty and the agony of longing.

The silence seemed to roar.

He stepped closer, his eyes locked with hers. 'I miss you, Alice. So much.'

He was so close she could see every golden striation in the dark velvet-brown of his eyes, every dark lash, the first hint of blue shadow upon his jaw line. She could smell the scent of him that she knew each night in her dreams. And she could not stop all that was in her heart to swell and respond.

'I miss you, too, Razeby.'

A noise sounded somewhere in the near distance, someone leaving their box and coming out into the foyer.

Razeby reacted in an instant. He grabbed her hand and pulled her with him down the closest passageway that led from the foyer. Halfway along, he guided her along another passageway and then into another recess that led from it. He backed her against the wall, shielding her from view of anyone who might happen to pass. Except there was nobody else down this maze of passageways. No footsteps. Not even any noise from the auditorium. Only the sound of her breath too loud in her ears and the hard frenzied thud of her heart.

He was standing too close, his fingers still wrapped around hers. She knew she should not be here with him, that she should disengage her hand and walk away, but she did none of those things.

The touch of him, the feel of him… He rubbed his thumb against her fingers, in that small familiar gesture.

'We shouldn't be doing this,' she whispered, but her fingers entwined with his.

'We shouldn't,' he agreed as his free hand moved to gently cup her cheek. And in his eyes she saw all of what had always raged between them.

'Razeby,' she whispered. There was so much they could not say, so much tension, so much longing. She could feel it sparking in the air, like the terrible hush before the ferocity of a storm, feel it whispering across her skin and throbbing in her blood.

'Alice.' His eyes darkened. There was a fierceness to the handsomeness of his face, a torment that mirrored her own. She wanted him as she had never wanted him before. She needed him. It had been so lonely without him.

His hand slid round to the nape of her neck, then up into her hair, holding it firm. 'Alice,' he said again and his voice was hoarse and tortured.

Their eyes were locked only on each other, the moment stretched to a roaring eternity. And then, at last, he angled her face, and his mouth descended to crush hers.

Razeby. His name echoed through her mind, through her very being as she gave herself up to him, yielding to the fierce possession of his lips, giving all her heart had to give and receiving all of his in return.

There was nothing of the theatre. Nothing of shame or guilt or anything that was wrong. There was only this moment, this man that she loved with all that she was. He was the other half of herself. Her heart. Her very life. Here before her, like breath to a woman who had been slowly suffocating.

'Razeby.' This time the word escaped aloud, as her teeth scraped his chin, as her hands slid within his waistcoat and pulled his shirttails loose from his breeches that she might touch the familiar warm nakedness of his skin.

There could be nothing of resistance. The torrent that whirled between them was too strong. She surrendered to it, giving herself up to his kiss and all of the fury and passion and love that was in it. Against her thigh she could feel the hard press of his arousal and she longed for him, wanted him, needed him. She could not stop herself. Her hand slid to touch him there in that most private of places, feeling the large rigid bulge through his breeches.

He sucked in his breath, jerked beneath her fingers. 'I need you, Alice,' he whispered hot and harsh against her ear, biting gently at its lobe so that the fire in her thighs flared hotter and higher.

'I need you, too,' she admitted, and her voice was breathless as his.

All of time seemed to stop. Their eyes held for the expanse of the moment. They both knew it was inevitable. They both knew they were powerless against the force of what raged between them. In the silence all around the raggedness of their breath was deafening. Their gazes clung as the moment stretched beyond endurance. Trying to fight it and failing.

'Oh, Razeby,' she whispered. And then the last of their resistance, if there had ever really been any, crumbled. Razeby backed her against the wall and pulled her skirts up, sliding his fingers against her slick wetness.

Her fingers fumbled with the buttons on his breeches. His own closed over their tremble for a moment, looking deep into her eyes as he made short work of the buttons and freed himself from his drawers.

She moved her hand to stroke the silken length of him.

He wrenched her skirts higher.

She wound her arms around his neck as he lifted her up and plunged his heated length into her.

She gasped her relief, welcoming him back to the place where only he belonged.

'Do you want this?' he whispered. 'Do you want me?'

'You and no other, Razeby,' she replied with ragged breath.

'You and no other, Alice,' he said and thrust within her.

It was everything that was right, this mating, this coupling with the man that she loved. She needed him. She needed this physical joining with him, this reunification of two halves to make a whole. She met his every urgent thrust with the power of her own, groaning aloud at the ferocious intensity of it. So much need, so much love that she did not know if she could bear it. Their bodies strove together, rode together in unfettered abandon until they gasped aloud, rocking and exploding simultaneously in a union of utter love. And the glory of it was blinding. Alice ceased to exist. Razeby, likewise. There was starlight and sunlight and time itself seemed to shatter into a silver white myriad so that there was nothing, absolutely nothing save the merging of their two souls.

She cleaved to him and he cleaved to her.

'Alice,' he whispered and it seemed that every stroke of love that beat in her heart for him echoed in that one word.

'My love,' she whispered, unable to help herself.

He kissed her, and she could taste the salt of tears on her lips, but whether it was from his eyes or her own she did not know.

In the distance a bell rang, sounding the start of the interval.

Their bodies did not want to part.

There was the opening and shutting of doors, the hum of voices not so far away in the foyer.

And still he stood there inside her, their hearts beating in unison.

His eyes held hers.

She took his dear, dear face in both her hands, stroking his skin, staring into his eyes with all the love that she felt for him, her heart tender and aching. 'This is impossible, Razeby. You know that, don't you?'

'I know.' He closed his eyes and touched his lips to her forehead. 'God help us both, Alice,' he whispered.

Footsteps sounded, coming down the corridor. Yet still she could not move. It was Razeby who made them both decent, Razeby who shielded her from the view of whoever passed. The footsteps did not stop, just continued until they receded into the distance.

'There you are, Alice,' Tilly exclaimed and linked her arm through Alice's as she stepped alone into the now-crowded foyer. 'We wondered where you'd got to.'

Ellen was there, her perceptive eyes scanning Alice's face. 'Are you all right?'

Alice felt her cheeks warm beneath the scrutiny. 'Of course I am,' she said and turned her gaze back to the brash safety of Tilly.

After the interval was over they returned to the auditorium. And when the players were once more playing upon the stage and the lights had dimmed and the audience settled again within their seats, Alice's eyes found Razeby's box. He sat there, cool and dark and handsome. And across the distance and all of those people his gaze was not upon the stage or on the rich young woman who sat by his side, but on Alice.

God help them both, indeed.

After the theatre was over and the Darringtons and his mother delivered safely home, Razeby sat alone in the study of his town house in Leicester Square. An oil-painted portrait of his father, the seventh Marquis of Razeby, painted by Sir Joshua Reynolds, looked out at him from above the fireplace. A man so much like himself that it was like looking at his own reflection. The same dark hair, the same brown eyes, the same cleft in his chin. His father had been twenty-nine years old when the portrait had been painted. The same age as Razeby was now. A year later his father was cold in the ground. Dead at only thirty from a consumption of the lungs.

But he had done his duty and left behind a son to carry on the name and line. And Razeby had known his whole life that he must do the same.

'Was it ever the same for you?' he whispered and wondered for the first time at his parents' marriage. He did not think so. They had married young. His mother was the daughter of a minor baron. But he had never before thought to question whether his parents had been happy together. Whether they had been in love. Or if there had been another woman before her, a woman his father could not marry…a woman whom he loved.

He poured himself another brandy and drank it too quickly.

'Hell,' he cursed beneath his breath. Hell—for, in truth, that is what he felt he was in. Every time he closed his eyes it was Alice's face he saw, that shy and joyous smile that made his heart fill with a warmth, those beautiful blue eyes either teasing and playful, or dark blue as a summer midnight, half-closed in passion. There had been a bond between them right from that first night in the Green Room. She could tease him and beguile him. She could make him feel comfortable, at ease and excited all at once. He felt as though she understood him completely and that he understood her. And he missed that easiness, that natural affinity, that connection. In the meeting of eyes, in words, in a smile and in laughter. He missed just being with her. For him there had never been another woman like her. And there never would be. She was the one, in truth, just as he had told her that day in the Royal Academy.

He took a swig of the brandy. He had been under the same sentence his whole life, knowing what was coming. Knowing he would not live beyond thirty. And because of that he had made damn sure that he had lived his life. Squeezing every last drop from it, living every minute, taking it right up to the brink. But that had been before Alice.

Before Alice he had thought that living life to the full was about indulging himself, thrill seeking, hedonistic pleasures. That was what Alice was supposed to have been. An affair. One last blast in the dying light of the day. Something meant to last a few weeks until he got the lust and passion for her out of his system. But being with her had changed everything. Now he understood the difference between pleasure and happiness. Now he understood what it was to love.

He topped up the brandy glass and, sipping the rich heat of its contents, stood by the window watching the quiet darkness of the night. In his nose was the scent of Alice and on his body was the feel of hers. And he knew after what had happened between them in the theatre tonight that he could not marry another woman.

Love or duty?

Such a big question. A conflict that had battled within him since meeting Alice Sweetly. But after tonight there was no other choice he could make. He stood there and watched the dawn break through the darkness of the sky.

It had rained in the night, but this morning the sky was blue and the sun filtered in through the windows of the rented rooms in Mercer Street. Alice pulled the blanket tighter around her and thought of last night at the theatre. Her body felt alive, blooming from his touch. And yet her heart ached all the more. She was angry at her own weakness, but she knew now that the strength of what was between them was greater than all else.

She desired him. She longed for him. She loved him. And what had happened between them had been as natural as breathing. She could still smell his scent upon her, still feel the caress of his fingers upon her skin, still hear the whisper of his words against her ear. And if he came to her right now, even knowing that to love him was wrong and that it would only make things worse, she knew that she would do the same again.

She thought of rich Miss Darrington sitting beside Razeby in his theatre box. It did not matter that it was Alice who Razeby had made love to in the quiet corner of the theatre, it was Miss Darrington, or a woman like her, who he would marry. And that woman who would bear his children. And that thought served only to break her heart a little more.

In future she must avoid him completely, must walk out of the room when she saw him, no matter how blatant it was before all London. And never, ever be alone with him. It was the only way. Now that she knew she could not trust herself when it came to him.

It was late afternoon the next day that the maid came to Alice's bedchamber to tell her that Lord Razeby was waiting for her in the parlour.

She felt her heart skip a beat and her stomach give a somersault as she seemingly calmly set down the duster and jar of polish upon the dressing-room table. 'I told you that I was not at home to any visitors.'

The maid's cheeks coloured. 'He was most insistent, ma'am. I couldn't stop him.'

Alice gave a nod, knowing that she was being unfair; the girl would not have stood a chance against Razeby at his most determined. 'Tell him I'll be down shortly.'

But as she spoke the words there was a knock at the bedchamber door and she knew it was him standing there on the other side of it even though he made no move to open it.

A whisper of panic fluttered through her. She closed her eyes trying to control it. And knew she was going to have to fight not him, but herself, to send him away.

'It's all right, Meg, you may let him in and then leave us.'

The girl gave a nod and a curtsy, then did as Alice bade.

Razeby just stood there, leaning against the door frame.

'You shouldn't be here, Razeby.'

'I came to speak to you.'

'We did quite enough speaking last night at the theatre.'

'Not nearly enough.' His words made her heart flip-flop and her blood rush all the faster.

'What happened last night shouldn't have. We both know that. This is only making it worse. You have to leave. Now.' Before she yielded and made love to him again. 'I've got nothing more to say to you, Razeby.'

'But I have certainly got something more to say to you, Alice.'

Chapter Sixteen

Razeby paused. 'There is something I wish to ask you, Alice.'

'Then go downstairs and wait for me in the drawing room. We can talk there.' She was too conscious of the bed behind her and the way her body was already reacting to his presence, and the throb of her heart.

But Razeby's shoulder did not shift from where it leaned against the door jamb. His eyes dropped from her face, moved slowly over her body, before moving on to the gleaming polished surface of the dressing table, complete with its cloth and pot of beeswax and lavender polish, before returning again to her face.

'Are you feeling a little anxious, Alice?' he asked in a low velvet voice that stroked all the way through her. She shivered and he smiled.

Considerably so since his arrival. She glanced down at the plain worn apron still tied tight over her dress and blushed. Her fingers were trembling as she made to unfasten the tapes, pulling them into a knot in her fluster.

'Allow me.' He walked slowly to close the space between them. She closed her eyes as his fingers brushed lightly against the small of her back.

'You really shouldn't be here, Razeby.'

'So you have already told me.' He smiled again and the apron gaped free.

She swallowed and, after easing it over her head, paid unnecessary close attention to folding it into a small neat square.

Razeby took it from her fingers and slipped it into the pocket of his tailcoat.

'You aren't playing fair,' she whispered and turned to look up into his eyes.

'Fairer than you realise,' he said.

They looked at one another and she felt that same anguish and love vie in her heart.

'What do you want?'

'You,' he answered.

She sighed and closed her eyes. 'It's impossible,' she whispered beneath her breath. To resist him. For things to continue in this way. 'We can't do this. *I* can't do it. Don't you understand?'

'I understand too well.'

'Then why are you here?'

'For you.'

'I don't understand.' She shook her head, confused, hurt, both wanting him to leave and needing him to stay.

'I love you, Alice.'

'Oh, God!' she gasped and clutched a trembling hand to her mouth. 'What are you doing to me, Razeby?'

'Telling you the truth. Asking you to marry me.'

She gaped at him. Her knees felt weak. The blood roared in her head.

He caught her to him, holding her upright.

'This jest is too cruel,' she whispered and she was shaking like a leaf.

'It is no jest.'

She stared at him, wondering if he was drunk. 'Have you been at the brandy?'

'Not a drop has passed my lips today.' He smiled at her and inside her chest her heart felt like it blossomed.

'You can't marry me.' she said fiercely.

'Why? Won't you have me?'

'I'm an actress, Razeby.'

'I know what you are.'

'We're not like Venetia and Linwood. She might have been an actress, but her father was a duke. And Linwood's neck was in a noose. All of London understood why they married. And can forgive them because of it.' She swallowed. 'But it isn't the same for us. Look at me. I was born and brought up in a one-bedroom cottage outside Dublin, barefoot and lucky to have a single dress to my name. I was a whore in a bawdy house!'

He just held her gaze with steady brown eyes.

'I'd ruin you. And Razeby. All that your family worked so hard for. London would crucify us both were we to marry.'

'They would,' he agreed. 'And I would never leave you to face their wrath.'

'You're a marquis, Razeby. There's no getting away from that.'

'Is there not?'

She wrinkled her brow in confusion and shook her head. 'You've lost me.'

'I do not have to be a marquis.'

'If you haven't been on the brandy you've run mad.'

'I am thinking more sanely than I have done in weeks.'

'Then please tell me what you're talking of because I don't understand what you're saying.'

'It comes down to duty or you, Alice. And I choose you.' She stared at him, unable to believe the words he was saying. Like those of a dream, more than she could ever have hoped for or imagined.

'I do not have to be the Marquis of Razeby. I will give it all up for you; let Atholl run the place. He has a good head on his shoulders. And he will need something to focus upon when he returns home to England. He's not going to be going anywhere else for a very long time.'

'You can't just give up an inherited title, can you? I didn't think it worked like that.'

'It does not. But if I were to disappear, taking nothing more that the clothes I stood up in…' He raised his brows. 'We could run away together, Alice. Go abroad. After a certain amount of time had elapsed I would be declared dead and the title and estate and all that goes with it would pass to the next male in line—which is Atholl. And the seat of Razeby would continue in a fashion.'

'You're serious!'

'Never more so.'

She was reeling, shocked, hardly able to believe that he was willing to give up all that he had been born to, all that he cared for and loved, for her.

'I want you as my wife, Alice. And if this is the only way that I might have you, then it is what I shall do. So, Alice—' their gaze had not separated for a moment '—will you marry plain James Brundell?'

It seemed that her heart had swelled to fill all of her chest, and it glowed with a rainbow of glorious colour. He loved her. He wanted her for his wife. It was her heart's desire. He was her everything. *Yes!* she wanted to say. *Yes!* To yell it from the tree tops and press her mouth to his and kiss him with all that was in her heart. And if she did not love him so very much she would have done just that. She would have wrapped her arms around him and told him that she would marry him whatever name he called himself, if had not one farthing to it, and they had to live together in a one-room shack for the rest of their lives. But she did love him, and because she loved him she knew she could do none of that.

'What you're proposing is of such magnitude for your life, for your people, for all that you have been raised to be.'

'That is my decision to make.'

'You're talking about walking away from everything you are. From everything you love.'

'Not everything.' The look in his eyes was fiercely possessive.

'To be declared dead and have another man step into your shoes… I can't let you do that, Razeby.'

'We all die sooner or later,' he said softly, and there was a calm acceptance upon his face as he said those words.

'But to walk away from your duty would grieve you for every hour of every day,' she whispered.

He did not deny it. 'Not having you would be a worse death. I choose the lesser of the two evils. You shall not dissuade me from it, Alice. My mind is made up.' It was the truth. She recognised the stubborn determination in his eyes.

He was selling his soul to have her. And it really would destroy him. Maybe not today or even tomorrow. But the day would come eventually. And by then it would be too late to rectify. There would be no going back. And she could not let that happen.

'I'll come back to you. Move back into Hart Street as your mistress. Marry your Miss Darrington, or whomever you will. We can be discreet. I can bear it, Razeby.'

He smiled at her, and touched his thumb ever so gently to the centre of her lips. 'But I could not.' He looked into her eyes. 'It is you that I want, Alice, you that I love. I cannot marry another.'

She could have wept from joy and from sadness. Razeby, a man to whom honour and duty was everything. His love for her would tear him apart. Already she knew what she was going to have to do. There never really had been any decision to make, other than the way she must be sure to do it.

'I...I need some time to think, Razeby.'

'Not Razeby any longer. Just plain James.'

'James, then.' She smiled to soften her reply.

But he did not return the smile. 'What is there to think about?'

'Everything,' she said. And nothing. 'It's not every day a girl gets asked to wed.'

'I suppose not.' He smiled that glorious smile of his and gave a nod. 'Twenty-four hours, Alice. Not a minute longer. And I will be back for your answer.'

He kissed her fiercely with all the same passion and love that she could feel racing and throbbing through her own body. She clung to him and when he would have left she did not let him go, but held him to her and stroked his face, and kissed him more tenderly and with all the love that was in her heart.

'Let me love you, Razeby...' she said and did not speak the rest of the words. *One last time.*

He could not deny her, not when his body longed for hers and he wanted to climb in that bed with her and love her with everything that he was. A thousand times over and it would never be enough. He wanted her. All of her. For ever.

She unfastened the buttons of his breeches, pushed aside his drawers and freed his manhood into her hands. He was hard for her. Aching for her. She closed her hand around him and moved him within. Softly at first and then more firmly. He clenched his jaw to keep from losing control and caught hold of her wrist to stop her.

'On the bed. Now,' she whispered.

He peeled off his tailcoat, threw his waistcoat to follow and, pulling her into his arms, backed them both to the bed.

'I am yours to command,' he said as he gathered her skirts high and laid her gently down upon the covers. His gaze swept over her fair hair tumbling from its pins, at her kiss-swollen lips and the dark desire in her eyes, and the place between her legs that was so ready for him. He covered her body with his, their mouths clinging together, sharing lips and breath and tongues. But when he would have slid into her she inched her body just out of reach.

He groaned and made to capture her, but she stayed him.

'Not yet,' she whispered into his ear. 'I want to see you. I want to touch you. And taste you.' She stared down into his eyes.

Together they rolled on the bed so that she was on top and he beneath.

She unfastened his cravat and it was gone. She pulled the shirt up high to expose his chest. He peeled it over his head and threw it away.

'I want you naked,' she said.

'And I, you. I will take off the rest of my clothes only if you take off yours.'

'It's a deal.' She smiled, teasing him in that familiar way she had always done.

They stripped, and when he lay down on the bed again she came to him naked as the day she had been born, her straight pale-blonde hair freed from its pins to brush against her breasts, the pale rose tips nosing through its lengths. She straddled one of his thighs, kneeling there so that he could feel her warmth and moisture against him.

His manhood stood high to attention. She leaned over him, her long hair and her nipples brushing against his chest as she reached her lips to touch his. She placed one gentle kiss against his mouth. One on his breast against his heart. Then slid lower, to place another on his navel, dipping her tongue within to taste him there. Her mouth slid lower, following the line of dark hair, to the turgid thick length of his manhood. She kissed the tip of him and he almost came. She licked the length of him and he gasped aloud. She took him in her mouth and worked him gently.

'Have mercy, Alice, or I will not last any longer.' His whisper trembled.

She let him slide free. 'With you there can be nothing of mercy.' Words they had so often used in their play. 'I must be cruel to be kind, Razeby,' she said with the strangest expression on her face, but she did not take him in her mouth again. Instead, she kissed the other parts of him that made him a man. Stroked her hands slowly up the dark smattering of hair that dusted his belly, over his stomach, over his ribs and the length of his arms, from the tips of his fingers all the way up to his shoulders, as if she were trying to memorise every part of his body.

She kissed the hollow of his throat. Each shoulder. His Adam's apple. And then she looked into his eyes and watched him as she moved her legs to straddle him and lowered herself to take him into her body.

They sighed together in the relief and ecstasy of their reunion, their breaths mingling to become as one. Their gazes stayed locked as they moved together, as they found the place that only they could reach. And afterwards he gathered her in his arms and he held her and felt their hearts race together. She stroked his face, traced the line of his eyebrow, kissed his eyelids, the tip of his nose, the cleft of his chin.

There was such tenderness and love in her touch, in the way she looked at him, in her whisper of his name.

'You are mine, Alice. And I am yours.'

She smiled, but there was a sadness in her eyes.

He kissed the sadness away and held her as if he would never let her go. Come tomorrow he would save her heart, and his own, and lose his honour in doing so.

Alice lay in the bed long after Razeby had gone. Her body was contented from his loving, and when she slid her hand against the sheet that lined his side of the bed it was still warm from where he had lain. She loved him with every beat of her heart, with every breath in her lungs, with all that she was. But love wasn't all sweetness and softness and pretty things. Sometimes for love you had to make the hardest decision and do the most difficult thing in the world.

Alice had never loved before. She did not think she would ever love again. For her there was only, and would only ever be, Razeby. But he was the most determined man she knew. He had made up his mind and no amount of persuasion would turn him from it. To marry him was all she could ever have dreamed of. To be with him as his wife. To love him. And be loved by him. What more could there be in life? It was joy. It was happiness. If there could be heaven on earth, then to live like that with Razeby would be it.

But it would destroy him—and what happiness could there be in that?

So she would do the hardest thing in the world. To save the man that she loved she would sacrifice her own heart. And make him hate her for ever. It was as she had said, sometimes you really did have to be cruel to be kind.

There was only one way Razeby was going to let her go. One tack she knew would work for certain. And her heart shivered to take it, and her skin grew cold and clammy at the thought and she was so afraid, more afraid than she had ever been in her life, but she knew it was what she was going to have to do.

She closed her eyes and remembered the way he had loved her, the tenderness in his eyes. He would never look at her like that again. Never. She pushed the thought away and rose from the bed. She had to be strong enough for the both of them.

* * *

Razeby arrived at Alice's rented rooms at four o'clock the next afternoon, exactly when he had said he would—twenty-four hours after he had asked her to be his wife. She was dressed in the same yellow walking dress she had worn that day in Hyde Park and had wrapped a fawn cashmere shawl around her shoulders. There was a small fire burning on the hearth and the sun shone in through the windows, adding to the warmth of the room. But it did not matter how much coal she burned or how many layers of clothing she wore, she was frozen to the marrow and did not think she would ever feel warm again.

He was smartly dressed, wearing a black Weston riding coat and a pair of fitted buckskin breeches. The leather on his riding boots gleamed in the sunlight, as did the mahogany of his hair. He bore himself well, a slight arrogance in his walk, a confidence in the way he held himself that stemmed from being raised to lead. Everything about him spoke so loudly that he was born to be a marquis that she knew she was doing the right thing.

'So, Alice,' he said softly. 'I have come for your answer.'

Her stomach was balled so tightly she felt sick and her throat was sticking together so badly that she could not swallow.

'Will you marry me?'

Her heart was thudding hard and fast in the base of her throat. She forced her chin up, clutched the shawl so tight that her hands went numb. 'I'm afraid not. My answer is no.'

He gave a small surprised laugh, as if he did not really believe her. 'Do you think to save me from myself, Alice? Because if that is your game, I will brook no refusal.' He stepped closer.

Her heart missed a beat. 'This is no game.' She swallowed and took a step in retreat. 'I'll not marry you, Razeby.'

'Why not?' He cocked an eyebrow and his gaze bored into hers. 'I know that you love me.'

'No. You're mistaken. I don't love you. I've never loved you.' She looked away to tell the lie.

'I do not believe you. You cannot even look me in the eye to say it.'

She curled her hands so that her nails dug into her palms, forced herself to meet his gaze. 'I don't love you, Razeby.'

'And what happened between us yesterday?'

'Was sex.'

'It was a damn sight more than sex.'

'I made you think that. It's what whores are paid to do and I'm good at my job.'

He grabbed hold of her arm, hauled her to him, staring mercilessly down into her face. 'Never call yourself that word again. Do you understand?'

She nodded, afraid of the power and strength of what she saw in his face.

Something of the tension in his grip relaxed. 'Besides,' he said softly, 'I did not pay for yesterday, or the time in the theatre.'

'Consider it a couple of goodbye liaisons, for the sake of our previous arrangement.'

'I am prepared to give it all up for you and you tell me you will not have me?' He gave a laugh of incredulity and stared at her as if he did not believe her.

'Well, you see, that's the problem, Razeby.' She had thought so carefully all through the night of the words she must say—the words that would convince him. Re-hearsed them in her head again and again. But now that it came to saying them they stuck sharp as fish bones in her throat. 'I'm...' She took a breath and forced them to her tongue. 'I'm not interested in a man without money or title. A man who cannot keep me in the manner to which I've become accustomed. I don't want to be a poor man's wife. I don't want to flee to another coun-try. Or spend the rest of my life in a hovel, cooking and cleaning, with laundrymaid hands and scrabbling to make do and mend and put food on the table. I've been there. I've done that. I came to London to escape pov-erty and I'll not go back to it to be your wife.'

He stared at her in silence as if it took some time for the words to sink in. 'So it is not me you want at all,' he said slowly, 'but my wealth, my title, my power?'

She nodded, making sure she did not look away. Delivering every last piece of the lie while meeting his eyes.

'If it was not about love, but only gain, why did you not take the dresses, the bracelet, the money?'

'To pique your interest. It was all just a game to get you back.'

'You made me believe that you loved me.'

She swallowed and the air in her nostrils seemed chilled as ice and that in her lungs sharp as the prickle of pins. What was it he had said that day in the Exhibi-tion Room? *Clean and quick is the best way of severing something that one has no wish to let go.* 'I never said those words, Razeby.' Her voice was quiet as she deliv-ered the blow that would sever them for ever. 'Not once.'

She saw the words hit home. Saw the realisation in his eyes. It had worked, just as she had known it would.

'Neither you did,' he said softly. 'How remiss of me not to notice.'

The tension was stretched tight between them. She had not known that she could be so strong or so callous. To stand there second by second, minute by minute, and coldly, deliberately break his heart...and her own.

She forced her lips to curve in the echo of a smile. 'You're a nice man, Razeby—kind-hearted, generous. Great in bed.' She swallowed and the smile wavered before she forced it harder. It felt like there was something wrapped tight around her throat. 'But you see, the reason I was attracted to you was because you were a marquis and rich and high up, and good-looking, too. I know what that makes me, but then I've never pretended to be anything else.'

Razeby said nothing. He stared into her eyes, his face a mask of anger and darkness and disgust that she did not recognise. But better his contempt and loathing a hundred times over than let him destroy himself. If he thought her a selfish whore over whom he had made a mistake and had a lucky escape, then he would be glad to walk away and leave her. His wounds would heal in time. She did not think of her own. He would marry some rich, suitable woman. Breed his heirs upon her. Care for his people and his lands. Be the great man he had always been destined to be.

She could feel the intensity of his anger, the barely leashed rage, the darkness of emotion. And against her face was the warmth of his breath—but not from passion, not from loving. The intensity in his eyes was searing. She did not know how much longer she could endure it. Part of her was so close to falling to her knees, to blurting all of the truth, to wrapping her arms around him and cradling him to her, and telling him that she loved him. And another part, the strong part that knew she would move heaven and earth to save him, stood there quiet and resolute.

He did not say a word, not one word. Just took some coins from his purse. He put the purse away again and held out his hand, palm flat, offering her the two gold sovereigns that lay glinting upon it.

She knew what they were. She understood what he was paying for—their loving of yesterday and in the theatre. She stared at the coins and could not move.

'Take them,' he said in a deadly quiet voice.

The final test. The final sacrifice that must be made.

She reached out her hand and took both sovereigns from where they lay.

He curled his lip with disgust and gave a tiny disbelieving shake of his head. Then he turned, and without a glance back strode out of the bedchamber. She could hear the hurried, purposeful tread of his boots on the stairs, and across the hallway, the almighty slam of the front door that reverberated throughout and made the whole house tremble. And she did not move, just stood there, frozen in horror and shock and pain at what she had just done. Stood there, and stood there, while time ceased to be and somewhere around her was a whole world moving on.

She did not know how much time had passed before she heard the girl's voice. 'Are you all right, ma'am?' The youngest maid, Rosie, stood wide-eyed and timid outside the open bedchamber door.

She nodded. 'Go,' she managed to whisper.

But the maid just stared at her with horrified fascination and concern.

'I said, leave me.' Stronger this time.

The girl bobbed a curtsy, shut the bedchamber door and the light footsteps hurried away.

And still Alice stood there. Unmoving. Frozen. Staring at the floor, blind to the pale Turkish rug and the dark polished floor boards. Blind and deaf and dumb. Slowly she turned and walked to the bed, sat down on the edge of it. It felt like there was a great band of iron wrapped around her chest, crushing her, making it hard to breathe. She felt hollow where she had placed her hand within her chest and ripped out her own heart.

Razeby was safe. But the cost had been herself. All of herself. All of her heart. Everything she was. Every one of those words of deceit had been a cut to her own soul. In hurting him she hurt herself a hundred times over. In freeing him she sentenced herself to a living death. She felt numb, shattered, disconnected. There was nothing she could do or say or think.

She sat there, and the seconds stretched to minutes and the minutes to hours. She sat there and the sun moved away to set in the west and the daylight faded and the darkness came. And all the while her right hand was curled tight and hard.

A knocking sounded. The older maid, Meg, opened the door a crack and peeped in. 'Shall I bring you up a tray of dinner, ma'am?'

'Go away,' she said and her voice sounded like someone else's.

The door closed again.

She leaned to the side. Lay down on the bed, her feet and legs still dangling over the edge. She lay there, eyes open, staring into the darkness. Until the sounds of the carriages and the passers-by faded to nothing and there was only silence. Until, eventually, the silver of the moon crept in through the window and moved its way, inch by inch, across the room to light the curled tight fist of her right hand lying on the counterpane, white and bloodless as a dead thing. She looked at it as if it were not a part of herself. Slowly, she loosened the fist, uncurling her fingers inch by tiny inch until they lay flat and stretched, her palm exposed in full. She stared at the two large coins that lay upon it. Gold painted Judas silver by the light of the moon.

The pain hit her then, savage and merciless, and black beyond all despair. And all of the barriers crumbled, and the breaking was so sudden and swift and complete that there was nothing she could do to stop them. She wept, as she had not wept in all these weeks. She wept for the loss of the man that she loved and the loss of the woman she had been. She wept and she did not think that she would ever be able to stop.

Three days later Alice packed her travelling bag, and left her rooms in Mercer Street. She caught the mail to Southampton, boarded the first boat she could find and went home to Dublin.

Chapter Seventeen

There was silence in the drawing room of the Darrington town house in fashionable Upper Grosvenor Street.

Miss Darrington took a tiny sip of her tea. Her golden hair was perfectly coiffured, her body robed in an expensive pink silk.

'So what is your preference for the colours of flowers for the wedding breakfast table?' Mrs Darrington enquired of him.

'I am content to leave the decisions on such matters to yourself and Miss Darrington.' Razeby said. 'I am sure you will make an admirable selection.'

Mrs Darrington smiled and nodded.

'Such a pleasure that you have decided to ally yourself with our family. And with such eagerness for the nuptials.'

'There is no point in delaying when the decision has been made,' he said.

'A man after my own heart, Lord Razeby,' agreed Mr Darrington. 'Seven weeks should be more than long enough. Although Mrs Darrington is already getting herself in quite the flutter over arranging so speedy a wedding.'

Razeby forced a smile that could not touch his eyes. 'Such is the prerogative of ladies.'

Mrs Darrington gave a nervous giggle. 'La, there is so much to be done!'

'So much indeed,' said Miss Darrington. 'Perhaps seven weeks is not long enough. There is lace for my dress, the silk... Perhaps it would be better to defer the wedding until—'

'Seven weeks will be more than enough time,' Mr Darrington interrupted, fixing his daughter with a warning eye.

'If Miss Darrington is in agreement?' Razeby looked at her.

Miss Darrington gave a nod.

Seven weeks and he would stand before an altar and make Miss Darrington his wife. It would be done.

'More tea, Lord Razeby?' Mrs Darrington asked.

'Thank you,' he murmured and allowed her to fill his cup.

The clock on the mantel ticked its slow steady rhythm in the background. The large bouquet of flowers that Razeby had brought sat beside it in a cream-and-blue glazed vase.

'To marriage, Lord Razeby.' Mr Darrington raised his teacup as if making a toast.

Razeby raised his teacup in return. 'And duty,' he returned and smiled a cold hard smile that did not touch his eyes.

Alice climbed down from the cart's seat and walked up the garden path of the small cottage that lay on the outskirts of Dublin. The surrounding trees were all in bud, the first signs of green touching their winter-stripped branches. In the garden the heads of the daffodils had withered, but their leaves still grew thick and lush amongst the long untended grass through which a carpet of early bluebells was woven in vibrant splendour.

She felt a sense of relief and of home coming to be here. The air was cleaner than in London, and sweeter. Just a breath of it felt like it cleansed all of London's filth from her lungs.

Mr MacCormack lifted her travelling bag down from the back of the cart and set it down by the doorstep. 'Your mammy will be glad to have you back home for the visit, Miss Flannigan.'

The doxy, Miss Rouge, and the actress, Miss Sweetly, had been left behind in London. Here, she was plain Alice Flannigan, the same as she had been born, on the outside. But inside...that was a different story all together. She smiled at the old man and gave him a few extra coins as a tip and he ambled away, tugging the peak of his soft cloth cap as he did.

The front door still had not opened. And from the cool grey sky overhead came the first smir of rain. From inside the cottage she could hear squabbling voices and the running patter of small feet.

She raised a gloved hand and banged all the harder on the door. 'Mammy, are you going to open this door, or leave me standing here on the doorstep for the rest of the day? Anyone would think you're not wanting to see me.'

The door opened. Her mother stood there, staring in

disbelief. 'It's yourself, Alice. All the saints in heaven be blessed. I didn't know you were coming for a visit.'

Visit. Alice smiled again and did not correct her mother's misconception, just as she had not corrected that of the old carter.

Her mother took her face between her work-worn hands, her eyes raking her face, filled with welcome and with the sheer joy of reunion. 'Oh, but it's good to see you again, Alice, truly it is.' And something inside her suddenly welled up so that she felt like weeping and she could only be glad when her mother pulled her against the familiar old pinny and hugged her. Alice embraced her mother just as if she were a small girl again, squeezing her eyes shut, struggling to stopper the tears.

'It's good to be back, Mammy!'

'Look at us out here on the doorstep. Come in. Come in.' Her mother took hold of her arm and drew her inside.

The cottage interior was darker than Alice remembered and much of the furniture was missing.

Six-year-old Annie sat on her older sister Jessie's knee, having her hair combed. Molly was sitting in the only armchair in the room, weaving strips of rags to make a rug. They all looked at her, smiling but shy as if she were some stranger come to visit. She went to each one in turn, chucking their chins and teasing their hair just as she had done when they were small, and kissed their cheeks. From outside came the sound of wood being chopped and shrieks of laughter of girls playing in the background.

'Christie! Maggie, Cathy! Our Alice is back!' Her mother wrenched open the window and shouted out at them to come in. Alice's eyes moved to the small three-legged stool which was the only place that her mother could be sitting. There were two iron buckets set before it. One held dirty water, the other glistening newly washed potatoes. By her feet sat a small scrubbing brush and an old cloth potato sack.

'You'll be wanting a drink of water, Alice. Or I've nettle tea in the pot.'

'Water would be grand, Mammy. But you sit yourself down. I'll fetch it myself.'

'Indeed, you will not.' Her mother was already bustling through to the kitchen to fetch the water.

Thirteen-year-old Christie came in, the sleeves of his shirt rolled up, looking more grown up than she remembered.

Alice dropped a kiss on his cheek. 'Look at you, Christie! You've taken a stretch and no mistake. You're taller than me now.' And thin as a bean pole.

He blushed a vivid red, grumbled a protest and pulled away, but he was smiling all the same.

'He's the man of the house now,' her mother said as she came back through from the kitchen carrying a cup of water and a slice of bread.

'Where's our David away to?'

'Took the King's shilling at the beginning of last year and has been away fighting in King George's army ever since,' her mother explained. 'He sends money when he can.'

Maggie and Cathy were red-cheeked from the fresh air, their clothes ragged and worn from being passed down through so many older sisters before becoming their own.

'You look like a grand lady, Alice.' Cathy smiled

and touched a hand to the dark-blue skirt of Alice's travelling dress.

Alice smiled and hugged each of her little sisters, glad in heart to see them, but shocked at the level of poverty she saw around her.

'Christie, bring your sister's bag in from the front step. The rain's coming on.'

Her brother went to do as he was bid.

'And where's all the rest of them?' Alice asked looking round for the rest of her sisters.

'Our Martha's away married to a fella in Kilteel.'

'Married?' Alice's eyes widened.

'He's a shepherd and got his own cottage. They got married last summer just in time for the arrival of the baby, thank the Lord.'

'That's good news.' Alice smiled and felt something shift inside her.

'And our Mary and Bernadette both managed to find positions in the same big house in Dublin.'

'That's grand.'

'It is,' her mother said, but Alice looked in her mother's face and saw the lines of worry that had not been there two years ago when last she had seen her.

What are you not telling me? she wanted to ask. Where had all the money she had sent gone? Her eyes moved over the bare poverty-stricken room and those she loved. But there would be time enough for such questions later. For now she was just glad to be away from London and the terribleness of what she had left behind there. Glad to be home with the secrets of which she tried so hard not to think.

* * *

It was the afternoon of the next day before Alice learned the truth of what she had come home to.

The cottage was empty save for Alice and her mother. Molly and Jessie were out in the back garden, pegging clean washing on a line.

'So this Mr Feeney that you married—' Alice said carefully.

'It turns out we never were married after all. The dirty lying scoundrel already had a wife and six wee ones in Dublin!' Her mother interrupted. 'They say there's no fool like an old fool, and he had me reeled in all right, hook, line and sinker.'

'You weren't to know.'

'Maybe not,' her mother muttered. 'He was a charmer right up to the moment on Christmas Eve when he told me he was going back to his wife. I only discovered once he'd gone that he'd run up debts all over the place and relieved me of my savings before leaving. The bastard!'

'And you've been struggling to get by ever since.' She knew now where the new clothes and furniture had gone, bit by bit.

'We've managed up to now.'

'Thank God the cottage is bought and paid for.' *With the money that Razeby had given her.* 'At least he couldn't touch that.'

Her mother looked away, an uncomfortable expression on her face. 'It's not quite so simple, Alice.'

'I had the lawyer put the deeds in your name.'

'Everyone thought we were married. Even I thought we were man and wife. My property became his.'

There was a sense of dread in Alice's stomach. 'What did he do?'

'He mortgaged it behind my back. Gambled away the money on the horses. The first I knew of it was some gentleman at the door telling me he's the new owner and that he's putting the rent up. He's charging a fortune.'

'But I've been sending money.'

'Not enough. He's asking such a lot. And we can't go without food or coal. And he's putting the rent up again. Where on earth can I find more money? He says we owe months in arrears and that he'll turn us out in the street if I don't pay.'

'Don't worry, Mammy. I'll sort it out.' She thought of her savings at the bottom of her travelling bag.

'And that's not the worst of it.' Her mother looked at her.

How much worse could it get?

'It's our Molly.'

Alice hid the worry from her face and waited.

'Some lad from the village has got her pregnant. She's four months gone and he won't marry her. What am I going to do, Alice?'

Alice thought of Razeby and all the pain of that last scene between them, all because she refused to yield to her heart and marry him. Irony could be very cruel. Taking her mother's hand in her own, she patted the work-roughened skin. 'I've some money put by. There's enough for the cottage and for the baby when it comes. And to see you all right for a while.'

'You've still got your fine acting job at the proper theatre?'

Alice nodded. 'I've still got my fine acting job.' But

she'd walked out on Kemble and the theatre season was coming to an end.

'Oh, thank God!' Her mother's face crumpled with relief and she squeezed her eyes shut. 'What on earth would we do without you, Alice?'

Within the ballroom of the Earl of Misbourne's town house situated only a few houses along the street in Leicester Square from Razeby's own, the first ball that Venetia and Linwood were hosting was in full swing. Most of the *ton* were present, with only a few small exceptions who refused to accept Venetia into polite society. Not that their absence would have any effect on the ball's outcome. Linwood and his father, Misbourne, had used their contacts to land the Prince of Wales himself as a guest. And as the Prince was now on the floor dancing with Venetia, her acceptance by the *ton* was guaranteed. Miss Darrington had excused herself to go to the ladies' withdrawing room and showed no sign of hurrying back, much to Razeby's relief. He stood alone with Linwood in a corner of the room, both of them sipping champagne as if they were enjoying themselves, when in truth neither of them were; Razeby knew that Linwood felt the evening as much a strain as himself.

'I have seen the change in you, Razeby.'

Razeby ignored the comment. He kept his mind focused on his marriage ahead, of his duty, steering his mind coldly, ruthlessly from dwelling on anything else.

'I am telling you this as your friend because it has not gone unnoticed by the rest of London. Indeed, I wonder that Miss Darrington has agreed to marry you.'

Razeby thought of the woman who had not. The one

woman to whom he had offered everything that he was, only to have it thrown back in his face as not enough.

'It is hardly surprising that she has spent so much time in the withdrawing room thus far this evening,' added Linwood.

'It is a marriage of convenience for us both. She understands how these things work.'

'Maybe,' said Linwood. 'But are you going to tell me what is going on, Razeby?'

'I am marrying Miss Darrington is what is going on.'

'And Miss Sweetly?'

'Alice and I are no longer together.'

'I had worked that one out,' Linwood said. 'She is gone from London. Walked out on Kemble and the theatre. Venetia went looking for her. She thinks Alice might have gone home to Ireland.'

'I do not give a damn where she is.' He felt the simmer of red rage at the edges of his mind and in his chest was that familiar lance of pain that cut deep whenever he thought of her.

Linwood's dark eyes seemed to see too much. 'The last I saw you, you were harbouring feelings of a more tender nature towards Miss Sweetly.'

'I have changed my mind.'

'So easily?'

He gave a nonchalant shrug of his shoulders, but Linwood was not dissuaded.

'Damn it, Razeby. You were talking of marrying her!'

Razeby glared at his friend.

Linwood held his gaze with those calm black eyes. 'If you are truly done with her, then all well and good. But I do not think that to be the case.'

'You are mistaken.'

'Am I? Is that why you punched Devlin the other night?'

'He suggested going to the Green Room of the Covent Garden theatre.'

'He was trying to cheer your ill humour!'

Alice's name whispered unspoken between them.

'I have no wish to visit the Green Room of any theatre.' Razeby stared straight ahead, his jaw stiff and stubborn. Both of them knew the significance of the Green Room in Razeby and Alice's relationship, but neither man made mention of it.

He had loved her. And believed she loved him. He had almost dishonoured all that he was as a man, turned his back on the one thing he had to do in his life, given it all up for her—a woman who had taken his heart and trampled it into the ground. What an actress she was. She had fooled him completely and utterly.

The bitterness of the illusion she had spun seemed to gnaw in the pit of his stomach. He did not even think of telling Linwood the truth. That she had rejected his offer of marriage—that she had ripped out his heart and ground it to a pulp before his very eyes. That he was such a fool that he had been prepared to put his honour aside. It was too raw, too intense, too private. Too damn shameful! He had not come to terms with it himself, let alone start revealing such vulnerabilities, even to Linwood.

Linwood said nothing, but Razeby could feel his friend's discerning gaze upon him.

He glanced across and saw Miss Darrington re-enter the ballroom.

There was still time enough before his thirtieth birthday. He had to stay focused. And do what had to be done.

Alice sat in the lawyer's office in Dublin beside the man she was paying to represent her. Over on the wall were square-shaped box shelves, each one filled with scrolls piled high, every scroll tied with a red ribbon. The light from the office window lit the faded brown leather of the seats a warm chestnut and glanced off the glass of the pictures on the wall. A grandfather clock in the corner of the room ticked slow and steady, punctuating the silence. Tiny specks of dust floated in sunlight, softening the drab interior of the room. Alice, dressed in her best blue day dress and pelisse, sat across the desk from the lawyer and tried to keep calm.

'A thousand pounds? You cannot be serious, Mr Timmons.'

'If you wish to buy the cottage, Miss Flannigan, that is the price Mr Lamerton is asking.'

'For a cottage in the country, with its roof in need of a new thatch?'

'He has offered to re-thatch the roof as part of the selling price.'

'Then you can tell him he may keep it. There are other cottages to be had in the village.'

'Mr Lamerton owns all of the properties in the village.'

'There are other villages nearby.'

'There are, Miss Flannigan. But you seem not to be aware that Mr Lamerton inherited some considerable acreage in the area from his late uncle. He is a landowner of wealth and influence. Perhaps your mother might consider moving out of the parish.'

'No.' Alice knew that her mother had been happy in the village. She had friends there. And besides, the house represented much more than four walls and a roof over their heads. After the years of living on the street, of shifting from a shared room in one relative's house to another, it had been the one point of stability in their lives. Her mother had always sworn she would never move again. Never go back to that life of constant shift and insecurity. 'I would not ask that of her.'

'The price is unreasonable, I agree, Miss Flannigan, but there is little else I can do.'

A thousand pounds. Alice's savings. From her time with Razeby. And her earnings from the theatre.

'Maybe I could speak to Mr Lamerton about reaching some arrangement over the payments for the rent that is outstanding.'

And Lamerton would have her mother over a barrel for the rest of her days. 'A thousand pounds and my mother would own the cottage outright?'

The lawyer nodded. 'That is the case, Miss Flannigan.'

'Tell him I will give him nine hundred and arrange myself for the roof to be thatched.'

'I will make the offer, as per your instruction, Miss Flannigan.'

In the crowded bedchamber of the little cottage Alice stole from the bed she shared with her sisters and crept through to the living room. The moon was high in the sky, its quiet silver light spilling in through the small lead-latticed window. She stood by the window and looked up at the moon, the same moon that shone down on Razeby in London. She wondered how he was and what he was doing. Every time she closed her eyes she could see his face.

The night was the cruellest time, for he came to her in her dreams, always in tenderness. He made love to her and gathered her in his arms and told her that he loved her. And always, always, it ended with those words that she had spoken, those lies and deceptions. And him staring down into her face with such anger and disgust. And always in the darkness it seemed that she could feel the press of two golden sovereigns against the palm of her hand. And every night she wept silently in the darkness.

She stood there and watched the full moon. Once upon a time she would have wished on it. But she did not do that now. A month had passed since she had come to Dublin. The cottage was paid for. A new fresh thick thatch upon the roof. Furniture and new clothes bought. The larder stocked full and ten bags of coal emptied into the coal cellar. And all save five pounds given into her mother's hands. But the money would not last for ever. She could not shirk her duty. It was time to go back to London. Besides, there was another reason she could not stay here. But she did not want to think of that right now. Not until she was sure.

Chapter Eighteen

It was two weeks until Razeby's wedding.

He sat in White's Gentlemen's Club with a group of his friends and pretended to laugh at some crude joke that Fallingham had just cracked. Devlin was guffawing by his side, the drink flowing freely.

'Another three bottles of champagne,' Razeby said.

'Steady on, old man, someone might think you are celebrating getting yourself enmeshed in parson's trap,' Bullford teased.

'Happens to the best of us, as Linwood will tell you.' Razeby grinned as if his heart were not shattered and aching.

Linwood gave the tiniest incline of his head, but said nothing else.

'So how do you wish to celebrate your last night of bachelorhood when it comes, Razeby?' Devlin's words were already slightly slurred. 'The boys and I have been discussing it. And we were thinking a night out at a certain colourful establishment—Mrs Silver's House of Rainbow Pleasures, to be precise. You could sample

one of every colour. Maybe we all could. And afterwards swap notes.'

The words touched a raw nerve. None of them knew
the truth, save for Linwood. The identities of Mrs Silver's girls were a closely guarded secret. He thought of
Alice working in that place as Miss Rouge and his stomach twisted tight into a small hard knot. The thought
of even entering the brothel made him feel sick. Yet he
showed not one sign of his discomfort.

Across the table Linwood's gaze met his and held
for the smallest moment before moving away to the
rest of the group.

'Hardly original,' Linwood drawled. 'Besides, he's
tasted them all already.'

He had tasted one and one alone and she had snared
him and bound him to her in ways he had never imagined possible.

'I concede there is something of the truth in that,'
agreed Razeby, although he did not say which half of
Linwood's sentence was the truth, and which the lie.

'Linwood's right,' said Bullford. 'You will have to
come up with something better than that, Devlin.'

'If you are so smart, you come up with a better idea,'
said Devlin.

'Maybe I shall, old man. There's time enough yet to
think about it.'

Razeby lifted one of the bottles of champagne
from the silver bucket of ice that the footman had just
brought. He gave the bottle a shake then, laughing as
if he had not a care in the world, popped the cork and
necked some of the erupting froth to the cheers of his
friends. He wiped a hand across his mouth as if were
enjoying every dissolute moment and passed the bottle

to Devlin, who did the same. 'And in the meantime why do we not take our champagne through to the gaming room and play a few hands on the tables?'

'Now, that is a damnably splendid idea,' said Fallingham and, taking out his snuff box, offered it round.

Razeby's gaze met Linwood's across the table, and there was nothing of laughter or mock merriment in either man's eyes. Razeby drew his friend a tiny nod of gratitude of what he had just saved him from. Linwood reciprocated in the same way. In the carousing and drunkenness of the others, no one else noticed.

It was almost dusk when Alice knocked on the front door of Venetia and Linwood's apartments in St James's. The hackney carriage waited out on the road, with her travelling bag still stowed inside. She pulled again at the voluminous dark hood, checking that it shrouded her identity from any of Venetia's neighbours who might be chancing to look from their windows and see the lone woman standing there. A breeze stirred the dark shroud of the cloak around her.

The footman let her in. But when he would have taken her cloak she declined, only followed him through nervously to the drawing room.

Venetia was on her feet to greet her. 'Alice!' She came to her and took her hands in her own. 'Thank the Lord! I have been so worried over you. Come in, sit down and take some tea. Your cloak…' She gestured to the butler who hovered, ready to take it from her.

But again Alice shook her head, waiting until the manservant left before she sat spoke. 'I know the hour is late and I've no wish to embarrass you amongst your neighbours.'

Venetia sat down on the sofa beside her. 'That is foolish talk, Alice, and you know it.'

'I didn't come to stay, only to...' she hesitated for the smallest of moments '...to ask a favour of you.'

'Anything,' said Venetia.

'You own a charity house out in Whitechapel. One that provides shelter for certain women and their children...'

'I do,' said Venetia and Alice could see the curiosity and concern in her eyes.

'May I stay there? It would just be for a short while, until I get myself sorted out.'

Venetia met her gaze and held it. Alice glanced away, afraid of what her friend would see in her eyes.

'You may not,' said Venetia quietly.

Alice stared round in shock. She had not thought Venetia would refuse her. 'I wouldn't ask it of you, Venetia, but I've nowhere else to go,' she admitted out of desperation. 'And you needn't worry that I'd speak anything of your connection with it. I know you hold it as a secret. I would say nothing.'

'Alice.' Venetia took her hand in her own. 'I know you would say nothing. But you cannot stay there. It is in Whitechapel, for heaven's sake. No. You will stay here with me. I insist upon it.'

'I can't stay here. Only think what it would do to your reputation. The *ton* would have a field day if they knew I was living under your roof.'

'The *ton* do not need to know. We can be discreet.'

'But what of Linwood? He won't like my being here one little bit.'

'My husband will understand my wish to help my best friend. Please stay, Alice.'

'I...' The temptation pulled at her. She knew she would be safe here with Venetia. Besides, she knew that having the celebrated Miss Sweetly in their midst would do neither herself or the refuge any good.

'I take it that is your hackney carriage waiting outside?'

Alice gave a nod.

Venetia instructed her butler to see to Alice's luggage and send the carriage away.

'I'll stay only for a few days. Then I'll find somewhere else.'

'Are you forgetting that you sheltered me, Alice, when my home was lost? I do not. You are welcome to stay here as long as you wish. I will be sincerely glad of your company.'

Alice smiled a smile of relief. Venetia was good to her; she always had been.

'Have you eaten?'

Alice shook her head. 'I'm just off the stagecoach from Southampton. I was back in Ireland visiting—' She stopped mid-sentence. 'Is Linwood at home?'

'He has business round at his father's.'

Alice felt herself relax a little, afraid that where Linwood was, Razeby might appear.

Venetia looked down into her face. 'Was everything all right with your family, Alice?'

'No.' She smiled. 'Not really. But it is now.'

'Then you had better tell me about it.'

Alice sat at the breakfast table the next morning in Venetia's apartments. Venetia sat opposite her, not yet dressed, still wearing her dressing gown wrapped around her. Alice had put on her pale-green afternoon dress and pinned up her hair.

'Won't you eat something else?' Venetia asked.

Alice shook her head. 'I'm not hungry.'

Venetia topped up both their cups of coffee and spread some honey across her fresh bread roll. 'It is Razeby, is it not?'

Alice said nothing, just forced herself to nibble on the dry roll on the plate in front of her.

'What happened between the two of you?'

'Nothing happened.' She could not meet her friend's eyes.

'You will have to hone your acting skills better than that before you go back on stage,' Venetia said quietly, but she did not press her for the answer.

Alice glanced away and massaged the tight spot of tension that ached between her brows. 'How is he?'

'Like a different man.'

She closed her eyes at that.

'He is engaged to be married to Miss Darrington.'

'I am glad of it,' she said. And she was, truly she was. It was the best she could do for him.

'The wedding is set for two weeks' time in Westminster Abbey.'

'So soon?' she whispered and swallowed.

She glanced up to see Linwood in the door frame and felt her face pale.

'Miss Sweetly.' He gave a small bow of his head. Unlike Venetia, he was fully dressed in a smart dark-green tailcoat and buckskin riding breeches.

'Lord Linwood,' she murmured as she rose and gave a small curtsy. She resumed her seat too quickly.

Linwood helped himself to a selection of breakfast

items from the heated silver trays on the sideboard.
As he lifted the lids the food smells wafted strongly
in Alice's direction. Bacon and eggs and kippers. Her
stomach tightened.

He sat down by Venetia's side, opposite Alice.

She bit her lip, averted her gaze from his heavily
laden plate and tried not to breathe through her nose.

'I hope your trip home to visit your family went
well,' he said.

She nodded and knew she could not keep staring
in the opposite direction. 'Very well, thank you.' She
forced herself to look at him, and those black eyes were
so perceptive that she wondered what Razeby had told
him of her. Her gaze dropped and she found herself
looking directly at his plate of food.

He cut into the fat fillet of kipper and the smell hit
her all the stronger.

Alice gagged and, clutching a hand to her mouth,
fled from the room.

Venetia found her in the little bedchamber up in the
attic, kneeling over the chamber pot, retching up the
remains of the half bread roll she had eaten. She came
into the room, shut the door behind her and opened up
the window.

Alice sat on the bed, leaned back against the wall
and breathed in the cool, fresh morning air as Venetia
sat beside her.

'Sorry,' Alice said. 'It must have been something I
ate at the coaching inn yesterday.'

'But you did not eat anything in the coaching inn
yesterday, did you, Alice?'

Alice swallowed and took a deep breath. 'No.'

'How many months gone are you?'

Alice did not even try to deny it. Venetia would know the truth of it sooner or later, and in a way it was a relief to be able to tell someone else. 'I've missed two lots of my monthly courses.'

'Does Razeby know?'

'No!' She sat bolt upright and the dizziness swam in her head, so she eased herself back against the wall again. 'And don't you dare tell him, Venetia. Please, I beg of you!'

'I will tell him nothing that you do not wish him to know.'

'Thank you. I don't want him to know anything of it.'

'Why not? He is not an unreasonable man, Alice. You will need a means of living for you and the baby when it comes. Razeby would hate to default on his duty.'

Alice smiled at that—a bittersweet smile at the remembrance of how much Razeby had been prepared to give up for her.

'It is his child, too, Alice. And whatever has happened between the two of you, I am sure he would take care, at least financially, of both you and the child you have made between you. You should tell him at the very least.'

'I cannot.' *The child you have made between you.* She felt the tears prickle in her eyes and pressed her hands to her face to hide them. 'You have no idea, Venetia. What I did to him…the terrible things I said.' She swallowed and swallowed, but the tightness in her throat would not alleviate. The scar of that terrible day in that bedchamber in Mercer Street was still vivid and throbbing in her memory. 'I lied to him. I made him despise me. I made him think the very worst of me.'

'Why would you do that?'

She looked up at her friend, knowing she was going to have to tell her the truth. 'He asked me to marry him. He wanted us to go away, to the Continent, to live. He was going to give it all up for me. His birthright, his heritage, his title, his people. Everything that is so important to him. Everything that he has been raised the whole of his life for. I couldn't let him do that, could I? No matter how much I want to be with him.'

'So you turned him down.'

Alice nodded. 'In the worst way possible. There was no other way he would have believed me otherwise. He's a very determined man, is Razeby.' She clutched her bottom lip hard with her teeth to stop herself from crying, but it was useless, the tears spilled over her eyes just the same. 'He thinks me the most callous and worst of whores. God only knows what he'd do if he knew I had his babe in my belly. I doubt he'd leave his child to be raised by the woman he believes me to be. And I couldn't let that happen. I won't risk that happening. Not when it's all I've left of him.' She looked at her friend. 'Oh, Venetia, what am I going to do?'

'We'll find a way, Alice.' Venetia put her arm around her. 'I'll help you.'

'I can't stay here, unmarried and with a belly that will swell to notice soon enough. I wouldn't do that to you, Venetia.'

'I will find rooms for you in the country. I will take care of the money and—'

'No.' She shook her head. 'I can't let you do that,' she said, knowing what would happen to the fragile reputation that Venetia had worked so hard to build. Besides, there was also her family back in Ireland to think of. 'I will find another way. I have to.'

'Alice, the theatres are closed for the summer. And when they open again you will not be in a position to hide your condition.'

'I know. But my mind is made up, Venetia. You're my friend. And you've already done so much for me. Getting me out of Mrs Silver's and all. But enough is enough. I won't ruin your chances of happiness in your new life. I'll leave this very minute otherwise.'

'You can be a most stubborn termagant when you choose to be, do you know that, Alice Flannigan?'

Alice smiled even though the tears were still rolling down her cheeks and she could not seem to stop them. And then she thought of Razeby again. 'You won't tell him, will you, Venetia?'

'I will not tell him.'

Alice gave a sigh of relief. 'Thank you, Venetia. For that and for letting me stay. Linwood's not too angry, is he?'

'He is not angry at all. He, too, remembers how you took me in after my house burned down, before we were wed. He is not what you think him, Alice.'

'He's Razeby's friend.'

Venetia gave a little wry smile that did not touch her eyes. 'I cannot deny that.'

'How is your head this morning?' Linwood asked as he and Razeby trotted their horses through a deserted Hyde Park early the next morning.

'Absolutely fine.'

'Then you did not accompany Devlin to that tavern in the docklands?'

'I did. It proved to be an interesting distraction.' Anything to take his mind off mulling over what a fool he had been over Alice.

'Do you know Miss Sweetly has returned to London?' Linwood asked.

Razeby's heart skipped a beat and for that small moment he could say nothing. Then the anger and determination kicked in and he recovered himself. 'I did not. Nor is it any of my concern.' His voice was cool. His eyes belying nothing of the small curve of his lips.

'Should you choose to call upon me at home, it will therefore not discompose you to know that Alice is a house guest of Venetia's for some short while.'

Razeby said nothing, but he gave a small acknowledging nod of the head to his friend. 'I will bear it in mind.'

They rode on in silence, Razeby determined not to ask one question about her and Linwood revealing nothing.

He should be glad of that, Razeby thought. There was nothing about Alice Sweetly that mattered to him anymore. That was what his head was saying. What he felt in his heart was something else all together. But Razeby had done with listening to his heart. So he did not ask. And Linwood…he did not tell.

Chapter Nineteen

Alice walked along Oxford Street the next morning. She had thought long and hard through all of the days past over her options. It was as Venetia had said. The proper theatres had closed for the holidays. And even if they had not, she was not entirely sure Kemble would have her back after the way she had walked out on him. There was no point in approaching any of the other so-called theatres. She could not dance, or hold a tune. She could not twist her body into gymnastic shapes or ride bareback on a horse. She had never been on a horse in her life, if it came to that. And she could not play a single musical instrument. She liked to draw and colour, but again, she thought the standard was insufficient to find employment through that avenue. She could launder and wash and scrub and polish as good as any maid. But the agency had turned her away, saying that without a single character to her name, or any experience, she would not find work in service. She had an excellent memory, but no employer had need of that. Even Mrs Silver would not want her with a babe in her belly, though in truth she could not stand the thought of any man other than Razeby touching her.

So she spent the day trawling the streets of London looking for work in any shop that she thought might hold the slightest chance of employment. Although in her heart she knew even if they did take her on, she was just deferring the problem for the future. Once the baby began to show, they would not have her, and the money was unlikely to be good enough to last her through. But in the end, there was nothing to be considered. Some respectable shop owners recognised her as the famous Miss Alice Sweetly and sent her packing immediately. Others would not interview her without previous experience of working in a shop. And the one establishment that showed a measure of interest needed her to record all sales in a ledger and write the customer a receipt and, given that there were only two words that Alice could write, she made her excuses and left again.

She knew that Linwood's sister was visiting Venetia this afternoon, so she did not return to the rooms, but instead headed for nearby St James's Park. There was a nip in the air, but other than that the day was fine and bright. She stayed clear of the more fashionable routes, walking along a quieter line of trees until she found a wooden park bench. Her feet and back ached from all the walking and she was tired. It seemed she was always tired these days. So she sat down in the sun and rested. She could hear the chime of St James's clock and did not intend on returning to Venetia's apartment until after six, to ensure that any visitors would have long departed.

A few people passed. Two ladies walking. An old man. A boy who looked like he was running an errand. And a gentleman on horseback. She kept her face averted from the latter, although she knew he was not Razeby. Half an hour elapsed. She felt better for the rest, and for the fresh air. And then she heard the jangle of a horse harness.

'I thought it was you, Miss Sweetly.' She glanced up to find the Duke of Hawick standing there on the grass, leading a large chestnut horse by the reins. He removed his hat and held it in his hand beside his riding crop.

'Your Grace,' she said and, getting to her feet, gave a small curtsy.

He bowed. 'Have you been away? I have not seen you in a while.'

'Visiting my family in Ireland.'

'How pleasant for you.'

'It was.'

'I trust you had a good trip.'

'Very good, thank you, Your Grace.'

He smiled and his teeth looked remarkably white against the pale golden tan of his skin. 'What brings you out here to the park?'

'It's a pleasant day. I thought to take some air.'

'The day is fine indeed. I have been taking something of the air myself. Brought Legion out for a bit of a canter.' He gave the chestnut horse's neck an affectionate half-rub, half-pat. 'Do you ride, Miss Sweetly?'

'Unfortunately not.'

'You prefer to enjoy the view on your own two legs, or perhaps in the safety of a carriage.'

'It's a less dangerous pursuit.'

He smiled again and his dark blonde hair fluttered in the breeze. 'I suppose that depends on whose hands are upon the ribbons.'

'I suppose you've the right of it.' She smiled and wished he would go away.

'We never did get to have that evening alone.'

'We didn't.' She glanced away, feeling awkward and a little vulnerable. 'I really should be getting on... If you'd excuse me, Your Grace.' She got to her feet.

'May I be as bold as to escort you home? I do not like to think of any woman walking home alone at this time in the day.'

'I thank you for your kind offer, but it's not late and I'll be quite safe.' She gave him a small curtsy and made to walk away, but Hawick came, still leading his horse, to walk by her side.

'I would be remiss in my duty as a gentleman if I were to agree. Where are you staying these days, Miss Sweetly?'

She realised her mistake. She could not tell him without drawing scandal upon Venetia. 'With a friend,' she said and did not elaborate. 'But I wasn't intending heading home immediately. I've a few chores to attend to first.'

'Anything that I may be of assistance with?'

'I appreciate the kindness of your offer, and I thank you for it, but there's nothing with which you can assist me.'

He gave a nod of his head, but he did not take his leave of her, just continued to walk slowly by her side.

There was a small time in which they walked in silence.

'Perhaps you will think me too bold and too hurried in my approach. But I am a man who has learned from past experience...' he paused for the tiniest moment and she knew he was referring to events of last year when all of London had known how long and hard he angled to make Venetia his mistress without success '…that it is best not to dally in negotiations or protracted games when it comes to such matters. I see what I want and I will have it…or not.'

She felt her stomach tighten and her heart beat harder with a sudden nervousness.

'I have made no secret of my admiration for you, Miss Sweetly.'

She kept on walking, very slowly, by his side and did not look round at him.

'And indeed your absence seemed only to cement my feelings on the matter…'

Her heart began to thump in earnest. She knew what he was going to ask her.

'You are a lady without a protector. I am a gentleman who would be happy to offer that protection.'

'Your Grace…' She stopped then and turned to him.

'I am not prepared to undergo prolonged negotiations by letter and note. I have found a more direct approach preferable, and therefore I hope you do not find my open discussion of terms to be offensive. To come to the point, Miss Sweetly, a hundred pounds a month, four new wardrobes of clothes a year, all outings to entertainments included, a furnished house in Sackville Street with a complete staff and all running costs met, and the use of a carriage and four. The agreement in full detail to be drawn up in writing between us, naturally.' He smiled charmingly, but there was a slight hard edge to his clear blue eyes.

A hundred pounds a month. Even if she were only with him for three months that would be three hundred pounds. It was enough to find somewhere safe to stay, enough to survive on for a good while if she was careful. And yet she knew too well what being any man's mistress entailed and the thought of that reality with another man... What she really wanted to do was to tell him to go away and never come near her again, that she had no desire to sell herself to him or any other man. She wanted to shout at him that she was not some cheap whore to be sold to the highest bidder without any consideration for her heart or desire. But Alice knew she could not do that. She bit her lower lip and looked away. Because the reality was that she *was* a whore and the only thing she had left to sell was herself.

That strange hungry sickness was gnawing in her belly and that same slight faint feeling was in her head. She thought of the baby that was growing inside her, her baby and Razeby's, and the knowledge instilled a fierce protectiveness in her, a searing determination that she would do anything and everything to protect their child. She could see the green of the grass beside the pale-fawn material of her slipper and the polished gleam of the toes of Hawick's black-leather riding boots standing not so very far away.

'You surely can't expect me to give you an answer right now, Your Grace.' She raised her gaze to meet his.

'That would be unreasonable. And I am not an unreasonable man. I would have your answer by the end of the week. I can be found here exercising Legion most days at this time. Or you may send a note to me at my town house.' He slipped a card from his pocket and offered it to her.

She said nothing, but she took the card from him.

'Such a pleasure to have met you here this afternoon, Miss Sweetly.' He took hold of her gloved hand

and pressed a kiss to it. After a bow he placed his hat on his head, slipped one foot into his stirrup and mounted his horse. He looked down at her from where he sat for a moment, then he gave a small smile, and with a nod of his head, rode off in the direction from which he had come.

She watched him ride away and the thought of what he was proposing made the queasiness rise in her stomach. She took a deep breath, stowed the card inside her reticule and kept on walking.

Alice sat on the edge of the bed in the tiny bedchamber in Venetia's attic in her long plain-white nightdress. The house was in darkness and silence. From somewhere outside she heard the cry of the watch.

'Two o'clock and all is well.'

The soft patter of rain sounded against the window and the darkness of the night sky was complete, the moon and stars shrouded by thick charcoal-streaked clouds. The candle, which sat on the cabinet by the side of the single bed, burned lower and she pulled the wool shawl more tightly around her shoulders to ward off the night's chill. In her hand she held the card that Hawick had given her that afternoon in the park. A smooth, thick white card, printed with expensive black ink, but the words that were there could have said anything. It did not matter how many months she had studied letters and words, they were always just a strange jumble of symbols and patterns that made no sense.

Hawick had had famous mistresses in the past. Indeed, his negotiations to make Venetia his mistress when she was still an actress and before she had married Linwood were renowned. He was reputed to have offered her ten thousand pounds and still Venetia had turned him down. Twelve hundred pounds was a far cry from ten thousand, but it was still a fortune in money, even if she was not able to stay the course to collect all twelve hundred. Once he discovered she was pregnant, he would not want her in his bed.

She wondered how many months it would take before it became obvious. It would be difficult to hide from him given what it was he wanted from her. She closed her eyes at that thought, unable to bear it. But she knew that beggars could not be choosers. She had made her bed and now she must lie in it, quite literally.

She clutched a hand to her stomach and tried to stopper the tears. Tears and sensibilities and regrets would not provide for the baby, she told herself angrily. And it was not as if she had not slept with men in order to survive before. Men that she was not attracted to. Men that she had not loved. But the little voice at the back of her mind whispered that that had been before Razeby. And Razeby had changed everything.

But she could not stay here. She would not ruin Venetia's chance of happiness and acceptance. And she could not go to Ireland and put her own problems on to her mother, not when her mother had aged ten years in the last one and was already worried sick over their Molly. Alice was the one who solved her family's problems, not added to them. And come a week Tuesday, Razeby would be married to Miss Darrington.

When she thought it all through like that there was not really any decision to be made. All this weeping could not be good for the baby. She forced herself to breathe, to wipe away the tears from her cheeks. Then she climbed beneath the covers of the bed, blew out her candle and lay there in the darkness.

'Miss Sweetly.' Hawick smiled and drew the horse to a halt some little distance from the bench on which she sat waiting for him the next day. 'I am delighted to see you again, and so swiftly following our previous meeting.'

There was no sunshine today. The sky was a light dove grey and the grass beneath her feet was still wet from the earlier shower.

'Your Grace.' She stood and drew him a small curtsy. And did not resume her seat.

He removed his hat and came to stand before her.

She could not smile, could not speak anything of the niceties and prevarications that she should. The rehearsed words came to her lips. 'With regard to your offer of yesterday...'

His blue eyes were trained on hers.

'For two hundred pounds a month, I will accept.'

'One hundred and fifty,' he said with a smile.

'Two hundred,' she repeated and loathed herself for what she was doing.

He looked at her a moment, let his gaze move down over her body, blatantly appraising what he would be getting for his money. Her breasts felt larger than normal and more tender. Hawick's eyes lingered upon them. There was no other visible evidence of the baby's presence...yet.

When his gaze came back to her eyes he smiled again. 'You drive a hard bargain, Miss Sweetly. But two hundred it is.'

The relief flowed through her.

'I will have my lawyer draw up the contract. To take effect from...shall we say tomorrow?'

'Tomorrow? So soon?' The words were out before she could prevent them.

'Unless you have a reason to delay?' The hard look was back in his eyes. He raised his eyebrows ever so slightly and waited for her reply.

Delay would only make it worse. So she shook her head.

'Where shall I send the carriage for your move to Sackville Street?'

'There's no need for a carriage. I'll make my own way.'

'If that is your preference.'

'It is.'

'The house is Number 44.'

'You have leased it already?'

'I own the street,' he said.

'Oh, I did not realise,' she replied.

They looked at one another.

'Until tomorrow, Miss Sweetly.' Hawick took hold of her hand and it was all she could do not to snatch it from his grasp. He took it to his lips and kissed her gloved fingers, holding her gaze with his own as he did so, so that she saw the lust there and the arrogance and sense of ownership. A ripple of panic shivered through her. She lowered her eyes that he would not see it and curtsied.

'Your Grace,' she murmured.

'I would offer to walk you home, but I have a feeling that you will refuse me that pleasure.'

'Your feeling is right, Your Grace.'

'But you will not refuse me tomorrow, will you, Alice?'

'No. I'll not refuse you tomorrow,' she said quietly.

He smiled at that and, mounting his horse, rode away.

Chapter Twenty

Alice finished the last of her explanation and turned away from the expression in Venetia's eyes.

'You do not have to do this, Alice. You can stay here.'

'I can't stay here, Venetia. We both know that. You're risking much in just having me here for a few days. If it gets out, it could undo all the good work that your ball accomplished.'

'Alice...' Venetia's brow furrowed with concern as she came to take her hand, but she could not deny the truth; they both knew Alice's presence here was a liability. 'You can stay at the house in Whitechapel, it is a rough part of town, but there would always be food and shelter. They would not turn you away.'

'I know.' But it was too late for that. Besides, Alice needed to earn money for the baby and for her family back home in Ireland. She smiled to soften the refusal. 'I didn't unpack my travelling bag. I'll leave for Sackville Street first thing in the morning.'

'What are you going to do when Hawick discovers you are pregnant?'

'I'll deal with that when it happens.'

'If you change your mind about Hawick, or if there is trouble with him or anything else, you must come to me. Promise me that, at least.'

'There won't be any trouble.' Alice said it with a confidence she did not feel.

She felt Venetia's hand squeeze around her own. 'Promise me, Alice.'

She looked into her friend's eyes and saw the compassion and concern in them. She remembered all that they had shared and how very much Venetia had done for her.

'I promise,' she vowed but she knew she would not risk ruining Venetia's reputation unless it was a matter of utter desperation.

Venetia hugged her and they both wiped the tears from their eyes.

The next afternoon Alice faced Hawick across the finely furnished drawing room of the town house he kept for his mistress in Sackville Street. Upstairs in the master bedchamber her travelling bag was already unpacked, her dresses hanging in the wardrobe, her underclothes folded neatly in the drawers.

'So let me get this straight—you are telling me that you have your monthly courses and cannot sleep with me this night?'

'It is most unfortunate in its timing.' She looked him boldly in the eye to tell the lie.

'Unfortunate indeed,' he drawled and did not look pleased. 'You made no mention of it yesterday...when you were abroad in the park. Does not such a malady usually keep women housebound?'

'It only came on this morning,' she said and saw his

gaze drop to where her fingers were worrying at the crocheted strap of her reticule. A little spurt of fear rippled through her at the direction of his interest and she threw it down on to the corner of the sofa behind her, casually, as if the reticule and its contents meant nothing to her. She wondered what he would do if he were to open it and discover the letter and the engraved silver pen from Razeby.

'You are not having doubts over our arrangement, are you?'

'Of course I'm not.' Another lie to compound all the others. 'I can't defy nature, now can I? No matter that I would wish it otherwise.' She smiled teasingly and forced herself to touch her lips to his cheek.

'How long do your courses last, Alice?' he asked, and for all the intimacy of the question the strange thing was that she was thinking that at no point had he asked her permission to call her by her given name.

'Only a week.' It was the longest she could ask for without arousing his suspicion. And until she had at least his first payment in her hand she could not afford to do that.

'Next Saturday?' He raised a brow to ask the question.

She nodded.

'Then I will wait a week,' he said and traced along the edge of her bodice, his fingers skimming the skin of her breasts that were constrained within it. 'And hope our union is all the sweeter for it.'

She nodded again, but her flesh was crawling where he touched her and the sickness in her stomach was not from the baby.

She had a week's graciousness. One week. And then

there could be no more deferring. She would have to give Hawick what he was paying for. She heard the retreat of Hawick's footsteps. Heard the close of the front door. She sagged back against the wall and prayed that the days would pass slowly.

Razeby had prayed the same thing. But the week during which he spent too few of the days with Miss Darrington and too many of the nights carousing in White's or some gaming hell, trying hard to prove to the world that he was having a great time in his life, passed in a blur of speed. That he was just making the most of his remaining bachelor days, rather than hiding a man whose life felt like it was falling apart. He did not want time to think, to brood, to ponder. He spent every night in company and then, when it was late and he was alone in his town house, he drank himself into oblivion.

Saturday came. Saturday. He lay in his bed and winced against the lance of sunshine that crept between the curtains to impale his eyes. His stag night. Three more nights and he would be standing before an altar with Miss Darrington and, once the deed was done, this torment would be over. Once she was his wife and he had begotten his heir upon her, he would welcome his thirtieth birthday and the end it would bring. He had spent a lifetime dreading it, doing every damn thing to deny it. Now he longed for it and the relief it would bring. For only that final end would wipe the spectre of Alice from his mind. God help him, nothing else did.

The clock downstairs in the hallway struck midday. He pushed back the covers, sat up and swung his legs over the edge of the bed. He sat there, naked, unshaven, feeling dreadful; too many late nights, too much brandy and wine and champagne. Too many cigars. And not a one of them salved the anger that raged in his blood or the bitter taste in his mouth...or the damnable ache he would not admit to another living soul that throbbed in his chest.

He leaned forwards, elbows on knees, hands cradling his head, wondering how the hell he was going to get through marrying Miss Darrington on Tuesday when he did not even know if he could maintain this façade through the night that was to come. He raised his head and peered across the room at the black domino that hung on the outside of the changing screen and the black face mask that hung by its side. No matter that he did not feel one bit like celebrating, a stag night at a masquerade ball was preferable to one spent in Mrs Silver's high-class brothel. With a snarl he crushed the thought of Alice that had crept into his head and rang the bell for his valet.

At four o'clock that afternoon Hawick arrived at the house in Sackville Street in which Alice had spent the week alone in the bedchamber, feigning a woman's condition that was the very opposite of the condition which beset her body.

'Alice,' he said, capturing her hand in his and touching it to his lips.

She ignored the string of maids and footmen that hurried past them carrying parcels and packages and long covered garments on hangers and managed to resist the urge to snatch her hand from his grasp.

'Won't you come through to the drawing room?' she offered. 'I'll have some tea brought up for us, or something stronger, if you prefer.' Anything to keep him occupied so that he would not kiss her or get other even worse ideas.

He gave a nod of agreement and followed her as she led them through to the drawing room. 'I trust you have recovered from your affliction.'

She was so tempted to beg just one more night, but she knew she could not do that. 'Indeed.' She nodded. 'I'm my usual self, Your Grace.'

'I am relieved to hear it.'

She said nothing.

'And I think, given the intimacy of our…friendship, that you may dispense with "Your Grace". My given name is Anthony.'

'Anthony,' she said, and the smile she forced to her face felt more like a grimace. 'But "Your Grace" comes so readily to my lips.'

'Well, we'll have to see what we can do about changing that tonight, will we not?'

Her stomach clenched tight at the thought. She smiled all the harder to hide her dread.

'In view of your recovery and to celebrate our new arrangement, I have a little surprise planned for tonight.'

'A surprise?' She tried to sound pleased rather than worried.

'A ball,' he said, 'with a little twist to make it a bit more exciting. I thought we could attend.'

'That would be a grand way to spend our first night together,' she said. All the while she was out with him in public there was a limit to the intimacy of what he could do. And then she remembered Razeby and the Covent Garden theatre and what they had done there in that public place.

'I love to dance.' The dance floor would be safe.

'Good,' he said. 'I'll look forward to our dancing together.'

The smile was starting to hurt her mouth. 'I'll ring for the tea, shall I?'

'I did not come here for tea, Alice.'

'No?' It came out a little too high pitched.

'Let's go upstairs.'

'Upstairs? Isn't it a little early in the day for—'

He laughed and, taking her hand in his, led her up the stairs to her bedchamber.

Her knees were knocking by the time she got there. The sweat prickled beneath her arms and her hands felt both clammy and chilled.

He stopped her outside the door. 'Close your eyes,' he instructed.

'Why?' she asked suspiciously.

'Because if you do not it will spoil the second half of the surprise I have waiting for you inside.'

'To be honest, I'm not great on surprises, Anthony.'

'Trust me, you'll like this one.'

Alice was not so sure, yet she could do nothing other than close her eyes.

She heard him open the door, then he took hold of her arm and guided her inside.

'You can look now.'

She opened her eyes and there laid out on the bed before them was a dress of brilliant scarlet silk, the bodice sewn with a thousand glass beads that glittered like rubies in the sunshine. The neckline plunged indecently low. The silk of the skirt was so sheer as to be almost transparent. Beside the dress was spread a scarlet domino with a deep-cowled hood. And positioned between them on the bed sat a Venetian mask to match their colour precisely. It was adorned with tiny glittering glass beads and vibrant red feathers, and from either side there was a length of thin scarlet ribbon that would bind it to her upper face.

Whatever horror Alice had been anticipating, all of her expectations paled into insignificance beside the reality of what lay upon that bed. The dress and the mask were similar to those she had worn as Miss Rouge during her time in Mrs Silver's brothel.

'For every woman needs a new dress to attend a ball. And none more so than for a masquerade ball.'

She felt a dizziness swim through her head at the shock of seeing the outfit and clutched a hand to the thick mahogany poster of the bed to support her. Her heart was hammering in her throat and it felt like her stomach had dropped clear of her body, through the floor beneath her feet into the drawing room below.

'It's red,' she said in a stilted voice that sounded nothing like her own. She turned her head to look at him, wondering if somehow he knew the secret of her background—that she had been the woman forced to play Miss Rouge behind the mask. Wondering if this was some cruel torture he was inflicting upon her.

But Hawick's gaze held only lust and appreciation. 'I have always found red to be a most stimulating colour.'

'I've never thought of red as a colour that suited me,' she said carefully through stiff, cold lips.

'On the contrary, I think it will suit you very well indeed.' He paused and stepped closer, brushing his fingers against her *décolletage*.

She could feel the heat and moisture of his breath against her forehead. She could smell the cologne scent of him too strong in her nose.

'Wear it for me tonight, Alice,' he commanded, and she knew she could not refuse without raising his suspicions as to her aversion to the colour, or their arrangement, or both.

'Of course.' She nodded.

She saw his gaze was focused on her breasts, watched it drop lower to sweep over the rest of her. He skimmed a hand against her buttocks, making her jump.

'You seem a little nervous, Alice.' His gaze met hers.

'You're a duke, for goodness' sake, Anthony. That's enough to make any woman nervous,' she said by way of excuse and prayed with all her might that he did not mean to take her right here and now.

'I wish I had time to show you that you have nothing to be nervous about right now, but, unfortunately, I have another commitment elsewhere. So we will just have to wait until after the masquerade.'

She could barely contain her relief. Her smile was all genuine this time.

'I will pick you up at nine,' he said.

She nodded and did not think to ask what colour of domino he would be wearing.

The bell of St James's Church sounded ten o'clock. The sky overhead was as dark as the long dominoes and moulded black face masks that Razeby and Linwood were wearing within the dimmed interior of Razeby's town coach.

The coach slowed as it approached the Argyle Rooms on the north side of Little Argyle Street at the corner of King Street. The entire building lit up the darkness of the night with the candlelight from the huge crystal-dropped chandeliers glittering through the windows that lined the west ballroom and the flambeaux that flamed in their holders high on the wall outside the magnificent front door.

'Go in without me. I will join you later. There's something I have to do,' Razeby said.

'You do intend on coming later?' Linwood asked.

'It is my stag night. I can do nothing other. The *ton* will expect a dissolute celebration of the end of my bachelorhood—and we shall not disappoint them.' He glanced across at his friend, glad of the shadowed gloom of the interior. 'I am glad it is not Mrs Silver's House to which we go this night.'

Linwood gave a nod of acknowledgement. 'This thing you have to do...'

'It is closure, Linwood. Something I should have done weeks ago.'

Linwood gave a nod, but he made no move to leave. 'Razeby...' Linwood leaned forwards '...there is something that I think you should know, concerning Miss—'

But at that very moment the coach door was opened by the footman.

'I will tell you later,' said Linwood and climbed from the coach, leaving Razeby inside alone. The door closed again and he was off and travelling through the night towards Hart Street.

Inside the house everything was just as he had left it. The candles had been lit in the hallway and the main rooms as he had instructed. A low fire burned on each hearth, so that the house was warm in contrast to the chill that clung to the night air outside. He had not slept here in weeks, but everything was prepared just as if he was due to arrive, just as Alice had run it.

He set the black Venetian mask he was holding down on the opened surface of the bureau as he surveyed the room around him. A small fire burned on the hearth just as it had done when he and Alice had spent their evenings in here. Darkness already shadowed the skies outside and although the candles of the chandelier had not been lit, those of the wall sconces and on the branch upon the occasional table blazed. The room had a comfortable atmosphere to it as if Alice and he still lived here. The faint scent of lavender and beeswax polish still hung in the air.

Tomorrow he would terminate the lease. And there would be no trace left of his life with Alice. He did not even know why he had kept the place on. Why even now he felt reluctant to let it go. It was nothing but torture to realise what a fool he had been and how close he had come to throwing everything away for a cold-hearted harlot. His jaw tightened. His father would have turned in his grave. His mother would never have forgiven him. He wondered if he ever would have forgiven himself. Looking back at those days, he could barely believe he had even considered such a ridiculous course of action. Some kind of madness had fixed himself upon his brain…upon his heart. And Razeby swore that in the short time he had left that nothing would ever affect him like that again.

He let his gaze wander around the room, from the two armchairs on either side of the card table where Alice and he had played *vingt-et-un,* to the sofa on which they had played games of a more intimate nature and the rug before the hearth on which they had made love. There was a bitter taste in his mouth. He hardened his heart and his expression and made to pick up the face mask from the bureau, remembering all the times he had come in and caught her hiding secret letters, her fingers stained with ink, her cheeks flushed with embarrassment. His eyes narrowed at the memory. He felt the suspicion stir through him as he wondered just who the hell she had been writing to so often.

He left the face mask where it was and searched the bureau.

In the pen holder lay an old cheap pen, its nib blunted from excessive use. Of the expensive silver pen he had bought for her and had engraved there was no sign. She had probably hawked it, he thought sourly. Most of the compartments and drawers were empty. There were a few stubby pencils, some eraser putty and a stick of sealing wax in one. And in another, a pile of his old letters, letters that his footman had brought following their daily delivery to his town house each morning. Letters that he had dealt with here and left with Alice to be burned. He frowned and pulled the pile out, wondering what she had been up to.

The letters appeared just as he had left them, until he turned them over. Across every sheet of paper were lines and lines of letters of the alphabet. A row of a's followed by a row of b's and so on, pages of them, like pages from a copy book, crudely formed as if from the hand of a young child. Some had been written back to front or upside down. He leafed through the pages and then he stopped dead, for there was a page on which two words had been copied again and again and again. The pages underneath were the same. The same two words painstakingly practised until she had written them perfectly—*Alice* and *Razeby* and between the two words a heart. Razeby felt his chest tighten and his own heart shift. At the bottom of the pile was a sheet on which she had sketched a pencil portrait of him. It was roughly drawn, but it had captured his likeness, and in it he was smiling at the artist, smiling in a way he no longer smiled any more.

Oh, God! He understood what she had been doing all of the hours of all of those days and why she had not wanted him to see them. And he understood, too, why he had never seen her read a newspaper, or receive a single letter, or ever even sign her name. Alice 'heart' Razeby—she did not know how to write the word 'loves'. Alice loves Razeby. Not Razeby 'heart' Alice, as he had had engraved upon the silver barrel of the pen.

In his head he heard again those words that had haunted his nightmares and made him turn his hurt into bitterness and anger. *I never said I loved you. I never used those words.* Both carefully and callously uttered. She had not said them, but she had written them again and again when the cost of doing so was very great. And as he stood there his blood trickled cold against his neck, there was a sinking realisation in his stomach and he had the horrible sensation that he had got this all wrong.

Alice loves Razeby.

He folded the pile of letters, placed them in his inside pocket and grabbed the black face mask from where it sat on the bureau. The length of his domino swept out like a great black wing behind him as he left the room.

Chapter Twenty-One

The masquerade ballroom was crowded.

Up on the balcony a small orchestra was playing. The high stone ceiling curved around the haunting baroque-inspired melodies so that the music seemed to come from the surrounding walls. The crowd was colourful as the courts of fifty years ago. Men and women wore dominoes of peacock colours, their upper faces hidden by intricate white or black masks similar to the ones that both Alice and Hawick wore. It seemed the masking lent an air of liberation and sensuality and barely suppressed recklessness to the night. Alice was very conscious of the scarlet that she wore. Beside her Hawick had chosen black, like many of the other gentleman that packed the floor.

She thought she had escaped Miss Rouge and all that time in her life had held but, garbed in the bold sensual scarlet silk and with Hawick's hand possessive against her arm, she knew she was that woman once more. Miss Rouge, a harlot, a whore who must sell herself to the highest bidder. The one mercy that would make the night bearable was the mask that covered her face, so that all of London would not know her shame.

She closed down that part of her mind. Did not let herself think. Refused to feel. So the woman by Hawick's side moved and danced and replied when she was spoken to, but she was not Alice, she was an empty façade. She was Miss Rouge. And Miss Rouge could get through this night, when Alice could not.

Everyone was drinking, laughing, dancing. It felt like some Bacchanalian orgy from days of old. Hawick's hand slid beneath her domino, stroking against the small of her back, encircling her waist.

'Let us dance, Alice.' His breath was hot against her cheek. She could smell the tang of red wine on his breath. She let him guide them out onto the dance floor and take her hand in his as the music began again.

The hammering of the brass knocker against its strikeplate resonated through the street all around. The front door opened to admit him. Razeby did not wait for an invitation, just stepped past the gaping butler into Linwood's hallway.

'Lord Razeby to see Miss Sweetly,' he said.

The door closed behind him. The butler's cheeks flushed as he tried to speak firmly, but politely. 'There is no Miss Sweetly here, my lord.'

'I know damn well she is here, so fetch her and be—'

Venetia appeared in the doorway that led into the drawing room, dressed in a dress of pale fawn. She was as calm and confident as ever she was, with that air of assertion. 'Razeby,' she said in her smooth low voice.

'I know she is here, Lady Linwood, and I am not leaving until I have seen her.'

Venetia nodded her assurance to the butler and dismissed him before she addressed Razeby. 'You are supposed to be at the masquerade ball for your stag night.'

'I am going nowhere until I have spoken to Alice.'

Venetia's brow furrowed ever so slightly, the one small sign of discomposure. 'Has Linwood spoken to you?'

'Of what matter, ma'am?'

She shook the expression away with a small half smile. 'No matter,' she replied smoothly and paused before adding, 'Alice is not here.'

'Do not seek to deceive me. Linwood told me you have been sheltering her since her return to London.'

'She was here. And now she is gone.'

'Gone where?'

'What do you want with her?'

'I have discovered that she has not been entirely honest with me.'

He thought he saw something shift in Venetia's eyes, but when she looked at him again her expression revealed nothing.

'Where is she, Venetia?'

'You will find out soon enough.'

He arched an eyebrow and felt his nostrils flare. 'Which means?'

Venetia's gaze was steady and composed as it held his.

'Please, Venetia…' he begged. 'I love her.'

Venetia glanced away. 'Oh, Alice,' she whispered softly beneath her breath and closed her eyes. She took a deep breath before she looked at him once more. 'She does love you, Razeby, no matter that it may appear otherwise. All that she has done, all that she does…she has her reasons. She would not stay here or let me help her because she was convinced it would turn the *ton* against me. Her family has troubles of its own. And there are other complicating factors at play of which I can say nothing. Had you come last week...' He saw the concern and worry on her face and the tiny furrow that wrinkled her brow. 'You are too late, Razeby.' She hesitated and he saw the pain in her eyes. 'She is gone to Hawick a week since, to his house at 44 Sackville Street.'

'Hawick,' he said and even to his own ears his voice sounded too quiet and loaded with danger.

'I am sorry.'

But Razeby was already halfway down the stone stairs that led from the front door down on to the street.

Alice felt the surreptitious caress of Hawick's hand against her hip as he turned her on the dance floor.

'Red becomes you well, Alice, but I am in anticipation of divesting you of it tonight,' he whispered close by her ear. Her stomach tightened with trepidation, but she was saved from having to answer by the steps of the dance which drew them apart.

She stared through the crowd towards the exit, wishing with all her might that she might turn away from what lay ahead, thread her way through the bodies on the dance floor to walk out of the hallway, out of the main door and keep on walking away from Hawick, away from this nightmare. As she looked she saw at the edge of the dance floor was a group of men cloaked in black dominoes like so many others, but who had not yet fixed in place their masks. Alice stared in horror as her eyes moved over the faces that she recognised too well: Devlin, Fallingham, Bullford, Monteith and Linwood.

Her heart stumbled and gasped. Her stomach plummeted in fear and dread. Her blood ran cold as ice as her eyes scanned frantically for the sixth member of that male party, dreading to find him. Her heart was hammering so hard and fast that she felt herself tremble, her blood roaring in her ears. Of all that she had thought she must endure this night... Please, God, she begged, do not let him be here, for she could not bear Razeby to see her with Hawick, to see her dressed like this. God must have heard her pleading. Razeby was not there with his friends. And for that she could only be grateful.

Across the dance floor Linwood's dark gaze shifted to meet hers. And she felt her blood run cold and her face burn with shame for she knew that the viscount recognised her. Then the bodies on the dance floor moved to block her view and she saw him no more.

She glanced longingly at the exit. But Alice could not run away from her responsibilities. She turned her gaze away and followed the steps of the dance that led her back to Hawick.

'Miss Sweetly is not at home.' The footman standing at the door of 44 Sackville Street was young, still wet behind the ears, but he knew who was paying his wages. 'Nor is His Grace the Duke of Hawick.'

'Where have they gone?' Razeby asked in a deceptively soft voice.

'I'm not at liberty to say, sir.'

'Of course not.' Razeby smiled. 'One must have

trustworthy staff. It would be more than your job's worth to tell me, I suppose.'

The young man gave a nod.

'How much *is* your job worth?' Razeby leaned against the door jamb in a relaxed fashion.

The footman looked uncomfortable.

Razeby smiled again and, slipping a wad of white banknotes from his pocket, began to flick through them. 'This much?' he asked after a few pound notes had passed and saw how the footman's eyes were transfixed by the sight. 'Or perhaps this much?' He fanned through half the pile. 'Or, maybe even a little more?' He opened out the whole wad of notes and smiled at the footman. 'Two hundred pounds, such a lot of money for such a little answer. London is a busy place, in which I could have heard the same answer from any number of sources.'

'His Grace took Miss Sweetly to the grand masquerade ball at the Argyle Rooms.'

Razeby smiled and handed the money to the footman, who slipped it straight into his pocket before glancing around suspiciously.

Razeby climbed into his waiting coach and tied the black mask in place across the upper half of his face.

In the heaving masquerade ballroom of the Argyle Rooms, Razeby wondered how the hell he was going to find Alice and Hawick. The crowd was a rainbow of coloured dominoes and masks. Most of the men had opted for black, while the women were in gold and silver, white and yellow, blue and green. The music swayed and lilted, reverberating throughout the stone walls of the hall.

Razeby wove his way through the revellers, past footmen who waited with silver salvers laden with glasses of champagne. The light glittered on the jewels on the women's masks and around their bare throats and *décolletages.* It was one of those rare events in which *ton* and *demi-monde* mingled side by side and all of scandal and intrigue and whispered debauchery was acceptable behind hidden identities.

He saw Linwood and the rest of his friends, their smart white-tie evening wear hidden beneath the shrouds of their black dominoes, but their faces un-masked. He gave a grim smile, knowing that they had deliberately removed their masks that he might find them.

The music played on, the sets moved upon the floor. Razeby made his way to Linwood. 'Linwood.'

'Razeby,' said Linwood and tied his mask back in place as did the others once they saw him.

'Alice is here with Hawick. I need to find her.'

Linwood's eyes glittered black as the devil's behind his mask. 'This is your stag night. You are marrying Miss Darrington on Tuesday.'

'Am I?' he muttered. His jaw clenched tight. 'I will have the truth from Alice regardless of what happens on Tuesday.'

'Razeby…' Linwood lowered his voice and leaned closer '…there is something you should know before you see her. I am sworn to silence, but you are my friend, and you did ask me to tell you if I were ever to know that all was not well with Alice.'

Razeby stilled, seeing the intensity in Linwood's eyes, and waited with a fear beating in his chest.

Linwood hesitated for a second before saying, 'She is carrying your child.'

'God in heaven,' Razeby whispered, then gritted his teeth with determination. 'How the hell am I going to find her in here?'

Linwood's eyes gestured to the figures moving in unison upon the dance floor. 'Perhaps with a deal less difficulty than you anticipate.'

And there, in the middle of the floor, dancing with a black-cloaked man was a woman in a scarlet-silk domino that swirled around her legs when she moved to reveal the figure-hugging scarlet dress beneath. Her fair hair hung long and straight and wanton over her shoulders in such contrast to the current fashion. And across her eyes and nose was tied a scarlet Venetian mask with holes cut for the eyes. Miss Rouge for all the world to see. His heart skipped a beat. He knew what being Miss Rouge had done to Alice, knew how very much she loathed even to see the colour. He pushed emotion aside, sharpened his focus.

'Be careful how you do this, Razeby,' cautioned Linwood.

'I am done with care.' Razeby gave a hard smile. 'I need to find myself a dance partner. And so do the rest of you. It is my stag night, after all.'

The dance came to a halt and Hawick kissed Alice's mouth, hard and brief, right there on the dance floor. No one seemed to mind. Other men were kissing their masked ladies, too.

'Shall we have a little rest for a while, over in the corner?' he breathed so close to her ear that her skin crawled.

The next dance was called.

'Can we not stay upon the floor a little longer? Please, Anthony?'

'It is a progressive dance. Are you so eager to find yourself a new partner, Alice?' He smiled as if joking, but there was no joke in his eyes.

'The dance will deliver me back to you. One turn round the circle.'

'I do not know if I wish to wait that long.' Hawick's gaze drifted lower to linger upon her exposed *décolletage* where the scarlet domino gaped. 'I want you, Alice.'

'What an impatient man you are,' she managed.

'Only when it comes to you.' He smiled.

And so did she, but the horrible sensation in her stomach churned all the more.

Upon the dance floor, the ladies formed one large circle, the gentlemen a slightly smaller inner one, like dark masked ravens in their black dominoes. Each faced their own partner. The music started up once more. The ladies curtsied. The gentlemen bowed.

The melody played and Hawick took her in his hold. They moved with and around each other, dancing the steps before Hawick handed Alice on to the next gentlemen and received his new lady in her stead. And so she gradually passed on from one gentleman to another.

Every gentleman that Alice partnered was garbed in the same long black-silk domino, overlying the same black-and-white formal evening wear. Every face was obscured with the same dark domino mask. She did not speak to them, barely even looked at them, feeling only relief that they were not Hawick. The music with its slight macabre undertone seemed to resonate through her. She moved through the dance, its every step taking her further away from him, through one man and then the next, dancing with each one in turn until they handed her on. Five men, all tall, all dark, all masked, all in black dominoes. And on to the sixth. She stepped in towards him and something made her glance up into his face. And masked though it was, what she saw there made the breath catch in her lungs.

The eyes behind the mask glittered too dark, too familiar. Even masked she would have known him anywhere. Her heart leapt into her throat. Her blood rushed too hard, pounding loud in her ears. She swallowed hard, forced herself through one step and then the next. He reached out, caught her hand in his and, even had she not recognised him through the mask, her skin thrilled to his touch and her whole body reacted to his proximity, making it impossible not to realise his identity.

He pulled her close to turn her beneath his arm, and the scent of him, so familiar, sent a shiver of longing all the way down her spine. It was only halfway through the turn that she realised he had shifted them both out of the circle. The space closed invisibly behind them, and when she looked more closely she realised that the men with whom she had danced before Razeby were all of Razeby's friends. But she was already being hustled away.

'Alice, you did not really think to escape me so easily, did you?' Razeby whispered into her ear as he steered them both to be swallowed up by the surrounding crowd. She tried to turn, but his grip was unyielding. She could do nothing other than go where he directed her, away from the dance floor, threading a path through the close-packed bodies out into the crowded hallway where he pushed her against the recess of a wall and, shielding her with his body, unfastened the ties of her domino. The expensive red silk slipped to land on the floor by her feet.

'What are doing? You can't just—'

'I thought you did not like red, Alice.'

'You know I don't, but—'

He unfastened his own domino and swept it around her shoulders, enveloping every inch of the indecent scarlet dress in which Hawick had dressed her with the black silk. For a moment she yielded to her instinct, snuggling into his domino, breathing in the scent of him, before common sense reasserted itself. Razeby stepped closer still, until his body was hard against hers and her face touched against the lapels of his black evening tailcoat.

'What are you—?'

But his fingers were untying the red mask that hid her face. Throwing it to the floor as if it were a piece of worthless tat.

She gasped and had to crick her neck to stare up into his face. 'Would you reveal me to all of London that is here? Have mercy on me, for pity's sake, Razeby, I beg of you.'

'I have told you before, Alice, that when it comes to you, I have no mercy.' His voice was hard, but from his pocket he produced a plain black Venetian mask and tied it where the red mask had been.

'Razeby...' She hated to say the words, but knew that she must tell him, now, before any more harm was done. 'I'm with Hawick now.'

'Are you? I do not see Hawick out here.' He smiled, but it was a chilling smile, a dangerous smile. 'Besides,

I want to talk to you, Alice.' And the quiet, determined, angry way he said it stroked a shiver all the way down her spine. 'Shall we go somewhere a little quieter?'

He took hold of her arm, in a grip that was firm but unbreakable, and led her up the staircase towards the upper floor. Behind them the crowd closed and the scarlet domino and mask were trampled underfoot.

Upstairs he drew her into one of the dark shadowy private rooms that led off the main floor. Beside the brightness of all the candles and crystal of the ballroom and hallway the room seemed to be in blackness. It took a moment for her eyes to adjust enough to see the soft flood of moonlight that glowed through the window.

'You're marrying Miss Darrington on Tuesday. I'm Hawick's mistress. What more is there to say between us?' She tried to make her voice sound as if she did not care, but it was impossible. It hurt to look him in the eyes, knowing the truth of what she had done to him and the truth of their child within her belly. But she could not look away.

'What more indeed?' he said quietly and behind the mask his eyes looked blacker than Linwood's. 'How about the truth, Alice?'

Her heart gave a stutter. 'I don't know what you mean.'

'Shall we start with this?' From inside his tailcoat he produced some sheets of paper folded over.

Oh, God! She knew what they were before he opened them up and showed her. She dropped her gaze, biting at her lip and feeling the shame scald her cheeks.

'You said that you did not love me. But...' He had found the sheets on which she had written both their names together a hundred times or more.

'Idle scribbles,' she murmured and could not look at him.

'I do not think so, Alice.'

'I have to go. Hawick will have noticed I'm missing.'

'You are not going anywhere.' He stepped closer, backing her against the wall, catching hold of both her wrists and securing them behind her back. 'There is another matter of which you have been remiss in telling me.' He held both her wrists in one hand, leaving the other free to brush gently against her lips.

Her breathing grew heavy. She was too conscious of his touch, of his body so near to hers, of the dangerous quiet control that barely leashed the force of his anger.

He trailed his fingers slowly over her chin, traced them down over the column of her throat.

'Please, Razeby,' she whispered. 'Don't do this.'

But the dark eyes just glittered dangerously behind the mask. 'Why not?'

'You know why not!' she cried, her voice hoarse with emotion.

His fingers trailed against her collar bones, then lower over her *décolletage,* tantalisingly close to her breasts, so pale and barely concealed by the blood red of the dress. 'Because of what is in here?'

She gasped and arched as he slid his fingers beneath the bodice to cover her heart. Beneath the dress she wore no shift, no underclothes of any description. He stroked gently against the aroused peak of her nipple, before capturing the fullness of her breast, making her heart thrill and thud to his touch.

In one smooth movement he had ripped the bodice of the dress open, the tear of silk a hiss in the silence between them. Her breath grew ragged as his hand explored lower, over her rib cage, over her stomach, sliding tortuously, slowly, to her abdomen where it rested flat against her skin and what lay beneath. He could not know, she told herself.

But Razeby lowered his voice and looked directly into her eyes. 'Or what is in here?' he said.

Chapter Twenty-Two

Alice closed her eyes against the accusation she saw on Razeby's face.

'Venetia told you,' she whispered.

'Not Venetia,' he corrected. 'Her lips were sealed, on that secret at least.'

'Then how…?' She opened her eyes and looked at him.

'It does not matter,' he said harshly. 'What does matter is why the hell you did not come to me? You are carrying our child, Alice. Did you honestly think I would have turned you away?'

'You don't understand…'

'Damn right, I do not understand!' he snapped. 'Were you even going to tell me? Or perhaps you were planning on cuckolding Hawick?' He stared down into her eyes with a ruthless and tightly coiled rage she had never seen there before.

'No!' she cried, horrified at the suggestion. 'How could you think I'd do such a thing?'

'I wonder,' he said.

She caught her breath as the words cut her, but she

knew she deserved his wrath. After what she had made him believe of her, she could not blame him for thinking so badly of her.

'Hawick would have to be a complete fool to believe the babe his, when I'm two months gone and haven't even slept with him.'

'You have not slept with him? How have you managed to avoid it when you have been with him for a week?'

She sagged back against the wall. 'The oldest excuse in the book.'

'How ironic.'

She said nothing, just averted her gaze to a distance beyond him.

He removed his hand from where it lay warm and flat and possessive against her belly. The chill of the night air against her naked skin made her feel its loss all the more. Capturing her chin between his fingers, he brought her face round, forcing her to meet the full raze of his gaze.

'What did you think he would do, Alice, when he discovered you were carrying my baby? Keep you on as his mistress? Claim my child as his own?'

'Stop it!' she cried. 'He would have turned me off without a farthing more.'

'And yet you went to Hawick knowing that, rather than come to me,' he said in a hard voice.

'I never went to Hawick. He came to me. I've nothing else I can do to earn a living.'

'You are an actress.'

'The theatres are closed for the holidays, Razeby. I've not a penny to my name. Do you think I'd be selling myself to Hawick were there any other way? I can't read and write. I can't write entries in a cash book or receipts for customers. I can't sew or sing or dance. Without a character they'll not take me in a shop or a workshop or in service. And I won't ruin Venetia's chances of happiness in her new life. What else could I do?'

'You could have come to me,' he said harshly.

'When I had worked so hard to make you believe me a cold heartless whore who had used you for your money and was moving on to the next man who could offer her more?' She stared at him incredulously. 'I couldn't come to you. What sort of man would leave his child to be raised by a woman like that?'

'You thought I would take the child from you to raise myself.' His voice sounded suddenly weary. He rubbed a hand against his forehead as if it ached there and glanced away.

She nodded. 'Wouldn't you have?'

'It would never have come to that.'

'Why not? Don't you want the child?'

'Oh, I want the child, all right. But you see, I want you, too, Alice.'

'Even after I made you believe…' She let the words peter out, realising just how much she had admitted.

He smiled a hard smile. 'You admit that you lied to me.'

She swallowed and tried to look away, but he held her chin and would not let her.

'You love me.'

She pressed her lips together to stop them from trembling. It had gone too far for lies. He knew too much. He knew the truth of her. He knew of the baby. She closed her eyes to stop the tears, but they leaked out just the same.

His breath was a caress against her cheek. She felt his lips brush against her mouth, her cheek, her ear. 'Answer me, Alice,' he demanded.

She opened her eyes and looked into his, 'Of course I love you, Razeby. I've always loved you. Why else did I refuse to marry you?'

'You were trying to save me from myself. It was my initial gut instinct to your refusal. I should have listened to it.'

'I couldn't let you give up the Razeby estate and title, all that you had worked so hard for, your birthright, your heritage. It's your duty, your destiny. Razeby needs you. You would have regretted it for the rest of your life.'

'What is left of it,' he murmured beneath his breath. Then more loudly, his voice still harsh, 'You were right, Alice. It would have been a mistake to turn my back on Razeby and my duty. If a man does not retain his integrity, he ceases to be much of a man. I will not dishonour either Razeby or myself.'

She nodded and her heart ached even as she smiled her approval and understanding.

'So I suppose I should thank you for breaking my heart and putting me through sheer hell.'

'If it's any consolation, I broke my own in doing so.'

'I do not doubt it.'

They looked at one another through the moonlight.

'We have much to discuss, Alice. But not here. I am taking you home to Hart Street.'

'We can't!'

He arched an eyebrow and the dark dangerous look in his eyes made her shiver. 'I will brook no refusal.'

'What about Hawick?'

'Do you want me to kill him?' he asked softly.

'No!' The word shot from her mouth because she did not know whether he was serious or in jest. 'He could sue, and the last thing you need is a scandal.'

'Do not worry, I will sort matters with Hawick.' He brushed his lips against hers, as if sealing a promise, and only then released her bound wrists.

Wrapping his domino more tightly around her to cover her semi-nakedness, he scooped her up into his arms and carried her down the stairs, through the crowded hallway and out into the night.

The house in Hart Street was exactly as she had left it. In every detail. All the servants were still in place. There were flowers in the hallway vase. Lamps were aglow.

It felt cosy and warm and safe. As if she had never left.

He took her straight upstairs and into the bedchamber, kicking the door shut behind him, before setting her down on her feet.

A small fire burned on the hearth, casting their shadows to dance upon the walls.

What had happened between them the last time they were in this room seemed a lifetime ago.

'Take off that dress.' She saw the way his expression hardened when he looked at the remains of the dress that still hung on her body.

She stripped it off, letting it fall on the floor around her ankles like the blood of her shame.

'I couldn't tell him of Miss Rouge. He didn't understand when I said I didn't like red.' She stared at the dress, remembering the horror of everything that it represented for her and wondering if she would have been able to go through with it tonight with Hawick, had Razeby not saved her.

She let the silk fall away and stood there naked. Razeby's glance held hers, then he lifted the dress from where it lay and, taking her hand in his, led her to the fireplace.

He passed her the crumple of red silk and she threw it into the flames. Hand in hand they stood there and watched it burn, watched in silence until it curled and blackened and crumbled away to ash.

Turning to him, she looked up into his face. The tears were spilling from her eyes to roll down her cheeks, but they were tears of love and relief, tears of what just being with him at this moment meant. 'I don't know why I'm crying. I hardly cried all my life. And now I just can't seem to stop. I've turned into a watering can.'

He smiled and gently kissed away her tears.

He did not say a word. Just stripped off all of his clothes until he stood naked before her. Her man. Her lover. The father of the child that grew within her. A child made of their love. He was so tall and strong and handsome...so beloved.

She reached out her hand and laid it against his heart, feeling the rhythm of its strong steady beat. He captured her fingers, placed a kiss in the very centre of her palm that had lain against his heart. There was no need for words.

He carried her to the bed. And he made love to her. And she made love to him. And it was the gentlest, most moving moment of her whole life. A merging of hearts and souls. An acknowledgement of a love that defied all. And afterwards he held her in his arms and looked deep into her eyes. He said nothing in all those minutes. Just studied her.

His own eyes looked dark and serious in the amber glow of the firelight.

'You do know that I am not going to let you go, Alice?'

She smiled at that, but there was a sadness in her heart. 'You are marrying Miss Darrington on Tuesday.'

'How can I marry Miss Darrington when I love you and you love me, and...' his gaze dropped to her belly '...you are carrying our child?'

She swallowed. 'Are you asking me to be your mistress?'

'Not my mistress. And not asking.'

Her eyes widened as his meaning hit home. 'We can't marry, Razeby!'

'We can't not, Alice.'

She stared at him.

'What would you not give to protect the babe in your belly from hardship and censure and danger? What would you not give to ease his way in a difficult world?'

'Nothing,' she said. 'I would give my all.'

'And so, too, would I, Alice.'

She could feel their hearts beat in unison, hear the soft sound of their breath as they lay there.

'Would you have our child bear the label of bastard? Would you deny him the protection of my name, my wealth, my rank? Or our son his birthright, to accede to Razeby and inherit all that he is due?'

Her heart swelled with the enormity of what he was saying, what he was offering. She stared into his eyes, knowing he was right. 'No,' she said softly. 'I would not.'

'The child changes everything, Alice,' he said.

'Yes,' she whispered. 'Yes, he does.'

Their eyes held, locked in such tenderness.

He smiled. 'You do know you are going to have to marry me?'

She smiled, too. 'I suppose that I do.' But the tears began to spill again, tears of happiness and of joy.

He reached out and wiped each precious one away. 'Console yourself, my love.' A teasing light shone in his eyes. 'I am a marquis, wealthy, good looking and great in bed—or so I once was told.' He smiled with that wicked gleam that made her heart bloom.

'Stop it, you wicked man!'

They smiled together.

But as he looked into her eyes the teasing faded away. His gaze was soft but serious. Very gently he brushed a tender kiss against her lips. 'You are my love. You will be my wife and the mother of my child. And as such, there is something that you need to know, Alice. Something I probably should have told you a long time ago.'

A shadow moved in the depths of his eyes, and her heart tightened and she knew that something bad was coming, before he stoked her cheek one final time, before he moved away to sit naked on the edge of the bed.

How did a man tell the woman he loved such a thing? He did not know the words to say. They had been hidden for a lifetime, never spoken to another soul. Every single one that came to his tongue seemed clumsy and inadequate. He raked a hand through his hair and felt the dread seep through his blood. He took a deep breath.

Alice seemed to understand, for she rose and came to sit on the edge of the bed by his side and took his hand within her own.

'Start at the beginning, Razeby,' she said. She was so calm.

He nodded and did as she instructed. 'I was seven years old when my father's final illness claimed his life. He knew he was dying. On that last day he sent my mother away and bade me sit with him. The doctors had dosed him with so much laudanum, but he was still in pain.'

Alice did not rush him. She did not question. She was just there beside him, with him, and it was enough.

'He told me that my grandfather had died at thirty years of age. That he, too, was dying at thirty. That a weakness of the lungs runs in the men of our family. That it was some sort of curse from which we could not escape.'

Razeby closed his eyes at the memory. He saw his father frail and wasted in that dim-lit room and heard again that laboured and breathless voice. 'Marry and breed before you are thirty. Marry and breed an heir before it is too late.' Razeby spoke those same words aloud.

For Razeby and its future. Do you understand, James?

In his mind he saw the boy who had stood there and answered, *I understand, Father.*

'I held his hand and watched him die.'

'Razeby,' she whispered and her fingers warmed the chill from his own. 'That is much for a boy of seven to bear.'

He swallowed and turned his gaze to meet hers. 'I will be thirty in four months, Alice.'

It took a moment before the realisation crossed her face. 'You have lived your whole life believing that you will die at thirty,' she said slowly.

'It sounds ridiculous now I come to say it out loud.'

'You were seven years old, Razeby. It's only natural for a boy to believe his father's words and take them to his heart. Even a father who was dosed high on laudanum.'

Her words made him see it in a different way. When he looked back he saw how disturbed his father must have been by the drug and the prospect of his imminent death. 'They never left my heart. Beneath their shadow I sought hedonism and thrills and pleasure. I had a plan, you see, of exactly when to undertake that last task of duty.' He paused. 'And then I met you.' He threaded his fingers through hers. 'And I did not want to give you up. You changed everything. You changed me. I fell in love.'

She smiled and brought his fingers to her mouth and kissed them.

'It is why I did not ask you to marry me. I would have done it in a heartbeat, but we both know that the same people who love you as Miss Sweetly will despise you as the Marchioness of Razeby. I could not subject you to that cruelty, knowing I would not be here to protect you. But the baby changes everything.'

'Oh, Razeby,' she said with a sad smile.

They sat in silence and her eyes studied his. 'Your father was a sickly man.'

'Weak lungs, the doctor said. The same as my grandfather before him.'

'But not you.'

'We cannot know that.'

'You're forgetting, Razeby, I know exactly what you can do with that breath of yours. And there's nothing weak about it.' She arched her eyebrow, teasing him, but her eyes were soft.

He smiled.

'Atholl's father, your father's brother—did he pass away at thirty?'

'He died last year, aged fifty-seven, having drunk a bottle of port every day of the last twenty years.'

'No weak lungs there, then.'

'No.'

They smiled.

'My granddaddy used to say that the length of a man's life was as uncertain as the wind.' She smiled, but it had a poignancy to it. 'Thirty years, or three score and more, who knows? Why worry, Razeby? Just to live is the miracle. To love, even more so.'

'Maybe you have the right of it. You are my miracle, Alice.' She shone a light in the darkness and made it fade away.

'And you're mine. Come here, you foolish man.' She rose and moved to stand before him. sliding her hand to rest against the nape of his neck and pulled his mouth to hers. 'You should have spoken to me of your worry long ago.'

'I should have,' he admitted.

'What am I going to do with you, Razeby?'

'Do you wish me to give you a few suggestions?' He smiled.

'Maybe later,' she teased and then the teasing dropped

away and she kissed him in earnest, with tenderness and with love.

He wrapped his arms around her and they lay back on the bed and loved. And Razeby knew that she was right. Everything was going to be all right. Because of Alice and their love.

Razeby left Hart Street and had his coach take him directly to St James's and Linwood's apartments. It was midnight when he knocked on the door.

Linwood had not long returned from the masquerade. His black domino still lay over the back of the sofa where he had thrown it. The black Venetian mask sat on the occasional table alongside a half-full glass of brandy. Of Venetia there was no sign, but the door that led into Linwood's bedchamber was closed.

'Forgive the late hour of my call.' Razeby moved to take the wing chair opposite Linwood's and accepted the glass of brandy that his friend pressed into his hand. 'I am come from Hart Street.'

'You spoke to Alice?'

'I did. Thank you for telling me, Linwood, and for all that you did this night. But there is one more favour I must ask of you. And it is not an insignificant one.' He paused.

'I am listening,' said Linwood.

'When your father pulled strings with the Archbishop of Canterbury to arrange your marriage to Venetia…'

Linwood smiled.

On Monday morning Alice woke alone in a beam of sunshine shining through the window. She felt a feeling of warmth that she was here and safe with Razeby, even if he had not yet arrived.

Over on the little hearth the maid had already been in and lit the fire. The bedchamber was warm and cosy. All it lacked was Razeby.

She was about to get up when there was a knock at the door and the maid appeared carrying a tray of light breakfast—bread rolls and toast, butter and jam and honey, a pot of chocolate and one of coffee.

'Master's orders,' said the maid and sat the tray on the bedside table. 'I'll be back in half an hour to help you with your *toilette*.'

Alice glanced across at the emerald-green silk dress that hung ready and waiting for her, over the dressing screen, the dress that had so much significance for her and for Razeby. So much had happened to her wearing that dress. And today she would be wearing it when she married him.

She dressed carefully, hearing the front door open and the soft murmur of voices in the hallway downstairs as she did so, and knew that Razeby had arrived. He came to her, dropped a kiss on one exposed shoulder before leaning back against the bed post to watch while she pinned her hair up in the same simple style that he loved.

'How did Miss Darrington take the news?' She addressed his reflection in the looking glass.

'She wept,' he said.

Alice spun round to look at his face. 'Oh, I feel terrible!'

'Do not! They were tears of most adamant relief.'

'I thought she wished to marry you.' Alice looked at him quizzically.

'So did I, but it transpires that wish belonged only to her parents. I suspect that Miss Darrington's heart, like my own, is engaged elsewhere.'

'Oh!' Alice said.

'Oh, indeed.' Razeby smiled, his eyes moving over her in appreciative perusal. 'You look beautiful, Alice. But there is something missing.'

'What have I forgotten?'

'This,' he said and from his pocket he took a small black-leather box and handed it to her.

Within the box was the most beautiful emerald-and-diamond ring she had ever seen.

'To match the dress,' he explained as he slipped it onto her betrothal finger.

She touched the ring lovingly then slipped her arms around his neck and kissed him. 'Oh, Razeby,' she whispered. 'My love.'

When Alice walked into the drawing room half an hour later, on the arm of Linwood's father, the Earl of Misbourne, it was to find the room decked in the prettiest of summer flowers. The sunlight streamed through the window to light the room golden and bright as the love in her heart.

In the rows of chairs their friends sat dressed in their smartest: Monteith, Devlin, Bullford, Fallingham and Sara. Arlesford and Hunter and their wives. Ellen and Tilly. And Venetia.

Razeby, with Linwood as his best man, stood at the front of the room before a dark-robed priest.

Razeby glanced round when he heard her step,

watching her with love in those liquid brown eyes of his and smiling that smile that was all for her as Misbourne led her to him.

She placed her right hand in his and, before God, the priest and their friends, Alice married the man she loved.

Epilogue

Alice, Lady Razeby, stood on the small wooden bridge and stared down into the river. The water was shallow here and so clear that the sun peeked through the overhanging green canopy of leaves to glint golden shimmers upon the brown gravel of the river bed and the speckled trout that rested upon it. They were large fish, well fleshed, ripe for Razeby's fishing net if he saw them, but, much as she enjoyed the taste of fresh trout, she preferred that they remained free.

A soft breeze stirred through the surrounding woodland, bringing with it the sweet scent of wild summer flowers and the quiet drone of bees. From the branches overhead she could hear the cheery chirp of sparrows and from further afield the rhythmic cooing of a woodpigeon. All of it sounded against the gentle sound of the river's flow.

In that beautiful, idyllic, peaceful setting she slipped a piece of paper from her pocket. The paper was tattered at the edges, with creases that were well worn where it had been opened and folded closed again so many times. She let her eyes wander over the words that were penned upon it. The ink had faded a little with time and sunlight, but she knew each of those words by heart.

She traced her finger along each line, saying the words of the love letter that Razeby had written to her all those years before quietly to herself. She could read and write now, of a fashion, since Razeby had patiently taught her, but it was still a struggle for her and always would be. But Razeby had also taught her that it was nothing to be ashamed of and that it was no reflection upon her intellect. She smiled at the thought of the man she had loved almost from the first moment she had met him.

The sound of distant voices broke the still calm of the moment—a woman's voice, louder and more forceful than the rest, singing an old-fashioned nursery rhyme. Alice smiled all the more as the tramp of feet came closer along the woodland path and, folding the letter, she slid it safely into her pocket just as the littlest voice giggled and called out with excitement, 'Mama!'

She turned to the tiny child sitting on Razeby's shoulder, a boy whose light brown hair was a mix of her own blonde and Razeby's dark locks, and whose eyes were a rich warm brown all from the tall, handsome man who was his father.

'James junior caught his first trout,' announced the Dowager Lady Razeby, holding up a fine fat trout fixed to a string looped around her hand. She had hated Alice with a vengeance, but all of that had changed with the birth of James junior when the dragon dowager had transformed into a doting grandmother. 'My grandson is advanced for his years.'

Alice laughed.

Razeby lowered his head and lifted the little boy off his shoulders, passing him to her. James junior wound his little hands, all dirty from where he had been playing in the mud, around her neck and she kissed his soft baby cheek. 'He's a clever boy all right.'

'Just like his mama,' said Razeby and, sliding an arm around her waist, pulled her back to snuggle against him that he might drop a kiss on the top of her head.

The dowager began to sing again, the same old nursery song that Alice's own mother, who now lived with Alice's youngest brother and her sisters in a large house on the outskirts of the local village, had been teaching James junior.

Razeby joined in and so did Alice, and James junior clapped his hands together and smiled and smiled with his little chubby cheeks.

And Alice's heart glowed with happiness.

* * * * *

Dicing with the Dangerous Lord

For my big Wee Sister, Andrea —
lots of spicy bits because I know you like them!

Chapter One

Theatre Royal, Covent Garden, London
November 1810

The applause within the Theatre Royal at Covent Garden was deafening, even after the heavy red curtain had descended on Shakespeare's *As You Like It*, to shield London's most acclaimed darling of the theatre from the audience.

Miss Venetia Fox smiled and hugged her friend and fellow actress as they made their way from the stage. 'They are still on their feet, Alice.'

'I can't believe it! It's amazing! I've never seen a response like it.' Alice Sweetly's eyes were big as saucers. In her excitement her soft Irish lilt grew stronger.

Venetia laughed. 'You will get used to it.'

'You think this'll happen again?'

Venetia smiled at her protégée and nodded.

'You were right. Life doesn't get much better than this.' Alice's face was lit with the same euphoria that was flowing through Venetia's veins. Away from the glitz and glamour of the front of the house, the theatre's corridors were mean and narrow and the décor shabby, but it could not suppress the women's spirits.

Alice hesitated outside the door to the small dressing room that they shared and turned to look up into Venetia's face. 'Thank you, Venetia. For helping me. For persuading Mr Kemble to put me on stage with you tonight. For everything.'

'I knew you would be a star.' Venetia gave Alice another hug. 'After the green room we will celebrate.'

'Only after the green room,' Alice agreed. 'See, I'm learning to be professional, just like you taught me.'

Venetia laughed, and a joy welled up in her to see just how far Alice had come in the past year. Alice's face showed confidence, self-respect and excitement. Venetia felt like she was walking on air as she opened the dressing-room door.

She was still smiling as she stepped across the threshold and saw the bunch of roses that lay upon the dressing table. The smile dropped from her face and the lightness of her mood evaporated in an instant.

Alice chattered on oblivious, her face lighting even brighter when she saw the roses. 'Someone's ahead of the game tonight. Got in early before the others.' She touched a finger to the centre of the bouquet. 'Nice little quirk from the usual arrangement, too. Which one of us is the lucky girl, do you think?'

Venetia knew the answer to that question without reading the small white card that had been tucked within the brown paper wrapping the stems. There were twelve roses, soft and velvety and of the deepest darkest red, and nestling in the centre of their arrangement, in such contrast, was a single creamy white rose, just as Robert had said. It was the message for which she had waited these weeks past. It had been so long in the coming that she had almost forgotten what she had agreed to. Almost.

Venetia picked up the card with its scrawl of black ink.

'Looks like you've got yourself a new admirer. And one that hasn't signed so much as his initial.' Alice raised her eyebrows suggestively. 'Very mysterious.'

Not mysterious at all. Venetia forced a smile, but it felt wooden upon her lips. Her eyes moved over the card and she read aloud the single word written upon it in handwriting that she could not fail to recognise—*Tonight*.

'Sounds intriguing,' said Alice. 'Who is he?'

'I have not the faintest idea,' Venetia lied and threw the card down on the dressing table carelessly, as if it meant nothing.

'That'll put the cat amongst the pigeons with Hawick and Devlin,' said Alice. 'Hawick thinks he's about to close the deal.'

'Then Hawick is wrong.' Venetia did not rise to the bait.

'You're leaning towards Devlin, then?' There was a mischievous sparkle in her friend's eye.

'Alice!'

'I'm teasing you!' Alice grinned. 'But if I had a duke and a viscount fighting to make me their mistress, believe you me, I wouldn't be playing so hard to get.'

'Better to earn your own money than put yourself in a rich man's power,' Venetia said, but the rich man she was not thinking of was not the Duke of Hawick or Viscount Devlin, and the woman enslaved, not herself.

She moved her mind away from the past to focus on the evening ahead…and just how she must snare a different rich man's interest. According to Robert's covert floral message the man would be waiting in the green room at this very moment. He was just another arrogant lust-ridden nobleman, like any other. Except he wasn't. But she did not let herself dwell upon who he was and what he had done. Nor did she think about the danger. Instead, she focused herself with cool dispassion to the task that lay ahead.

'Hurry yourself and turn around, Venetia. They're waiting for us in the green room.'

'A little waiting will serve to whet their appetites all the more.' They were waiting. *He* was waiting. Venetia smiled a grim smile at the challenge ahead of her as she presented her back to Alice to unlace the bodice of her stage costume.

'I should not have let you persuade me into coming here.' Within the green room of the Theatre Royal, Covent Garden, Francis Winslow, or Viscount Linwood as he was known, moved his gaze over the mix of gentlemen and peers already flirting with those minor actresses who had come straight from the stage. The room was decorated in the rococo style, the green walls edged with elaborate gold-leafed plasterwork, and set with large ornate mirrors before which crystal-decked candles burned. From the centre of the ceiling a single chandelier had been suspended, studded with few enough candles to hide the shabbiness of the room's gentility.

'Why? Do you not want to see the celebrated Miss Fox, or Miss Sweetly?' The Marquis of Razeby raised an arrogant eyebrow.

'Some other time, perhaps.'

'Hell, Linwood, it will do you good and I tell you they are worth the seeing. If you thought they looked good upon the stage, wait until you see them up close. Miss Fox is all cool silver moonlight, and Miss Sweetly, all warm golden sunshine. Both divine in their own ways.' He moved his hands in the outline of the curves of a woman's body. 'If you know what I mean.'

'So I saw.'

'Which would you go for?'

'I am not looking for a woman right now.'

'Been a while since the last one.' Razeby arched an eyebrow.

'It has,' agreed Linwood. 'I have had other things on my mind. I still have.'

Razeby persisted. 'Maybe. But I think what you need is an armful of something warm and curvaceous and soft to distract you...'

'I do not wish to be distracted.' There was only one thing on Linwood's mind right now. And he would have given the world if it had been something as frivolous and meaningless and pleasurable as a light-skirt. But those days were long gone and, given the mess his life was in now, he knew they would never return.

'I have been working on Miss Sweetly and she is ripe for the plucking, but Miss Fox, well, she is a different story altogether. Sweetness versus sophistication. Can you imagine having both of them together? At the same time?' Razeby blew out a sigh.

He understood Razeby was only trying to help, but his friend knew nothing of the truth, of what had happened, of the things he had done. He pushed away the thoughts, the memory of that final scene with Rotherham. 'I will leave you to your actresses and your imagining,' Linwood said. 'And wait for you on the balcony.'

'Miserable sod!' Razeby smiled in his good-natured way and shook his head.

Linwood's lips curved in the ghost of a smile.

Venetia knew exactly how to identify the man for whom she was looking. *He carries an ebony walking cane topped with a silver wolf's-head in which the eyes are two set emeralds.* Robert's words rang in her head as she worked her way through the men around the green room, all the while scanning for the walking cane. There were canes aplenty, but not the one that she sought. Yet both it and its owner were here; Robert would not have sent the message had he not been certain. And then she noticed the dark red curtain, masking the French doors to the balcony, sway slightly in the breeze. A *frisson* of uneasiness whispered within her at the realisation of having to do this alone with him, out there in the darkness.

It took thirty minutes to reach the curtain, via Razeby and Haworth and Devlin. But then at last she was able to slip unnoticed behind it. The door was only slightly ajar. She took a deep breath, pushed it silently open and, closing it quietly behind her, stepped out into the cool dampness of the London night.

The moonlight silhouetted him where he stood looking out over the lamp-lit street; a dark, lithe figure, silent and unmoving as if he were carved of the same Portland stone as the balustrade that contained the balcony. Her gaze moved over the dark beaver hat and gloves held in his left hand, and then on to the walking cane in his right. The tip of it touched to the leather of his glossy black riding boot and beneath his hand she could see the glint of the stick's silver wolf's-head handle and the glow of two tiny green gems within. And in that small moment before he moved, all of Robert's warnings about this man and what he had done seemed to whisper in her ear, making her blood run cold. But even then she did not consider changing her mind. She stepped forwards, relishing the challenge.

He glanced round, half turned to her.

'Do you mind if I...?' She gestured towards the coping that topped the balustrade just along from where he stood.

'Not at all.' It was a smooth, low, well-spoken voice, not harsh and cold as one might have imagined for such a man. 'I was just leaving.' His expression was serious, unsmiling, nothing of the hopeful flirtation that was upon every other male face within the green room.

'Not on my account, I hope.' She kept her voice low and lazy and seductive as she strolled over to the balustrade, stopping, not too close to him but close enough, and looking not at him but out over the same view he had been watching. 'Who would have thought such a spot could offer such refuge?' She knew the way to draw a man into conversation, to entice his interest by offering a little of herself. It was a necessary skill of any successful actress and Venetia had spent years perfecting the method.

'Refuge?' he asked.

She kept her gaze fixed on the lamp-lit streets below. The breeze breathed its chill against her cheeks, against her exposed décolletage.

'A few precious moments of calm in a night full of frenzy and demand.' She watched the carriages and the groups of gentlemen with their mistresses on their arms. 'I often come out here before the performance…and after. To think. I find it helpful.'

'You do not enjoy acting?'

'I enjoy acting very much. But not that which goes with it.'

'You mean the green room?'

'And more. But—' she inhaled deeply and slowly released the breath, and the chill of the night air lent it a misty quality '—it is all part of my job. Written into my contract, would you believe?'

'To entice and delight.'

'Some may call it that.' She leaned slightly closer to him, presenting him with a better view of her cleavage. 'But in reality to generate interest in, and donations to, the theatre. You paid more to visit the green room than you did for your theatre ticket, did you not, sir?'

'I did.'

'To be seduced.'

'By you, Miss Fox?'

'Perhaps...' She let the word hang in the air as a suggestion before lowering her voice as if they were two conspirators speaking secrets. 'Or then again, perhaps not. We actresses are not supposed to tell. Such truths quite spoil the illusion.' She smiled, but only because the role called for it, then glanced across at him, and looked at the murderer properly for the first time. At his olive-skinned face with its chiselled angles and planes that lent him a handsomeness she had not expected. At his dark hair that hung in ebony-sheened waves, and his eyes that were black as midnight and held such dark brooding intensity within that had nothing to do with their colour. His gaze met hers and it was as if he had stroked a finger down the naked length of her spine.

She stared into those dark compelling eyes and her heart gave a stutter and her stomach turned a somersault. She stared, shocked and unable look away. The moment stretched between them and all the while he held her imprisoned in that steady, scrutinising gaze as surely as she did any other man's. Her heart was pounding as she finally managed to tear her eyes away and lower her gaze. With a determination of iron she masked the fluster, reined herself in, but all the willpower in the world could not suppress the shiver that rippled right through her. It took every ounce of her experience upon the stage to regain her poise before she could look at him once again.

'The nights grow colder and an actress can hardly wear her woollens and flannels to work,' she said by way of excuse, knowing that he had seen the shiver.

'Indeed.' His eyes moved over her dress, over the bare skin it revealed and the pale swell of her breasts before coming back up to her face. 'That would not do at all.'

Play the part. It is just another role. He is just another man. 'So...what is your excuse?' She held his gaze, her appearance once more the cool, calm, enticing Miss Fox, but beneath the surface her composure was still ruffled. 'Why are you braving the chill of a November evening instead of enjoying the hospitality of the green room?'

His eyes moved back to the Bow Street view. 'I have things on my mind.'

'You disappoint me. There was me thinking that you had come outside alone to wait for me.' He glanced round at her and she curved her lips to show that she was teasing him, even though her heart was still beating that bit too fast. 'Things from which an evening at the theatre cannot distract you?'

'Quite.'

'They must be serious or perhaps it is a comment upon Miss Sweetly's and my acting abilities.'

'Rest assured your acting abilities remain unchallenged.'

'You flatter me. And flattery is not permitted out here. I have a rule that it must remain confined to the green room.'

'The truth is quite the contrary, Miss Fox. I enjoyed the performance very much.'

She smiled a wry smile and let her gaze wander back to the view. 'In that case I am intrigued as to precisely what it is that so preoccupies your mind, sir.'

The sounds from the streets below drifted up to her. The silence seemed so long that she wondered if she had gone too far in asking so blatantly.

'Trust me, you do not wish to know.' And there was

something in the way he said it, a dangerous, haunting honesty that quite chilled her to the bone.

She turned her gaze away, watching the view once more so that he would not see the truth in her eyes. 'We all have things on our minds.'

'Learning your lines, or deliberating in your choice of Hawick or Devlin?' he asked.

'Not quite,' she said, and thought with irony of just what she had come out here to do to him.

'Then what, may I ask?'

She looked at him across the small distance and wondered, just for the tiniest of moments, what he would do if she were to tell him and the thought made her smile in earnest. 'You are asking me to spill my secrets and you have not even told me your name, sir.' She arched a perfectly groomed eyebrow, the ultimate *femme fatale*. 'What manner of woman do you take me for?'

He glanced at her again, the dark eyes studying her face.

Their gazes held and even though she was prepared this time, the same prickling sensation stroked against her nerves. Her heart was racing and not only because she feared that he meant to walk away.

'Forgive me,' he said at last and gave a small bow of his head. 'I am Linwood.'

'I am pleased to make your acquaintance, Lord Linwood,' she said with mocking polite formality.

'And I yours, Miss Fox.' Just the sound of his voice, rich and dark as chocolate, sent goose bumps erupting over her body.

She focused. Breathed. Let her gaze drop to his lips, to linger there for the smallest moment before returning to his eyes.

'So now we are properly introduced.' She lowered the pitch of her voice.

'We are,' he agreed.

She smiled, a slow, seductive, suggestive smile.

'You can go ahead and tell me what is on your mind,' he said.

'Oh, you really do not wish to know, Lord Linwood. Trust me.' It was a parody of the words he had used to her.

'*Touché*, Miss Fox.' There was a hint of amusement in his voice, although his face betrayed nothing of it.

Her mouth curved as she turned her attention once more to the London streets beyond and below. 'So what brings you to the green room tonight? I have not seen you here before.'

'I accompany my friend Razeby. To use your own words, he wishes to be seduced, or, perhaps more accurately, to do the seducing.'

'And you?'

'I am not in the market for a mistress, Miss Fox.'

'Nor I in the market for a protector.' Her eyes were cool and disdainful with truth.

'Hawick and Devlin seem to be under another impression.'

'Hawick and Devlin are mistaken.' She let just enough steel show.

His eyes slid to hers. He paused. 'And had I come outside alone to wait for you…?'

'Just the two of us, out here, alone in the darkness…' She raised her eyebrow ever so slightly. 'Who knows what might have happened?'

Neither made any move, only looked at one another ᵃcross the small space of darkness. She stood still, calm, ⸻ of her posture inviting, alluring, sensual. And ⸻ on her lips was the merest suggestion of a

The balcony door opened. 'Linwood, I—' Razeby halted at the sight of her. 'Forgive me, I did not realise—'

'If you will excuse me, gentlemen.' Only then did she break the gaze that bound her and Linwood together, and took her time over a small desultory curtsy. 'Lord Linwood.' Her eyes met his one last time before moving to Razeby. 'Lord Razeby.' And as she passed Linwood she leaned close enough to smell his cologne and whispered softly for his ears alone, 'Until the next time, my lord.'

She walked past Razeby into the green room, without a backward glance at either man, even though she could feel the weight of both their gazes following her.

And just like that, the matter was begun.

Chapter Two

Venetia's heart was still thudding too fast as she closed the door behind her and made her way across the room.

What had just happened between her and Linwood was something which, despite all the men she had dealt with, Venetia had never experienced before. Linwood was not what she had expected. Yes, he was most definitely dark and dangerous, but there was something about him. Something both disturbing and fascinating. She quashed the thought in its inception, unwilling to admit even to herself exactly what it was she had felt on looking into Lord Linwood's eyes. It was too late to change her mind, and even were it not, she had no intention of turning away from this. The first step of the plan had been completed. She and Linwood were introduced. The seed had been sown. It had begun. And the next time it would be easier…now that she knew what she was up against.

'Are you all right, Venetia?' Alice whispered by her side, her eyes scanning her face.

ac. Venetia smoothed her expression into its small calm everything betraying nothing of her thoughts. 'Of course.'
in her eyes and k and Devlin have competition tonight.' Alice smile and so much more

gestured with her eyes to the corner of the room. 'More admirers.'

Venetia followed her friend's gaze over to the group of gentlemen waiting there, some holding large bouquets of flowers, others clutching bottles of champagne. Their faces were flushed from too much drink, their eyes arrogant and eager and lustful as they met hers. Men used to using women, men used to holding all the power. Men over whom she now held power of a sort. Walking away was not an option. Not for any actress, least of all for her. She had not lied to Linwood in that respect. Just the thought of him sent ripples of unease spreading through her, like a pebble thrown into a still lake.

As if summoned by her thoughts she saw Linwood and Razeby slip back into the room from the balcony. Linwood's dark gaze sought hers across the room. She met his eyes and held them for just a second longer than was decent. Her heart missed a beat, stuttered, but no one in the room would have known. She was as poised and confident as ever she was—an act perfected by years of practice and determination.

He drew her the slightest incline of the head in acknowledgement.

And in return she let the hint of a smile play on her lips before deliberately turning her attention to Alice while he still watched.

'They're coming over.' Alice's focus was fixed on the gentlemen in the corner.

Venetia nodded. This was her job and she was good at it. It paid her well—very well—and let her run her own life. With a single look she could quell a conversation when it had overstepped the mark, and stay a wandering hand. She sparkled and enticed and then enforced her limits with an iron hand and was trying to teach Alice the same.

'Have a care over Quigley, he is not so harmless as he appears,' she whispered the warning to her friend. Pushing Linwood from her mind, Venetia turned to face the men and the rest of the night.

It was at Viscount Bullford's ball two nights later that Linwood saw the enigmatic Venetia Fox again. He watched her in the ballroom, with her almond-shaped eyes, smiling that small seductive smile. There was definitely something fluid and feline in the way she moved. Men watched her with greedy eyes of which she was either unaware or did not care. She appeared relaxed, polished, comfortable in her own skin; seductive, but not in the way he had thought she would be. Not blatant and too readily available. Rather, tantalising but untouchable. The dress she wore was the colour of a glass of red wine held up and viewed before firelight—a deep translucent red that made the darkness of her hair only darker and the whiteness of her skin a shimmering pearl pallor.

He watched her manage Razeby and Monteith, Bullford and Devlin, and even Hawick, flirting with each of them in turn, if it could be called that, for despite the smoulder in her eyes he noticed that she kept each one at arm's length. Venetia Fox was very much in control of the situation. And although every man in the room was panting after her, she allowed not one of them to touch her as they must have been longing to. No wonder men were willing to bid so highly for her. And then he remembered what she had said of illusion and this flirtatious socialising being a part of her job. It was a dangerous game for any woman to play, but especially for one as beautiful as Venetia Fox.

He watched her because she was fascinating. He watched her because she was the only thing in all of these weeks past that, for the few moments he had been with her, had stopped him thinking of other, darker, things. It was the reason he was here tonight. *She* was the reason he was here tonight. Not that he had any intention of taking this flirtation any further.

Her gaze met his across the room and held for just that moment too long before she turned it back to the man with whom she was speaking.

He waited until she slipped out onto the balcony before following her. She was standing there, staring out over the moonlit garden when he appeared. He did not say a word, just walked up and leaned on the balustrade's stone coping just along from her and looked out over the garden.

'We have to stop meeting like this,' she said without looking round and he could hear the tease in her voice. 'People will start to gossip.'

'Are you afraid of gossip?'

'On the contrary, you know that I am obliged to court it.'

'Then you should be glad that I am here.'

'Should I, indeed?' She turned her head and looked at him then. There was an edge to the words that made him unsure if she were glad or angry to see him. Her eyes held his and there was a certain coolness in them before it faded. He watched her gaze drop to his hat and gloves he carried in one hand and his cane in the other. She arched a sultry brow as if questioning if he meant to leave.

He set them down on the flat coping surface before him.

She returned her gaze to wander over the darkness of the garden, but not before he saw the small satisfied curve of her lips. They were not the small rosebud lips so sought in women, but full, passionate lips that reminded a man of the erotic pleasures a woman's mouth could bring.

'Another refuge?' he asked.

'You know all my secrets, Lord Linwood.'

'Not all.'

'No, not all,' she said as she turned to look into his face. He saw something flicker in her eyes, something that was not quite in keeping with the rest of her, something which he could not quite discern. But it was gone as quickly as it had appeared. 'And I do have so many.'

'I am intrigued, Miss Fox.' It was the truth. She was the most celebrated and coveted actress in all London. Bewitching. Beguiling. Yet cool. Her reputation preceded her. Linwood had never met a woman like her.

'By my secrets or by me?'

'Both. But I thought you desired flattery to be confined to the green room.'

She laughed, her eyes silver in the moonlight beneath the dark elegant curve of her brows, her skin pale and perfect as porcelain. 'I will tell you one of mine if you tell me one of yours.' Her voice was husky and as alluring as that of a siren. Her gaze held his boldly. The sensual tension tightened as the silence stretched between them.

All around them was darkness, as dense and black as the secrets he carried in his heart, secrets that he would take to his grave rather than spill.

'Would you really, Miss Fox? Tell me your darkest secret in exchange for mine?'

She glanced towards the star-scattered inky blue of the night sky, before returning her gaze to him. Her eyes seemed to glitter in the moonlight. 'No,' she said softly, surprising him yet again with her candour. 'I would not. Would you?'

'I think you already know the answer to that question.'

'I do.'

'It seems we are two of a kind.'

'Perhaps, when it comes to secrets.' She looked directly into his eyes and again there was that coolness and distance. 'But then again, I doubt you are anywhere as good at guarding your secrets as I am at guarding mine.'

'I think you underestimate me, Miss Fox.'

'No, Lord Linwood, I assure you the underestimating is all on your half.'

'That sounds like a challenge.'

'I do like a challenge,' and her eyes held his and seemed to smoulder. The silence stretched between them, brimful with desire, before she turned her gaze to the garden once more. He felt the stirring of excitement, the need to know more of her. He studied her profile and did not want to take his eyes from her.

'Were you on stage tonight?'

'I am on stage every night. And every hour of every day. It is the price any actress must pay if she wants success.'

'Are you on stage now, Miss Fox?'

She did not hesitate in her answer. 'Of course.' Another answer so contrary to everything he expected. And through him, over him, in him, he could feel the pull of the power that she held over men.

'Are you always so honest?'

'I am an actress, Lord Linwood. I am never honest.' She smiled again and this time so did he, he who in all these past months had so rarely smiled.

'And what of the real Venetia Fox, as opposed to Venetia Fox the actress? What of her?' Questions he would never have asked any other woman. And yet he asked her, for he found that he wanted to know the answer.

'What *of* her?' She looked at him.

'Is she content to stay hidden in the shadows of the divine Miss Fox?'

'Divine…? You are flattering me again.'

'And you are not answering my question.'

'Then the answer is that she is very content to stay hidden.'

'May I meet her?'

'You would not care for her in the slightest.'

'Why not let me be the judge of that?' He was flirting with her, angling to catch just a little more of this fascinating woman—Linwood, to whom flirting and women should have been the last thing on his mind.

'Expose myself to a stranger?' She arched one perfectly shaped dark brow and leaned towards him ever so slightly so that he could not prevent his gaze sweeping down to the luscious curve of her breasts and imaging them naked and exposed before him. He knew she was toying with him, just like she toyed with all the others, but right at this moment in time he did not care. She was all that stood between him and the dread and bitterness of his memories and thoughts.

'Maybe we will not always be strangers, Miss Fox.' His gaze held hers.

'Maybe,' she said and smiled a slow sensual smile.

The music floated out from the ballroom, the notes so sweet and clear on the night air. 'The Volga,' she said. 'My favourite dance.'

His eyes held hers. 'I am afraid I do not dance tonight, Miss Fox.' How could he, when so much hung in the balance?

She stepped towards him, slowly closed the distance between them until the hem of her dress was practically touching the toes of his boots. She angled her face up to his, and her eyes glittered full with secrets, and her lips made him want to place his own against them, to kiss her, to taste her, to take the temptation that she offered. It had been such a long time since he had had a woman. But when he would have yielded she moved her mouth away to whisper against his ear, and he could feel the warm caress of her breath against his cheek and smell the bittersweet heady scent of neroli, her lips so close yet not touching.

'I was not asking,' her whisper enunciated so clearly that it stroked the nerves that ran from his neck all the way down to his manhood. His blood stirred hot.

She paused before retreating beyond his reach.

'Perhaps…we might go for a carriage drive one afternoon.' The words were spoken before he could think better of them.

She held his gaze, her eyes the cool white-blue of sunshine on a winter sea, alluring and remote both at once so that he was sure that she meant to refuse him.

'Perhaps,' she said enigmatically. The light in her eyes changed to a teasing smoulder before she hooded them beneath her long black lashes and walked away, with that signature slow sensual sway of her hips, back into the ballroom.

The clock in the small parlour chimed eleven as Venetia topped up first Alice's coffee cup and then her own.

'In answer to your question, yes, it went very well last night. Razeby has offered me a thousand pounds a year to be his mistress. That, and a house in Hart Street, just over the back from here. Imagine that. We'd almost be neighbours. And he'll see that the house is furnished with only the best, so he says. It's nowhere near what Hawick offered you, I'm sure, but more money than I'm ever likely to see.'

'Do not rate Hawick's offer so highly, Alice.'

'I heard on the grapevine that he offered you ten grand.'

'You should know better than to listen to gossip.'

'But it must have been a high sum all the same.'

'Good enough, but nowhere near what you imagine,' Venetia lied and thought of the astronomical amount of money the Duke of Hawick had actually offered her. Some men thought they could buy anything, that it always just came down to the price. It was all she could do to stop her lip curling at the thought.

'And still you turned him down.'

Venetia sipped at her coffee and knew she must be careful in what she said. Alice's attitude was understandable. It was Venetia who, for her own very personal reasons, was at odds with what was considered normal within the acting profession. 'What answer did you give Razeby?'

'I told him I needed time to consider his offer. I wanted to speak to you first.'

'And what are you thinking?'

'Whether to hold out for more money.'

Venetia looked into her friend's eyes.

'Please don't look at me like that.' Alice averted her gaze to the corner of the room. 'I already know what you think of a woman selling herself to a man. But…a thousand pounds a year is so much.'

'It is. But after your success in this run, Mr Kemble will increase your wages. He has no choice if he wishes to compete with other theatres who would offer you better. I know that you send money to your mother. If you need some help financially…'

Alice shook her head. 'I couldn't allow you to do that. You've already done so much for me, Venetia. Besides, it isn't just about the money. Razeby's a marquis and he's young and handsome and I…I like him. It would be no hardship to be his mistress.'

'Alice, Razeby may be all those things, but do not be fooled by his charm, he is a rake, every bit as much a gentleman of disrepute as the rest of that crowd. You have to be aware of that.'

'I'm under no illusion, Venetia. Believe me, with my

history I know how these things work. I'm not a fool, just practical. And I may as well get the best price I can.'

'Well, in that case...' Venetia gave a sigh '...hold out for more. Do not name your price. Do not appear persuaded or that you have reached a decision. Entice him with less rather than more. And, most importantly, do not so much as let him touch you until you have the arrangement legally drawn up, signed and a copy of it in your own hand.'

'Yes, ma'am!' Alice grinned. And then the grin faded, to be replaced with a thoughtful look. 'Razeby said something...about you and Viscount Linwood. I saw Linwood in the green room the other night, but I hadn't realised that you were with alone with him out on the balcony.'

Venetia did not deny it. Nor could she explain what she was involved in. Not even to Alice. She gave a tiny shrug as if it meant nothing.

'You're never alone with men in private places, Venetia. It's the thing you're always warning me against.'

'I made an exception for Linwood.'

Alice frowned. 'You should be careful of him.'

'Why?' she asked slowly. 'Do you know something of him?'

The pause before Alice answered was just that little bit too long. She shook her head and glanced away. 'Not really.' Then bit her lip. 'You aren't...*interested* in him, are you?'

Venetia smiled to reassure her friend. 'I am as interested in him as I am in Hawick or Devlin or any of the others. Which is not at all.' But she was lying. She was very interested in Linwood, just not in the way that Alice thought. She did not allow herself to think of the unprecedented response she had felt on looking into his eyes, on being close to him, on spending just that short time within his company. 'What have you heard of him?'

'Nothing specific.' Alice did not meet her gaze. 'Only that he's a dangerous man to get involved with. And, as they say, there's no smoke without fire, Venetia.'

'Indeed.' Venetia had listened to Robert's suspicions about Linwood and a fire that had razed an entire building to the ground and destroyed the possessions accumulated across a man's lifetime.

The two women moved to talk of other things.

Venetia did not see Linwood the next night. She left Alice to Razeby and the green room and slipped out of the theatre by the stage door into Hart Street. Her carriage was waiting outside as usual, to take her home. As her footman opened the coach door she drew him a nod and, pulling the long black cloak tighter around her shoulders, climbed inside. The door closed behind her with a quiet click and the carriage was pulling away along the street before she saw the man lounging in the corner of the opposite seat. For a moment she thought it was Linwood and gave a small shriek before realising the man's identity.

'Robert!' she chided, pressing her hand to her chest. 'You frightened me!'

'You need not be so jumpy, little sister. I am not Linwood.'

'You should have warned me you were coming.'

'I could hardly do that now, could I?'

She gave a sigh, knowing her half-brother was right.

'How do matters progress with the viscount?' he asked.

'I have secured his interest.'

'I did not doubt it. Your talent is unsurpassed. Who else could feign an interest in such a man?'

She looked away, unable to meet his eyes in case he saw the truth in them. She did not tell him that Linwood was a man who could have had his pick of many women. Not because of his handsome looks, but because of the danger and darkness and mystery that emanated from him. He was what other men were not. Acting an attraction to him was uncomfortably easy, even knowing what he had done.

'This is one role I do not like playing, Robert.'

'Understandably so. But it is the best way.'

'As you said.'

'I hate asking this of you, Venetia.' Robert's face looked grim. 'Maybe I should call the villain out and be done with it.'

Venetia looked across the carriage at him. 'He would kill you.'

'Such confidence in me,' he said drily.

'We both know of what he is capable and I would not have you risk your life.'

'I know and I am glad of your concern for me.' He took her hand in his and gave it a little squeeze of reassurance before releasing it again. 'We must proceed as planned. It is our best chance of bringing Linwood to justice.'

She nodded.

'Have you learned anything of use yet?'

'Nothing so far, except that he is definitely brooding upon something dark.'

'I expect murder on his conscience might have such an effect.' Robert's voice was low and serious. 'But a beautiful woman can always make a man lower his guard and loosen his tongue, even a man as careful as Linwood.'

She said nothing, just kept her mind focused on why they were doing this.

'When are you seeing him again?'

'He does not know it yet, but Monday night. At Razeby's dinner party.'

'Good.' Robert rapped on the roof of the carriage with his cane and the carriage drew to a halt. He looked at her through the dim light. 'You will be careful, won't you, Venetia?'

'Am I not always?'

Robert gave a low laugh before kissing her cheek and disappeared like a shadow into the darkness of the night. And when the carriage drove on, Venetia thought of Linwood. A man who had killed. A murderer. The only man that stirred a whisper of desire through her. She pulled the soft fur-lined cloak all the tighter around her, but it did nothing to warm the chill that crept in her bones.

Chapter Three

Linwood stood alone in the crowd of Razeby's drawing room and wondered if it was Razeby or Venetia Fox who had lied. Razeby's words from that afternoon played again in his head.

'I am not gammoning you! I tell you, Miss Fox *did* send a note not two hours since. She will attend my little dinner on the proviso that she is seated next to you.' There was an excitement in Razeby's eyes as he had paced the drawing room of Linwood's apartment. 'So much for your denials that anything happened between the two of you on the green-room balcony, you sly dog!'

'We exchanged polite conversation, nothing more.'

'I do not know what you said to her, but evidently she liked it. She has never attended one of my dinners previously. Indeed, she has never attended any dinner held by a gentleman.' He had given a wry smile. 'God only knows why, but it seems that the divine Miss Fox is interested in you, Linwood.'

Linwood had shaken his head to deny it, but Razeby's words had kindled something within him. Since then the pulse of desire that he felt for Venetia Fox had beat all the harder. What man would not respond to a woman like her?

'Naturally I sent a note back by return, saying that the seating arrangements would be to her preference and that I looked forward to seeing her.'

The two men had looked at one another.

'You cannot let me down, Linwood. You will have to come now.' Razeby smiled before adding, 'To have Venetia Fox grace my little soirée will be quite the coup. And you do owe me one.'

And so here Linwood was, waiting only for her.

He stood alone, the glass of champagne in his hand untouched, the bubbles rising in a riotous frenzy through the pale golden liquid. All around him the conversation buzzed loudly. Snatches of other people's conversations reached his ears. Men's talk of horses, gaming and politics. Women's, of fashion and wealth and men. There was the chink of glass and silver as footmen glided silently through the small crowd, topping up glasses. And the high, tinkling, affected laughs of the women, mistresses and actresses and courtesans, not a respectable one amongst them. The latter were all beautiful creatures, all expensively and provocatively attired, their necklines so low as to reveal nipples that had been rouged to attract even more attention, the skirts revealing, even transparent in some cases. It was most certainly a *demi-monde* affair. And then all at once the talking seemed to fade away to leave a hush.

He saw the almost imperceptible effect that rippled through the room the instant she appeared. All eyes riveted to the door. In the men there was a sudden gleam of both interest and appreciation, a puffing out of chests, a preening, a sharpening of expression that was almost predatory. And beside them the change did not go unnoticed by the women who stood by their sides. While their men's darkened with desire, the women's eyes narrowed. Linwood did not need to look to know that it was Venetia

Fox that stood there in the doorway, but he looked anyway…and was not sorry that he did. The murmur of conversation began again.

Venetia saw Linwood almost immediately. He was standing by the farthest window, alone, unsmiling, emanating an air of such dark, brooding intensity as if to ward off any that might approach him. Their eyes met through the crowd and her stomach tumbled and swooped and that tiniest of moments stretched and expanded to fill the room and render it empty save for the two of them. With every beat of her heart she could feel something of him calling to her, every thud that reverberated through her chest; inside knowledge spinning a false sense of connection between them.

'Miss Fox, so delighted you could come this evening.' Razeby's voice smashed the illusion, bringing her back to reality, allowing her to break free from Linwood's gaze. She smiled at Razeby with gratitude.

'It is a pleasure to be here.'

'A glass of champagne, first, and then allow me to introduce you to a few of my friends before we go in to dinner.'

She saw the way his eyes flickered towards Linwood before coming back to hers.

She met Razeby's gaze boldly, almost daring him to say something of the request she had made, a hint of amusement playing around her lips. She knew that he would have told Linwood.

Razeby made no mention of it; he was too shrewd for that. She drew him a small wordless acknowledgement and accepted the crystal glass of sparkling wine, touching its rim to her lips without actually drinking anything of it. Then she allowed Razeby to make his introductions without a single word or glance in Linwood's direction.

And all the while, she prepared herself and focused her mind on what she was here to do—to see that a man guilty of murder did not evade justice. It was the least she owed to Robert and to the man she could only ever call Rotherham, even if he was so much more.

The forest-green silk she was wearing had cost her a fortune, but was worth every penny. Both the cut and colour suited her well and gave her a confidence in her appearance. The skirt clung just a little to her hips and legs, the neckline showed the promise of her breasts. To Venetia it was like donning her armour. She knew her weapons well and wielded them with expertise.

She exchanged pleasantries with Fallingham, Bullford and Monteith. Spoke to Razeby and Alice, who, having taken her advice, was wearing an almost-virginal gown of cream silk that Razeby seemed to be having trouble keeping his eyes from. Until, eventually, she found Linwood before her.

'I believe that you have already been introduced to Lord Linwood?' Razeby said for the benefit of those that surrounded them. She knew her every move was being scrutinised, that who she spoke to and what she said had every chance of appearing in tomorrow's gossip sheets.

'We have met,' she said and her eyes touched Linwood's and, despite how much she had steeled herself against it, she felt that same nervous fluttering in her stomach.

'If you will be so kind as to excuse me, for a moment...' Razeby melted away, leaving her and Linwood alone in the crowd.

'Miss Fox,' he said, his eyes never leaving hers.

'Lord Linwood.'

The dinner gong sounded before Razeby's butler announced that dinner was served in the dining room.

'Allow me to take you in to dinner.' Linwood's voice

was low, the words polite, assertive rather than forceful, but there was something in the way he was looking at her that made a shiver run over her skin.

'What a pleasant suggestion,' she said and arched an eyebrow ever so slightly. Both of them knew it had been her suggestion. He was cleverer than most men, she thought, more perceptive.

'I thought so.' His smile was small, secret, the jest shared between just the two of them.

She flexed her lips in return and, tucking a hand into the crook of his arm, let him lead her into the dining room.

The food was exceptional, as it ever was at Razeby's table, guinea fowl and peacock, goose and a pie of turkey and ham combined. A medley of the sweetest quinces, potatoes sliced and scalloped in a cream sauce with capers, rabbit jelly, spiced leeks and ginger-fried cabbage, and an enormous tart, each slice of which contained a different honeyed fruit, and on a fine glass dish all of its own a rich plum pudding. But afterwards, had he to say what they had eaten Linwood could not have told them. His attention was too much on the woman by his side.

She did not flirt. Indeed, she did nothing of what he expected. Rather, the conversation between them flowed easily and naturally. They spoke of Bonaparte and the war that was raging across the Continent, of the exhibition at the Royal Academy of Arts and Captain Diamond's wager with Milton. Anything and everything, but nothing that touched anywhere near the subject of Rotherham and all that worried him.

The time passed too quickly, too comfortably. Just an hour in her company and already he felt something of the darkness lift from him. The burden that he carried grew light. She engaged him completely, making him forget in a way that his family and friends and everyday life could not. And when the plates were cleared away and the table brushed down, he found that he did not want her to leave.

'I believe our evening is at an end, Lord Linwood.' Even just the sound of her voice stroked against him to both soothe and excite. He breathed in the scent of neroli that seemed to follow wherever she went and watched her beautiful face and those clear pale eyes that only hinted at the mysteries that lay beneath.

'It does not have to be,' he said in a voice that was for her ears only.

They looked at one another, her eyes scanning his as if she would take the measure of him.

At the head of the table, Razeby got to his feet. 'And now I have a surprise. Something new to bring to my table. A feast for both the eyes and the lips.'

The double dining-room doors opened and six footmen, three on each side, carried in what looked to be a long silver salver on which lay a masked naked woman who had been strategically and artistically decorated in fruit. Sliced oranges overlapped sliced lemons and limes, apples, green grapes and red ones, blackberries and gooseberries—the rainbow medley lay against her skin and over it all a fine white powder of silvered icing sugar had been dusted. He doubted that any of the men would be wondering where the hell Razeby had found such a variety of fruit so late in the year.

'Ladies and gentlemen, I give you Miss Vert.' Miss Vert, whom no gentleman in the room could fail to be aware of, was a courtesan from the London's most famous high-class bordello, Mrs Silver's House of Rainbow Pleasures.

Razeby's footmen placed the salver on the table before them.

Linwood felt Miss Fox stiffen beside him. He glanced

round at where she sat on his left-hand side and caught
the look that passed between her and Miss Sweetly. Miss
Sweetly gave a tiny shake of her head and smiled at Miss
Fox, then the younger actress's gaze shifted to his, lingering there for only a moment, before moving back to Razeby
by whose side she was seated. He saw Razeby thread his
fingers through hers where their hands lay on the table,
uncaring of who saw it.

He and Miss Fox were seated close to Razeby at the
head of the table. Miss Vert's head lay on the salver before
them, so close that he would not have had to stretch out his
arm if he wanted to touch her, so close that he could see
the slight quiver of the soft green feathers and glittering
glass beads that made up the mask that hid the upper half
of the woman's face. Against her mouth a cherry had been
placed like a glossy red pearl on the cushion of her lips.

'Something beautiful to grace the scene while the l
adies withdraw to their own refreshment and the gentlemen enjoy their port,' Razeby said.

The room was filled with lewd laughter and ribaldry,
even though the women's chair legs were yet scraping the
floor and not one of them had left. But then they were the
demi-monde and did not warrant handling with the same
consideration accorded to the respectable women.

Venetia Fox's expression had not changed. It remained
unfazed, controlled, unreadable, yet Linwood could sense
that it was as much a mask as the green feathers of the
courtesan spread out on the table before them. Her eyes
met his and for the smallest of moments they were un-
guarded and he saw in them outrage and anger and a
strength so formidable that it shocked him. Not one word
passed her lips, not so much as a frown marred her face,
but the tension that rolled off her in great crashing waves
was a living, breathing, palpable thing. He wondered that

no one else in the room seemed to be aware of it. And then the door closed as suddenly as it had opened and there was nothing there to suggest that she was in any way discomfited.

'If you will excuse me, Lord Linwood,' she said in a voice that made him doubt what he had seen in her eyes. And then she was gone.

Venetia asked the footman to fetch her cloak, then discreetly took Alice to one side in the hallway instead of entering the drawing room with the rest of the women.

'Come with me. Do not stay here.' Venetia spoke low and urgently, for her friend only. But Alice shook her head.

'I think Razeby means to increase his offer and I know how to handle him.' She touched a hand to Venetia's arm. 'You shouldn't trouble yourself about Ellen...' her eyes slid in the direction of the dining room they had just left '...Miss Vert, that is. Razeby won't let anything happen to her and he's paying her well enough.'

'The woman in there, Ellen...was she a friend of yours?'

Alice nodded. 'Still is. All Mrs Silver's girls look out for one another, always.'

'Tell her she can come to me. Tell her I can help her to leave Mrs Silver's just like I did you.'

'She doesn't want to leave. She earns more money than I do. And she likes what she does.'

'Does she like being at the mercy of all those men in the dining room right now?'

Alice glanced away, an uncomfortable expression on her face. 'It's the way of the world, Venetia.'

'Just make her the offer, Alice.' Venetia looked at her friend. 'Please.'

Alice nodded. 'I will, but I know what she'll say.'

The two women looked at one another.

'I will see you back at the house later.'

'Maybe.'

Venetia knew it was pointless to argue with Alice. 'Remember what I said about holding out despite all of Razeby's persuasions.'

Alice nodded. 'I will.'

The footman arrived with her dark fur-lined cloak, sweeping it around Venetia's shoulders. She thanked him before he disappeared into the background once more.

'And I'll convey your apologies to Razeby.'

'With the utmost insincerity, please.' Venetia smiled and watched her friend slip into the drawing room.

'Has my carriage arrived?' she enquired of the same footman who had brought her cloak.

'It has, ma'am, but there's been an accident involving two carts along at the junction. None of the carriages can get out that way. They think it will be an hour before the road will be cleared. Shall you be joining the other ladies while you wait?'

The ribald laughter of the men sounded from the dining room, stoking the disgust and anger in Venetia's belly. 'No.' She would be damned if she'd stay in this house a moment longer. Her stomach cramped tight at the thought. 'My home is not so far. I will walk.'

'Walk, ma'am? Alone, ma'am?'

'Positively scandalous, is it not?' She smiled at the footman, who was staring at her as if she had grown two heads, and swept through the door that he scrambled to open.

It was a relief to feel the chill of the night air against her skin and in her lungs. And even more of a relief to hear the front door close behind her. She instructed her carriage to wait in case Alice decided to use it. Her slippers made no noise against the pavement as she made her way past the few carriages that waited there, along to the end of the street and past the scene of the collision of the two carts.

She thought of Miss Vert lying there on the salver, exposed and vulnerable, and the thought made a hollow of her stomach. She thought, too, of Linwood in there with the other men, feasting upon the woman, and a wave of disgust flooded through her blood. She walked on, turning down Bear Street and heading towards Cecil Court. She was listening, watching, aware of the darkness that surrounded her and the emptiness of the streets. There was a risk in walking, especially alone, but the thought of staying in that house, knowing what was happening in the dining room, made the risk one she was prepared to take. Ten minutes more and she would be home. Ten minutes more and she would be safe.

The street lamps in this stretch had not been lit, which whetted her nervousness all the more. She found herself walking faster and clutching all the tighter to her reticule. A small dark shape darted out from the stairs that led down to beneath the door of the smart town house she was passing, making her start and inhale a breathy gasp. The cat mewed at her before running off into the night, its sooty fur merging with the blackness of the night. She gave a small shaky laugh, annoyed at herself for being so jumpy, telling herself not to be so ridiculous...just as the two men stepped out from where they had been sitting on the same stone-hewn stairs and, side by side, sauntered towards her.

Venetia stopped.

'Didn't mean to startle you, ma'am.' The man's voice was as rough as he looked. He was about thirty years of age, of medium height and bulky build. A dark cap had been pulled over his head, hiding his hair. There was a sleazy insolence in the way he was looking at her that negated the politeness of his words. His companion was younger, with a face that had been ravaged by the pox and eyes that threatened violence and more. Venetia's heart began to thud in earnest.

She saw their gazes wander over the heavy fineness of her long cloak, over the small glittering reticule, the handle of which was looped around her wrist beside the sparkle of her diamond bracelet, before sweeping back up to her face.

'Bit dangerous for a lady to be walkin' the streets all alone at this time of night,' the bulky man said. 'Especially one that looks like you.'

Venetia did not deign a reply.

'But then again, maybe you're no lady.' That brazen appraisal swept the length of her body again, as if he could see through the thickness of the cloak that shrouded her. 'Ain't you that actress?'

Her mouth felt as arid as a desert as she hid her hands and the reticule within her cloak.

The man saw the slight movement and laughed. 'That's not gonna help you, darlin'.'

'Perhaps not,' she said, 'but this might.' She slipped her hand from the cloak and aimed the small ivory-handled pistol at the ruffian.

He smiled, but she saw something flicker in his eyes. 'So you want to play it the hard way?'

Her own lips curved in the semblance of a smile. 'Walk away now and I will not shoot you.'

'I don't think so, lady. Besides, I doubt you even know how to—'

'Oh, but I assure you....' her finger squeezed before the sentence was finished '...that I do.' The shot was loud for such a small weapon.

'You shot me!' He stared at her as if he could not believe it, clutching at his blood-seeping thigh.

Venetia began to run, but the other thug tackled her as

she passed, grabbing her and holding her in a vicelike grip that she could not escape.

'We gotta get out of here, Spike. The noise of the shot'll have the watch here. What will we do with her?'

'Bring her with us. I've got a score to settle with the bitch.'

Venetia tried to control the panic.

'I do not think so.' A voice sounded from a little away, a voice that was low, but so deadly and certain that it cut through the night like an arrow, and made her heart tumble with recognition: Linwood.

'Who the hell are you?' Spike asked.

'That is irrelevant. Move away from the woman.' The expression on Linwood's face did not alter. It was closed, indifferent almost. And all the while his gaze remained fixed and steady on the villain. There was an unnerving stillness about him, a calm that was more dangerous than any swagger or shouted bravado. The very air was ripe with danger, the threat so real that only a complete fool would fail to recognise it.

No one moved. No one spoke. But Venetia felt the villain's fingers tighten around her arms.

And even though she was waiting for it, holding her breath in expectation, Linwood's move, when it came, still shocked her. He lashed out quick and deadly as a viper, the wolf's-head of his walking cane flashing silver in the moonlight as he swung it to land hard against the head of the villain who held her, sending the villain reeling and freeing her. Then Linwood kicked the leg of his accomplice that held her bullet. The man screamed with pain as he crumpled to writhe in agony on the pavement.

Linwood did not even look at the men he had felled. Just walked up to her and, taking hold of her arm, guided her briskly away down the street. By the time the doors of the surrounding houses had opened and lanterns were being held aloft, Venetia and Linwood had been swallowed up by the darkness. Only when they turned the corner into the next street, the street in which she lived, did Venetia stop and stare up into his face.

'What are you doing here? I thought that you were still at Razeby's. I thought you were…' *Eating fruit from a courtesan's naked body like every other debauched gentleman in the marquis's dining room.*

'The after-dinner entertainment was not to my taste.'

Her eyes searched his, looking for the lie and finding no hint of it.

'And then I learned that you had decided to walk home alone.' He sounded as if he were distinctly not amused. His face was as stern as when he had faced the two ruffians. 'A foolhardy decision, Miss Fox, and I had not thought you foolish.'

She flushed beneath the harshness of his criticism, knowing he was right and balking all the more because of it. 'I had no mind to stay in that house a moment longer. Besides, I was not exactly defenceless.'

'So I saw.' And she was not sure if he meant what he said or was being ironic. Her cheeks burned hotter. They both knew what would have happened had he not arrived.

'Next time, wait for me.'

'Next time?' she demanded, her temper sharpened by her wounded pride. 'I believe you are a trifle presumptive, my lord.'

He said nothing, gave no hint of reaction upon his face. Just looked at her and there was something in those dark eyes that made her feel ashamed of her pettiness.

'Forgive me,' she murmured, glancing away. 'I am grateful for your intervention.'

She turned her eyes back to his and they looked at one

another through the darkness. She should feel as afraid of him as the two ruffians that they had left behind. But what she felt was wary curiosity and physical attraction, not fear.

'I will see you safely home, Miss Fox.' He did not offer her his arm. He did not smile.

She gave a nod, knowing that she was close to ruining all that she had worked upon with him, knowing that she should say something to redeem herself and the situation, but unable to do so. She felt uneasy, uncomfortable, shaken more than she wanted to admit. Not by the two men, but by Linwood.

They walked side by side, in silence, an awkwardness between them that had not been there before, only stopping when they reached the front door of her home.

'Goodnight, Miss Fox.' She felt as if there were a hundred miles between them, that all of the rapport that had flowed between them earlier in the evening had gone, that she was in danger of losing the game when it had barely begun. He rapped the knocker on her front door, then walked away.

'Linwood,' she called out, before she could change her mind.

The dark figure stopped by the railings. He turned slowly and looked at her, and the light of the nearby street lamp illuminated him in its soft yellow glow. She walked slowly towards him, ignoring the front door opening behind her, walked right up to him, her gaze never breaking from his, reached her face up to his and brushed his lips with her own.

'The next time I will wait for you,' she said softly.

She saw something flicker in the darkness of his eyes, then she found herself in his arms, his mouth upon hers, kissing her.

Linwood's mouth was masterful. He kissed her and she

forgot what any of this was supposed to be about. He kissed her and Venetia had never known a kiss like it. Her heart thundered, her pulse raced, every inch of her skin shimmered with a desire that was all for him. She had never experienced anything so raw, so powerful, so shockingly arousing. Her body melded to his, her arms winding themselves around his neck as she clung to him, wanting him with a passion that roared in her ears and fired her blood to unbearable heat. His tongue stroked against hers, lapped, teased, enticed, and her own leapt to meet it. He kissed her and everything else in the world seemed to slip away and the heat for him, the desire for him, roared with a primitive ferocity.

She broke the kiss, drawing her face back and staring into his eyes, those dark dangerous eyes that hid so many secrets. She was shocked at her loss of control, shocked at the strength of feeling coursing through her, at the blatant physical desire that had her body pressed to his and a heat scalding the tender skin of her thighs. She stepped back, opening up a space between them, feigning a control she did not feel.

They stared at one another through the darkness, both their breaths loud and ragged in the still silence of the night. The tension hummed in the small space between them. She did not trust herself to speak, only to turn and slowly walk away into her bright-lit hallway. Only then did she glance back to find him still standing there, watching her. Their eyes met once more before the door closed and her butler turned the key.

She sagged back against the solid support of the thick oaken barrier, wondering if he was standing out there still. Her legs felt weak. She touched a finger to her kiss-swollen lips.

'Are you all right, ma'am?' Albert, her elderly butler, peered at her with concern.

She nodded. 'Perfectly.' She forced a smile to allay the worry from his face. But it was a lie. Venetia was not all right. She felt hot, aroused and more disturbed than anything by her reaction to Viscount Linwood.

'There is no need for a night porter tonight. Miss Sweetly will not be home until tomorrow,' she said and made her way towards the large sweeping staircase.

'Very good, ma'am. I'll send Daisy up to attend you in your bedchamber.'

'Thank you.'

But even when her maid had helped her to change into her nightdress and Venetia had climbed beneath the bedclothes she could not sleep. She could not even lie still, let alone close her eyes. There was a tension throbbing through her that had not been there before. Her body felt restless and twitchy, her mind, milling a thousand thoughts.

The after-dinner entertainment was not to my taste. Linwood's words seemed to have etched themselves upon her brain. It should not have mattered to her in the slightest. Even if he had climbed upon Razeby's dining-room table and ridden Miss Vert before them all, such an act paled in comparison to what he had done. And yet Venetia found that it did matter, very much. He had not stayed to indulge a base appetite with the other men. He had come after her. And only because of Linwood was she lying here safe now within her own bed. There was a heavy irony in that. And in the fact that she was attracted to him...and he to her. She squeezed her eyes shut, knowing that it made her objective both more difficult and easier at once. The sooner she discovered something useful against him, the sooner all of this would come to an end. But she would have to be careful, careful in a way that neither she nor her brother had ever contemplated. Careful not of Linwood, but of her own response to him.

Chapter Four

Linwood stood alone in his rooms, gazing down into the dying embers of the fire. The open newspaper still lay on the table behind him, the *London Messenger,* the newspaper that Linwood owned, discarded where he had left it earlier that day. The last rallying flicker of the flames danced upon the crystal glass held within his hand, burnishing the brandy within a rich deep auburn. He swigged a mouthful, relishing the smooth aromatic burn against his tongue and the back of his throat, and for the first night in such a long time he had not given a thought to Rotherham.

Her image was etched upon his mind. It seemed that he could still smell the faint scent of her perfume and taste her upon his lips. And just the memory of that kiss, of her body against his, and all that had flared between them, made him hard. He wanted Venetia Fox. He had wanted her since that first night on the green-room balcony. Linwood had had his share of women, but none compared with her. She was a woman more beautiful than any other. Intriguing. Irresistible. And it seemed that the attraction that he felt for her was reciprocated. There was definitely something of a connection between them. Desire rippled through him. Maybe Razeby was right. Maybe a little distraction would be no bad thing. Maybe then he would be able to sleep at night without first drinking half a bottle of brandy.

He set the glass down on the table, and as he did so his eye went to the article uppermost on the neatly folded page; the same article he had read and reread since yesterday. *Lord Dawson of Bow Street announces that the shooting of the Duke of Rotherham was murder.* His arousal was gone in an instant. His mind sharpened. The problem was not going to go away. He had the horrible feeling that instead of the ending it should have been, Rotherham's death had started something, something that, if not contained, would destroy them all. He could not afford distraction, even distraction as enticing as Venetia Fox, not when he had a murder to hide. He lifted the bottle of brandy and topped up his glass.

Venetia was still out of sorts the next afternoon. Because of what had happened the night before with Linwood. Because he had not yet called upon her, even though, had he called unannounced, she would not have received him. And because of what Alice was now saying as she sat opposite her in their drawing room.

Venetia studied her friend's face, the pallor of her skin and shadows beneath her eyes that betrayed a night spent not in sleep, and the triumph and the excitement that radiated from her every pore.

There was an uncomfortable silence, in which Alice had the grace to blush.

'You have accepted Razeby's offer.' Venetia could not keep the disappointment from her voice.

'He's offered me two thousand a year, and the house in Hart Street. How can I refuse?' She paused. 'Please understand.'

'You are placing yourself at his mercy, Alice. What happens when he tires of you and takes a new mistress?'

She shrugged. 'If it happens, then I'll move on and find another protector.'

'*When* it happens.'

'I'm going into this with my eyes wide open, Venetia. I've made up my mind.'

'Flirt with him, tease him. Sleep with him if that is what you so truly desire, but do not give yourself into his power.'

'It's too late,' said Alice. 'I've accepted him.'

'It is never too late,' said Venetia.

'Really it is.' Alice's gaze met hers. There was a small silence. 'I want him,' she said simply, as if that explained it all. 'I want this. Please be glad for me, Venetia.'

Venetia gave a sigh, followed by a smile of resignation. 'If you are happy, then I am glad.'

Alice smiled. 'And what of you, last night? Linwood came looking for you. Did he find you?'

'He did.'

'And?' Alice demanded.

'He walked me home.' She made no mention of the ruffians who had attacked her, or of Linwood saving her.

'You really do like him, don't you?' Alice looked worried.

She could not like a man like Linwood. Not when she knew the secret he was hiding. And yet… She thought of the way he had not taken part in the feasting upon Miss Vert; the way he had come to protect her, instead. And the dark sensual attraction that simmered between them. 'He is different to any other man I have met.' It was the truth.

'Venetia…' Alice chewed on her lower lip. 'You should be careful of Linwood. He's not a good man.'

A chill stirred in Venetia's blood. Her gaze sharpened.

'That is the second warning you have given me of him, Alice. If there is something I should know…'

Alice bit her lip again as she always did when she was uncertain or worried.

'I concede I have an interest in him, if that makes a difference in your decision to speak.'

'I swore I'd never tell, but…' Alice hesitated. 'I think you need to know, Venetia…the part with Linwood at least.'

Venetia nodded, her senses quickening, her heart beating that bit faster. 'Go on.'

'It was when I worked for Mrs Silver. Linwood came to her House of Rainbow Pleasures and—'

Venetia felt her stomach contract and a sudden sick feeling of dread. 'Linwood was your client?' she whispered in horror.

'No!' Alice glanced up, shocked at the suggestion. 'Not mine, or any of the other girls. No,' she said again and frowned as if the memory was unpleasant. 'He came for information. Offered a fortune for us to betray one of our own.'

'One of your own? I do not understand.'

'The identity of one of Mrs Silver's girls. As you know, none of us ever revealed our faces or our real names in full. But this one girl, well, it was a bit more than that. We were all sworn to extra secrecy over her. Paid a lot of money to keep our mouths shut. So I can't speak of her, but I can tell you that Linwood offered much money for even the smallest scrap of information on her.'

'He wanted her?' Venetia's voice was quiet.

'Not in the way you're thinking. There was a big scandal over the girl and a certain eminent nobleman. Linwood wanted information, for himself, for his father and their newspapers. He owns the *London Messenger*, you know.'

'I did not,' said Venetia, making a mental note to inform Robert of that fact at their next meeting.

'He's dangerous.'

'Did he threaten you?'

'No, nothing like that. He and his father are reputed to have been up to all sorts of shady dealings. He's handsome, Venetia, handsome as the very devil, and with something of that same darkness about him. I would that you would take Devlin or Hawick instead.'

'I do not want Devlin or Hawick.'

There was a silence.

'Then be very careful over Linwood, Venetia.' The same words Robert had used. 'He is cold and untouched by emotion. Nothing affects him. Linwood may make for an exciting lover, but…he's dangerous.'

And Venetia meant to discover precisely how dangerous.

Linwood sat in his box in the Theatre Royal that night and watched Venetia Fox upon the stage. That she could absorb him in the story she was weaving upon the stage, even though he had seen the play already, rather than studying the woman herself, was testament to her acting abilities. He dragged his attention away, swept his gaze over first his mother and then his sister sitting by his side. Marianne's focus was intent upon the play, the emotions that played across her face showing that she was caught entirely in the fate of the character Venetia was portraying. There was a contentment and a confidence about his sister these days, and Linwood was glad of it. His eyes moved to the man responsible, her husband who sat on the other side of the box, Rafe Knight.

He waited until the interval, then left with Knight to fetch the women refreshments.

'You saw yesterday's copy of the *Messenger*?'

'Of course.' Knight's mouth tightened. 'The Bow Street office has discovered that Rotherham did not die by his own hand.'

Linwood thought of the rumour of suicide, the seeds of which his own newspaper had sown.

'Murder or suicide, either way there will be an end to it now,' said Knight.

Linwood shook his head. 'There will be questions and digging into the past. An investigation risks stirring up that which should remain hidden.'

'The bastard is causing trouble even from beyond the grave.'

'Maybe you should leave town, take Marianne to the country for the winter.'

'We're better off here, knowing what is happening. If the truth comes out...'

Linwood felt his face harden. 'It will not come out. I will see to that.'

The two men looked at one another with respect. Neither liked the other, but they were united in a common cause.

Knight gave a nod. 'You have not asked me.'

'And you have not asked me,' said Linwood. 'It is better if we leave it that way, for Marianne's sake.'

Knight gave a grim nod of agreement.

It was the night after Linwood had brought his family to the theatre. Venetia's night off, if attending Fallingham's ball could be described as such a thing. She was so busy keeping track of where Linwood was in the ballroom that she did not notice Hawick's approach.

'Venetia...' His voice was low and possessive. She felt her heart sink even as she turned to face him.

'Your Grace.' She curtsied.

Hawick's gaze lingered over her breasts as he spoke. 'Come now, there is no need for such formality between us.'

'There is every need and I do not wish to insult you,' she said.

'As if you could ever do that.' He arched an eyebrow. 'Are we not *friends*?'

'In as far as men and women can ever be friends.'

He laughed.

She smiled up at him, her smooth practised smile that held just the hint of seduction.

'Are you enjoying the ball?'

'Indeed. It is a sumptuous affair, your Grace.'

'My name is Anthony, Venetia. I would that you used it.'

She smiled again, as if in agreement, but she did not use his given name. 'Lord Fallingham has gone to much expense.'

'It is nothing compared to the ball I will give for you.'

'We have been through all of this before.'

'Indulge me,' he whispered.

She smiled and looked into his eyes. 'You know that I indulge no one save myself.'

He smiled. 'You are a cruel woman, Venetia.'

'But an honest one.'

He laughed again. 'Come place your hand within my arm and let us take a small promenade around the room.'

Despite the antipathy she felt towards Hawick and his arrogance, she tucked her hand into his elbow and let him lead her round the edge of the ballroom. She was confident in her ability to remain in control, but when they got to the small exhibition room in which Fallingham had his collection of antiquities, Hawick made a quick unexpected move and, before she realised what was happening, he had steered her into the exhibition room.

'Your Grace! I must protest.' Venetia had spent a lifetime avoiding situations such as this. She knew that flirting with men in the safety of a crowd was one thing, but being alone with them in private was quite another.

Hawick was dressed more expensively than any other man or woman in the room. With his title and riches and classically handsome looks she supposed he was the epitome of what most women in her position sought. But Venetia had no intention of ever being any man's mistress. Hell would freeze over before she would put herself in that position—selling herself to some rich man, letting him take everything of her before he grew tired and cast her aside as if she were a worthless piece of rubbish. Echoes of her childhood whispered through her mind, fuelling her determination and disgust all the more.

'I am sure that you will agree it is far beyond the time that we spoke with a degree of privacy, Venetia.' His eyes, so clear and blue, bored down into hers. 'Enough of letters and notes and conducting our negotiations in public.'

The moon lit the gallery in soft silver, casting shadows before the carved marble statues, gifting them with a life they did not possess.

'Stay here and contemplate what you will. If you will excuse me, I have other dances to dance.'

He caught her wrist as she turned to walk away, pulling her back to him. 'Not until we have spoken together.'

She raised her eyebrow and looked pointedly at where he gripped her, before shifting her gaze to his. There was nothing of enticement now, only cool wrath.

'Please, Venetia,' he begged, but he did not ease the tightness of his fingers around her wrist.

'Very well,' she said, trying to control both her anger

and the little germ of panic. 'As you are so impolitely insistent.'

'Let us not prevaricate any longer. You know that I want you, that I have wanted you for months. I have offered you more than any other woman and always it seems the sum is never quite enough.'

'You misunderstand, Your Grace—'

But he held up his other hand to stop her. 'And now Devlin is on the scene, bidding against me.'

'You are mistaken.'

'I do not think so, Venetia. Your ploy has worked.'

'Ploy?'

'Using Devlin to drive up your price.' He smiled. 'I know the game as well as you, and, indeed, I commend you on the way you have played it. I bow to your shrewdness.' His fair hair glinted silver in the moonlight as he bowed his head to her in acknowledgement. 'You win. You shall have whatever you want. *Carte blanche*. I am yours to command. Name your price and I will pay it.'

'As I said, you misunderstand me, Your Grace.'

'On the contrary, I think I understand you very well, Venetia.'

'I am not for sale.' She spoke slowly, coldly, all the while holding his gaze with an implacable force that matched those of the words. 'So if you would be so kind as to release my wrist I do not believe we have anything more to say to one another.'

She saw the flare of incredulity in his eyes.

'What new tactic is this?'

'No tactic. It is the truth.'

'We have been in negotiations for months.'

'No, we have not. You have sent me letters making offers. I have never replied to a single one of them.'

There was a silence in which the light in his eyes hardened. 'You led me to believe...'

'If I did, then I apologise, for it was never my intent.'

'Never your intent?' The incredulity was still there, but laced with anger this time. 'I beg to differ, madam. You have been teasing me, cultivating my interest all of these months past.'

'I have made my position clear.'

His eyes narrowed. 'Have you already reached an arrangement with Devlin?'

'I have not,' she said with a calmness that belied the harried beat of her heart and the prickle of fear that was driving it even faster. 'Although it would be none of your business were I to do so.'

'You think to make a fool of me before all of London. To dangle me from your fingers for yours and the *ton*'s amusement.'

'This conversation is at an end.' She tried to wrench her wrist from his grip, but Hawick's fingers tightened, imprisoning her.

'Not yet, Venetia.'

She felt the spiralling panic and quelled it with a will of iron.

'You go too far, sir.'

'Or not far enough.' He leaned closer and the brandy was strong upon his breath. His eyes stared down into hers for a moment and she could see in them both anger and lust.

'Unhand me!'

'I do not like to be made a fool of.'

'The ballroom is full,' she threatened.

'But we are all alone in here, Miss Fox.' His free hand ranged over her hip, over her buttock, pulling her close enough that her thigh brushed against his arousal. 'Besides, they all know the situation between us.'

'No!' she snapped. Her mind was whirring. She knew she could not start screaming like a débutante. And he was right, no one would believe her. She felt the blood drain from her face. 'Release me,' she said again, more fiercely this time, and struggled against him, but his mouth was already moving to take hers.

'I believe the lady does not wish your attentions, Hawick.' The familiar voice came from the shadows, low in volume, but loud in menace.

Hawick's gaze shot round as Linwood stepped from the corner of the room. The moonlight cast his features in stark relief, making his dark hair look only darker and his eyes as black as the devil's. His features were as perfect and cold and sculpted as those of the marble statues that surrounded them. The wolf's eyes in his walking cane glittered as hard as his own. In the moonlight and shadows, he looked like the most handsome, most dangerous man in the world. Danger and threat exuded from his every pore. Everything of his stance, everything of his posture was sleek, poised and watchful, and yet with that underlying edge of aggression.

'This is between me and Miss Fox. You are not stupid, Linwood. I am a powerful man, a rich man.' Hawick glared at Linwood. 'If you know what is good for you, you will turn around and walk away.'

'That sounds like a threat.'

'Take it as you will.'

The tension in the small gallery bristled. Venetia's heart was beating so fast she felt sick. She held her breath, waiting for Linwood to do just that. Turn. Walk away. Leave her to Hawick.

'I am not going anywhere,' Linwood said in his quiet, dangerous voice.

The silence that followed was tight and tense. The two men watched one another, like two dogs with hackles raised.

'Oh, I see,' said Hawick with the air of a man making a discovery. 'It's not Devlin bidding against me, after at all, is it? It's you.'

'Step away from Miss Fox.'

'And if I choose not to?' Hawick said.

Linwood looked at Hawick and the expression in his eyes was one of absolute violence, a declaration that nothing was too far, a promise of death. She felt her blood run cold just at the sight of it. Hawick must have seen it, too, for where he held her still she felt the change in him.

'Get out,' Hawick said to her and, releasing his grip on her, pushed her across the gallery towards the door. 'But know that this is not finished between us, Venetia.'

'It is more than finished, Hawick,' said Linwood darkly.

'We will see about that, Linwood.'

'Close the door behind you, Miss Fox,' said Linwood.

She hesitated to leave, afraid of what might happen between the two men. Hawick was taller and heavier than Linwood, but Linwood was lithe and lean and strong, and with such dark deadliness about him.

Linwood's gaze met hers for the first time since he had interrupted Hawick.

She gave a nod and, turning, hurried from the gallery, leaving the two men alone.

Venetia took her time threading her way around the periphery of the floor, as if she were as cool and unfazed as ever when the truth was quite the opposite, until at last she found Alice.

'You enjoying yourself?' Alice looked happy.

'As ever.'

'Bleedin' hell!' Alice blurted, but she was no longer looking at Venetia. She was staring instead at a point somewhere in the distance over Venetia's shoulder with a look of fascinated horror.

The faces around them were staring, too, at the same thing that held Alice transfixed. The music came to a natural halt and in the gap there was the spread of the hushed murmur like a wave across the ballroom.

Venetia felt the shiver of foreboding ripple across her scalp and all the way down her spine. She did not want to look, but she was already turning, just as everyone else was.

Hawick was making his way through the crowd towards the door. The white of his shirt and cravat was splattered scarlet with blood and he was holding a large bloodied handkerchief to his nose.

Venetia's eyes widened.

'What on earth happened to him?' Alice whispered.

Venetia gave no reply, even though she knew the answer very well. She watched Hawick like every other person in that ballroom.

'Devlin?' Alice murmured almost to herself. A number of others must have been having the same thought, for once Hawick disappeared through the door, all heads turned to find Devlin. But Devlin stood at the farthest side of the room from the gallery, by the French windows, looking as shocked as the rest of Fallingham's guests.

Venetia took a deep breath and accepted a glass of champagne from a passing footman, even though inside she was still shaking and her mind was reeling from the shock. All she could think of was how close she had just come to ruin, and that the man who had saved her was the one man she had thought would not. To shoot a man, unarmed and with his leg not yet fully recovered from a hunting accident, as he sat at his own desk—it took a certain type of villain to do that. Across the ballroom chatting to Razeby she saw Linwood. His dark gaze met hers across the floor and held. It lasted for only the briefest of moments, then the dance progressed and the bodies of the dancers hid him from her. And by the time the dance progressed again he was gone.

Her heart was beating fit to burst, her blood rushing too fast. She lowered her gaze, composing herself, conscious that Miss Fox must maintain her cool, collected air. So she held her head high and nodded as if she were listening to Alice's chatter. The music played on, sweet and loud and vibrant, but all that Venetia could hear was the echo of Linwood's voice playing again in her mind. *I am not going anywhere.*

He had saved her. Again. The uneasiness stirred all the more in her breast and she wondered if what she had learned of Linwood so far would disquiet her brother as much as it did her.

Chapter Five

There was a note from Linwood the next morning.

> *If it is not presumptive of me, may I request the plea-*
> *sure of your company this afternoon for a drive in*
> *Hyde Park?*
> *Your servant,*
> *L.*

His letters were angular, sharp, boldly formed by a pen
nib pressed firm against the paper, the ink a deep opaque
black, expensive as the embossed paper upon which the
words were written. As she read the words it seemed that
she could hear the rich smooth voice speaking them, the
slight irony of his reference to 'presumption' following her
taunt the night he had saved her from the ruffians, and see
the dark handsome face, all cheekbones and harsh angles,
with its lips that could drive every last vestige of sense
from a woman's head.

She screwed the cut sheet of paper into a ball, her fingers curling tight, crushing it within, tempted to throw it
onto the coals of the fire and watch it burn away to nothing. She did not want to go driving with him, not when,

against all rhyme and reason, he made her feel the way he did. Aroused. Attracted. Out of control. She squeezed her eyes shut, knowing that she could not refuse him. This was part of what she had agreed to do, the game she had willingly entered into. With a sigh, she carefully eased the paper open, smoothing out every crease she had inflicted upon it. She stood by the window and stared at the paper for a long time in the cold autumn light, thinking of the man who had written the words and of the man he had murdered in cold blood. Then, taking a deep breath, she sat down at the small desk within her little parlour. She slipped Linwood's letter into the drawer, then set a clean sheet of paper before her. Taking up her pen, she dipped it into the inkwell and began to write.

When Albert told her Linwood was waiting in her drawing room she felt a sense of dread and beneath it, for all she would deny it, a stab of satisfaction that he had come. Part of her wanted to have Albert send him away, and part, for all she was loath to admit it, was eager to see him. She felt unusually unsettled and told herself that she could not send him away, that she had a job to do here, that that was the only reason she must see him. She sat in front of her dressing table, staring into the oval peering glass and seeing nothing. Deliberately slowing her actions, she took her time inserting the wire of the pearl-drop earrings through the lobes of her ears, before smoothing butterfly fingers over the soft white-rabbit fur of her hat and checking the pins that held it in place.

Her dress and matching pelisse were of icy blue silk, the same colour as the sea on a sunny winter morning, clear and pale as her eyes. She was stalling, making him wait, calming herself as she did just before any performance, except that she had never felt this nervous before any other role. Taking a deep breath, she moved to resume the game.

'Lord Linwood.'

He was standing by the fireplace, dressed in a midnight-blue fitted tailcoat, buff-coloured breeches and glossy black riding boots, as if he had known the colour of her outfit and dressed to complement it. Every time she saw him she felt that same small shock at the effect his dark handsome looks had upon her. Her eyes moved over him, noting that his hat, wolf's-head walking cane and gloves, were still in his left hand, even though Albert must have offered to relieve him of them. The dark eyes met hers and she, the famously cool, calm and collected Miss Fox, felt herself blush. And that small betrayal made her angry and determined—which was exactly what she needed to be when she was with him.

She saw his gaze rove over her.

'You are beautiful.'

'You flatter me.'

'You know I do not.'

They looked at one another and all of her body seemed to shimmer with the memory of the kiss they had shared.

'Hyde Park,' she said.

'Unless you have another preference.' And there was that same darkness in his eyes that had been there before he had kissed her. The air seemed too thin for her lungs, making it hard to breath and the atmosphere was thick and writhing with sensual suggestion. Images flashed in her mind. Too real. Too potent. His lips on hers, their tongues entwining, breathing his breath, tasting him, feeling the hard muscle beneath her fingers, her palms; the flickering flame of desire that just the scent of him seemed to fan to an inferno. She stepped back from him, from temptation, from danger.

She shook her head, the small lazy smile that curved her lips in such contrast to the race of her heart and the simmer of her blood. 'All in good time, my lord.'

He drew her a small nod of acknowledgement, as if what would happen between them had just been agreed. Her heart fluttered with fear, but she had already turned away and was walking out of the room, out of her house, towards Linwood's carriage.

He sat with his back to the horses, giving the direction of travel to Miss Fox.

His gaze studied her as he leaned back against the squabs. She was a woman he could have looked at for a lifetime and never grown tired. She appeared as relaxed, as cool and in control as ever she had been. But when he looked into those clear pale eyes, it was as if she had drawn a curtain behind them to hide herself from him.

'A new landau.' She stroked over the leather of the seats and bolster, the soft pale-cream kid of her gloves so stark in contrast to the black leather interior of the carriage.

'My father's,' he said.

Her fingers touched the small neat coat of arms embroidered upon the bolster. 'The Earl of Misbourne. Does he know that you are using it to squire actresses about London?'

'One actress only,' said Linwood and deliberately did not answer the rest of her question.

'And yet you have taken an apartment in St James's Place when your father's house is not so very far away.'

'You have been enquiring about me.' The realisation would have been a compliment to any man's ego and Linwood was no exception.

'No more than you have been enquiring about me. You knew my direction without my telling you the other night.'

'Then it seems we both are caught with an interest in the other.'

She glanced away, as if unwilling to admit it.

'And yet you are not looking for a protector,' he said in a low voice.

'Nor you for a mistress,' she replied silkily.

She looked over at him, her eyes meeting his so directly that he felt the desire lance through him swift and sharp. Her mouth curved to a small enticing smile that did not touch her eyes, before she turned her attention to their surroundings.

They had entered through Hyde Park Corner, taking the fashionable route along Rotten Row, although the lateness of year and the chill in the air meant the park was relatively quiet. They passed only two other carriages, one a group of elderly dowagers, who, having scrutinised the occupants of the landau, turned away as respectability deemed they must. And the other, the Duke of Arlesford and his wife. The two men exchanged a look that held distinct animosity, but Linwood was not troubled by it.

Overhead the sky was a clear white-blue and the sun hung so low that its pale dazzling light made him narrow his eyes. The chill in the air held the dampness of autumn and the leaves on the trees rustled in the flame-vivid colours, littering the grass around them. But the vibrant vital beauty of the surroundings paled to nothing against the woman sitting opposite him.

'Your performance the other night was excellent.'

She seemed to still and, for a moment, he saw the flicker of confusion and a slight underlying fear in her eyes. 'My performance?'

'I brought my mother, my sister and her husband to see the play.'

She closed her eyes and smiled, and he could sense the release of tension, the relief that flowed through her in its place. He wondered at her reaction, but when she opened her eyes she was her normal self once more. 'I saw you there, in your father's box. How did your mother and sister find the evening?'

'Most enjoyable.'

'Your father did not accompany you?'

'He did not.' He did not expand upon it.

The breeze stroked against the fur of her hat, so that it quivered soft as down. They drove the rest of the time, speaking occasionally of nothing important, small things, and silences that were comfortable. He had never known a woman who did not try to fill them. Eventually the carriage reached the north-east Cumberland Gate. Her eyes moved to sweep over the greenery of the park and above to the sky and the sunlight. She inhaled deeply.

'Such a fine day,' she murmured almost to herself, 'too often I see only evenings and nights', and then she turned her gaze to him and smiled such a radiant warm smile. 'Thank you for bringing me out in it.'

'You are welcome', and he felt his own mouth curve in response to the pleasure that lit her face.

'Perhaps I could tempt you to a hot chocolate at Gunter's?' he asked as they left the park. Anything to prolong this time in her company.

'You really have been enquiring of my vices, Lord Linwood.' She smiled again.

And so did he.

And then the carriage turned into Park Lane and the sight there that, for Linwood, shrivelled all the sunshine of the day to darkness.

A costermonger's barrow had overturned not far from the corner, spilling shiny red-and-green-striped apples across the road. Children swooped like starlings, chattering and grabbing and quarrelling with each other over the spoils. Linwood's carriage was forced to stop directly outside the place he least wanted to be—the lone dark scar in the row of pale Portland-stone town houses.

Venetia stared at the charred wreckage of the burnt house, wondering if it were fate or Robert's intervention that had brought the carriage to a halt at this very spot.

'The Duke of Rotherham's house,' she said softly and the companionship that had been between her and Linwood only a moment early was ripped away, exposing it for the sham it was, even though it had felt real enough to fool her.

Linwood said nothing, but she sensed the change in him without even looking. Or perhaps the change was all in herself.

'Apparently it was an act of arson.' Venetia kept her voice light as if it were not a matter of such consequence of which she spoke.

'Was it?' All of Linwood's reserve and caution had slotted back into place.

'Someone must have disliked Rotherham very much indeed.'

'So it seems.' His expression was closed, cool, almost uninterested in the subject.

She turned her eyes to his, held his gaze with her own. 'Did you know him?'

'Of a fashion. My father and he ran together when they were young.' His eyes did not so much as flicker. 'Did you?'

She felt caught unawares by his question. She doubted any other man would have asked it of her. 'Only a very little,' she answered, and it was not a lie. 'He was a patron of the theatre.' But Rotherham had also been a lot more than that to her.

'What was your opinion of him?'

She thought carefully. 'He was a cold, precise man who liked things his own way, cruel in many respects, arrogant and rich, a man with too much power and yet one who did not default from his duty.'

'Duty?' Linwood gave a small ironic laugh.

'He was a man of his word, to the letter,' she said, knowing that, much as she had disliked Rotherham, she would defend him over this.

'He was most certainly that,' said Linwood with a hard edge to his tone as if he were referring to something specific that had happened between the two men in the past. 'It seems that you knew Rotherham more than a little.'

Her heart gave a judder at his words. The seconds seemed too long before she found a reply. 'Hardly,' she said in a lazy tone she hoped hid the sudden fear coursing through her. Linwood could not know, she reassured herself. Hardly anyone knew. But it reminded her of how carefully she must tread in this game they were playing.

'Did you like him?' he asked.

'No.' Another truthful answer. 'I tried, but I could not.'

His eyes studied hers, and in the silence she could hear the thud of her heart and feel the goose-pimpling of her skin. The game intensified. 'And you?'

He shook his head. 'I doubt there is any who could claim otherwise.'

She moved her face to the derelict house once more, studying the charred beams and great blackened stones.

'Yet even so, to burn a man's house to the ground...'

She kept her gaze on the ruined remnants of the once-fine

building, asking the question without looking round at Linwood. 'Why would anyone do such a thing?'

He shrugged his shoulders. 'I am sure they had their reasons.'

'Does any man deserve such hatred, such utter abhorrence?'

'Some men deserve much more,' said Linwood and his eyes grew colder and darker as he said it.

'Like murder?' she asked softly and arched her brows.

'Undoubtedly.'

She swallowed, shocked at his honesty. The air seemed to chill around them, the wind picking up in the cold grey light and rendering the silk of her walking dress and pelisse too thin against it.

'He is dead,' she said.

'He is,' said Linwood and did not sound the least remorseful over it.

They looked at one another, the mess of apples and hubbub in the street around them forgotten.

'It does not bode well to speak ill of the dead,' she warned.

Linwood was not perturbed. 'I doubt that even Rotherham can return from the depths of Hades to haunt us.'

'You sound sure that he is in hell.'

'I am.'

'And the hand that put him there? What of that man?' Her heart was beating hard and fast at her own audacity, and at his. The honesty of the conversation lent it an air of intimacy, of secrets confided between lovers. She was afraid he knew her game, afraid of his answer, afraid of the desire that simmered between them.

His eyes studied hers, the tension stretching so tight between them that she could not look away even had she wanted to.

His face lowered ever so slightly towards hers, but whether he meant to kiss her or to whisper the answer she did not know. She leaned in to meet him, wanting it either way.

And then his tiger was shouting that the road ahead was now clear, and the spell that had bound them alone together in the middle of a busy street was broken. There was nothing she could do to capture it back. With a lurch, the carriage started on its way again.

She wondered what she would have done if he had confessed his guilt in that moment or if he had kissed her so publically in broad daylight, and the thought made her shiver.

'You are cold.' He was a man who missed nothing.

'A little,' she admitted. The damp chill seemed to have seeped into her very bones.

He took the travel rug from his seat and tucked it over her knees.

'Would you mind if we postponed our trip to Gunter's until another day, my lord?'

'As you wish.'

There was an awkward silence.

'I have shocked you with my blunt talk,' he said after a moment.

'I am not a woman so easily shocked.' Yet she was shocked by the level of the hatred for Rotherham that she had glimpsed in him, and, even more, by the way that Linwood made her feel. It took all of her acting skills not to show it, to resume once more the mantle of the cool, unruffled actress. On the seat beside him lay his cane, the silver wolf's-head of the handle watching her, its emerald eyes clear bright green in the daylight, so piercing that it seemed they could see beneath all her disguises to the woman beneath. She turned away from the wolf's gaze, closing her mind to such foolish imaginings.

'Do you work tonight?' he asked.

'I do.'

'And tomorrow night?'

'That, too.'

A silence.

'I am free on Sunday night,' she offered.

'I am otherwise engaged on Sunday,' he said. 'And it is not an appointment I can change...or forgo.'

'How unfortunate for you,' she said drily.

He smiled at that. 'We could take tea at Gunter's on Friday.'

'We could,' she said in a tone that neither agreed nor disagreed with the suggestion.

His carriage came to a stop outside her house and Linwood climbed down, taking her hand to help her down the steps. She could feel the warmth of his fingers through the leather of their gloves. His hand lingered a second longer than it should have.

She looked into those dark eyes and, standing this close in the harsh clear daylight, could see that they really were black, rather than a dark brown. No one had black eyes, save for Linwood...and the devil.

'Two o'clock,' she said, then lowered her lashes and made her way to the front door that stood open for her entry. She did not look back at him, just let Albert close the door and kept on walking all the way up to her bedchamber where she stripped off her gloves and moved to the shadowed edge of the window. Linwood had climbed back into his landau, but it had not yet drawn away.

Even from here she could feel the danger that exuded from him...and the attraction. As if sensing her focus, Linwood glanced up at the window and, even though she was hidden, his eyes seemed to meet hers, as if he could see her as clearly as if she stood in full brazen view. Her heart stumbled. She held her breath until he turned away and gave the order to drive on.

She watched the landau and the dark figure within until she could see it no more, wondering at how much she had told Linwood, she who normally told little of the truth. This was turning out to be a game like no other she had played. A game of higher stakes and one in which she must reveal more of herself that she was used to. But sometimes to breach an opponent's defences it was necessary to lower a few of your own. A very dangerous game indeed. And one she knew she had to win.

Linwood dreamed of the charred remains of Rotherham's house that night. And of the fires that had transformed it from a fine mansion to the black skeleton it now was; flames that had illuminated the London night sky for miles around and generated a heat that had smouldered for a week. It was a dream that had haunted him often, but this time it was different. This time, the dark figure by the window, the figure that he always willed in his heart to be Rotherham, seemed to shimmer and morph amidst the golden roar of the fire. He strained forwards, his eyes stinging and raw from both the smoke and the heat, desperate to see Rotherham burn, but it was not the duke he saw standing there, but a woman, a woman with dark hair and a white slender neck, a woman whose lips had so often teased and enticed with the hint of a smile, and whose eyes, so pale and so beautiful, only hinted at the woman within. The woman was Venetia Fox.

She stood there calm and still as if she accepted her fate was to burn, but in her eyes he saw fear. He was running towards her, running to save her, running so hard that his lungs were bursting and the coppery taste of blood was in his throat and on his lips. But it was too late and, as he watched, the flames exploded to consume all around them and he knew with a terrible certainty that he had destroyed her. And in his chest were the same feelings of anger and worry and loss that he could not rid himself of.

He woke with a start, the sheets and bedclothes twisted around his legs, his skin beaded with sweat even though the room was chilled. He was breathing hard and his stomach was balled with dread and with fear. The dream had felt too real and more disturbing than those that usually troubled his nights. He threw the covers aside, climbed from the bed and moved to the window, where he opened the curtains, staring out over the darkened street. The street lamps had guttered to nothing and the moon had long since set. He stood watching until the frenzied thump of his heart had slowed to its normal pace and the sweat dried cold upon his skin. Venetia's appearance in the dream was no doubt due to their being stopped outside the burnt remains of Rotherham's house that day, and the subsequent conversation that had ensued. He supposed that her interest in Rotherham was only natural, but that knowledge did not make him feel any better. Linwood did not return to bed, only found the bottle of brandy and poured a stiff measure, then sipped it until the dawn light crept across the sky.

When Venetia came off-stage the next night a flurry of flowers were delivered to her dressing room. There was an enormous bunch of lilies, large and trumpeted, their centres laden heavy with vibrant orange pollen and a perfume so overpowering that it lay heavy in the small dressing room. A lengthy love poem was contained within Devlin's note that accompanied the flowers. Venetia knew that he had no interest in love, only sex, and that he thought she was his for the buying. She folded the note over and left it where it lay without reading the poem. In addition to the lilies were four bouquets of roses and two of chrysanthemums, all from different admirers. And, on its own, a single spray of small cream-coloured flowers that she did not recognise amidst some glossy green leaves. The card was merely signed *L*. The flowers stood out amongst all the others because they were not showy or beautiful or colourful. She bowed her head and sniffed their perfume, then she understood.

'You're smiling, so I'm thinking they must be from Linwood,' said Alice.

'Indeed, they are.'

'Not exactly flowers to woo a woman.'

'Quite the contrary,' said Venetia quietly.

Alice's expression showed her disbelief. 'What are they?'

'They are the flowers of the Spanish Orange tree.' Venetia passed the spray to her friend.

Alice gave the flowers a cautious sniff. 'Oh!' Her eyes widened. 'They smell exactly like you.'

'My perfume is made from their blossom.'

'He's a clever one, all right.'

Not so clever to see through her, Venetia hoped. But, as the subtle bittersweet scent of the flowers drifted up to her nose, she could not help feeling a pang of worry.

Linwood did not come to the green room that night and Venetia was relieved. She knew that Robert would be waiting for her. And she knew that the game with Linwood was heading in a direction she had not foreseen.

She hesitated by the small stage door of the theatre that night, her eyes scanning the darkness for her half-brother.

'I am here, Venetia.' Her name was a whispered hiss. 'Robert.'

He climbed into the carriage after her. The door closed with a thud and then they were off.

The carriage had long since disappeared into the darkness when the shadow finally moved from the periphery of Hart Street into which the stage door of the Covent Garden theatre exited. A figure stepped out from where it had stood, hidden by the darkness, poised still and silent beside the damp stones of the opposite wall. He watched for a moment longer before he turned and walked away, retracing his steps silently back down the road towards the busy throng of Bow Street. There was no one to witness his progress, none to know he had ever even been there, and, even had there been, the man remained faceless in the dark moonless sky. When he reached the street he disappeared into the straggle of the crowd, just one more theatre-goer who had lingered to talk or for other more licentious pursuits. But beneath the glow of the street lamps two tiny sparks of green fire glowed within the head of his walking cane.

Chapter Six

'Good idea of yours to come for an early morning ride, Linwood.' Razeby smiled and sat easily as the two horses walked around Hyde Park. 'Told you a bit of distraction would do you the world of good.'

'More than you can know.' Linwood's mouth gave a cynical smile.

'So how is the mysterious Miss Fox?'

'Mysterious,' said Linwood, and thought of how he had waited in the shadows of Hart Street to surprise her after the play, only to find himself the one surprised by her clandestine meeting with Rotherham's bastard son—Robert Clandon. He wondered just what the hell Venetia Fox was up to—bedding Clandon while she played him? Or perhaps, given her significant interest in Rotherham the previous day, something rather more daring and dangerous. Either way, Linwood meant to discover more.

Razeby laughed.

The morning air held a slight mist, through which the sun filtered in pale white beams. The horses beneath them snorted, their breaths puffing white and smoky as Trevithick's 'Catch Me If You Can' locomotive had been in his steam circus.

'What is mysterious is how the hell you have managed to secure her interest when all others have failed. She turned down Hawick and rumour has it he offered her twenty thousand a year. And Devlin, who I know for a fact offered her ten. And I know that you have not the blunt to surpass that.'

'Maybe Miss Fox is not for sale.' He had thought the words she uttered in Fallingham's antiquities room were the truth. But now, in light of Clandon, he was not so sure of anything about her any more.

'That little spat with Hawick the other night. It was you, was it not?'

'I do not know what you are talking about.' Linwood kept his mouth shut. Just as he always did. He was not a man given to revealing secrets—his own, or anyone else's.

But Razeby was not fooled.

'You are as secretive as her.'

Linwood said nothing.

'Well matched, I would say.'

Linwood gave a smile. 'Perhaps we are,' he conceded.

'I knew you liked her.'

'I have never denied it.' Even now, he did not. For he *was* attracted to her. He *did* want her. Her double dealing did not change that. Only made him more careful, more cautious. Indeed, given Clandon's relationship to Rotherham, and Venetia's questions on the duke, he had a positive duty to discover her more fully.

Razeby gave a quiet laugh and shook his head.

'What do you know of her?' Linwood asked the question behind his suggestion for the morning ride.

'It is serious, then?'

'I think perhaps it is.' In a way that Razeby could not appreciate.

Razeby raised his eyebrows at his friend's admission.

'Well, in that case...' He rubbed a buff-coloured gloved hand against his mount's mane and the horse blew an appreciative wicker. 'Her name has been linked with a number of high-profile men of the *ton* over the years, Hawick and Devlin being just the latest two. Never takes a man home from what I hear.'

'Who are the other names on the list?'

'Arlesford, Hunter, Monteith, and even York himself.'

'Robert Clandon?'

'No.' Razeby frowned his perplexity. 'Unless you have heard something that I have not.'

Linwood shook his head. 'I must have been mistaken.'

'I would not have had Clandon down as her type.'

'What is her type?'

'You, seemingly.' Razeby smiled.

Linwood ignored the remark. He was too aware that Venetia Fox's interest in him might not be all that it seemed. 'Which of the men on your list was she mistress to?'

'Ah,' Razeby said. 'That is not clear. She plays her cards very close to her chest does our Miss Fox, and a very nice chest it is, too.' Razeby grinned at his own jest. 'Also insists that the men in her life follow suit. The slightest indiscretion and she turns to ice. Come to think of it, maybe that is why she likes you.'

Maybe, but Linwood was not entirely convinced. 'And her background?'

'Truth be told, no one knows much about Venetia Fox before she was famous, except that she came up under Kemble's wing at the Theatre Royal in Covent Garden and has stayed loyal to him and his theatre ever since. They say she comes from respectable stock—that her father was a younger son gone into the church, and that Miss Fox was the only daughter of him and his good lady wife. It certainly adds to the mystique that surrounds her—there is something titillating about a priest's daughter who should be so very good, but turns out to be so enticingly wicked and wanton. But whether there is any truth in the story...' Razeby gave a shrug '...your guess is as good as mine.' He paused. 'If you are so interested, I'm sure the Order of the Wolf could find out all about her for you.'

'The Order has better things to do.' This was not a matter to be taken to the secret society of which both he and Razeby were members. The society existed for bigger, more important things, to see that right was done. Its members included some of the most powerful and influential men in the country, politicians, nobility, even royalty, whom he could not risk drawing more of their interest to Rotherham's death.

'It has, but matters are quiet for now, and I am sure if you were to mention it in the right ear...'

But Linwood shook his head. 'I will deal with it myself.'

'As you wish,' Razeby said. 'I would not look too hard if I were you, Linwood. She is an actress. And no actress gets to where she is without having a past that is less than lily white. But then you are planning on bedding her, not marrying her. And in that, experience in the bedchamber is no bad thing.'

'No doubt,' said Linwood ambiguously.

'But enough talk of Miss Fox. The mist is lifting and Monty's growing impatient.' Razeby's horse gave a little twitch as if to demonstrate his master's words. 'A monkey that I will reach Hyde Park Corner before you.'

Linwood gave a nod, accepting the wager, and the two of them spurred their horses to a canter through the drifting sunlit mist.

As arranged Linwood called for Venetia the next day at two. Although the day was fine he was travelling in his town coach rather than the landau. Although the curtains were open and the sun shone in through both windows, the atmosphere within it held an intimacy.

He had arranged for a hot brick for her feet and a sheepskin rug should she need it. The day held an autumn chill, but with her legs so close beside Linwood's Venetia felt nothing of the cold. She was too conscious of his presence, of the intimacy of the situation, of the role she was playing. Yet the strange tension that was between them, that had been between them from the very start, was nothing of play acting. It was as real as the shiver that swept over her skin at his mere proximity and the somersault of her stomach every time he touched her. She was playing a woman in lust, when in fact that's precisely what she was, no matter how distasteful, or how much she did not want to admit it.

They spoke little. No inconsequential talk. Nothing to break the ice of the tension that was between them. When they reached Gunter's he helped her down from the carriage. Taking his arm, she walked with him towards the tea room. But as they would have entered a man was leaving. An elderly gentleman, well dressed, walking with a cane in his right hand, while his left arm hung at an unnatural stiff angle by his side. The grey of his hair was peppered with its original black. A neat trimmed silver beard did not disguise the haggard, ravaged face, the lines etched there or the suffering within those dark secretive eyes that seemed so familiar.

Beneath her hand she felt the muscles of Linwood's arm tense, and the stiffening of his whole stance.

'Francis,' the man breathed softly. Venetia knew without being told who he was. The years had not been kind to the Earl of Misbourne, yet she could see in his face the man he had once been, a man that in his youth would have looked very like the one standing by her side.

'Sir.' Linwood's voice was cold and formal with nothing of affection or the respect she had expected for his father. Indeed, his expression was harsher than ever she had seen it.

'We have not seen you in a while.'

'I have been busy,' replied Linwood.

She could sense the strain between the two men, the unwieldy awkwardness that lay between them.

She saw Misbourne's eyes flick over her.

'May I introduce Miss Venetia Fox. Miss Fox, the Earl of Misbourne...' the slightest of pauses before adding ' ...my father.' There was an unmistakable bitterness to that last word.

Misbourne and Venetia made their devoirs before Misbourne turned his attention back to his son. 'You will come for lunch on Sunday?'

'I am busy that day.'

'Then a brief visit whenever you can manage...for your mother's sake. You know how she worries over you.'

Linwood gave a stiff nod before saying, 'If you will excuse me, sir.'

'Of course.' She saw something of pain flicker in Misbourne's eyes.

A small dip of the head in acknowledgement and the moment was over, Misbourne walking away, while inside Gunter's tearoom Linwood and Venetia were shown to their table, but she saw Linwood's eyes follow the figure that receded into the distance along the street. And she felt like she had had a glimpse into something very private, an anger and vulnerability that Linwood did not want the world to see.

He caught her watching. The look in his eyes was poised, waiting, defensive almost. But then the waiter was there, pencil and paper in hand, ready to take their order. Venetia turned her gaze to him, and, with a smile, asked him to list the choice of cakes for the day, giving Linwood the dignity of the space to regroup himself, even though Linwood's proximity robbed her of her hunger and the scene that had just played outside Gunter's front door seemed to echo between them.

'So,' she said softly when the waiter left.

She saw Linwood tense slightly.

'Do you come to the theatre tonight?'

'I do,' he said, and there was a peculiar look in his eyes—was it relief or gratitude? 'There is a certain actress I have a mind to see.'

'You did not tell me you were a fan of Miss Sweetly.'

He smiled. His hand moved to lie flat upon the table, close to hers but not touching in this so public and respectable place. Yet she could feel the pull of their fingers, the sensation as if he had stroked his over hers. She turned her palm over and saw his gaze drop to where the buttons of her glove gaped to reveal the soft white skin of her inner wrist. And when his eyes met hers again it was as if something passed between them, something shared, something that she did not quite understand.

'You know my interest is not in Miss Sweetly.' His voice was low, intimate, velvet.

She held his gaze and kept her words as quiet as his. 'And yet you recognise her from her days before she came to the theatre.'

He did not pretend to misunderstand. 'I do.'

She had heard it from Alice's mouth. She wanted to hear what Linwood would say. 'Were you her client?'

He raised an eyebrow at her bluntness, then gave her back as good as he got. 'I have no need to frequent brothels, Miss Fox.'

'That is not what I asked you.' It was nothing to do with

what she was supposed to be gleaning from him, nothing to do with Rotherham. It should not have mattered to her in the slightest. But in a perverse sort of way it did. Very much so. She found she was holding her breath for his answer.

'I was not her client, or that of any other woman of the night.'

'But you offered to pay her.'

His eyes did not waver, just stayed focused on hers.

'I did, indeed.'

It felt intense and dangerous and very personal, even though they were sitting here sipping tea and eating scones with cream and jam with the most respectable of London's *ton* all around.

She leaned across the table to drop the words more quietly than the others. 'For sexual congress?'

He gave a half laugh, half smile at that. 'Have I not already told you that I do not pay for sexual congress?'

'Again, Lord Linwood, you have not answered my question.'

'And you do ask so many, Miss Fox,' he said in a soft voice.

She felt a little stab of apprehension. Neither his expression nor the intonation of his voice revealed anything more of his meaning. But her doubt was soothed when he continued, 'I am sure that Miss Sweetly has already told you the details of what I wanted from her.'

'Then it may surprise you, as much as it surprised me, that she did not.' She frowned slightly at the memory. It was hypocritical to feel hurt that Alice did not trust her with the details, given there was so much she, herself, was hiding, but she felt it all the same. 'You wanted information, but about whom she would not divulge.'

There was a pause. She saw his gaze drop to where her

hands lay upon the table, to where she was worrying at the button on the wrist of her glove. She stopped what she was doing and, lifting her delicate cup from its saucer, took a sip of tea before meeting his gaze once more.

'She really did not tell you.'

Venetia said nothing.

Linwood's gaze was dark and steady. 'It is irrelevant to what is happening between us, Miss Fox.'

'Is it?' she asked. 'You paying for information on one of Mrs Silver's girls?'

'I am the owner of a newspaper with an interest in such stories. Have you never done anything that you regret?'

'I take care not to.'

He gave a nod of almost mocking congratulation.

'Have you any other regrets, my lord?' She arched her brow, her eyes as serious as his, daring him to tell her of Rotherham.

'Something of the devil's blood runs in my family, Miss Fox. A man cannot live a lifetime with such blood in his veins and not have regrets for the actions he has taken... even if they were for the best of reasons.' His eyes were steady upon her, controlled, watchful in a way that made her feel like he could see right through her game.

Both his words and the look in his eyes made her shiver. She steered the conversation to safer ground, but it did not ease the tension that had appeared between them. It made her uncharacteristically nervous so that she was relieved when the time came to leave and he took her home. The journey was conducted in silence. Even when they came to a halt outside her house and Linwood helped her down from the coach he did not say a word, making her fear that she had gone too far in her questions of Alice and the brothel and Rotherham.

'Good afternoon, Lord Linwood.' She made to walk away.

He let her take a few steps before the words slipped from his lips, faint and gentle as a lover's caress and with such a sincerity of feeling that it stroked a shiver from her scalp all the way to the tips of her toes. 'You should know, Venetia, that I do not share. If you are mine, you are mine alone. As I am yours alone.' He paused. 'And if not, then we have nothing more to say to one another.'

She froze, her heart suddenly galloping, afraid of what he meant, afraid of where this thing between them was going, then turned to face him.

They stared at one another across that small space and all the street surrounding them seemed to fade to nothing.

'Good day, Miss Fox.' Linwood bowed, climbed back into his carriage and drove away, leaving her standing there still staring after him.

Three nights later Venetia arrived early at Razeby's small private soirée he was holding in celebration of his new arrangement with Alice. Her friend was glowing in the role of the marquis's hostess. She stood by his side, greeting each of their guests as they arrived.

'I'm so glad that you're here, Venetia.' Alice smiled, then lowered her voice to a volume that was intended for her ears only. 'I've invited Linwood for you, even though it goes against my better judgement.'

'Thank you.' Not for the first time Venetia wished she could tell her friend the truth of what she was doing.

She had spent the past days worrying over Linwood. Now she did not wait for the viscount to come to her, but threaded her way through the room towards him.

'Miss Fox.' Fallingham bowed when he saw her. 'You know Linwood, of course.'

'Of course.' She slid her gaze to the man who made her blood thrum and her heart thunder.

Linwood drew her a small bow. He said nothing, but there was something in his eyes when they met hers that made his parting words after Gunter's resonate between them. Three nights of pondering and still she could not decide if it had been a warning or a question, or both. Asking her to go beyond what had up until now been nothing more than flirtation and warning her that he would not tolerate unfaithfulness in the same breath. Both question and warning disturbed her far more than they should have. She felt like the game was moving in a direction she had not foreseen, one that was both frightening and enticing.

'Miss Sweetly has done Razeby proud,' said Fallingham, drawing her away from her thoughts on Linwood.

'Indeed, she has, Lord Fallingham.'

'It is good news about their arrangement.' Fallingham was all politeness, but he was unable to resist a quick glance at her breasts.

Venetia could not bring herself to agree. 'He makes her happy,' she conceded and could not understand why, despite all of her warnings, Alice was so intent on being with Razeby.

'As she does him. He is putty in her hand.'

I doubt that. Venetia smiled and did not say the words. She was under no illusions as to how Razeby saw Alice. He would use her and dismiss her just like every other man of his ilk treated every woman of Alice's and hers.

'A toast to Miss Sweetly and Razeby.' Fallingham raised his glass of champagne.

Venetia raised her glass. Linwood did, too, but only Fallingham drank the champagne. Venetia noticed that Linwood did nothing more than touch the rim of the glass to his lips, in the same way as she did.

Their eyes met, each knowing the other's secret.

Linwood's eyes were dark and intense, and she felt the shadow of his last parting words still upon her. *Was she his?* It was the question she had asked herself these three nights past. She knew her own strength, knew her purpose in this game, knew she must not lose focus. If Linwood chose to raise the stakes a little, then Venetia believed herself more than capable of rising to the challenge. Besides, if the answer to his question was no, then she knew that he would walk away and Robert's plan would be lost. And beneath all of those rationales was another reason that she could not quite bring herself to admit.

'Ah,' Fallingham smiled. 'Here comes Clandon.'

In her shock Venetia sucked in a mouthful of champagne and had to swallow it down, half choking in the process.

'My dear, Miss Fox, please allow me...' Fallingham was poised with handkerchief in hand, ready to dab in all the wrong places. She ignored him, turning her gaze to Linwood's and accepting the plain white handkerchief that he offered without a single word.

She pressed it to her lips, as if kissing it, as if kissing him, before returning the handkerchief to its owner.

Fallingham seemed to realise that he was staring at the pocket into which Linwood had just slipped the handkerchief. 'Just toasting our hosts, Clandon,' he said. 'You know Linwood, of course.'

She felt a pang of annoyance that Robert had not warned her he would be present. She did not look at him.

Robert gave a nod, but barely glanced at Linwood. The air between them was all cold formality. She watched Linwood's eyes move over the black band of grief around Robert's arm.

'So sorry to hear about Rotherham,' said Fallingham. 'Terrible way to lose a father.'

'Indeed,' murmured Clandon and his eyes held the sudden shimmer of tears before he glanced away and cleared his throat.

She saw the sympathy in Fallingham's gaze.

Linwood's expression remained its usual unrevealing, unsmiling mask.

'But I am confident that our justice system will find the perpetrator.' Robert sounded as pompous as their father had been.

'Indeed,' agreed Fallingham. 'Have you been introduced to Miss Fox?'

Robert's eyes met hers. 'I have not yet had that pleasure.' He bowed and looked at her with a degree of calculated interest that made her uncomfortable. 'Miss Fox.'

Her brother was better at this game than her, she thought.

She curtsied. 'My sympathies on your loss, Mr Clandon.'

'Thank you.' Robert's gaze moved from her to Linwood, as if in expectation of him adding to the condolences, but Linwood remained stubbornly silent. The awkwardness of the moment stretched. The two men faced one another, neither seemingly willing to back down.

'Clandon, you must allow me to introduce you to our hostess, Miss Sweetly,' Fallingham said, placing a hand on Robert's arm and defusing the situation by leading him away in the direction of Alice.

Venetia waited until her brother was out of earshot before she spoke. 'You did not offer him your condolences.'

'Because I am not sorry that Rotherham is dead.' Linwood was watching her, his expression daring a response.

'That is a dangerous thing to say when the authorities are searching for his murderer.'

'Maybe I like to live dangerously...' he stepped closer, his breath brushing her cheek as he whispered by her ear '...as dangerously as you, Venetia.'

Greensleeves was being played on the piano in the background, the notes soft and sweet and melodic. The room was bright with candlelight reflected from peering glasses and the thousand shimmering crystal drops that lined the heavy chandeliers overhead and sconces patterning the surrounding walls. All around them was the chatter and buzz of conversation—the deep tones of a man's laughter, the flirtation of a woman's response, the chink of glasses and somewhere in the distance the pop of a champagne cork. All of it was as nothing. Venetia and Linwood might as well have been alone. All of the pretence and flirtation fell away. She could feel the beat of her own heart—fast, hard, loud, and the way her pulse throbbed in her throat. Strings of bubbles fizzed from the glass in her hand. She watched their tiny trails, her mind sharpening, focusing, before she raised her eyes from the glass and looked into his. Black eyes that seemed to reach inside her and see too much, black eyes that lit a part of her she had not known existed until him.

'I do not know what you mean, my lord.' The words were breathy and low, and not through artifice. He could not know the truth of her, of what she was doing to him, could he? Maybe it was her own guilty conscience that gave his words another interpretation. And despite that danger, she had never felt more aware of him as a man or of the strength of the sinuous desire that rippled between them.

'There is an unanswered question between us, Venetia.'

There were many unanswered questions between them,

but she knew the one to which he was referring—the same one that had haunted her dreams for three nights. *If you are mine, you are mine alone... And if not, then we have nothing more to say to one another.* The echo of those words seemed to whisper between them.

'We cannot have you keeping Miss Fox all to yourself, Linwood.' Devlin arrived with Mrs Silver on his arm, breaking apart the intensity of the moment.

'Indeed?' said Linwood but his eyes stayed fixed on Venetia.

Linwood let the questions hang between them, the ones he had asked and the ones that were silent. That Clandon and Venetia had pretended not to know one another was a sign that boded ill. Was she spying for her lover? Or was Rotherham's illegitimate son paying her? He remembered her strange response to his allusion to her performance, and he thought again of her questions that seemed to edge more and more around Rotherham and the duke's murder. And he understood now what lay behind them. Clandon and Venetia thought him guilty of Rotherham's murder. It was a bittersweet realisation.

Mrs Silver, madam of the highest-class brothel in St James's, was wearing her customary muted dove-grey dress, as sober and respectable as those worn by her girls were provocative and revealing. Mrs Silver might have been accompanying him, but Devlin's gaze was engaged entirely on Venetia, lingering over the curves that the audacious scarlet gown revealed too well. Venetia stepped closer to Linwood.

'Miss Fox.' Devlin kissed her hand. Venetia accepted his greeting with grace, but she did not allow her hand to linger in Devlin's possession, withdrawing it immediately and slipping it casually around Linwood's arm. It was a statement to Devlin and perhaps something of an answer to himself.

'Linwood.' Devlin's gaze was cool and appraising, observing the message Venetia's body was so clearly sending. Then to Venetia, 'I saw your play the other night. Splendid performance. As usual.'

'Thank you. You are too kind, sir,' Venetia said and she smiled with her eyes, if not with her mouth, in that bold, provocative way he had come to recognise.

'Have you seen it, Mrs Silver?' Devlin asked the woman by his side.

'I have not, sir.' Mrs Silver smiled, but her gaze, when it finally moved to Venetia, was cold.

He noticed that neither woman actually spoke to the other.

'May be I shall get up a little party and take you,' Devlin said, but his focus was once more on Venetia, more specifically on the smooth white skin that the neckline of the scarlet dress revealed.

'Such a delightful offer, but unfortunately I am engaged every night of this week, and next,' said Mrs Silver.

Venetia's mouth curved up ever so slightly at the edges, but the atmosphere between the two women was so frosty that Linwood wondered how Devlin failed to notice. 'If you will excuse us…' And with the smallest of curtsies Venetia and Linwood were drifting away towards the other side of the room.

'Do you have your answer, Lord Linwood?'

He looked into those beautiful silver-blue eyes and all that they were hiding. 'I am not sure that I do, Miss Fox.'

'You wish me to spell it out, my lord?'

'I wish to be certain of where we stand.'

She held his eyes for a moment longer. 'Very well.' She

released his arm, stepped to stand before him and reached her lips to touch his ear. 'I am yours. And yours alone.'

Even knowing what he now knew of her, even with the worst of his suspicions he felt the words stroke against him as if she had boldly traced her fingers against the length of his manhood.

Her gaze moved to his once more.

'I am glad to hear it.' He captured her hand in his, a small surreptitious movement, but one of possession before the crowd all the same. He would take what she offered because Linwood knew it was always best to keep one's enemies close, and play them at their own game. And more than that, he wanted to ensure that Clandon's suspicions remained focused on him alone.

And he would take what she offered, because, despite everything, he wanted her.

Devlin and Mrs Silver walked past them again. He saw the veiled hostility in Venetia's eyes as she looked at the woman—and her realisation that he had seen it when she returned her gaze to his.

'It seems I must work a little harder upon my acting skills when it comes to Mrs Silver.'

'There is nothing wrong with your acting skills, when you choose to employ them.'

Her hand went very still beneath his.

'Ever the flatterer,' she said, choosing to take it as a compliment, but well aware of the edge to their conversation.

'Never the flatterer, but then you know that of me, by now.'

'I suppose that I do...even if I know little else of you.' He wondered if she realised how close to the edge she was treading.

'What precisely is it that you wish to know, Venetia?' The nub of all that was between them.

'All that you are, my lord.' She looked into his eyes and beneath his hand he felt the stroke of her fingers against his palm before she slid them from his reach. He managed to prevent a blatant arousal, but only just.

'You do not desire much.'

'No.' She smiled that dangerous seductive smile. 'Only you.'

This time he did not smile in return, just pinned her gaze with his and did not let it go. 'Then I shall tell you that which you want to know, Miss Fox.' He lowered his voice to a whisper and breathed the rest of the words into her ear. 'When you tell me what I want to know.'

'And that is?' Her whisper sounded breathless and he could feel the warmth of her breath against his cheek and the line of his jaw.

'All that you are, Venetia Fox.' He moved his face to stare down into her eyes.

'A pact of honesty?' She sounded amused, but there was a little flicker of something else in her eyes, something that looked triumphant.

'We are sworn to speak the truth or say nothing at all.'

They were still standing too close, their faces poised as if they were about to kiss, as if they were the only two people in the room, as if there was no crowd surrounding them.

'Do we have a deal, Miss Fox?'

She glanced down, her long dark lashes hiding her eyes, hesitating just long enough that he knew her glimmer of unease. But when she raised those beautiful pale eyes to his once more she showed nothing of disquiet. He had to admire the steeliness of her nerve.

'We do,' she said smoothly.

'Let us seal our agreement.'

'And do you have a suggestion for how we might do that?' They were words designed to torture him. She was a woman who knew her power. Images of her naked and beneath him, of his mouth upon hers, of him riding her, swam in his mind. He thrust the imaginings aside with the ruthless hand of a master.

'In the conventional way…for now.' He took her right hand in his, a handshake in all except that they were standing so close it looked like the touch of two lovers. 'Since it binds us in honour.'

She said nothing but beneath his hand he felt the tiny shiver go through her as she understood that she was, in truth, honour-bound.

And only then did he smile.

Chapter Seven

It was a little after three the next afternoon when Linwood learned something of what lay behind Venetia Fox's dislike of Mrs Silver. The sun shone bright through the window of White's Gentleman's Club, lighting the elegant large room in pale white light, bleaching the colour from the dark-mahogany wood panels that lined the walls and the deep rich blue of the curtains and warming the room in such contrast to the icy temperatures outside. The room was almost empty. A few elderly peers were dozing in the line of high-back leather-wing chairs. Old Lord Soames was reading his newspaper, hard of hearing and oblivious to the loud snores of one of his neighbours. The ticking of the grandfather clock was slow and steady and comfortable. Linwood and Razeby were drinking coffee at the far end of the room, discreet and away from the famous bow show-window.

'Alice worries over her friend's association with you.' Razeby sipped at his coffee.

'That does not surprise me. Miss Sweetly thinks me the very devil.'

'Ah, but I learned a few things about your Miss Fox that might.' Razeby smiled.

'Go on.' Linwood was careful not to sound too eager.

'I understand from Alice that you know of her secret—that she was in the employment of Mrs Silver.'

'I hope she made it clear to you the nature of our dealings. That we did not...'

'She did.' Razeby smiled. 'She is the sweetest little thing.'

'You were telling me of Miss Fox,' Linwood prompted.

'Ah, yes.' Razeby collected himself from his thoughts of his new mistress. 'I thought you would be interested to learn that it was Miss Fox who persuaded Alice to leave Mrs Silver's and join the theatre. She took her under her wing, made her her protégée. Alice is eternally loyal and grateful, of course.'

'Of course. Old news, Razeby.'

'But Miss Fox's offer to Miss Vert on the night of my little dinner gathering is not.'

Linwood stilled and raised an eyebrow.

'To help her "escape" Mrs Silver's establishment. Little wonder Mrs Silver is outraged, even if Miss Vert declined the offer.'

Linwood thought of the barely concealed dislike he had witnessed between the two women and he knew exactly what Razeby was insinuating. 'Miss Fox is poaching Mrs Silver's girls.'

'So it seems.'

Linwood remembered the night the green-masked courtesan had been the table decoration at Razeby's. He remembered, too, the fierceness of Venetia Fox's reaction on seeing Miss Vert's display.

'Alice let slip one other interesting little titbit.' Razeby looked like the cat that had got the cream. 'Did you know that all of the maids in Miss Fox's employ were once ladies of the night? All rescued by Miss Fox.'

'I did not.'

'According to Alice, Miss Fox has very strong feelings when it comes to prostitution.' He paused. 'It does make one wonder as to why.' *And to Venetia Fox's personal history.* Razeby was too diplomatic to say it.

'Indeed, it does.' Linwood met his friend's eyes. 'How much do you think Miss Sweetly knows?'

'Ah, there is the rub,' said Razeby. 'Very little, I am sure. It seems Miss Fox keeps her secrets all to herself.'

But she would reveal them to him. One by one. Until he knew all that there was to know of her.

Venetia Fox sat opposite Linwood in the town coach that night. The lantern within had not been lit. The bright silver moonlight and the dull fiery glow of the street lamps that spilled in through the coach's windows were enough to see each other by. The roads were busy already with carriages that queued to take their occupants into Covent Garden and the theatres that lined it.

'Traffic jams at theatre opening and closing times. It is the disadvantage of living so close to Covent Garden, although they do not usually affect me,' she said.

'Why so?'

'Because I am in the theatre hours before the curtain goes up.'

'And hours afterwards?'

'Not quite so long, but enough time for the jam of coaches to have disappeared.'

'Along with the gentlemen waiting for you.'

She held his gaze boldly. 'It is the occupational hazard for any actress.' And so it was. But not whatever was between her and Clandon.

'You could always leave by the stage door.' He was testing if she was adhering to their oath of speaking the truth.

There was a small pause before she admitted it. 'I do,' she said.

'I will remember.'

Her eyes met his across the carriage. 'Are you planning to surprise me one of these nights?'

He smiled, and did not tell her he had already done that. 'If I told you, it would not be a surprise.'

'You do not need to wait in the darkness and cold of Hart Street...when there is the warmth and comfort of a dressing room within.' She would not want him chancing upon her liaison with Clandon.

'Then I will come to your dressing room...should I wish to surprise you.'

There was a small silence.

'I would like you to come.' She glanced away. 'But I confess that I do not like surprises.'

'Neither do I,' he said. 'But sometimes they are worth the discomfort.' Ambiguous words—that could be interpreted in many ways.

'Perhaps,' she agreed. But her eyes held his too boldly, in that way he was coming to recognise as her defence against a threat.

The tension notched a little tighter. Two people engaged in a duel of truths and deception...and desire.

He backed off a little, easing the pressure, changing the subject. 'So how do you find being in the audience instead of upon the stage?'

She gave a shrug. 'In truth, I cannot enjoy it. I analyse the actors, I watch for the cues and the shifts in scenery. For me the theatre is always work, whether I am on the stage or seated in the plushest of boxes within the auditorium.'

'Then why are you coming to the theatre tonight?'

She looked at him, and the moonlight emphasised the

darkness of her brows and hair, and the pale smooth beauty of her face. 'Do you really need me to tell you?'

'I could hazard a guess. But given our recent…agreement, I thought I would just ask you.'

'Very well.' Her eyes held his. 'I accepted your invitation to the theatre tonight so that I might spend the evening in your company.' She paused. 'Why did you invite me?'

'Because I wanted to be with you, Venetia.' He was not lying. Even were it not for Rotherham he would not have turned away from this game. He enjoyed her company, even knowing that there was so much she was hiding. In a way he did not blame her, for was not he just the same? Hiding greater secrets than she would ever guess.

She smiled.

'We do not need to go to the theatre to be together,' he said.

'But you have bought the tickets. Our seats will remain empty. And I would not inflict that upon any performer.'

He tapped his walking cane on the roof of the coach, stepping down from the carriage when it came to a halt. A couple of ragged prostitutes approached him. He gave them the tickets and more money than they could earn if they lay on their backs for a week before climbing back inside.

She was watching him with a strange expression on her face. 'You surprise me.'

'And you do not like surprises.'

'I like that one. It was a kind gesture.' He remembered then what Razeby had told him of Venetia Fox's strong feelings on prostitution.

'Perhaps they can lose themselves in a different world tonight.'

'More likely they will sell the tickets and spend it with the rest of the money on gin.' She sounded saddened, yet resigned to the fact.

'At least they have the choice. Either way, the seats shall not go empty.'

She was silent and it seemed that she was studying his face through the shadows and the moonlight. 'If not to the theatre, where shall we go?'

'Anywhere that you desire. The choice is yours to make. Where in all the world would you most like to be right now, on this clear starlit night?'

She smiled, knowing that he could not realise just how his description of the night touched her. Memories of the past, both happy and sad, whispered from the corners of her mind. She wondered if she dare reveal so much, by telling him. But one had to be daring when one diced with the devil. 'You will be disappointed.'

'With you, Venetia, that is not possible.'

'Very well.' She paused. 'I should like to be in the glass-house in my garden.'

If he were surprised, he did not show it. 'Then to your glasshouse we shall go.'

She hesitated, looking across into his face, wondering at the man he was. 'We could walk to escape the traffic jam.'

He reached through the darkness and took her hand in his. 'Then, Miss Fox, please allow me the honour of ac-companying you to your glasshouse...on foot.'

'I would like that very much, Lord Linwood.'

They smiled at one another, a warm genuine smile that seemed to bind them together, before he slipped outside and spoke to his coachman.

Linwood did not put the step in place, but lifted her down onto the ground, sliding her close so that she could feel his body against hers, all hard, strong muscle, making her feel that she had never been more conscious of him as a man. She breathed in the scent of him and felt her blood stir in response. It was with reluctance that she stepped away to accept the arm that he offered, resting her fingers lightly in the crook of his elbow as if they were a respectable couple. Together they walked off down the street gridlocked with carriages, away from the theatre and the hubbub of busyness.

They spoke little as they walked, and yet that same feeling was there between them, that same parry and thrust of attraction in this strange duel she was dancing with him. The excitement, and the thrill of walking the knife edge of revelation. Telling truths that she had not revealed to anyone else. Tempting the same from him. Together in a game of intimacy and passion, of trust and deceit. Her reveal. His reveal. Turn and turn about. But his arm was solid and real and warm beneath her gloved fingers, and she held on to him a little more tightly against the chill of the night.

It did not take long to reach her house. Albert's face registered surprise to see her, and even more so to see Linwood step out of the shadows behind her.

'Please come in, Lord Linwood.' She was very conscious of the door closing behind them and of the fact that this was the first time she had invited a man, any man, into her home.

Albert moved to take her cloak, but she shook her head. 'Thank you, Albert, but no. Lord Linwood and I will be in the glasshouse.' The butler's eyes slid to Linwood before coming back to her.

'Very good, ma'am,' was all he said, but she knew what he was thinking, knew what all her staff would think. Not that she could let their opinion or anyone else's stop her. Her heart was tripping a little too fast and she could feel the warmth of a blush touching to her cheeks.

Linwood followed her downstairs and into the kitchen

at the back of the house. Neither of them spoke as Albert lit her a lantern and passed it to her.

'Will you be requiring anything else, ma'am?'

'No, thank you, that will be all.' She lifted the heavy key from the peg on the wall beside the door, feeling the comfort and familiarity of the metal within her hand.

He opened the back door for her and she walked through it just as she had done a thousand times before. Except this time it was different.

The moonlight was so bright that there was no need for the lantern. She held it out before her regardless, tracing her steps along a path she knew so well she could have walked it blindfold. It was a narrow path, bordered by bushes and flower beds in which the blooms had faded and died with the summer. Behind her the tread of Linwood's shoes made no noise, but she was acutely aware of his presence. She could feel him there, even though there was no contact between them. Sense him as if all of her senses were sharper, more sensitive than usual.

In the centre of the garden, largely hidden from view from her house and those surrounding, the glasshouse stood, dark and silent and inviting. The key turned easily within the lock, and as the door swung open the moonlight rippled and shimmered upon the glass of its panes.

She hesitated, that moment seeming to stretch. The wind whispered through the branches of the trees and the few leaves that still lingered on their witch-finger branches. And across her mind crept a tiny doubt, that she was making a mistake in bringing the enemy within her castle walls, and to this secret place above all others.

Linwood, the wind seemed to whisper. *Linwood,* calling his name.

She turned to him, looking up into the face of the handsome man standing so silently behind her. She knew the risk she was taking in bringing him here, the even bigger risk of their being alone. Dicing with the devil, indeed. Taking his hand in her own, she led him across the threshold into the glasshouse.

Chapter Eight

Venetia set the lantern down on an old oak work bench. Contrary to Linwood's expectation there were no flower pots, no trowels or gardening implements. Only the work bench, a heating stove and a broad day bed, in dark leather, that would not have looked out of place in an upmarket drawing room.

'No gardening,' he said.

'No gardening at all,' she confirmed with a secret smile. 'I come here most nights that I am not working, although I have been rather remiss of late...due to other distractions.'

He smiled at that. 'I have been a little distracted recently myself.'

'Only a little?' she asked.

He smiled again. 'I concede it is very much more than a little.'

She leaned back against the potting bench, watching him. 'I have never brought anyone here before. Not even Alice.'

The lantern was behind her so that her face was in shadow. The smell of night was in the air all around them—damp and cold and fresh.

'Then I am honoured, Venetia.'

The silence stretched between them but it felt natural and comfortable.

'This glasshouse is the reason that I took the house.' She surveyed the place with obvious tenderness. 'I think I fell in love with it from the very first moment I saw it.' She smiled, an inward smile, almost as if she had forgotten he was there. But then she returned her gaze to him. 'Have you worked it out yet? What I come here to do?'

'Escape?' he offered.

She smiled, more fully this time. 'I suppose there is something of that in it. But there is more. Take another guess.'

'Learn your lines.'

'You are not trying, my lord.'

He stepped closer. 'You truly wish me to guess your secrets?'

The tension and hints of darkness suddenly whispered between them.

She did not answer his question, only told him another truth. 'Many men have tried. None have succeeded.'

He smiled at the challenge. 'You have told me that you come here only at night and that it is always alone. There are no books or scripts, no candles or lanterns save the one you have brought to light our path. Therefore, you do not read or learn your lines here. And when I look around the key piece of furniture is a day bed on which you might lie in comfort.'

'Indeed.'

'You come here to…'

'To…?'

Their eyes met and held.

'To stargaze.'

She gasped her astonishment and then laughed. 'You are quite correct!'

'You are a secret astronomer, Miss Fox.'

'Hardly. I am ill educated, but I like to look at the stars, at their wonder and beauty and brightness.' She glanced up to the roof as she spoke and he found his gaze following, but all he saw was the reflection of the lantern and their own faces.

He leaned across and closed the lantern shutters, blinding its light, and rendering them in a darkness that was almost complete.

She did not move and neither did he. Just stood motionless and close while their eyes adjusted to the blackness that enveloped them together. And when they looked up again, the glass was not there, only the black velvet of the night sky and the brilliance of the diamond jewels studded within it.

He heard the sudden release of her breath, but whether it was in awe of the stars or that she had been holding it, he did not know.

'Is it not a wonder?' she asked with an innocence that was contrary to all of her usual polished sophistication.

'Indeed it is,' he said, and he was telling the truth, although it was not the stars to which he was referring. It was a wonder to see her like this. See the real woman beneath the mask she presented to the world. 'Look over there in the southern part of the sky—that is Pegasus.'

She tilted her head and he felt the brush of her hair against his with the movement and smelled her perfume. 'I cannot see it.'

'See the square shape of the four stars at the bottom?' He pointed.

'Oh, yes...' He could hear the smile in her voice. 'I have looked at those stars all these years and never knew what they were before.'

They stood silent and watching. And then she dropped

her gaze to his, as if she were weighing him up, and massaging a hand lightly against the nape of her neck as she did so. 'There is a more comfortable way to do this.'

He did not need to look at the day bed to know what she meant.

'To stargaze only,' she said, her voice the cool impenetrable Miss Fox once more. And then more gently, more honestly, 'You do understand what I am saying, Linwood, do you not?'

'Perfectly,' he replied, sensing the tension and debate within her.

He waited until she was settled upon the day bed before he lay down by her side, taking care not to touch her.

They lay in silence for a while, both looking only at the sky overhead and its myriad of stars.

'Now I see Pegasus more clearly,' she said.

'It is the autumn signpost in the sky.'

'Named from the mythological winged horse?'

'The very same—if you have a very good imagination and look at it upside down then you may just see the front of the horse.'

She tilted her head towards him as she stared up into the sky.

'The star right up there, the small bright one, is the North Star, by which travellers may guide their journeys,' he said.

'Ah, so that is the North Star. I thought it was supposed to be the brightest star in the sky.'

'It is a common misconception. There are many bigger and brighter stars, although not all that we see up there are stars, some are planets.'

'How interesting. Tell me more.'

'That little circle of stars beneath the Square of Pegasus

is part of Pisces—the two fish. The Circlet of stars represents one of their heads.'

'Which stars make up Virgo, the Virgin?'

'Virgo is not visible at this time of year. You will have to wait until spring to see its constellation. But that other group next to Pegasus and Pisces, see there…' he pointed to the stars '…is Aquarius, the water bearer.' She briefly touched a hand to his, following his gaze.

'Those five little stars clustered together are known as the Water Jar.'

'I see.'

He glanced across at her, watching her rapture. 'I enjoy the night sky, too, Venetia.'

'So it seems.' She rolled onto her side to look at him. 'When I was a little girl I used to look up at the stars through my tiny attic window. I always said that when I grew up I would have a house with a roof made of glass that I could lie in bed and view them all the better.'

'And you did.'

'Yes,' she said softly, and she smiled at him in a way that revealed this was something more important to her than just stargazing. In telling him this, in bringing him here, she was sharing something very private to her, something that seemed to go beyond the game they were playing. She watched him across the small distance of the daybed's pillow for a few seconds in silence before asking, 'How did you learn all of this?'

'At Eton. At Oxford. From my father's books.'

'You are a scholar.'

'No.'

She paused, studying him for a moment in silence before reaching a hand to his face and tracing her fingers against his cheek. 'You look like your father.'

He clenched his teeth to stopper the bitter reply.

'I could not help but notice that matters did not sit comfortably between the two of you the day we met him outside Gunter's. I thought it was because you were with me.'

'Why should that make a difference?'

She gave a tiny shrug of her shoulders and he saw the way the dark cloth of her cloak shifted to reveal the smooth white skin that lay beneath. 'Your father is an earl. You are his son. I am an actress.'

'I am not ashamed of you, Venetia. And who I choose to spend my time with is no business of my father's.'

'You sound angry with him.'

'Sometimes it turns out our fathers are not the great men we grow up believing them to be. We are a disappointment to them, and they to us. Or perhaps yours was different and I speak only with the bitterness of my own experience.'

She glanced away, a sudden uneasiness in her eyes. 'Matters between me and my father sat as uncomfortably as yours seem to do. He was very far from being a great man, although he thought that he was.'

'Was?'

'He is dead.'

'I am sorry.'

Her eyes studied his and there was the strangest expression in them.

'And your mother?' he asked.

'She died when I was ten years old.'

'I am saddened by your loss at such a tender age.'

'It was a long time ago. And I learned very quickly how to stand on my own two feet.'

'A gentleman country vicar and his lady wife who married beneath her.'

'You have been making more enquiries about me,' she teased, lightening the mood.

'I have.' He made no pretence at denial. 'Is it true?'

She laughed and it had a bitter ring to it. 'Hardly. Fantasy is so much more enticing than the truth, do you not think?'

'That depends,' he said. 'On what lies beyond enticement.'

She lowered her gaze, the sweep of black lashes feathering against the pallor of her cheek.

'Venetia.' Her name was soft and smooth as silk upon his lips, the intimacy of it making her remember the feel of those lips upon hers.

'Linwood…'

'Not Linwood,' he said softly and, reaching across, skimmed the pad of his thumb against her cheek in a single caress. 'My given name is Francis.'

She scanned those dark eyes, feeling the butterflies fluttering madly in her stomach. 'Given names are for families and close friends, and for lovers.'

'And what are we, Venetia?' There was a blunt honesty to the question that seemed to reach within and touch her.

She hesitated to reply, only held his eyes, not with bold seduction and power, but seeing something of the man beneath. 'I do not know.' All the madness that was rushing through her blood, the fast hard pound of her heart, the way her body came alive beneath his touch, his kiss. 'You are not what I expected.'

'And what was it that you expected?' he asked softly.

She reached her hands up, cupping them gently against the strong hard lines of his jaw, holding him there. 'Not this,' she whispered and placed her mouth against his in soft surrender. 'Never this.'

She kissed him gently, cautiously, afraid that the kiss would not be all that she remembered and even more afraid that the memory was true. Their lips teased together, touching, tasting, feeling, while their eyes clung together.

And then his mouth moved to take hers and she knew that her memory had not played her false. She closed her eyes and gave herself up to the kiss, and to him, yielding to the madness that was thrumming through her veins.

The scent of him, the feel of him, the taste of him, stripped away all of her pretence. He kissed her and the woman that met his kisses with passion and with need was all Venetia. Something in her sparked to life, something real, something that only he could fire. He was in her blood, in her heart, in her mind. She drank him in, revelling in the sensation, sinking into it, opening herself, allowing all her defences to crumble. Venetia had been kissed by men before, but not like this, never like this. It made her forget herself, made her forget who she was, who he was. There was only him, only this moment, only his mouth on hers, wooing and demanding both at once, firing a passion that only he awakened, and the overwhelming need for him.

She kissed him harder, faster, with all the rage of urgency that was surging through her. He pulled her into his arms and her body answered the call of his, cleaving to him, wanting him so much that it hurt. Her mind was spinning, her body quivering beneath the masterful caress of his hands upon her back, her breasts, her waist, her hips. She was breathless, reeling, dizzy with desire. The last thread of sanity dangled dangerously close to breaking. She placed her hands on his chest and broke her mouth free from his.

His eyes were black as the devil's and just as dangerous. Their gazes clung together, their breaths hard and fast, her breasts brushing his chest with every rise and fall.

'Do you see?' she whispered, staring into his eyes. She held him tight, knowing that were she to let go she would fall into this thing that was yawning between them.

'I do,' he said. His voice sounded as breathless as hers and he stroked a hand against her hair.

She was not acting. She was not playing a game. This felt more real than any other thing in her life. And much more powerful. She struggled to hold on to the vestiges of control, forcing herself to think of Robert, of Rotherham, and the fact that Linwood had put a bullet through Rotherham's head. She pulled herself free of him, knowing that all the while he touched her she could not think straight. She felt breathless, shaken, shocked by how much she wanted him. It felt more than physical, it was every aspect of him that drew her to him. And the more she came to know him did not dissuade her as it should, but, in contrast, served only to attract her all the more. It took every ounce of her willpower to draw the veil of Miss Fox over her and stop this before it went too far; all of her years of acting experience to feign a control and calmness she did not feel.

'I think that is quite enough stargazing for one night, Lord Linwood,' she said in something of Miss Fox's cool voice and got to her feet. But there was a breathlessness to her words that she could not completely disguise and inside her chest her heart was racing and her blood was rushing, and every part of her longed for every part of him. And Linwood looked at her with those dark dangerous eyes as if he knew.

Linwood glanced around the ballroom the next night at the members of the *ton* who mingled with the *demi-monde* in this world of fashion and frippery, without seeing them. He was thinking of Venetia and what had passed between them in the glasshouse. She had revealed something of her true self. Although she was a talented actress he had seen enough of her to tell the difference between when she was acting and when she was not. And he did not think that last night had been about acting. Last night there had been a vulnerability to her, an honesty, a degree of trust, in revealing those parts of herself that she kept hidden. She seemed genuinely shocked and confused by the searing attraction that existed between them, as if that had not been a part of the plan, if indeed there was anything of a plan between her and Clandon. The way she had looked at him as she uttered those words, a look that was nothing of artifice but open and real. *You are not what I expected.* He had thought of it all the night through. She was not what he had expected. None of this was what he had expected. He wondered what she would do were he just to confront her over Clandon, but he knew he could not risk tipping off Rotherham's son that he was wise to him, not when there was so very much at stake. And so he must play this game every bit as much as her—to control Clandon's suspicions, and because he was fascinated, and more, by the woman who was Venetia Fox.

'You are woolgathering, Lord Linwood.' Venetia's voice broke his reverie.

'Caught in the act,' he replied.

'In such a calculated gentleman? I do not think so.' Her lips curved ever so slightly in that small half smile, and her eyes were teasing. The open emotions of last night were gone. She was once more the seductive Miss Fox.

'I take issue with your estimate as to my character.'

'You should not.' She leaned closer as if confiding a secret, and he could smell the bittersweet scent of her perfume with its hints of the exotic and erotic. The scent of it was still upon last night's tailcoat hanging within his wardrobe. 'I like calculation in a man.'

'Really?' he asked quietly and held her gaze steadily. 'It did not seem that way last night, Venetia.'

He saw the faintest tinge of colour touch her cheeks and something falter in her eyes before she glanced away.

And when she looked at him again there was an iron resolve in her face. 'Let us go in to supper.'

He glanced across at the queue that was forming to go in for supper.

She raised an eyebrow. Her eyes were cool, almost challenging, but her mouth was sultry. 'I had a little private table set up for us in the conservatory.'

'I am privileged indeed.'

'More than you realise, Linwood,' she whispered in a voice that was like the sensuous stroke of silk and let him take her arm.

Together they left the main ballroom and headed into the adjoining conservatory. The doors were not closed and the piano still played, its soft lilt carrying through from the ballroom. Anyone might stroll in, if they so chose, but the plants and bushes and trailing vines, some of which were made of silk, lent the room a private secluded air, even if it was all of an illusion. And amidst all of the plants, by the side of a small fountain from which water ran in a lulling trickle, a small, round cast-iron table had been set for two. A large silver ice bucket sat in a stand by its side and contained within was a bottle of champagne. In the middle of the table, beside a silver casting of cockerel, was an opened bottle of claret.

She took her seat and only when she was settled did he take his. A footman appeared and poured first her champagne and then his, before disappearing as silently as he had arrived.

He ignored the champagne and lifted the claret, pouring two half-glasses and offering one to her.

She accepted with a smile, a genuine smile of amusement this time.

'Why do you order champagne, Venetia, when you do not drink it?'

'You are very observant. No one else ever notices.'

'Another part of the illusion?'

'One cannot have an actress who does not drink champagne.'

'Imagine the scandal if you were to demand tea instead.'

She laughed and he smiled, and the initial awkwardness of their meeting was gone, replaced with the affinity that was growing between them.

'A toast to new friends,' she said and held up her glass.

'To new friends,' he echoed and they chinked their two glasses in a touch, the fine crystal glasses lingering together too long before finally parting. Their eyes met across the table and held as they each drank the claret.

A footman's approach interrupted the moment. Linwood saw the fleeting expression of horror that crossed Venetia's face at the servant's whispered words. But then it was reined under her usual smooth control once more. The footman faded.

She got to her feet.

And he to his.

'I am afraid I must leave you for this evening, my lord. My presence is required elsewhere.'

'Bad news?'

'Yes.' She did not elaborate. She held out her hand for him to kiss and he took it in his own as if that was what he meant to do. But he did not kiss it.

'Let me come with you.' No matter how transient it had been, he had seen that look of horror and he felt a genuine concern at what might have caused it. He wondered if Clandon was blackmailing her.

She smiled and shook her head, withdrawing her hand

and turning away to leave as she did so. 'Thank you for your offer, but I must refuse.'

He said nothing more. Just stood there as she began to walk away. Three steps, three soft wiggles of those hips and then she stopped, hesitated for a moment as if thinking, before glancing back at him.

'It is a matter of some discretion. A…secret,' she said.

'I am good at secrets.'

'You are,' she admitted.

The silence stretched between them. Still she did not walk away.

Finally she relented. 'I would be glad of your company, Linwood.'

He felt a stab of both satisfaction and relief at her words.

Their leaving together when the night was so young did not go unnoticed. There were whispers and stares, but if Venetia was conscious of them she did not show it. She did not hurry across the ballroom, but he could sense her focus, her purpose, and he admired how smoothly and quickly she dealt with those who would have delayed her. Then they were out in the hallway, the footman delivering her cloak, which Linwood slid into place, and out of the door and into her waiting carriage.

The coachman seemed to know where to go even though she had not issued him with any instructions. The door closed behind them and they were off at a brisk pace, heading in the opposite direction to that which would lead them to the house in which Venetia Fox had made her home.

Chapter Nine

'What you see tonight, Linwood…the place to which we are going… My association with them is not widely known and I would prefer it remain that way.' Venetia's eyes held his.

'None shall hear of it from me.'

'Thank you.' She withdrew her gaze, shifting it to stare out at the dark shadowed buildings past which they rushed. There was a tiny furrow between her brows, as if she were preoccupied with concern.

She did not speak again. And neither did he.

The street lamps revealed enough to show him the direction they travelled. They journeyed on, leaving behind the wealth and elegance of Upper Grosvenor Street, travelling through the heart of the city and heading east through the banking area, rushing onwards until the streets narrowed and became more pot-holed, and the houses that lined the streets were the crowded slums of Whitechapel. Little wonder the celebrated Miss Fox had asked for discretion. Such surroundings were not conducive to her sparkle and glamour. He wondered just where the hell they were going and in what she was enmeshed. And for the second time that night he thought of Clandon.

The carriage slowed quite suddenly and halted outside a building that looked as dismal as the rest.

'We have arrived,' she said and pulled the deep black hood of her cloak to cover her head.

He could smell the stench of poverty in the street even before the footman opened the carriage door.

Part of Venetia wondered at the risk she was taking at bringing Linwood here, but another part felt it was the right thing to do. *Yielding confidences. Winning his trust.* She justified his presence as part of the game, but the truth was she was glad of having him with her to face this. And if he did speak of this night and betray her, then there was nothing so very much to be lost. No one could prove anything through the association. Her secrets would still be safe. She did not glance back at him, just walked on, knowing that he would follow.

The windows at street level that overlooked the pavement had been smashed. Great shards of glass lay like spun sugar across the pavement. She heard the crunch of some crumbs of it before Linwood took her arm, steering her free of it.

'The glass will pierce your slippers,' he murmured.

There was no need to rap on the knocker, for the door had been kicked in, the fresh gouges raw and pale in the darkness of the door frame. Venetia used the knocker anyway, giving two light taps, before pushing the door open.

'Oh, Miss Fox!' Lily's face was white, the lines of worry etched clear upon it. 'Thank God you're here! Sadie said we shouldn't disturb you till morning, but the door is busted and the windows, too, and I didn't know what else to do!'

'You did the right thing in sending for me,' she reassured Lily.

As they moved through the hall into the little parlour Venetia stopped and stared around her at the room that was barely recognisable. The furniture had been thrown around, the curtains torn from their poles, the pictures upon the walls and ornaments that had made this place a home smashed and broken.

'What happened?'

Lily shook her head. 'It was like this when I got back. Whoever they were, they knew where to find the money. It's gone. All of it.'

Venetia glanced at the surrounding devastation. The door creaked as the wind played against it and pushed within. The room was freezing, the grate black and dead with burnt-out ashes.

'Is anyone hurt?'

'Sadie. She was the only one here. The rest of the girls were out. Still are.'

'Where is Sadie now?'

'Upstairs in her room.' Lily's mouth tightened.

'How bad is it?' Venetia felt her stomach tighten with dread.

Lily's eyes slid to Linwood, as if only noticing him standing in the background for the first time, and then back to Venetia. Venetia saw the question in them and felt a *frisson* of guilt that she had brought him into this place of safety.

'He is trustworthy.' Her eyes met Linwood's across the room and, contrary to everything that she knew of him, it felt like the truth. Her heart gave a little spur at the admission, before she turned back to Lily.

Lily did not look persuaded, but she gave Venetia a nod. 'The animals took the goods by force and without paying, if you catch my drift. All four of them.'

Venetia felt herself blanch. 'Have you called the doctor?'

Lily shook her head. 'She won't see one.'

Venetia struggled to mask the horror from her face and the nausea that was swimming in her stomach. And then Linwood was by her side, his hand upon her arm, both reassuring and strengthening. 'Go to her. I will do what needs to be done down here.'

She hesitated, uneasy at leaving him down here alone, and afraid of what she would find upstairs.

'She needs you, Venetia,' he said.

She nodded, knowing he was right, and with a glance at Lily slipped away.

Sadie's physical hurts were minor, but Venetia knew that, however much Sadie told her she was all right, the mental scars of what had happened tonight would never leave her. It was the risk that every woman who sold herself ran, the nightmare which they all feared. But even though the nightmare had become a reality for Sadie, Venetia knew it would not stop the girl from selling herself again at some point in the future. It was why this house existed. It was the little she could do. She stayed with Sadie until there was a knock at the door and Lily appeared with a doctor.

'Your gentleman friend insisted upon it. Supplied the geld up front, too.'

It was the start of a very long night. Looking back at it, Venetia wondered how she could have got through it without Linwood by her side. They worked together, side by side with the women who returned, wearing their skirts short enough to show the red-flannel petticoats beneath. Sweeping up glass and destruction, fixing what they could. Linwood left and when he returned he had a team of joiners in tow, although God only knew where he had found them at this time at night. And in the lateness of the night they boarded the windows and patched up the front door.

* * *

Dawn was crawling across the sky, diluting the inky darkness in ever-lightening hues by the time Venetia and Linwood eventually left. The streets were empty, the rumble and roll of her carriage wheels loud in the silence.

She looked across the carriage at him. His waistcoat and shirt were marked. There was a rip beneath the arm of his fine dark green tailcoat, where he had been lugging furniture, and his boots were coated in dust and scuffs. The pale silk of her skirt was grubby, and the threads pulled, where she had been kneeling on floorboards. Her hair was dangling free from half of its pins. She scraped it back, feeling tired and dirty, angry and sad with what had happened at the refuge house in Whitechapel.

'How long have you been supporting them?' His voice was quiet and held nothing of judgement.

'A few years,' she said and hoped he would ask nothing further. She was so tired she doubted she could guard her answers carefully enough. 'It is a charity that helps women and their children should they wish a means of survival other than that of the oldest profession. And the house we have just left, a place that they may stay however long they choose.'

'A worthwhile cause.'

'I am glad you agree. There are many that do not.'

'How was the woman they…hurt?' She heard the slight catch in his voice. He sounded as concerned as Venetia felt.

'Her physical injuries are small enough. But who knows what scars such an ordeal leaves upon the mind? She will survive. Women are strong. They have to be.'

'Maybe not always as strong as they seem,' he said softly, and she knew it was not the women in Whitechapel of which he spoke.

Her eyes met his across the carriage. 'That is why they

need smoke and mirrors,' she admitted. And she smiled a sad smile. 'Thank you for coming tonight. Thank you for staying. And for everything that you did.'

'You are welcome, Venetia. I am glad that you allowed me to help.'

She glanced away, and when she looked at him again she spoke the truth that was in her heart, 'You are not the man London thinks you.'

'Nor you the woman.'

'Maybe we are two of a kind indeed,' she murmured the words he had spoken on a moonlit night upon a balcony.

He reached out his hand to her, offering it to her. And she accepted what he offered, folding her fingers around his as she moved across the carriage to sit by his side, their hands still entwined together. It felt right and good, reassuring and soothing after all the distress she had witnessed this night, and the uncomfortable memories that such places always stirred in her.

'I fear for those women.' She stared into the distance and saw not the carriage, but another familiar scene from across the years. 'The men who did this are probably employed by one of the local bawdy houses at which the women used to work.'

'Then there is a good chance that the Bow Street Runners will find the villains.'

She shook her head at his naivety. 'The constables will do nothing. This is not the first time there has been trouble, although it was not so bad the last time. The women are prostitutes, the law will do nothing to protect or help them.' Her voice was bitter, but she was too exhausted to disguise it. 'Forgive me,' she said. 'I do not mean to lecture you.' She leaned back against the seat and him. 'I fear I am too tired for politeness.'

His arm curved around her, gentle and supporting.

'Rape is a deplorable crime. The men who did this will be found, Venetia, and punished. On this occasion I am sure that the Bow Street office will be more alert to its duty.'

She was too tired to understand what it was he was saying. Her mind was slow and heavy with fatigue. His body felt strong and warm, and safe. She relaxed against him, gladdened by the feeling that he seemed to care, about justice for a poor woman who had been raped, and about her. 'I fear that you are wrong, but hope with all my heart that you are right.'

'Justice will be done, Venetia.'

'Will it?' His words were strangely bittersweet. Justice for the women. Justice for Rotherham. She did not want to think of the latter implication. Not right at this moment. She threaded her fingers through his and laid her head against his shoulder as the carriage made its way across a still-sleeping city and did not think, but just let herself be with him.

Venetia retired to bed as soon as she arrived home, but her sleep was not uninterrupted. She dreamed of Linwood.

In the dream she was standing in her bedchamber. It was daytime, she could tell by the way the cold stark light flooded in through the windows, but even so she was wearing her new black-silk evening dress, the one she had been saving for a special occasion, the one that would shock and stir scandal that could only do the theatre, and herself, good. Her hair was pinned up, a few curls arranged to trail artlessly against her neck and the edges of her face. She faced the man sitting on the edge of her bed. A man who was fully clothed, dressed all in black as if their outfits had been deliberately matched. A man who was silent, and whose ebony-dark eyes were filled with passion and with secrets.

'Do you want me?' she asked in a low sultry voice. And she did not know why the answer was so very important, just that it was.

Linwood gave no reply. He did not need to. She could see the answer in the way he looked at her, see it in the tension that ran through his body, hear it in the whisper of the air all around, and feel it in the atmosphere that strained between them.

Her gaze dropped to the pistol that she held in her hand, an old-fashioned duelling pistol just like her father's. It felt too big and heavy, but she held it still and true in its aim at his heart and did not let it waver. Her eyes moved back to his face.

Linwood did not look at the pistol, not even when she pulled back the cock ready to fire or when she moved her finger to rest lightly against the trigger.

'Linwood.' She said his name loud and clear and began to walk towards him. 'Linwood', again, this time softer, the word almost a caress upon her lips. She walked until there was no more distance between them, until the muzzle of the pistol nosed within the lapels of his jacket to press against the clean white linen of the shirt that covered his heart. And it seemed as she stood there she could feel the beat of his heart vibrate all the way through the length of the pistol, feel the slow steady thud in her hand and her heart.

He whispered a word, one solitary word. 'Venetia.' And then he leaned forwards and took her mouth with his. And the kiss changed everything. *He* changed everything. The pistol was no more. He kissed her and she yielded to him, to the need that had been growing within her since the very first moment they had met. His hands were on her breasts, on her hips, stripping away the barriers between them. Touching her in a way no one else could. Caressing her, kissing her until Venetia could not fight it any longer, until they were naked together, until she was pushing him back flat on to the bed, until they were rolling together in a tumble of limbs and the heat between her thighs was a pulsing inferno of need. She splayed her legs, opening herself to him, needing him, wanting him, straining for what only he could give her.

'Yes,' she whispered. 'Yes', when all through the years she had said no. Linwood's eyes, deep and dark and smouldering, stared into hers as he positioned himself between her thighs, the tip of him teasing against her, so tantalisingly close, the moment stretching to an eternity of longing.

'Francis,' she whispered his given name, her use of it finally admitting what they were to one another. 'Francis!' She cried it out loud, needing him, wanting him to take her and make her his.

She woke with a start, her heart pounding in a frenzy, her blood rushing wild and torrential. Her breath was ragged and fast and loud in the silent darkness of the bedchamber. The dream was still heavy and vivid upon her. It seemed so real, so very real that she craned her neck to stare around her, looking for the man from her dream. But the crack of silver moonlight showed nothing but her own bedchamber and a hearth on which the fire had long since died.

Her breath blew puffs of mist into the night-chilled air, but although beneath the heavy weight of the blankets and covers she was trembling it was not from cold. Quite the reverse. Her body was aflame and hungry with desire. As she shifted her nightdress rasped coarse against her swollen nipples. And between her thighs burned a need frightening in its strength. A throbbing. An ache. A yearning for the touch of a man with a handsome face, unsmiling, dangerous, with dark, dark eyes that spoke to her soul.

She touched where he would have, sliding a trembling hand between her legs, to the place that was slick and wet with desire. 'Francis,' she whispered as her finger touched, and her body's response was swift and unexpected. She gasped aloud, her body arching and exploding with a shimmering sunburst of sensation that took her beyond the curtain-dimmed loneliness of her bedchamber, soaring high to a place she did not know.

Her heart was racing when she returned to her body. The haze of desire cleared, leaving her with a cold, clear realisation. She rolled onto her side and hugged her arms around her, feeling guilty and ashamed and more alone than ever, because the boundaries between pretence and reality were blurred, and of that which was happening between her and Linwood she no longer knew what was play-acting and what was not. The man she was coming to know was not the one she had expected to find. To the man she was coming to know she was in danger of yielding all that she had sought through the years to protect... her body, her respect...and maybe even something that touched dangerously close to her affections. And that was something that Venetia could not allow to happen.

The next day seemed to go wrong from the very start. She overslept, then woke late with a headache, feeling tired and unrested following the long hours of wakefulness in the night. She accidentally caught the skirt of her dress and tore it, there was a problem with the range, which meant the cook had been unable to heat water let alone cook anything, and she could not find the pages containing her lines and notes on stage direction. As if that was not bad enough, one of the horses had gone lame in a leg so there was a surgeon to organise and then a rush to catch a hackney carriage to the theatre.

She arrived late to find Mr Kemble in a black mood and the whole cast waiting for her. She had trouble remembering her lines and everything was going from bad to worse when she saw the small wiry man down in the stalls talking to Mr Kemble. There was something about him, an air, a bearing, that gave away his official position before she saw him slip the dark wooden truncheon into an inner pocket of his jacket—a Bow Street Runner. The uneasiness whispered through her like a winter wind through a graveyard.

'Gentleman from Bow Street office to see you when you've got a minute, Miss Fox.' The stage hand spoke quietly enough, but she knew that his visit would spark the curiosity of the rest of the cast.

'Have him come to my dressing room.'

All she could think of was that Linwood had been found out, that he had been arrested, charged with the murder. She could feel her heart in her throat; hear the way it made her voice ring higher. The nervousness threaded though her pulse, making her feel sick. She did not let herself look at him, just focused her mind on the lines, speaking them loud upon the stage until somehow she got through the scene. It seemed too long and yet not long enough before she made her way from the stage through the narrow corridors that led to her dressing room.

The man was leaning against the wall beside her door. 'Mr Collins of the Bow Street office.' He stepped forwards, introducing himself and slipping his baton from his pocket to show her the crest fixed to it. 'I wonder if I might have a word, Miss Fox.'

'Of course.' She preceded him into the dressing room

and waited until he closed the door behind him before she spoke again.

'How may I be of assistance, officer?' She did not sit down, just leaned against the edge of her dressing table, her hands holding loosely to it.

'Oh, no, Miss Fox.' The wiry little man shook his head and blushed. 'Nothing like that. I came to let you know the good news. We've closed one of our top priority cases. One in which you have an interest, although the office understands the requirement for absolute discretion...' his eyes glanced at her with undisguised admiration '...when it comes to your involvement in the matter.'

Something writhed in Venetia's stomach, something black that felt a lot like dread. She gripped hard to the dressing-table edge, even while her mouth curved in a cool smile and she held the man's gaze with a brazen confidence that belied all that she was feeling. Waiting. And waiting for him to say the words.

'We've caught them.'

The blood was thrumming so loud in her ears that she almost did not hear the last word. *Them.*

'Got all four of them locked up snug in the cells at Bow Street.'

'All four of them,' she repeated and suddenly realised that he was not talking about Linwood.

'They won't be bothering any women in Whitechapel again. Your charity works are safe, Miss Fox.'

The relief made her almost light-headed. She sat down in the chair, the thoughts whirring in her head. 'How did you come to catch them so quickly?'

'It was the strangest thing. Fifteen years in the service and never seen anything like it before, miss. All four of them had an attack of conscience. Came to the office and turned themselves in. Gave a full confession and everything. No need for the unfortunate victim…' he glanced down at his notepad '…a Miss Sadie Smith, I believe, to give evidence in court.'

'That is good news indeed, Mr Collins.'

'And it seems there will be no need to mention your association with the charity.'

'Even better.' She smiled. 'Thank you for coming to tell me.'

He smiled in return and gave a bow before leaving. The door closed after him.

Venetia did not move from her chair. Amidst the retreat of his heavy-booted footsteps along the corridor it seemed she could hear the echo of Linwood's words. *The men who did this will be found, Venetia, and punished. On this occasion I am sure that the Bow Street office will be more alert to its duty.* And she wondered at Linwood's far-reaching influence and how it might sway the solving of a crime— for good or for bad. It was a reminder of what Linwood was capable—and that chilled her, as did the realisation of her feelings when she had thought him caught. She stared into the peering glass and felt her blood run cold. It was a much more dangerous game than she had realised. She must take time away from him, must regroup and focus. He was a murderer, the man who had killed Rotherham, and she was in this to bring him to justice.

Chapter Ten

Venetia deliberately did not see Linwood for three days following Mr Collins's visit, by which time she had strengthened her resolve and cleared her head somewhat of the confusion of feelings surrounding him. She was shopping that day when she saw the two women walking in their direction on the opposite side of the street. She knew almost immediately who they were. The matron dressed severely in purple was Lady Misbourne, Linwood's mother, and the young, blond-haired woman by her side must be his sister, Lady Marianne, or Mrs Knight as she had only recently become in what had been a scandalously sudden marriage.

She studied the two for a moment, so clearly mother and daughter despite the differences between them. The older woman was taller, with a body thickened by the years. Her demeanour held an air of superiority and snobbery, and her face a faded beauty marred by weakness. Lady Marianne was smaller than her mother, a little pocket diamond as the gentlemen would have said. The women were engaged in conversation, Lady Misbourne smiling indulgently at something that her daughter had just said.

She knew the moment that the two women saw her.

Lady Misbourne's expression froze in horror, before she issued a curt instruction to her daughter.

'Avert your gaze, Marianne. This instant. We do not even see that woman's presence.' The words told Venetia that they were aware not only of who she was, but also of her association with Linwood.

Contrary to her mother's command, Lady Marianne did not look away. She was as fair as Linwood was dark, petite and very pretty. And from this distance her eyes looked as black as her brother's. There was nothing of condemnation in that gaze, only curiosity and considered appraisal.

'Marianne!' her mother snapped again and Venetia could see the outrage on Lady Misbourne's face.

But Lady Marianne did not appear to be ruffled in the slightest. She held Venetia's gaze, before turning her head to the front and walking on at the same unhurried pace, despite all her mother's consternation.

Venetia saw Lady Marianne again that evening, across the dance floor of the ball she was attending with Linwood. The days apart from him had fortified her confidence. Tonight she felt her usual poised, self-possessed self. In defiance of what had gone before between her and him—in the glasshouse and in the carriage after Whitechapel—or maybe even because of it, she wore the black-silk evening gown, so scandalously seductive in its cut and fitting. Every lady's eye was frowning upon it, every gentleman staring open-mouthed and drooling when their ladies looked away. And Linwood, well, she had seen the way his eyes watched her with such dark possession. It was her ultimate weapon. It gave her strength, to resist and to remember all that this game was about. She smiled and turned her attention to Linwood's sister.

By the girl's side stood a very tall, dark-haired man who,

by the subtleties of the body language between them, Venetia knew must be her husband. Lady Marianne had not snubbed her in the street, nor did she snub her now, even if every other lady of quality here was doing so. Their gazes met across the floor, fleeting and yet there just the same. Linwood saw his sister and her husband, too, his gaze sliding from the younger woman across the floor back to Venetia.

And even though the expression on his face was more closed than ever she knew that he had not expected Lady Marianne's presence. He showed not one sign of embarrassment, although the situation could be nothing other for him. The presence of his sister and his...inamorata. The word whispered a tingle down her spine that she deliberately ignored. It was hardly a fitting description of what she was to Linwood, but it was the impression that the *ton* was labouring under.

'You did not know your sister would be here.'

'I did not.'

'A trifle awkward for you...and for her,' she murmured.

Linwood said nothing, but she saw the tiny betraying flex in the line of his jaw. She should be glad of it, revelling in it, using the tactic to her best advantage. But when his eyes met hers she saw beneath the strong silent guise and it was not gladness or a sense of triumph that she felt but the uneasiness of his discomfort as surely as if it were her own.

'Linwood...and the divine Miss Fox.' Razeby's cheerful voice broke the moment as he sauntered up.

'Razeby.' Linwood gave a curt inclination of his head.

'If you will excuse me for a moment, gentlemen.' She drew her eyes from Linwood, glad of the interruption. 'I must powder my nose.'

She threaded her way through the crowd, smiling in

amusement at the shocked disapproving stares from the *ton*'s matrons and the wistful lascivious ones of their husbands. Linwood would certainly be black-marked for bringing her here, she thought. That he had defied their wrath to have her here with him was not something that she wished to dwell upon. Although the room was crowded a path opened up before her, some ladies and even the odd gentleman turning their backs to her. Venetia was not bothered in the slightest. She was well used to it; she was, after all, an intruder here in a place that was their territory. They would equally well have been just as unwelcome in the *demi-monde*.

When she walked into the retiring room the two matrons in there herded their young charges out, scowling, noses in the air, while the girls tried to steal surreptitious glances at the scandalous woman in their midst. The door closed with a resounding slam just in case she was not aware of their disapproval at her audacity to invade their world.

She had no need to use the chamber pots behind the screens. Instead, she stood before the large peering glass that had been set up within the room and reminded herself of what she had spent the past three days thinking. There was an attraction between Linwood and herself; she could no longer deny it. But what she felt for him was lust. And lust, no matter how strong, could be conquered. She was not some weak-minded, feeble-kneed woman to let herself be dangled like a puppet from the fingers of any man, and especially not Linwood. He had murdered Rotherham. The only reason she was here by his side tonight was part of this game to lure him into revealing the truth. There were questions to be asked, a tongue to be loosened, a murderer to be caught.

She fixed her hair and, removing a small pot of rouge from her reticule, applied a little to her lips.

The door opened.

Venetia did not even glance round, expecting the huff of disapproval and the slam, but there was only the quiet click of the door closing and the soft rustle of silk.

Within the peering glass, Venetia's eyes slid from her lips to the space behind her and saw Linwood's sister.

Lady Marianne did not look surprised to find her here. Their eyes held for a moment before she walked to stand by Venetia and share the peering glass. The reflected Lady Marianne smoothed a hand over the pale pink silk of her skirt. Venetia finished applying the rouge to her lips.

'So you are the famous Miss Fox.'

'And you are Lady Marianne.' Venetia offered the rouge pot to the girl with a slight arch of her eyebrow.

'Thank you, but, no,' Lady Marianne declined most graciously.

'Lord Linwood's sister,' said Venetia.

'I own that privilege.'

'I do not think your brother would approve of you talking to me.'

'Probably not.' Marianne smiled.

The two women looked at one another. Lady Marianne had the same eyes as her brother, eyes that showed a huge depth of complexity beneath the surface.

'But you make him happy when there has been much to cause him unhappiness. And so I approve of you, as long as you do not hurt my brother, Miss Fox.'

There has been much to cause him unhappiness. Lady Marianne's words seemed to catch at her. She brushed them aside, telling herself not to be so foolish. 'I am sure that your brother is more than capable of looking after himself.'

Lady Marianne gave the tiniest shake of her head. 'He is rather better at looking after others. But then I suspect you might know that already...' she paused '...since you are in love with him.'

'Lady Marianne—' Venetia stopped herself just in time.

'I recognise the way you look at him.'

'Really?' Lady Marianne's calm certainty irked her. The girl had no idea of the way it was between women like her and men like Linwood, even were the illusion that the *ton* thought true.

'Yes...' Marianne paused. 'Promise me you will not hurt him.'

She turned to the girl with a clever set down ready upon her lips, but there was something in Marianne's expression that she could not bear to crush. Instead, she gave a nod of her head. 'I should return to the ballroom. It would not do you good if it was realised that we had been in here together.'

Marianne smiled warmly. 'I do believe you have a concern for my reputation.'

Venetia left before Marianne saw anything more of the truth on her face.

Within the ballroom Razeby was still talking to Linwood.

'I seem to have developed something of a headache,' she said without any attempt at making it sound convincing. 'I wonder, Lord Linwood, if I might prevail upon you to escort me home.'

'But of course, Miss Fox.' Linwood's eyes were on hers; his face was serious, betraying not a single flicker of emotion.

She let a little smile tease around her lips and she held his gaze with a boldness that had the ripple of a whisper around them.

'If you will excuse us, Razeby,' he said.

The marquis raised his eyebrows and grinned, giving Linwood a knowing look.

She rested her hand lightly in the crook of Linwood's arm, as demure as any debutante, and together they left the ballroom.

When they were alone in her carriage and on their way along the road, he looked at her through the light of the flickering street lamps.

'Thank you, Venetia.'

'I am sure I do not know what you mean.'

He continued to hold her gaze and smiled, a real smile that transformed his face, and she felt her heart expand and flutter in her chest. She knew that he knew the truth, that she had left to spare his sister the embarrassment that their both being there was bound to cause, even if she had dressed it up as something else.

'She has the same eyes as you.'

'But a more tender heart.'

She thought of the night they had spent together in Whitechapel, of how he had cared about justice for a poor woman, how he had cared for her in the carriage afterwards and all that she had learned of him that vied against the terrible crime he had committed. 'I am not so very sure of that, Linwood,' she said softly.

He smiled again and the carriage rolled on towards King Street.

Linwood saw her again the next evening, in accordance with the handwritten note that had been delivered to him that same afternoon inviting him to dinner at her home. He had felt the heat curl in his stomach just reading it, at the thought of being alone with her in so private a place and all that such an invitation might mean.

The dining room of her house had that same elegance and sophistication as Venetia herself. The walls were a pale soft beige, the dressings all in matching caramels and taupes, creams and gold. Understated, tasteful, yet with a quality and class that many aspired to and few achieved. The long dining table was mahogany, carved by the hand of a master craftsman, the Turkey carpet thick and plush beneath the tread of his shoes. The fireplace was an Adams, an elegant design, inspired by the Doric columns of a bygone age. Above it was a large gilt-framed mirror and, on either side, a crystal-dropped wall sconce with a cluster of three candles. Opposite the fireplace was a large bow window, its cream curtains over-sewn with pale gold stripes, shutting out the rain and cold of the dark autumn night. On one of the walls he noticed a small Rembrandt. The lighting in the room was an unusual white-branched chandelier, hung with faceted crystals. It was lightweight compared to the heavy designs so currently in vogue, a combination of elegance and daring that was like that of Venetia herself, but then Venetia Fox was a woman who set fashions rather than followed them.

Linwood had thought of nothing other than Venetia in all of the past days. Whatever else she was, this attraction between them was real and solid, and escalating in ways he had not imagined. He had never wanted a woman as he wanted her. He had never wished to know one as he wished to know her. The desire was more than physical. He liked her. He admired her. He even respected her, his opponent in this game. A woman of courage and unflinching nerve, of confidence and strength, yet beneath it there was soft-ness and compassion and vulnerability. There was a con-nection between them, a strange bond that he had not felt before. She felt it, too. He could see it in her eyes, feel it in the way her body leaned in to his, hear it in her voice. The game was immersing them both. And he embraced it.

He waited until she took her seat at the head of the table, before taking his at the foot. Ten feet of solid polished mahogany stretched between them.

'Is it your own décor or that which came with the house?'

'All my own.'

'You have exceptional taste.'

She dipped her head in a tiny acknowledgement and her mouth curved in a smile.

'I could not help but notice the Rembrandt.' The painting was worth a fortune, more than even the highest paid and successful of all actresses could afford.

'It was a gift.'

'From an admirer?' He thought of Clandon and felt that same wariness and anger, but even Rotherham's bastard son could not have stretched to buy such a thing. And then he remembered Razeby's talk of Arlesford and Hunter, of Monteith and York.

'From my father.'

'Not a country vicar at all, then.'

'No.' She glanced away and he sensed her unease over the subject.

They fell silent as Albert and the footmen arrived, bringing an array of silver serving dishes to set upon the table between them. Two footmen remained, standing smartly against the wall, eyes fixed front.

'I hope you are hungry, Francis,' she said and met his eyes directly once more. It was the first time she had used his given name, and he understood its significance.

'Ravenous, Venetia,' he replied, but his eyes were not on the food, only on her.

She smiled as she helped herself to a variety of dishes.

Linwood waited until she had completed her selection before making his. 'The food is excellent.'

'I shall pass on your compliments to my cook.'

They talked of easy things, things that were comfortable, and over which they seemed to have much agreement. They talked and ate, while the footmen topped up their glasses with fine wine. There was no pretence of champagne when it was just the two of them.

It seemed too soon that the food was eaten.

The plates were emptied, the cutlery abandoned upon them. They looked at one another across the length of the table.

'Shall we retire to the parlour for a drink?'

'I would like that, Venetia.' He followed where she led, watching the hypnotic sway of her hips, smelling the subtle scent of her perfume in the air.

The parlour was a small room at the back of the house, furnished for comfort and privacy rather than show, but still with her recognisable stamp of elegance.

There was a small bookshelf, a proper desk rather than a lady's writing bureau, and a sofa and matching armchair positioned before a roaring fire. It was tidy enough, but not pristine as the other rooms had been. There were letters and newspapers piled upon the desk, a collection of pens beside them, a romance novel left abandoned on the table by the decanter and a newspaper balanced on the arm of the chair by the fire, as if she had been reading it earlier in the day. The whole room felt snug, warm, private, providing yet another glimpse into the life of the woman beneath the mask of the actress.

They were alone, no sign of the servants. He closed the door behind him.

'Brandy?' she asked.

He gave a nod. 'Thank you.'

She poured two glasses and passed one to him, lifting the other herself.

'To friends, Francis.' She raised her glass and held his gaze.

'Friends, Venetia.' He supposed that they were, of a sort, even if they were opponents, too.

They touched their glasses together and let them linger a moment before drawing away.

The brandy was smooth and mellow upon his tongue, as expensive as any in his father's cellar. He watched her take a sip, watched her swallow it down, her every action unmistakably feminine in contrast to the masculinity of the drink.

'Brandy, but not champagne?'

She smiled. 'Are you shocked? Rest assured, I do not normally invite gentlemen to dinner, let alone take brandy with them.' She moved to sit in the small armchair closest to the fire.

'Then I am the first?'

There was a sober expression in her eyes before she nodded. 'Contrary to what the world may think.' The knowledge pleased him more than it should have.

'Why not any of the others?'

'An unnecessary question.'

'Not to me.'

Her fingers toyed with the stem of her glass where it balanced on the arm of the chair, but her eyes, when they met his, were bold. 'Maybe the question you should be asking is why you?' Then she looked away, reaching to set her glass down upon the small table and inadvertently knocking the newspaper balanced on the chair's arm to the floor.

She bent to retrieve it, but Linwood was there first, their fingers tangling together against the crackle of paper. Their eyes met. Desire pulsed and throbbed between them. He stroked a thumb against her fingers and felt her hand open beneath his. Her eyes seemed to grow darker. He felt the tiny shiver that rippled through her, saw the way her lips parted slightly before she lowered her gaze and slowly withdrew her hand from his.

They rose together, their breathing in unison.

'The London Messenger,' he said.

'Your own newspaper.'

He gave a nod of acknowledgement and glanced down at the page she had been reading.

'The murder of Rotherham,' she said.

'Has done wonders for the paper's circulation,' he said and knew that the game had just racked up a notch. He kept his voice calm and steady, as if the subject matter meant nothing to him.

'That seems a harsh take.'

'I am a harsh man. And I have made no pretence of my feelings regarding Rotherham.'

'You have not,' she agreed. She gestured to the newspaper article. 'It makes no mention of the fire that destroyed his house.'

'Little wonder. The fire was three years ago.'

'Three years. How precise your memory is, Francis.' She was a worthy opponent, indeed. He knew where this was leading.

'Very precise.'

'One might wonder as to why.' She watched him.

'It is not every night that a duke's pile is razed to the ground. It was a spectacular blaze…by all accounts.' Thrust and parry.

The tension hummed between them. They were dicing closer to the edge than ever before.

She paused and in that tiniest of silences was the roar

of danger and desire. He knew the question that was coming next.

'Did you witness it?' she asked.

'You are very interested in Rotherham, Venetia,' he said softly.

'Is not everyone?' She held his gaze; watching him as carefully as he watched her. 'And you have not answered my question.'

'Half of London witnessed it,' he said.

'What sort of man burns another's home to the ground, and a duke's mansion at that?'

He thought of all the darkness of the past, and of Rotherham slumped dead across his desk with a bullet in his brain. He thought of Clandon's suspicions, and of the questions that were now being asked about Rotherham's murder. And he knew what he must do. He could see the flutter of the pulse in her neck, the dilation of the pupils in her eyes, each and every long dark lash that lined them. He stepped closer, moved his mouth to her ear. She made no move, stood as still as a statue, while all that was between them struggled and strained in the hiss of silence for release.

'A man like me,' he whispered. Her breasts rose and fell a little faster. He heard the soft quickening of her breath. 'But then you have known that all along, have you not, Venetia?'

She nodded as if she did not trust herself to speak. Her lips parted slightly. 'And the rest of it…?' Her chest held still along with her breath.

The air was so tense that it almost crackled.

He shook his head, but did not clarify if it was a denial of guilt or a refusal to answer the question. 'Let us not talk of the rest of it tonight.'

She released the breath she had been holding in a shaky

gasp. They stared at one another without a word, before she moved to stand before the fire, looking into the flames that flickered warm and bright upon the hearth.

In the silence he could hear the crackle of the coal and the slow tick of the clock on the mantel. It clicked forwards and the chimes sounded for the hour.

His eyes moved along the line of the mantelpiece, skimming over the expensive ornaments, drawn to the one that seemed out of place. It was a small vase, cream with pink flowers and green leaves painted upon it. Cheap and brash, pretty enough, but the kind that were sold on the penny stalls. And, moreover, it was in a poor state. A crack ran down its body and there were two chips in the rim, one small and one large. Both showed the terracotta of the clay beneath. It was the one single object that looked curiously out of place in the beauty and elegance of Venetia Fox's house.

They did not speak of the enormity of what was happening between them, of the layers of truth that masked deception and what lay beneath.

'It was my mother's vase,' she said without looking at either him or the vase. 'My grandmother, whom I never knew, bought it for her when she was a child. It is the only thing I have left of her.'

'It must be very precious to you.'

'It is.' There was the resonance of such sadness and regret in her voice that he felt something tighten in his chest.

She turned to him then.

They both knew what this was about—Rotherham. The golden light of the flames danced on her face. And there was something in her eyes, something behind all the sophistication and dangerous game they were playing with one another, something that seemed to reach inside of him and stroke against his soul.

He reached his hand to her, threaded it through her hair and angled her face to his. 'Too far for you, Venetia?' he murmured.

'On the contrary, not far enough,' she whispered, his eyes scanning hers.

She dropped her gaze to his lips before raising it once more to his eyes. And in them he could see the same need, the same longing as raged inside of him. Outside the rain pelted hard against the window, rattling loud as hailstones against the glass. There was the howl of the wind and the sway of the curtains that had been drawn shut across the windows. But they only had eyes for one another.

He lowered his face to hers and kissed her with the passion that had been smouldering the whole of this night. And in reply he felt all that was in her rise to meet him. And it felt like coming home. In some deep way that made no sense she was his destiny; this woman who knew her power over a man, who was yielding to him even as she enslaved him further. He plucked the pins from her hair, letting the long, dark, glossy lengths tumble free, running his fingers through its silken lengths as he had done so often in the erotic dreams that haunted his nights since meeting her.

He felt her hands slide against the nape of his neck, felt them thread through his hair as she returned his kiss with the same ardent passion that was throbbing through his blood. He slid his hands up over the bodice of her dress, over her hips, tracing the hourglass curve into her waist and back out again to the swell of her breasts, so white against the dark red silk that contained them. With one hand he held her, with the other he ran his fingers over her breast, moulded his hand to it, squeezing it gently and feeling her arousal.

'No corset…again,' he whispered against her mouth.

'I never wear one,' she answered in a breathless whisper. He found the bud of her nipple through the layers of silk and rubbed his thumb against it. She gasped and arched, driving her breast all the harder into his hands. He held her close, his hand against her back, while he worked the same attention on her other breast.

His hand possessed her breast as his mouth slid to her chin, to the slender edge of her jaw, so fine and so feminine, and lingered there before following down the column of her neck. She let her head drop back, exposing her neck to him all the more until he found the spot where her pulse throbbed and raced and thudded beneath his tongue. He licked her there, sucked her there, grazed his teeth gently against her, while his hand and his fingers and his nails emulated each action against her breast. He could feel her breath hot and hard against the side of his temple, hear the way it shook and trembled in her throat. He took her mouth again, kissing her lips before drawing back to look into her eyes. Their breaths came in unison, louder than the wind and the rain and the tick of the clock, masking all save the beat of their hearts. And all that was between them, that had always been between them, passion and desire and heat and need, rattled at the chains in which they had sought to bind it.

He reached his hand to the short sleeve of her dress, where it hugged her shoulder and arm. His fingers lingered there, poised against the edge of dark silk as he met her eyes again. Her breath was so ragged that he could hear it loud in the room. Keeping his gaze locked on hers, he moved his fingers slightly, sliding them beneath the silk to the skin beneath.

Her breath gave a tremble. She swallowed and wetted her lips.

He slid the sleeve lower, exposing the white skin of her

shoulder in full. His mouth touched where his fingers had been. He kissed there, then kissed the hollow between her collarbones. And as he did she kissed the top of his head, then drew his face up to hers.

'Francis,' she whispered and kissed his mouth. They kissed and he unfastened the hooks at the back of her dress until the bodice loosened and gaped, revealing the top of a thin white-silk shift which hugged her body. His hands traced over the shift, exploring her breasts as his mouth and hers mated again and again.

He slid the dress to tumble down her legs to the floor around their feet. She stood there, the thin white silk moulded to every contour of her body, masking her final nakedness from him. He ripped it open and it slithered with a soft whisper to land on top of the discarded dress. He cupped the curves of her buttocks, revelling in the feel of her before he lifted her to him and backed her flush against the wall beside the fireplace. She fastened her legs around him, her warm, moist core against his erection, their coupling prevented only by the barrier of his breeches and drawers.

'Venetia,' he whispered.

She kissed her name from his lips, stroked his hair from his face, the hard line of his jaw before kissing him again.

'Francis.' The pupils of her eyes were huge and dark. She was as breathless and lost as he.

He lowered his mouth, taking her breasts in his mouth, feasting upon each one in turn, driving them both on to what had always been inevitable from that first moment on the balcony.

'Venetia.'

His face came up to hers, his lips taking hers. He loosed a hand to find the buttons on the fall of his breeches, desperate to free himself and plunge the heat of his length into her, needing to love her, to make her truly his. He thrust against her, pressing her against the wall with a thud as she clutched him to her. From the corner of his eye he saw the flicker of movement and reacted instinctively to catch the small battered vase that meant so much to her as it fell from the mantelpiece.

He opened his hand between them and showed her the vase that lay there. 'Caught just in time,' he said.

She stared at the vase, with an expression of shock. Something of the shock was still in her eyes as she raised them slowly from the vase to look at him.

'Caught just in time.' Her whispered echo held an undertone of horror. He felt her withdrawal from him before she moved a single muscle of her body. She freed herself, slipped from his arms and carefully set the vase back in its place upon the mantelpiece before pulling on her dress to cover her nakedness and turning to face him.

He stared in her eyes, trying to fathom the sudden change in her. But she was looking at him with that cool seductive look that was her guard, the passionate unbridled woman he had held in his arms only moments earlier was gone.

'Venetia…' he started to say.

But she placed a finger against his lips. 'You may use my carriage. Goodnight, Linwood.' She rang the bell upon the little table.

'Linwood?' he said with a quietness that did not mask the anger beneath it.

For a second her gaze faltered, but only for a second. The small half smile did not touch her eyes.

By the time her butler appeared in response to the bell Linwood's breeches were fastened once more.

He met Venetia's eyes one final time, then, without another word, turned and walked away.

Chapter Eleven

As soon as the door closed behind him the smile fled Venetia's face. She squeezed her eyes shut as if that could block out what had just happened between them, all the confusion of emotions that were roaring through her, and listened to the receding tread of his footsteps down the stairs and across the marble tiles of the hallway. She heard the murmur of Albert's voice, the quiet opening and clos-ing again of the front door, and she could not help herself. She moved to the window, lifted the edge of the curtain to look down on to the street and watch him as he walked out into the rain. He glanced up to the window at which she stood, meeting her gaze for a moment, the expression of that handsome face as closed and dark and dangerous as the night she had first met him. She felt a heat rise in her cheeks, felt a wash of shame and regret and, beneath it all, something else that she did not want to admit. With-out waiting for her carriage he turned and walked away into the night, and as he did she saw the glint of the silver wolf's-head walking-cane handle in his hand. She knew she should let the curtain drop and turn away, but she just stood there and watched him until his figure receded and eventually merged with the darkness.

There was an uncomfortable squirm in her stomach and a dull heavy ache in her chest. She let the curtain fall back into place before she sagged against the adjacent wall. Her eyes moved to find the little chipped and broken vase upon the mantelpiece. She walked towards it and, as she reached the rug before the fireplace, felt the press of hairpins through the thin soles of her slippers. She stopped and looked down at the dark pins scattered over the pale sea of the carpet. Carefully, she gathered each one, her fingers moving over them soft as a caress, knowing that his had been the last touch upon them. She did not attempt to remedy her hair, just left it long and tumbling over her shoulders, and sat the small pile of pins on top of the mantelpiece beside her mother's vase. Her fingers reached to gently trace against the vase. *Just like her mother.* The words taunted through her head. She let her hand fall away and squeezed her eyes shut, balling her hands to fists, catching her breath. Never. But when she opened her eyes she was looking directly at the wall against which Linwood had pressed her and it seemed she could still feel the sweet caress of his hands, feel the heat and passion and tenderness of his mouth.

He made her forget all of her rules, made her forget who he was and what he had done. He had just admitted to her that he was responsible for the destruction of Rotherham's house. He was the man who had fired the bullet into Rotherham's head. Rotherham, as she always thought of him. Her father. And what kind of woman wanted a man who was capable of such things? Because she did want him. Wanted him so much that she ached in body and mind and spirit. She was fooling herself if she called it lust. Deep in her gut, in her very bones, she knew that what lay between them was much more than straightforward attraction.

He was clouding her judgement, swaying her from all that made her who she was. But when she looked in Linwood's eyes, she did not see a murderer, she saw a man who understood, a man that did not play by society's rules; she saw quiet defiance. He kept all of his emotions contained, controlled, and yet she had the feeling that he would move heaven and earth to do what had to be done. A man like herself. With as many secrets. A kindred spirit. Things with Linwood were spiralling dangerously out of control. She could no longer trust herself.

She clamped a hand across her mouth, afraid not of Linwood, but of herself. Just the thought of him made her pulse throb and her blood rush and her heart fill with yearning. When he touched her she was lost. The danger was too great to continue. She knew what she was going to have to do. It was fortuitous, indeed, that tomorrow was Tuesday.

Her eyes flickered again to the small battered vase. Maybe her mother was looking after her after all, better from beyond the grave than she had ever done in life.

Venetia's rehearsal at the theatre the next afternoon was the worst she could remember. She forgot lines, missed cues and could not focus. She could see the way the rest of the actors were looking at her. A worried-looking Mr Kemble called a break.

Alice followed her into the dressing room, closing the door behind her. 'What's wrong, Venetia?'

'Nothing is wrong,' she said, facing her friend squarely and letting a small careless half smile play across her lips as if she were still in control of her emotions. But she was lying. What was wrong was what was happening between her and Linwood. She could think of nothing else.

Alice's eyes scanned her face, with concern. 'You look like you haven't slept.'

'I slept like a baby.' Another lie.

'It's Linwood, isn't it?'

Her heart jumped just at the mention of his name. It took every last shred of willpower to maintain a calm expression and to hold Alice's gaze with her usual confidence. 'You are obsessed with Linwood, Alice.' But in truth it was Venetia who held that obsession.

'Venetia…' Alice sighed softly '…I'm worried about you.' She took Venetia's hand in her own. 'I've never seen you like this before. Please tell me what's troubling you?'

She only wished that she could. She shook her head and smiled to gentle the refusal. 'I am just a little out of sorts. It is my time of the month.' More lies upon lies. So many that she did not know what was real and what the lie any more. 'I will take a couple of days off and I will be better when I come back.'

Alice gave a nod. 'I've been too caught up with myself and Razeby. I'll come round tonight. We can have a good old chat.'

Venetia shook her head. 'Another night. When it is over.' This game of entrapment that was raging out of control between her and Linwood.

Alice looked at her strangely, as if she knew there was something more going on with her friend than the monthly female bodily function, but she did not probe with more questions, she just gave her a hug. 'I'm here for you if you need me, Venetia. Just remember that.' She pulled on her shawl. 'I don't like leaving you here alone like this.'

'Go,' said Venetia. 'Razeby will be waiting for you. Besides, I have plans of my own.'

'If you're sure…?'

'I am sure.'

The door closed behind her.

Venetia waited a few moments sitting there at the dressing table, with no costume to change or paint to remove. The theatre was silent, she knew that the oil lights at the front of the house would already be turned off and the little corridor outside the dressing room would soon be in darkness. She looked at her reflection in the peering glass and saw the uncertainty in her eyes and the smudges of sleeplessness that sat beneath them, and the pallor of her cheeks naked without a touch of her usual artifice to add colour to them. Wrapping her long shawl around her, she turned off the lamps in the dressing room and made her way to the stage door of the theatre.

Her carriage was waiting at the edge of Hart Street. The late afternoon was as dark and heavy as if night was already upon them. She stood there for a moment, before Robert stepped silently from the shadows and they climbed into her carriage.

'How does our plan progress?' He looked across the carriage at her.

'My job with Linwood is done. There is no need for me to see him again.'

Robert leaned forwards in his seat, a sharp look upon his face. 'It is barely begun. We agreed you would court him for three months, to find out all there is to know of the snake.'

And now that the time had come to tell him, the words seemed to stick in her throat and the hand of guilt lay heavy upon her shoulder. But she knew she could continue no longer in this game. She forced herself on. 'I have accomplished what we set out to do.'

His eyes narrowed as if he could not believe what she

was telling him. He stared at her more closely. 'What do you mean, Venetia?'

She swallowed, but no amount of swallowing would shift the great lump lodged in her throat. She had to tell him. She had to end it. 'Linwood was responsible for the fire that destroyed Rotherham's house.'

'He admitted it to you?' Robert's eyes widened, his brows lifted high.

She nodded, and could not bear to see the glee in his eyes. She stared down at her hands, fiddling with the buttons on the wrist of her glove, and could feel nothing of her brother's gladness and excitement.

He blew out a sigh of incredulity. 'I can scarce believe it.' He stared into the distance, smiling and stroking his chin before turning his gaze to her. 'And the murder...?'

She shook her head.

'I suppose he's hardly likely to admit pulling the trigger to the woman he's trying to bed.'

Yet her brother did not know how it was between her and Linwood. She feared that Linwood would tell her. And feared even more that it would make no difference to what was unfolding. The game would play out to the inevitable conclusion, if she let it. 'Why not?' She looked him in the eyes. 'He admitted arson, why not murder?'

'It is not the same thing, as well you know.'

'No, it is not the same thing at all,' she said quietly.

'The house burned to the ground, Venetia. It was an act of hatred and destruction. A clear message. Are you honestly telling me that you believe the man who did that is not the same man who put a bullet in our father's head?'

She knew that the argument made sense. The idea that another unrelated man had just turned up out of the blue to kill her father was almost ridiculous.

'We both know that he did it, Venetia.'

There was a small silence.

'Regardless, my part in this is over, Robert. You have what you need. I've done my duty. I will not see Linwood again.'

'Do not be so hasty, little sister.'

'My mind is made up, Robert.' Her voice was firm.

'Then unmake it. There is something I have not told you. A development.'

She felt her chest tighten in apprehension.

'My witness, the one who saw Linwood leaving our father's study that night, has disappeared. No doubt Linwood had a hand in it, with his...connections.'

She thought of the villains in Whitechapel who had turned themselves in for capture.

'Without our witness, the only evidence that ties Linwood to Rotherham is his admission to you...unless we find the murder weapon—dear Papa's missing pistol.'

'Even if he is guilty he could have disposed of the weapon.'

'No. Why take it, if he did not mean to keep it as a souvenir? It was not his and therefore could not have identified him. And yet he took it along with a book from our father's library.'

'I did not know a book was missing.'

'It was seen clasped within Linwood's hand as he left and there is a space on the shelf where it sat, a space that was not there when I visited our father earlier that day. If either were to be found in his possession...' He paused. 'Linwood will be out on Friday night. He has a meeting that starts at nine and will not finish until midnight.' He looked at her expectantly.

'Find someone else to do it.'

'That is not so easily done. Think how easy it would

be for you. Your association with him is known. It would be simple to gain access past his servants, to wait for his return, to search his private quarters…'

'Robert, there are rumours enough about my relationship with him. If I am seen going to his rooms at night, it is as good as admitting to all of London that I am his mistress.'

'You have been thought mistress to other men in the past. Such speculation has never bothered you before.'

But it wasn't the same with Linwood at all.

'You have to at least look, Venetia. One way or another it would prove his guilt…or his innocence.'

Those last three words seemed to echo within her. She met his gaze across the carriage. 'You are sure he will not be there?'

'I am positive.'

She swallowed. 'And after this, no more.'

'No more,' he agreed.

She gave a nod.

The carriage came to a halt by his usual alleyway. He brushed a kiss to her cheek, then opened the door and jumped down into the darkening gloom. She did not watch him go, just sat there with a tight knot in her stomach as the carriage rolled off to take her home.

She did not hear from Linwood that day, nor the next two. She told herself that she did not expect to hear from him, did not want to hear from him, but she was lying. Every time the door sounded she jumped and sat tense, holding her breath, waiting for the approach of Albert's footsteps to announce that Lord Linwood was in the drawing room, or, at the very least, convey a note written in that familiar hand. She was not at home to any other caller. And she should not have been at home to Linwood. But Linwood did not come.

* * *

Friday arrived and the hours of the day passed too slowly. The leaden sky outside, ominous and oppressive, seemed to mirror the waiting that stretched ahead. She tried to read the play's script, to learn the lines she could not recall, but nothing held her attention. She felt restless, agitated, unable to concentrate. She wished she had gone to the rehearsal, anything to distract her from this misery of thought. But she knew she could not have borne it any better than this.

Morning.

Afternoon.

Evening.

Eventually she entered the room she had not been in since that night—the parlour. A small fire burned on the hearth and the candles in the wall sconce had been lit.

The newspaper had been turned to the front page, neatly folded and sat on top of the pile of papers on her desk. The pile of hairpins had disappeared from the mantelpiece. And the vase sat in its rightful place.

She lifted the paper, kicked off her slippers and curled herself into the armchair. Then she read the report Linwood's journalists had written, even though she had read it a hundred times before. She glanced up at the vase. The clock struck nine.

She was quite calm as she rose to ready herself for the task that lay ahead.

The night was very still and held a cold dampness that seemed to seep into her very bones, or maybe it was only her own fanciful imagination.

Even the carriage horses seemed skittish.

Above there was no moon, no stars to light the sky, only a thick dark blanket of cloud and the soft patter of rain.

The carriage rolled on. She sat very still, focusing her mind. The journey passed quickly. Too soon she was in St James's Place. Her carriage rolled to a stop outside the address that was printed on Linwood's card. A glance up at the windows of his rooms. The curtains were drawn in both. One room was in darkness. In the other was the faint glow of light. Venetia pulled the deep hood of the cloak to cover her head, and stepped down from the coach.

Linwood's man looked surprised to find her there when he opened the door. She slid the hood back to reveal her identity.

'Miss Fox, to see Lord Linwood,' she said and held the man's gaze with a brazenness.

She saw his eyes widen. He hesitated only for the smallest second before inviting her in.

'I'm afraid Lord Linwood is not at home, ma'am.'

'I am content to wait,' she said easily and let the black velvet of the cloak slip from her shoulders.

Linwood's man caught it and folded it carefully over his arm, his eyes flickering over the bright scarlet of her dress and away again. He was embarrassed, as if this was not a situation with which he had ever had to deal, as if Linwood did not have women calling at his door in the night. And Venetia felt glad of it. She held the servant's eyes with a calm confidence and that same knowing curve of her lips.

He glanced away in clear discomfort, clearing his throat. 'It is likely to be some time before his lordship returns.'

'That is perfectly acceptable. I am in no hurry.'

She saw him swallow.

'This way please, ma'am.'

He showed her into a room that contained a desk, a bookcase, two winged armchairs and a sofa. A small fire burned upon the hearth and a candle burned at one end of the mantel. The clock in the centre of the mantel showed it was half past nine.

She sat herself down in the armchair closest to the candle.

'Shall I fetch you some tea, ma'am?'

'No, thank you,' she said. 'I have not come to take tea.'

He blushed as scarlet as her dress.

'What is through this door?' She gestured to the door at the side of the fireplace.

'The kitchen, ma'am.'

'And the other, at the far end of the room?' She did not look at the door in question, just kept her gaze fixed on his.

He hesitated for a second. 'Lord Linwood's bedchamber.'

'Ah,' she said softly, as if that was the very thing she wished to know, and smiled.

He lowered his gaze, his face scalding all the hotter. 'If there is nothing else, ma'am?'

'There is nothing,' she said.

He escaped to the kitchen, closing the door behind him.

Venetia rose and wandered about the room, evaluating where to start. She halted by the wooden bookcase, letting her fingers trail over the matching leather-bound books within, scanning the gold-lettered titles printed upon their spines. She paused at the stargazing section, trying not to think of the evening she and Linwood had spent together in her glasshouse, but the memory was vivid in her mind. Unable to resist, she slipped an astronomy book from its shelf and opened it...and there printed on that very page was an illustration of Pegasus. Something tightened in her chest at the sight of it. She closed the book cover with a snap and returned it to its rightful place.

There were books on the classics, books on history, on warfare and art. Books on hunting and on animals. Even one on the lives of wolves in Britain. All bound in a deep-blue leather that matched those in Rotherham's study. Short of taking every book from its shelf and examining it there was no way to tell if it had come from Rotherham's study or was Linwood's own. Nothing leapt out at her as being worth stealing from a dead man's library.

She turned her attention to his desk. It was similar in design to the one that sat in her parlour, except that a cover of dark blue leather sat beneath the silver pen-carrier and inkwell. On the desk's surface lay two sheets of blank white paper printed with his name and crest at the top, as if he was planning to write a letter.

Venetia had spent years studying people, watching what made them tick, all those little mannerisms of which they were unaware, all the little ways they betrayed themselves. All good fodder to bring to the roles she played, the characters she became. She thought of Linwood, of the type of man he was, the darkness that was in him, the absolute self-control. People thought him lacking in emotion, but she knew the truth, it was control and masking of emotion, rather than a dearth. She had never met a more passionate man. Everything about him was contrary to expectation. He thought differently to other men. He *was* different to other men.

She sat down in his chair, at his desk, trying to see what was before her with his eyes. *Where would he hide something that he did not wish to be found?* The answer whispered in her ear clear as if Linwood spoke it himself—in plain sight. She looked directly in front of her. On one side was the bookcase, on the other a painting of a racehorse standing before his stable.

She moved to stand before the painting. Then peeped behind it and smiled.

The picture was not heavy as she lifted it from its hooks

on the wall, and leaned it against the skirting below. And there, fitted flush into the wall was a safe box. It was locked, of course. Linwood probably carried the key with him, but he was a man who left little to chance and she knew there would be a duplicate key hidden in the room. She returned to the desk, sliding open the top drawer, and heard the front door sound, followed by voices, one of which she recognised too well.

Her heart turned over, then raced off at a thunder. Her stomach dropped to meet her shoes. Sliding the drawer shut as quickly and quietly as she could, she stepped away from the desk...just as Linwood came into the room.

Chapter Twelve

He did not smile. The candlelight played upon the harsh handsome planes of his face. His eyes looked black as pitch as they dropped to the painting that leaned against the wall before coming back to hers.

'I like to know the measure of the man with whom I am involved,' she said calmly, even though her heart was beating nineteen to the dozen.

'Involved. Is that what we are? Because after the way things ended the other night it seemed otherwise.'

The silence whispered.

He did not thaw.

'I see that I have made a mistake. If you will excuse me, my lord.' She made to walk by him.

He did not move to stop her, only spoke the words with that quiet intensity of his. 'Do you not want what you came for, Venetia?'

She stopped, her eyes meeting his, afraid of how much he knew, afraid he had won the game in earnest.

He flipped the head of the wolf's-head on his cane, and inside, tucked in the slot of a dark velvet cushion, was a small silver key. He removed it, slipped it into the lock of the safe and turned. The front of the box swung open. He stood back and gestured towards it.

'Go ahead,' he said. 'If you want to know so badly.'

She stared at him, her heart thumping madly, afraid to look, and even more afraid not to.

His expression was unreadable, but in that dark gaze that held hers she saw the flicker of something that made her feel ashamed.

The clock in the corner ticked, so slow and steady beside the spur of Venetia's heart. She stepped slowly to the safe. She could see straight away that it contained neither the pistol nor the book. There were several thick rolls of white bank notes, and, at the back, a calf-skin pouch of golden guineas, but it was not at them at which she looked. She stared only at the pile of assorted documents and letters. Only at the folded theatre playbill that lay on the top of it. The theatre playbill of *As You Like It*, starring Miss Venetia Fox and newcomer Miss Alice Sweetly, from the very first night she had met him. She lifted it out. Inside the playbill was a man's handkerchief, folded neatly, clean and white save for the clear rouge impression of a woman's mouth, where she had pressed it to her lips. There was an ache in her chest, a prickle of tears in her eyes as she raised them to his.

He said nothing, just stood there with dignity and his secrets laid bare.

She folded the playbill over the handkerchief, replaced them both in the safe box just as they had been.

'You have not examined the rest,' he said.

'I do not need to.'

They looked at one another.

'You dismissed me like one of your footmen, Venetia.'

'I should not have done that.' She glanced down at her

hands. 'There are things I have to ask you, things I need to know.' Questions all for herself and none for Robert.

He said nothing, just stood there and waited.

'You burned Rotherham's house.'

He was silent.

'What was between the two of you? Why did you hate him so much?' she asked.

She saw his jaw tense, the dangerous look that entered his eyes.

'Rotherham was a man who took what he wanted regardless of whom he hurt.'

There was a horrible feeling in the pit of her stomach, a sense of the horror that his words only hinted at. 'What did he do?'

'He hurt someone close to me. Hurt them very badly.' He looked at her and she could see the pain in his eyes.

'I am sorry,' she said, knowing the man who fathered her was fully capable of such cruelty.

'So am I, Venetia.' She felt her heart tremble at his words.

The silence was loud between them. The single key question that had been the start of it all remained unasked.

'You know who I am, Venetia. I have never pretended to be anything else. You have the measure of me.'

Her eyes met his again, seeing only the same man she had always seen. The man who seemed to call to her soul. Down where their hands rested, each alone, she shifted hers slightly so that her fingers brushed against his.

'Yes, Francis,' she said softly, her eyes searching his as if she could see into his very soul. 'I believe that I do.' And she took his face very gently between her hands and kissed him.

He stood stock-still at first, gave no response, but she could feel the stirrings beneath, sense the struggle that raged beneath that exterior of cool control. She kissed him again, plucking one kiss and then another softly from those firm sculpted lips, not with seduction but with a raw honesty of all that she felt for him—tenderness and understanding, desire and love. And he answered with a truth of his own, his mouth moving against her, kissing her with all that she had offered and more.

In his kiss, the barrier to all that he hid—passion and fire, gentleness and love—came crashing down. He kissed her with a strength of emotion that, now unleashed, towered above her. He kissed her mouth, the pulse-point in her neck. Kissed the length of each collarbone, and the hollow of her throat. His breath teased hot against the bare skin of her shoulders, making her skin tingle and shiver with longing for his lips. His hands slid around her waist, holding her to him, binding them together, as if she could ever want to be anywhere else. Their bodies had been made to fit together, breast to chest, thigh to thigh. He kissed her and everything of worry and responsibility and duty melted away. And with his lips upon hers she knew the truth—that for her there was only Linwood, that there had only ever been Linwood.

One hand slid to capture her breast, and she felt her body respond as if there were no layers of cloth to separate them, as if they were already naked and together. The other hand moved low, over her hips, caressing her, guiding her in this journey she knew now they had always been destined to make. He deepened the kiss, offering what only he could give, touching her, tasting her in a prelude of what was to come. And in the sharing of their mouths, and beneath the touch of his hands, she felt the flame of desire that had always burned between them flare and rage to a mighty inferno.

He unfastened her dress, freeing her breasts from her

bodice, taking them in his mouth, kissing them, tasting them, working each hard-tipped nipple with his tongue until her legs were melting and weak and she was clutching his head to her and arching against him, needing this and more, needing him, only him.

But Linwood pulled back, and his breath was as hard and fast as her own, his eyes dark and burning with a depth of desire and emotion she had never seen in any man's eyes before. He dispensed with his jacket, slipped off his waistcoat.

She reached out and pulled at his cravat, freeing him of it, her fingers sliding against the fine cotton of his shirt, needing to feel the skin beneath. He peeled it off over his head and let it drop away. The flicker of the candlelight danced upon the smooth sculpted muscle of his chest, down over the ribs of hard muscle that banded his abdomen. In reality his body was more magnificent than her imagination had ever dreamed. She reached out and ran her hands over him, stroking him, marvelling at how dark and golden his skin was beneath the whiteness of her fingers.

And then she was in his arms again and he was kissing her, their naked chests together, his fingers freeing her hair from its pins to thread within its lengths. Kissing her, touching her, teasing her. She could feel the press of his aroused manhood through his breeches, through her skirts. Their mouths clung as he backed her into his bedchamber.

His hands were gentle as they slid the rest of her clothing from her body, gentle as they laid her within his bed.

She watched him complete his undress in the candlelight, her eyes moving over the long hard length of him, knowing what was going to happen between them. And between her legs, so slick and heated, was an ache for him. Her eyes held his as the bed dipped and he finally covered her body with hers.

'Yes,' she whispered, just like in the dream. 'Yes.' And she opened her legs to welcome him in.

There was a calmness to the morning following the rain of the night before. The pavements were still damp, but the air touched a freshness against her cheeks and a sweetness to her nose. The dawn was only just creeping across from behind St James's church spire, the sky streaking washed-out shades of night to blue beneath a golden light. She breathed in deep, feeling a sense of gladness and wonder at the new day that she had not felt before, and within her chest her heart swelled with joy.

The surrounding houses still slept, blinds and curtains still closed over windows like eyes shuttered within a face. The street was empty, save for a solitary street sweeper, broom balanced across his shoulder like a musket as he made his way to work. On the railings that lined the low wall beside her, a robin sat perched, watching her, his little red breast vivid, his brown feathers fluffed like a ball. The door shut quietly behind her as she climbed into Linwood's waiting carriage and it rumbled off. She glanced up at the window of Linwood's bedchamber, to where he lay naked and sleeping within the great four-poster bed. And she smiled and thought that in all of the years of her life she had never felt so happy. Linwood did not have the pistol. And that had to mean he was innocent.

The house was awake and waiting for her when she reached home. She could see the way the servants looked at her, the slight embarrassed knowledge, the way they could not quite meet her eye. They all knew she had not come home last night. They all knew it was Linwood she was seeing. But she did not care, whatever the gossip. Nothing could dim the glow that she felt.

Her body was sore, but it was a good soreness, a feeling of satisfaction, of completeness. She washed herself in warm water, washed the dried blood smears from between her legs. And she remembered his tenderness, his gentleness, the way he touched her, the whispered words in the dark dawn of a new day. Then she dressed herself carefully, choosing a pale yellow dress that reflected her new lightness of spirit. Only then did she let her maid in to coil and pin her hair up in a demure style. She looked at herself in the mirror and despite the lack of sleep there was no need for rouge on lips or cheeks. She smiled, a smile of utter joy, and the woman in the mirror looked radiant. She was in love with Linwood and nothing else in the world seemed to matter. She was in love and she did not think of her predicament or of his, only that she loved him, and that her body still throbbed from it.

The clock on the mantel chimed quarter to the hour. Her maid helped her into her matching pelisse. She wrapped a scarf of gold crochet around her neck, fitted her beige kid gloves and left for the meeting with Robert.

Linwood woke to the sound of carriage and cart wheels on the road outside. He felt relaxed, at ease with himself, happy. It was the first morning in years that he did not wake with the dread and worry of the day that lay ahead. And there was only one reason—Venetia.

The bed beside him was empty, the sheets cool. He threw back the covers and padded through to the drawing room. His clothes from which Venetia had undressed him the night before had been folded into a neat pile upon his desk. Of Venetia's there was no sign. He smiled at her discretion as he headed back into the bedchamber and thought of how this strange game between them had played out. For all its risk, it had brought him Venetia. And he had fallen in love with her.

She was incomparable. Unique. A woman of passion and strength and yet with an underlying vulnerability. She was his, in truth now. And he was hers. He thought of their lovemaking, of its passion and gentleness, of the feel of her in his arms, of their bodies entwined afterwards. They had slept and loved, and slept and loved again, all through the night. And not once had he thought about Rotherham, or any of the rest of it. He had thought about Venetia. Only Venetia…and how much she meant to him. He smiled again as he glanced at the bed on which they had made love and in the light dimmed by the curtains saw the marks that marred the pale bed sheets.

He frowned, wondering what had caused them. Unmindful of his nakedness, he moved to the window and, wrenching open the curtains to let in the flood of daylight, turned to examine the bed more closely. And what he saw made his heart skip a beat. It was not possible, yet the evidence was before his very eyes. And then he remembered how very tight she had been, the way she had cried out and gripped so tightly to him as he had plunged into her. He had taken her with passion, with urgency, with no account of inexperience. He had never deflowered a virgin, until now. But he knew in the cold clear morning light that, contrary to all appearances and beliefs, Venetia Fox had come to his bed a virgin. And he remembered what had passed between them in her parlour, of the way she had come so close, then pulled away. He had thought it a deliberate and cruel teasing on her part—now he understood better. He needed to speak to Venetia. He raked a hand through his hair and rang the bell for his valet.

The theatre was empty and in darkness. The draught almost guttered the candle in her hand as she unlocked the stage door and opened it, letting Robert slip inside.

'How went it?' he asked as they walked down the corridor to her dressing room.

'Well enough.' She did not look at him, did not want him to see the truth in her face, just led him inside and sat the candlestick down on the dressing table as he closed the door.

'You found what we sought?'

She shook her head. 'He does not have them, Robert.'

'I hope you were thorough in your search.'

'I found his safe box, looked inside at that which he values, those things that he holds dear and most secret.' She felt her heart warm in the knowledge that thing was her. 'There was nothing of what was taken from Rotherham.'

'Did you check the bookshelves?'

'Linwood's library is bound in the same leather as Rotherham's, and there are many books within it. I saw nothing that stood out as having come from elsewhere.'

'Like finding a needle in a haystack.' He touched his thumbnail to his lips, rubbing the tip of it between his teeth.

'He does not have the pistol. You said yourself what that would mean—it proves his innocence.'

'Absence of evidence is not evidence of absence. He may have hidden it elsewhere.'

'Or not at all.'

Her brother hesitated before saying, 'We still have his confession to you…' Robert's eyes met hers and she saw the unspoken suggestion in them.

'No, Robert,' she said firmly and shook her head.

'It is enough to have him arrested. I have checked with a man of law.'

'I will not go to the police.'

'Even though he has admitted that he burned our father's house to the ground?'

'That does not mean he killed Rotherham,' she ground out.

'You forget, Venetia—the witness who saw him leaving Rotherham's house on the night of the murder. The witness who has, so conveniently for Linwood, disappeared.'

'The witness may have been mistaken. Or maybe he had a wish to implicate Linwood in the matter.'

'He is an honourable man and a most credible witness. Trustworthy. There can be no doubt that it was Linwood he saw.' Robert's gaze narrowed. 'I think you protest Linwood's innocence a little too strongly.'

She glanced away awkwardly before forcing herself to meet his gaze once more. 'Not at all.'

'You look different somehow, Venetia.'

Her heart skipped a beat, at how much Linwood's loving had changed her.

He studied at her more closely. 'You have done something differently to normal.'

'A new day dress and matching pelisse,' she said. 'From Madame Boisseron.'

'Very elegant. It suits you well.'

She gave a small half smile and was thankful that the light was so poor that he could not see the blush that was warming her cheeks.

'I take it you got out in time.'

She hesitated for a second too long.

'Venetia?' he pressed.

'Linwood came back early,' she conceded.

There was a silence.

'I was able to...manage the situation,' she said, unwilling to reveal to her brother just what had really taken place.

She saw him swallow and give a single nod.

'Does he suspect you?'

'I do not believe so.'

He smiled. 'I did not doubt you could do it.'

She could not return his smile. His words made her feel uncomfortable. She knew she should tell him, but what had happened between her and Linwood was too tender and private. She lifted the candle and, moving to the door, opened it. 'It is done. He does not have what you seek. I will be a part of this no more, Robert.'

'As you wish. You have played your role well, Venetia. And Linwood is none the wiser. You are a credit to your profession.'

His words sullied what had passed between her and Linwood, making it seem like something else. She felt sick at the thought. 'You should leave before you are seen.' She began to lead him along the corridor towards the stage door.

'The hour is still early enough,' he said. 'The streets are practically dead and we are the only two people in the building.'

'Even so, Mr Kemble will be here soon, and the set staff.'

'So they will.'

'We should not see each other again...for a while, Robert.'

'No, I suppose it would not do for our relationship to become common knowledge.'

'It would serve neither of our causes.' She shivered just at the thought.

'Goodbye, Venetia. And thank you.'

She nodded.

She turned the key in the lock behind him, leaning her back against the door and listening to the tread of his footsteps receding in the street outside. The relief was immense. The arrangement with Robert was over. Her brother had his mind made up. Nothing she said was going to change it. Yet their conversation had left a horrible taste in her mouth and an uneasiness in her stomach. She took a deep breath then walked slowly back down the corridor to her dressing room, conscious with every step of the ache and the tenderness between her legs. *Francis.* She wondered if he was awake yet, if he had seen her blood upon his sheets. And more than any of that, what on earth she was going to tell him when he came to ask her.

On the dressing table and rail she laid out her things ready for the night's performance. There was a faint sound from the corridor. She frowned, wondering whether Robert had returned or another theatre worker arrived. So she picked up the candle, moved to the doorway and peered out into the corridor.

'Mr Kemble?'

Silence.

'Is anyone there?' she called.

But the only reply was the echo of her own voice. There was nothing and no one, just the dim shadowed corridor. She shivered, chiding herself for own nervousness, and more glad than ever that the business with Robert was over.

She finished checking her costumes, then picked up her script and left by the stage door, taking care to lock it after her. The morning was fully light now. In the distance she heard a church bell chime nine. Out on the main street she could hear the rattle of carts and carriage wheels, the clop of horses and banging of doors; the rest of London had awakened. She pulled her shawl more tightly around her and climbed into her carriage that waited there in the alleyway. She did not look back out of the windows, just focused her eyes on the script in her hand, reading the words fruitlessly as her mind thought of Linwood and the passion and wonder of the night before. And so she did not see the dark figure that stepped out of the shadows and walked away in the opposite direction along the street.

Chapter Thirteen

Linwood stood at the window of his drawing room, staring out at the street below. All the lightness of the morning had expired. He had engaged in the game and he had lost. His stomach was filled with cold disappointment and the sickening realisation that what he had thought was happening with Venetia last night had been something else all together. A game that continued regardless. He had known the risk and accepted the gamble, staking his heart. And he had been bested by a master. Too beguiled by a beautiful face and a luscious figure, too engaged by a personality that flirted and parried and ensnared. She had filled his thoughts to the exclusion of all else, making him forget that which he needed to remember, making him believe that the feelings between them were mutual. Two cloths cut from the same die, both him and her, or so he had thought. But it was as much an illusion as the woman he had thought her beneath the facade of the divine Miss Fox. He had thought he could tell when she was acting and when she was not. But he had been wrong. Last night's performance had hoodwinked him completely despite all he knew of her. What an actress she was and he, a gullible fool.

In the daylight the blood on the sheets was a stark crimson. In the air he could still smell the scent of her perfume mixed with that of their lovemaking. Against the white of his pillow lay a single long dark hair. And it seemed he could feel again the satin of her skin beneath his hands, the soft sigh of her breath as he caressed her, the passion of her lips as they merged with his. He clenched his jaw so tight that it was painful and escaped to the drawing room, but the picture on the wall was not straight. And beneath was the safe box and all that she had seen within it, exposing the secrets of his heart for her to trample upon. He wondered bitterly that she had not told Clandon about that as well as everything else. He straightened the picture, as if by so doing he could wipe away her touch from it, and let his gaze drift to the bookcase. He stood there like that for a minute, feeling more alone, more hurt, more angry than he had ever felt in his life, which was ridiculous given all that had happened between his family and Rotherham. Then he reached out and rang the bell.

'Change the bedding, every last bit of it. Air the bedchamber and this one, too, anywhere that she waited. Leave no trace that Miss Fox was ever here.' He showed nothing of emotion on his face, just his usual deadpan serious expression. Then he took up his walking cane and walked out into the clear autumn day. He needed to think. About Venetia. About where the game went from here.

'Lord Linwood called for you, ma'am. I told him you had gone to the theatre.' Albert hesitated. 'I hope I did not do wrong in divulging such information. He was most anxious to see you and given that it was him...' The elderly butler cleared his throat and looked embarrassed.

'Did he say when he would return?'

'He did not, ma'am.'

All through the day she expected him to call. She waited for his note. Waited for the sound of his carriage wheels, of his horse, of the brass knocker striking against the plate of her door. But there was nothing. And as the day wore on the joy in her heart faded a little and in its place grew a feeling of unease and disquiet. Even if he had not seen the blood, even if he did not know, she had thought he would have been as anxious to see her as she was to see him. She forced herself to read her script, to focus on her preparations for the opening performance of *Rosina* tonight. But amidst all the excitement and nervousness that an opening night entailed, the worry over Linwood throbbed like a dull ache.

He finally arrived ten minutes before she was due to leave for the theatre. She was in the parlour, trying to compose herself for the performance ahead when her butler showed him through.

'Francis.' She smiled and went to him, feeling her heart sigh with relief to see him. 'Your timing is terrible. I must leave shortly for—' And then she saw his face, and she knew without him uttering a single word that everything had changed. She stopped in her tracks.

'Francis?'

'You were not honest with me, Venetia.' Both his voice and expression were as closed and controlled as the first night they had met.

'No.' She shook her head. 'I should have told you that I was a virgin.'

His mood was sombre, angry, nothing of what she had expected.

'That, as well,' he said.

Everything seemed to catch in that moment. Her heart, her breath, everything in the world all around her. Everything holding still, everything frozen with a sudden dread while she turned her eyes slowly to his.

'You were gone when I awoke,' he said.

'For the sake of discretion. I thought I would see you today. That we would talk.'

'And then I found your blood on my sheets.'

She swallowed and said nothing.

'I came here and learned you had gone to the theatre. I was desperate to see you. Desperate to know that I had not hurt you.' He gave a mocking laugh and shook his head. 'I went to the theatre. To the stage door…just as you had told me.'

She closed her eyes, knowing what was coming and needing to hear it just the same. Her heart felt heavy, pounding each beat with the same dread that was seeping like ice through her blood.

'When I came to your dressing room I heard a man's voice from within—Robert Clandon's voice.'

She pressed her fingers to her forehead. *Lord, no! Please, no!*

'The nature of your conversation stayed my hand upon the door, Venetia.'

She took a shaky breath, knowing that she had to face this head-on, that she could not shy from it. 'How much did you overhear?'

'Enough.'

She pressed her lips firm together and tried to swallow the lump that was pressing in her throat.

There was a knock on the door. 'Your carriage is waiting, ma'am.' Albert looked from her to Linwood and then back again. 'Please forgive my intrusion.' Then made a hasty retreat.

'Who is Clandon to you, Venetia?'

She shook her head. The one question which she could

not answer, not to him of all people. To open up her heart and lay bare the dark secrets of her past. Everything would be lost. And he would hate her for ever, if he did not already do so. 'He is no one.'

'No one,' he said softly. His eyes glittered hard and black. His face was all hard angles, angry and dangerous and heartbreakingly handsome. There was nothing of the gentleness, nothing of the tenderness that had been there last night.

'Just the man with whom you have been conspiring all along. I thought perhaps he was your lover, but after last night, I know that is not the case. What is your relationship—purely monetary?'

'You knew?' She stared at him aghast.

'Of course I knew. I have known all along. All those questions about Rotherham…' His eyes blazed with a black fury, but the rest of his face was cold and impassive. 'Clandon thinks I killed his father so he sent you to entrap me.'

She glanced away, knowing she could not deny it. 'Then why play the game?'

'For the same reason as you, Venetia.'

She faced him, head up, standing tall, dry-eyed and defiant even though inside she felt like she was dying. 'And last night…?'

'A fitting conclusion.'

His words pierced her heart like a dagger. She slapped his face and the sound of it echoed in the ensuing silence.

Linwood did not flinch, just stood there silent and strong as a rock, those dark, smouldering, dangerous eyes flaying her worse than any of his cruel words.

The air crackled between them.

'Clandon is right, you are a very good actress, Venetia. But it was worth it to have you in my bed and take from you what all the men in London could not.'

The breath was shaking in her lungs. 'Get out!'

His eyes held hers for a moment longer, his face dark and unsmiling. Then he gave her a small bow and turned and walked away.

The clock struck seven, but she made no move, just stood silent and still as a statue, all thoughts of the theatre and *Rosina* forgotten. She waited until she heard his footsteps reach the front door; waited until she heard the thud of the closing door, even though the tears were already spilling silently over her cheeks. Then she clasped her hands to her face and, for the first time since she was a child, wept as her heart broke apart.

There was an arctic coldness in Linwood as he walked away from Venetia Fox's house, angry and razing as the winter wind. He nursed the anger, embraced the icy blast of rage, because he knew what would be there beneath when they died away—a raw, weeping wound. His boots echoed against the pavement. The air was chilled against his face.

He walked and he did not look back.

He walked and told himself what she was.

Kept on walking away from her house, away from her. But no matter how far he walked, no matter the distance he put between them, he could not escape what was in his heart. He did not have to think about the route between her home and his, it was so engrained that his feet trod it without a single conscious thought. One street and then another. Past women who looked at him with wary eyes and men who were careful to give him a wide berth. He was halfway home when he realised that he had left his cane behind at Venetia's house. He, who had never mistakenly left the cane anywhere before. Part of him thought to keep on going and send a footman to retrieve it because he had no desire to see anything of her again. But he knew he could not do that. The cane was a symbol of his office in the Order of the Wolf. He had sworn to guard it with his life and never let it out of his sight. And Linwood was a man who took the oaths he had sworn very seriously. He stopped and began to retrace his steps.

The scent of smoke touched to his nose before he reached King Street, but he thought nothing of it until he turned the corner into the street and saw the commotion. His heart stopped and his stomach plummeted at the sight. Much farther along the street, from the house that was Venetia's, a flurry of people spilled out to crowd upon the pavement. And in the bow window of her drawing room, bright against the darkness of the night, was the flicker of golden flames. Then he was running, sprinting the length of the street. Venetia!

It happened so fast. From one small golden flicker of light within to the glass cracking and splintering, and the flames roaring to consume with a fury. By the time he reached her house the smoke was belching thick and black into the night and the flames licked like those on a bonfire. The crowd of servants in the street stared with smoke-blackened faces and eyes wide with terror. Maids and footmen alike shrieking, sobbing and wailing. Neighbours tumbled out onto the street in their housecoats and slippers. Someone already had a bucket in hand, the water in it a drop in the ocean that would be required to quench the blaze. He saw Albert alongside two footmen he recognised. But of all the figures, all the faces that he scanned, he could not find Venetia's.

'Venetia!' he bellowed, but in the chaos there was no answer. He made his way to Albert and when he got closer he saw that the old butler had Linwood's cane in his hand.

'Thank God you came back, my lord, she's still inside!' Albert cried and pressed the cane into his hand.

Linwood took the cane with a murmur of thanks. Then he pulled the handkerchief from his pocket, dipped it in the bucket of water as he passed and tied the wet handkerchief around his face. The front door was lying wide open. He walked into the hallway over which flames were already creeping.

The wooden balustrade was beginning to burn as he ran up the stairs, the smoke so dark and thick and acrid that it burned his eyes and made it difficult to see.

'Venetia!' he yelled. 'Venetia!' against the roaring fury of the fire.

And then he saw her through the smoke at the top of the stairs, a vision from his dreams, white-faced, her hair dark as midnight, the emerald-green of her dress vibrant beside the orange fire all around. She was coughing as the thick smoke forced her back.

Behind him the flames leapt up the staircase. He reached her, his body pressed against hers, pushing them both back into her bedchamber, slamming the door closed behind him, buying them a few precious minutes.

He saw the fear and shock in her eyes when she looked at him and he would have done anything to wipe it away and protect her.

'The stairs are gone,' he said.

Her eyes clung to his. 'There is no other way out, Francis. We are trapped.'

He shifted his gaze to the window.

She saw where he looked. 'We are one floor up. It is too high to jump.'

'Not if we break the fall.'

He wrenched the sash window up and the surge of cool air brought the fire through the door. He freed the sword from his cane, slashing the rope of the window's pulley system and ripping the cord out. The window thudded shut with a reverberating crash and the intensity of heat in the room was unbearable. He sheathed the sword into the cane, then tied a bowline at the end of the cord and looped it around the metal fastener of the window. The smoke was thickening as he smashed the cane's silver wolf's-head at the window, shattering the glass. He cleared the worst of the jagged edges and cushioned the cord across it. Then he climbed backwards through the window frame, cord wrapped tight around his hand, standing up to balance on the outer ledge. He reached his hand for Venetia. But she made no move to take it.

'The cord is not long enough,' she cried.

'We have no choice, Venetia, you have to trust me.'

She hesitated, glancing back at the flames splintering through the door, before meeting his gaze again.

'Please, Venetia,' he said and she reached her hand to his and let him pull her up to stand on the ledge by his side.

'Look at me, Venetia. Look only at me.'

She locked her eyes on to his.

'Hold tight to me. Arms round my neck. Legs around my hips.'

She fastened herself to him and he stepped off the ledge, the cord straining through his hands as they slid towards the ground. The rope ended twelve feet short of the ground, but he landed first and rolled, cushioning her.

Then he had her up in his arms, carrying her clear of the inferno to the safety of the distant road where the crowd was gathered.

The fire brigade had arrived, a bucket chain was in place, water sloshing everywhere in an attempt to bring the fire under some semblance of control.

When they were clear he sat her down on the pavement, kneeling down by her side. There were smears of soot on her face, her hair was dishevelled and the emerald silk of her dress was singed and tattered. Her eyes clung to his as if his body and hers still dangled entwined upon that cord from the window.

He took her hand in his and she looked down to where the rope had cut through the leather of his gloves and burned his skin. And when her eyes met his again he could see the tears that tracked through the soot on her face and feel the tremble that ran right through her.

He eased off his coat and wrapped it around her. 'Venetia…' he whispered as he gently stroked the long dark strands of hair from her face.

'Thank God, Venetia!' Alice Sweetly arrived, falling to her knees before Venetia, while Razeby stood by her side. 'We saw the blaze from my back-bedchamber window. When Razeby said it was your house I prayed that he was wrong.' And then Alice was cradling Venetia against her. 'Oh, thank God, you're safe!' she said again.

Razeby's gaze moved over Linwood's shirt before meeting his eyes. 'You all right?'

Linwood gave a single gruff nod.

Alice was still talking to Venetia. 'Don't you worry, Venetia. Everything's going to be fine.' Then to Razeby, 'It's all right if she stays with me isn't it? Can you carry her home?'

'Alice,' Razeby said gently and touched a hand to her arm, trying to pull her back, his eyes flitting to Linwood.

But Linwood was already on his feet with his cane beneath his hand.

'Look after her,' he said and turned and walked away into the night.

* * *

The next morning Venetia and Alice sat at breakfast in Alice's dining room when the front-door knocker sounded.

'Surely the reporters haven't discovered your whereabouts already.' Alice frowned.

Venetia gave a little sigh and pulled her dressing gown a little tighter around her. 'They would have found me sooner or later.'

'Heston will get rid of them. It's grand having a butler to do such things, isn't it?'

Venetia smiled at her friend. 'Things are working out well between you and Razeby.'

'They are.' Alice nodded. 'I'm happy.'

'I really am glad for you, Alice.'

They smiled at one another.

'Enough about me. We've got you to think about, Venetia. After last night we need to—'

But there was a knock at the dining-room door and Alice's butler appeared. 'There is a Mr Clandon at the front door to see Miss Fox.'

Venetia felt a flutter of panic.

'Then send him away. Miss Fox is hardly recovered enough to be receiving visitors.'

'The gentleman is being most insistent, ma'am. He says he will not move from the front step until he has seen Miss Fox.'

'Then fetch the footmen to see him off—'

'No,' said Venetia quickly. 'I will see him.'

Alice glanced round at her in surprise. 'If you're sure?'

'I am.'

'In that case, show him into the drawing room, Heston.' Then, to Venetia, 'Do you wish me to come with you?'

'Thank you, but there is no need.' Venetia shook her head. 'I will handle Mr Clandon easily enough.' She paused, seeing the look on Alice's face. 'He is…an old friend of mine.'

'Oh,' said Alice and she could see exactly what type of old friend Alice was thinking. 'I didn't realise.'

Venetia's cheeks warmed at Alice's mistake. She hated this subterfuge, all this misleading and dishonesty, but she could not very well tell her friend the truth.

She was so desperate to get her brother out of there as quickly as possible that she did not bother to dress before seeing him.

Robert was standing by the sofa, his face pinched and white, as she closed the drawing-room door behind her.

'I came as soon as I heard.' He came to her, his eyes scanning her face. 'I had to know that you were all right.'

'You should not be here, Robert. You risk too much.'

'Be damned to that, Venetia! You expect me to sit twiddling my thumbs at home pretending that all is well when I do not know the condition of my own sister? If you were hurt or at death's door? God damn it! I came past your house. I saw what little is left of it. I cannot begin to tell you what it felt like to see that smouldering black ruin. If you had any idea…' He turned away to control the extent of his emotion.

'Forgive me, I did not think.' She had not thought of Robert at all, she realised with a pang of guilt.

His eyes were filled with concern. 'Did you take any hurts?'

She shook her head. 'I am fine, really I am.'

'Thank God for that.' He blew out a sigh, closing his eyes and rubbing a hand against his temple. She could not help but notice the tremor in his fingers and knew how very frightened he had been for her. 'What the hell were you even doing in the house, Venetia? You were supposed to be at the theatre.'

She hesitated, not really wanting to tell him, but knowing that she should. 'Linwood came to see me.'

'Linwood was there?' The shock was transparent on her brother's face.

She nodded. 'We argued—he knows the truth, Robert. I did not realise but he has known all along.' When he was making love to her. When she loved him and thought he loved her.

'About me?'

'Of what you and I were about. The gathering of information, the seduction, the entrapment—whatever name it owns. He does not know you are my brother—he thinks I am in your employ.'

'He knows?' Robert's eyebrows rose. 'Little wonder you did not find the pistol if he was forewarned of your interest.' He paced, then turned to her suddenly. 'Tell me, was he present when the fire started?'

She shook her head. 'He had left some little time previously.'

'My God,' he whispered in a way that made her blood run cold. 'A man with a history of burning houses. A man who confessed a crime to you. A man who caught you searching his rooms and with whom you had argued. Who knew you had set out to seduce and entrap him...' His gaze shifted to hers and in them his thoughts showed clear.

'No! It was not like that.'

'Then what was it like?'

She shook her head, knowing that she could not reveal what had been between her and Linwood. Not even sure that she understood it herself. 'He would not hurt me.'

'Would he not?'

'It was Linwood who saved me and risked his own life to do so. Why would he do that if he started the fire?'

'Maybe he was seen. Maybe he realised it looked too

suspicious for him. Or he just wanted to play the hero. I do not know, Venetia.' He looked down, closed his eyes and rubbed at his forehead again, talking almost to himself. 'I honestly had no idea it would go this way.' He stopped and glanced up at her. 'I know you do not want to, but you are going to have to go to the police. Tell them about the fires, the one at our father's…and the one at your home.'

Her heart was beating very fast. 'No!'

'Yes, Venetia,' he insisted. 'He tried to kill you, for pity's sake! What are you going to do? Sit back and wait until he tries again? This has gone far enough. It stops here and now. I have already lost my father to that bastard and I will be damned if I let him have you.' He paused. 'Either you go to the police and tell them, Venetia, or I will.'

'You would not!' She stared at him in disbelief.

'Oh, but you know that I would.'

'If you do that, everything will come out about you and me and Rotherham, and about…my mother. All that I have gone to such pains to hide.'

'If that is the cost of saving your life, then it is small price to pay.'

'It would destroy me!'

'Hardly. He killed Rotherham. I am not going to stand back and let him kill you. So you go to the police today, Venetia. Or I will go to them tomorrow.' He looked at her. 'I know you do not like it, but it is for the best.'

They looked at one another for a moment and there was a stubborn determination in his eyes that she recognised from old. Then he gave her a nod of his head and left.

Chapter Fourteen

'Your drawing room reeks of soot and smoke.' Razeby poured them both a brandy. 'A trifle early in the morning, I know, but after last night, I think we can be excused.'

'The clothing I was wearing last night has been thrown out. I have bathed and scrubbed my hair and still I cannot get the stench of it out of my nostrils.' Just as he could not get the thought of Venetia from his mind. The image of her within that blaze, the feel of her in his arms as he carried her to safety and the way her eyes had clung to his. Linwood accepted the drink with thanks. 'Have you seen her this morning?'

Razeby shook his head. 'It did not feel right to stay over last night, not given the circumstance.' He took a sip of brandy. 'I'll visit Alice after this.' He paused. 'I take it you will be coming with me.'

'No.'

'I'll tell Miss Fox you will call upon her later, then?'

'I will not call upon her, either now or later.'

'But I thought...'

'Then you thought wrong.'

There was a silence

'Forgive me, Razeby.' Linwood met his friend's gaze. 'I am poor company of late.'

'Somewhat understandable, old chap.'

Linwood took a sip of his brandy. 'I am sure that Miss Sweetly will look after her.'

'No doubt,' said Razeby. He gestured down towards the group of reporters collected on the pavement outside Linwood's front door. 'How long have they been there?'

Linwood followed his glance with eyes that were still raw from last night's heat and smoke. 'Since dawn.'

'They think she is in here with you.'

He said nothing, but he felt the flicker of the muscle in his jaw.

'I take it from that you did not get much sleep.'

'Things on my mind...as ever,' said Linwood quietly. *Venetia Fox. What was between them. Robert Clandon. Rotherham.*

He could feel Razeby's eyes studying him, but he did not look round.

'You should try to get some rest,' Razeby said.

'When I have figured out something of this mess.'

The two of them moved to sit by the fire and finish their drinks before Razeby took his leave.

Linwood knew he should just let him go, should keep his mouth shut and say nothing. His friend was halfway across the room on his way out when he spoke. 'Razeby...'

Razeby stopped, his eyes meeting Linwood's.

Linwood hesitated, knowing that his words would betray something of his heart. 'You will let me know how she is?'

Razeby gave a nod. 'Of course I will,' he said softly.

Linwood moved to the window and watched Razeby leave. Only once his friend's carriage was out of sight did he turn away.

The room was very quiet. There was no noise save for the ticking of the clock. He poured himself another brandy and moved to the bookcase, letting his eyes meander over the leather-bound volumes, before they came to focus on one book in particular.

He could not regret that Rotherham was dead, no matter what else ensued from it. His eyes rose to the painting of the racehorse and he thought of the safe box that lay behind it, and Venetia, and the night he had loved her. He could not be in here without the memory haunting him so he rang the bell for his man and ordered his carriage be readied to take him to White's.

'Venetia?'

Venetia glanced up from where she sat staring into the fire to find Alice standing there, her friend's eyes moving over the untouched dinner tray.

'You've eaten nothing.'

Venetia shook her head. 'I have no appetite.' The dread was lying in her stomach, making it heavy and nauseous.

'You've not moved in the hours since Clandon left.'

She swallowed, pulling the dressing gown around her. 'I find my mind a little preoccupied.' Linwood had known all along. And all that she had believed that night in his rooms to be, all that she had thought she saw in his eyes and felt as his body loved hers, was illusion. He had taken from her all that she had to give—her trust, her body, her heart—as the fitting conclusion to a game. She was still reeling from the knowledge, still crushed from the realisation that she was every bit as foolish and weak as her mother had been, in loving a man that held her only in contempt.

'It's little wonder given how close we came to losing you.' Alice sat down on the sofa beside her.

But it was not that which held her rigid.

He tried to kill you, Venetia. She squeezed her eyes shut as Robert's words whispered through her head. But all she saw then was the look in Linwood's eyes when he had saved her from the fire, so vivid that it made her heart wrench even sitting here in this room with Alice. He had spoken not one word to her. Just set her down and walked away.

'You're pale as a ghost.' Alice frowned in concern and took one of Venetia's clenched hands in her own. 'And cold as ice. It's the shock setting in from last night. I came to tell you that an officer from Bow Street has called to speak to you about the fire. But I'll tell him to come back tomorrow when you're feeling better.' Alice made to rise.

'Please wait,' Venetia said quietly and stayed her friend with a light touch to her arm. Her throat tightened. She knew Robert would act if she did not. And she knew what that would mean.

'I'll wait,' Alice said calmly and sat back down by her side.

Everyone would know her secret. Everyone would know what she really was. She remembered the look in Linwood's eyes as he had admitted setting the fire and the hatred in his voice when he spoke of Rotherham. And that he had known she was working to entrap him. *Oh, God...* There was not really any decision to be made.

Robert had been right—Linwood was guilty. Everyone who had warned her had been right—he was dangerous. And yet still she hesitated.

'Venetia...' Alice said softly. 'The day's almost done.'

Her heart turned over. The last grains of sand slipped through the hourglass. Time had run out for Venetia.

Linwood was in White's, sitting with Razeby the next day, when the Bow Street officers came through the door.

He knew before they even looked his way that they had come for him.

'At last,' he murmured softly and felt relief that it was finally over. There would be no more searching, no more questions or investigation.

'Lord Linwood, you are under arrest, charged with the murder of his Grace, the Duke of Rotherham.'

He finished the last of his brandy from his glass, then got to his feet.

'I say, you cannot just come in here and—' Razeby started to protest.

'Leave it, Razeby,' Linwood said quietly. 'These gentlemen are here with a job to do.' He made no resistance as they placed the cuffs around his wrists.

'Linwood?' Razeby whispered and there was a look of shock in his eyes. The whole of the club was on its feet, watching while they led him out to the gaol cart. The buzz of voices gave way to an utter silence.

There was already something of a crowd waiting out on the pavement as they opened the black doors of the cart, placing him inside on the bare wooden bench like some common criminal. The straw that lined the floor was damp and dirty. The door slammed shut, the key scraping loud within it. There was the jangle of keys.

'Francis!' He heard the echo of shock in the familiar voice.

He turned his head to look through the bars of the tiny window and saw his father's face there, grey and horrified.

'Son?' his father whispered.

And when he looked into his father's eyes that were so like his own, he saw understanding.

Venetia got through the next days like an automaton. Life was going on around her. There was someone called

Venetia Fox living in that house with Alice, but it was not her. Venetia Fox was safe, both the charade she presented to the world, and the real woman beneath it, or so she told herself again and again, except that it did not seem to make her feel any better. There was a sick feeling in her stomach that would not go away and a coldness in her bones that nothing seemed to warm. She lay in the bed each night and could not sleep. She ate and the food turned to sawdust on her tongue. The pile of books and fashion journals Alice brought lay in a neat pile untouched on the table. She sat at night and stared into the flames of the fire and could not stop thinking of Linwood.

Alice took her to Madame Boisseron's and coaxed her to order a wardrobe of clothes to replace the ones lost in the fire, but the finest of silks were as sackcloth on her skin. She agreed to whatever designs Alice and the dress designer suggested. And when Madame Boisseron held a new green silk to her face and they placed her before the peering mirror, she could not bear to look at herself.

All the days seemed to run together. Venetia did not know how many or few had passed since Linwood's arrest. She sat on the sofa in Alice's little upstairs sitting room, letting the tea grow cold in the tea cup on the table before her.

'They're still out there,' Alice said from where she stood by the side of the window, sipping her tea and looking down at the crowd of journalists camped outside the front of her house.

'Are they?' Venetia did not even look round. Her voice was calm, empty of emotion and interest. Her eyes were trained on the low flicker of flames upon the hearth.

'It's ridiculous! You'd think the vultures would grow tired of the wait and go home to their wives.'

Venetia said nothing.

Alice walked over to Venetia, hesitating as her eye ranged over the barely touched tea to the newspaper that lay at the top of the pile. The paper's front page showed a sketch of Venetia and a bold headline. She placed her cup and saucer on the table and threw the newspaper into the fire before sitting down by Venetia's side. 'Razeby shouldn't have left that in here.'

Venetia did not need to read the paper's headline to know what it said. She had read the words a hundred times, poking at a wound that would not heal.

Murderous Lord Linwood caught by pillow confession to his mistress, the divine Miss Fox.

'I did try to warn you about him.' There was nothing of gloating in Alice's words, only genuine concern.

'You did.' Venetia did not look round at her friend.

'Did he really confess to setting the fire at Rotherham's house all those years ago?'

Venetia nodded and could not take her eyes from the coil and writhe of the newspaper as it turned black and disintegrated in the flames. It did not matter that it was destroyed—had she a pencil in her hand she could reproduce the whole article letter by letter, word by damning word.

'The newspapers are saying he started the fire at yours, too.'

She said nothing.

'You did the right thing, Venetia.'

'Did I?' she whispered.

'Of course you did.'

'Then why does it feel so wrong?' she asked, and still her eyes lingered on the newspaper, even though all that now remained of it was the pale delicate wafers of ash.

Alice stared at her.

'Had it been Razeby, would you have gone to the police?'

'I don't know.' Alice admitted. 'Besides, it's different with the way it is between me and Razeby.'

'Perhaps not so different as you think,' Venetia whispered.

There was a silence punctuated only by the tick of Alice's clock on the mantel.

'But it's not true what they printed about you being Linwood's mistress,' Alice said quietly. 'Is it?'

Venetia gave a sad hiccup of a laugh. The irony of the truth rammed the blade all the harder into her heart. 'No, I am not his mistress.'

'You didn't stay the night with him?'

There was a small silence.

'I did.'

'You slept with him?' There was incredulity in those words. 'But I thought…'

Venetia looked round into her friend's face for the first time. 'I love him, Alice.'

Alice stared at her, gaping with shock. 'But you can't, not after all that he's done. He tried to kill you, for God's sake!'

Venetia swallowed, but it did nothing to alleviate the hard lump lodged within her throat or the ache in her heart. Her gaze flitted back to stare at the flames.

The silence hissed.

'I'm sorry, I never thought…' Alice whispered and Venetia could hear the pity in her voice. 'Not Linwood of all men.'

'My mother once told me that we cannot choose whom we fall in love with. And she was right.'

She felt Alice take her hand in hers.

The clock ticked. Outside, life went on as normal.

'If you only knew, Alice, the whole sordid truth of it.'

'Oh, Venetia,' Alice whispered and hugged her. 'I'm so very sorry.'

Venetia closed her eyes, pulled the shutter down in her mind. Then she drew back and looked at Alice. 'I will go back to work tomorrow.'

'It's too soon.'

'I need to work, Alice. I cannot stay hiding here for ever. I have to carry on. The theatre, acting—it is all that I have. How else am I to survive?'

'I can lend you something if you need—'

But Venetia shook her head. It was not money to which she was referring. 'I will look for a new house, too. My presence here makes it difficult for you and Razeby.'

'Razeby understands. He's good like that. There's no rush for you to leave.'

'Thank you, Alice. You are a good friend to me.' But they both knew that she would leave as soon as she could.

'Visitors for you, your lordship!' The turnkey's voice rang out before there was the scrape of the key in the lock and the Newgate Prison cell door swung open.

Linwood was already on his feet, waiting in expectation. But it was not his father who was ushered into the cell. Instead, he saw his sister and her husband.

'What the hell are you thinking of, bringing her here?' he growled at his brother-in-law, Rafe Knight.

'Please do not be angry with him, Francis.' Marianne came to stand before him. 'I told him that I would come here alone if he did not bring me. And I would have done.'

Linwood gave a sigh and swallowed. 'You grow more stubborn since your marriage, little sister.'

'I do.' She smiled, but it was a sad smile. 'Oh, Francis!' She threw her arms around him and, with her face against his chest, hugged him tight.

He patted her on the back and stood there awkwardly until she released him. Her eyes roved over the cell, over the bed and its dark covers, over the washstand, the chest of drawers, over the small table and single chair. All of them new.

'Papa brought you all you need?' she asked.

He gave a nod.

'And they are feeding you decent food?'

'Our father has seen to everything.'

'Do you have candles to see by? And books to pass your time? I could bring you—'

'Thank you, Marianne, but really, I have no need of anything.'

She gave a nod. 'If you think of something...'

'I will ask.'

No matter that she was pretending to be strong and unmoved by seeing him here, he knew that she was not.

There was a silence—strained and filled with everything that they could not speak of.

'I wish...' He heard the break in her voice. She bit her lip and he could see that she was trying very hard not to weep.

'Rotherham is dead, Marianne,' he said. 'And it is an end to all that went before.' His gaze moved to Knight's. Knight's face was hard, but Linwood saw something that looked like gratitude and relief flicker in his brother-in-law's eyes.

'The price was too high.' His sister's eyes scanned his as she spoke.

'Maybe. But I do not regret what I do.'

'Francis,' she whispered, and the tears spilled over to run silently down her cheeks.

He smiled at her, knowing all that she had been through

these past years. 'You asked if there was something you might do for me.'

'Anything.'

'Do not come here again.'

She closed her eyes and gave a little sob. 'Please, Francis,' she whispered.

'Promise me, Marianne.'

She nodded. 'If that is your true wish, then I promise.'

Knight put his arm around her and began to steer her away. 'Come, Marianne.' She was weeping in earnest now.

The two men's eyes met across the cell.

Rafe Knight bowed his head in a gesture of acknowledgement. 'I will look after her, always.'

Linwood gave a nod. 'There is none who could do it better.' He knew that absolutely; the knowledge drove him on, even now. And even when the heavy iron door slammed shut behind them to leave him here alone once more.

In the theatre that afternoon Venetia watched the rehearsal with her understudy playing her part. She could hear Mr Kemble's voice talking about the play, about the delivery of her lines, about stage directions, about the audience, all the things that made up Venetia's life. All the things that had been so important to her. Except that now they did not seem so very important at all. She felt shallow, trivial, disconnected.

'Venetia?'

She blinked and realised that Mr Kemble was talking to her.

'Mr Kemble?' she said, the ghost of the self-assured woman she had once been.

'Are you sure you should be here?'

'Where else should I be?' The theatre had been her home, her family for as long as she could remember. If she were not here, she was afraid of where she would be, of what she would be doing. She had been afraid of that her whole life.

'The understudy can finish the run.'

'On the contrary, I will finish the run, Mr Kemble.' She had to. It was what she did. It was who she was. Wasn't it?

'Glad to hear it.' Mr Kemble smiled and lowered the volume of his voice. 'The place has been half-empty with Miss Bolton in the role. You know they only come to see you.'

She said nothing.

'I'll get the word out today that you're back on the bill on Friday night.'

She nodded.

'We're running a bit late for Miss Bolton's performance tonight. Go home, Venetia. Get some rest.'

Home. She did not have a home any more.

'I want you rested and at your best for Friday.' Then he hurried off to speak to her understudy, Miss Bolton.

Everything moved on around her, while she stood there forgotten. She turned and walked away.

On the coach ride back to the house she looked out of the window at a courting couple strolling along the pavement arm in arm. They were poor, she could tell from their clothes, but they looked at one another with shyness and excitement and affection. She turned her face away, but through the other window in an open-top carriage just across the road were Hawick and a young woman who looked both beautiful and happy. She remembered the night Linwood had saved her from the duke and she felt more miserable than ever.

At Alice's she made her way into the drawing room, peeling off her gloves and untying her bonnet.

Alice and Razeby were standing wrapped in each other's arms before the fireplace. They jumped apart as she entered the room.

'Forgive me.' She felt her cheeks warm. 'I did not realise…'

'Wait, Venetia,' Alice said, but Venetia was already walking across the room to escape. 'Razeby has come from visiting Linwood in Newgate.'

She stopped in her tracks. Stood there a moment and then, unable to help herself, turned slowly around. She tried to keep her face impassive, but her eyes met Razeby's and inside her chest she could feel the thud of her heart so hard and heavy that she wondered that he did not hear it.

'How is he?'

'As well as can be expected under the circumstances.'

Inside she felt a little more of her soul shrivel and die. She let her gaze drop to the floor and stared at the pattern on the Turkey rug, at the intricate intertwining of the gold wool with the blue. There was nothing she could say.

In the silence a piece of coal cracked and hissed.

'Miss Fox,' Razeby said.

She glanced up.

'He denies burning your house, but will say not one word on the rest of the charges.' Razeby paused before continuing, 'He means to offer no defence over Rotherham.'

'Oh, God help him! They will hang him!' She closed her eyes and clutched a hand to her mouth, afraid of what she had betrayed. Her blood ran cold, the tingle of it through her body making her shiver.

She saw Alice and Razeby exchange a look.

'Venetia…' Alice started to say.

'Please do excuse me.'

Alice made to follow her, but Venetia shook her head and fled from the room.

Chapter Fifteen

'They have found Rotherham's missing pistol, Francis.'

Linwood's father sat across the small table from him. 'Washed up on a mud bank of the Thames.' His father's brow was creased with concern. He had grown older and more haggard than the last time Linwood had seen him. There were bags beneath his eyes as if he had not slept in a long time. 'The evidence mounts against you.'

Linwood made no comment.

'Our own newspapers are handling the reporting of the story with sensitivity; the rest of them…well, you can imagine.'

'I can, indeed,' said Linwood.

There was a small silence before his father said, 'I have spoken to all that might hold sway over the case for when it comes to trial, called in every last favour, but…'

'Rotherham was a duke. And not all of the money or connections in the world can make the murder of a duke go away. An example must be made. A villain caught.'

'There is a way it might be done.' His father looked at him. 'Miss Fox's evidence is the linchpin in the case. Everything else can be explained away. But not that. If she were to disappear…'

'Do not dare touch her!'

'I meant money, a bribe. You always think the worst of me.'

'I wonder why.'

His father glanced away uneasily. 'I will give her every penny I have if that is what it takes.'

'I am warning you. Stay away from her.'

'Do you honestly think I am going to just sit back and watch you hang because of that whore?'

'She is not a whore, whatever you may think. And if I hang…well, some things are worth dying for, aren't they?'

His father closed his eyes and massaged his fingers against his forehead. 'Why the hell did you tell her?'

'We played a dangerous game together, Miss Fox and I. I took a gamble and I lost.'

'Do not think that she holds you or your plight in any regard. She returns to Covent Garden tomorrow night. The seats were selling for twice their normal price and there is not a one left to be had.'

'Promise me she will be safe,' Linwood said.

'I will not harm her,' his father said, but still Linwood was not persuaded.

'Swear it, on Marianne's life.'

He saw the pain in his father's eyes before he closed them. 'I swear,' he said with resignation and only then was Linwood convinced of Venetia's safety.

They looked at one another across the table.

'My dark deeds come back to haunt me, first with my daughter and now with my son.'

There was a silence.

'I should have been the one that killed Rotherham,' his father said.

Another silence.

'There is so much I never told you, Francis, so much

that I regret in how I treated you through the years. My father raised me hard. And I did the same to you. I thought I was doing the right thing. I thought it would make you strong to deal with the toughness of life. But I was cruel and too critical. For that I am sorry.'

Linwood looked at his father.

'I have made so many mistakes in the past, Francis. I have been a selfish, cruel and ruthless man, but know that I would give my life to rectify all that hurt Marianne… and you. I cannot change what happened with Rotherham. But I can tell you that I love you, that I was always proud to have you as my boy. I should have told you that a long time ago.'

The silence echoed between them.

Misbourne reached across and clapped a hand against Linwood's shoulder. 'Son.' He gave a gruff nod, then got to his feet. 'I will come again tomorrow morning, and every morning after that, until the trial.' Then he walked to the locked door and knocked upon it to be released.

'Thank you,' Linwood whispered, and could not bring the rest of the words in his chest to his mouth, lest they unmanned him.

Alice and Venetia sat opposite one another at the breakfast table the next morning, Alice with her pretty pink negligé showing from beneath her dressing gown, her legs bare beneath her skirts, Venetia wearing her new plain dove-grey day dress, her hair caught tight back, her face devoid of all artifice. The butler sat the large silver salver, piled high with letters, on the table before Venetia.

'Why don't you put them aside? Read them later when you're feeling better.' Alice's eyes were filled with concern.

Venetia shook her head. 'I should deal with them now. And I am fine, really, I am.'

'You don't look fine. You look like you haven't slept in days.'

Venetia smiled, but it was a smile that held nothing of happiness. She stared at her coffee cup. 'I can't stop thinking of him.'

'Little wonder after all you've been through. But you can't doubt that you did the right thing.'

'Can't I?' She glanced up at her friend. 'He will make no defence…' She winced. 'Without a defence there is no hope that he can escape a guilty verdict. That they will sentence him to hang is a certainty. Why would he do such a thing? It makes no sense.'

Alice gave a shrug of her shoulders. 'Maybe he's had an attack of conscience and intends to take what he deserves, but can't bring himself to make the admission.'

'I cannot rid myself of the conviction that there is something I am missing, that I have got this all wrong. It gnaws at me night and day.' She glanced down at her hands. 'That and the guilt.'

'You've got nothing to feel guilty over.'

'No?' She stared at her friend. 'My part in this is written in black and white for all London to read. I cannot hide from it. I was the one who went to the police to repeat the words he told me. Along with the rest of it.'

'Venetia, he tried to kill you! You'd no choice but to go to the police.'

She shook her head and thought again of the look on Linwood's face after he had rescued her from the fire. It was not that of a man who had just tried to kill her. What she had seen in his eyes reflected that which was in her own heart—hurt and disbelief and love. 'Alice,' she gave voice to the little quiet question that whispered in her ear through the long hours of the night, 'what if he is innocent?'

There was a stunned silence.

'How can you think him innocent? He's guilty as sin. With every day that passes they find more evidence against him. An innocent man would deny the crime, Venetia. He would stand up, hand on heart, and say he didn't kill Rotherham. But Linwood doesn't.'

And had the shoe been on the other foot, Venetia would have been saying the same thing to her friend. It was the logical explanation. It was what all London thought. But all London did not know the extent of what had been between her and Linwood.

'He has to be guilty.' Venetia could say the words easily enough, but they changed nothing of what she felt in her heart and in the very marrow of her bones.

She leafed through the stack of letters without opening them, knowing they would be yet more offers from newspapers for her side of the story, more offers from gentlemen eager to make her their mistress. And then her eye was caught by one letter different from the others. The top right-hand side was neatly printed with the mark that excused it payment of delivery. She pulled it out, discarded the others and turned it over to break the seal. There, printed on the reverse, was the name of the sender written in a neat hand—The Old Bailey Courthouse.

Her heart stuttered.

Her stomach turned over.

Her fingers stumbled as she broke the seal and unfolded the sheet to read the letter. The shock of the words penned there was so strong she felt physically sick.

'What's wrong, Venetia? You've gone chalk white.'

'The date for Linwood's trial has been set for two weeks' time.' Her lips felt stiff and cold.

'Better for you to get it out the way sooner rather than later.'

'I am called to attend and testify as the chief witness for the prosecution.' The piece of paper in her hand began to tremble. She laid it down on the table.

'They'll not let you out of it.'

To stand up and face him across a courtroom and speak the words that would tie a noose around his neck. She closed her eyes.

'You know that, don't you, Venetia?'

She opened her eyes and met Alice's gaze. 'Yes, I know.' And it seemed to Venetia that the words fell like shards of ice into the silence. She felt bloodless, chilled. And the pain in her chest was so bad that it made her want to gasp.

She swallowed and let her eyes move back to the letter. Then she folded it as if she were perfectly in control of herself and got to her feet.

'You've not eaten anything.'

'I am due at the theatre. I will get something there.'

Alice gave a nod. 'Tonight's performance sold out within an hour of the tickets going on sale.'

'So I heard.'

She walked to the door.

'Venetia?'

She stopped and glanced back at her friend.

'Are you going to be all right?' Alice asked.

She forced herself to smile, but it felt like it was tearing her lips apart. 'I will be fine,' she said. 'I always am, am I not?'

Alice nodded.

Venetia threw herself into the rehearsal at the theatre that afternoon, forced her mind to focus on the play, on the script, anything other than Linwood. She became Rosina and that was a lot easier than being Venetia. Everything was busy, everything rushed, urgent, demanding, intense, just as it was on every night of a performance except more so because everyone knew that every seat in the theatre would be filled, that every eye would be fixed on Venetia, every newspaper man ready to rush out and write up his report of *Rosina*'s leading lady. Venetia let herself be engulfed by it, swallowed up by it. It was what she knew, what she felt comfortable with.

She was fine all of the day and all of the evening, fine as they laced her into the old-fashioned dress of Rosina with its tight bodice that clung to her natural waist line. Fine as they untied the rags from her hair and unwound the wraps of hair so that they shimmered in a long mass of soft curls. Fine as they milled around her, painting her face, and touching her lips and cheeks with rouge.

There were only fifteen minutes to curtain up when they left her alone in the little dressing room to compose herself. But once she was alone she could no longer pretend that the spectre of Linwood was not haunting her. She sat at the little dressing table, very calm and very still, and felt the ache that had not left her chest since she had spoken to the Bow Street officer. She did not let herself look in the peering glass, just glanced at the notes she had written about Rosina, trying, and failing, to focus herself on the part she was about to play.

A sudden flurry of fast, light footsteps pattered outside in the corridor. Venetia glanced up just as the door was thrown open and a small dark-cloaked figure burst in. A finely manicured hand wrenched the cloak's deep hood back to reveal its wearer—Linwood's sister, Lady Marianne. The girl's eyes were dark and glittering and wild. Her cheeks were as pink as her lips. Some of her pins had been dislodged and half of her long fair curls had escaped to muss around her face.

'Miss Venetia Fox, how very happy you must be with

yourself!' Fury rolled off her in great waves. 'Your name is on every tongue in London, emblazoned across every newspaper! You have filled the entire theatre!'

Venetia rose to her feet, standing almost a head taller than Marianne. 'I understand that you are upset, Lady Marianne, but you should leave now.'

'Why? Because the truth does not make for comfortable hearing?'

'It would not serve you well if we were to be seen together. And I am due on stage shortly.'

'And that is all that matters to you, is it not?'

'I am sorry about your brother, truly I am.' The words sounded pathetic, even to Venetia's own ears.

'Sorry?' Lady Marianne stared at her as if she were the very devil. 'How can you be sorry, when it is your words that will hang him?' she demanded with a fierceness of which Venetia had not thought her capable.

The truth cut through all the pretence that Venetia had woven about herself to get through this day.

'How could you do it?' Marianne shouted. 'You were his lover! You shared his bed!'

'Lady Marianne—'

'You promised me that you would not hurt him! I thought that you loved him, fool that I am—but you have no care for anyone other than yourself!'

Venetia caught her breath. 'He set fire to my home,' she said, trying to make Marianne understand. 'He lied—'

'Never!' Marianne came right up to her, staring up into Venetia's face so that Venetia could see how much the girl was trembling with the force of emotion surging through her. 'My brother would never hurt you! And as for lying— he would rather say nothing than offer a lie! Anything he has done has only ever been to—'

'Marianne!' The tall, dark figure of Rafe Knight appeared in the doorway. In one swift smooth swoop he had his wife away from Venetia and in his arms. He stared down into Lady Marianne's face. 'This is not the way,' he said carefully, his eyes holding his wife's, and Venetia saw the urgent message that passed between Knight and Marianne. There was a fierce protectiveness in that gaze that would have razed all in its path.

Lady Marianne was breathing hard, but she calmed herself and gave a small nod to her husband.

Knight turned his eyes to Venetia and she felt herself quail at the hardness that appeared in them. 'You will forgive my wife, Miss Fox. She is naturally distressed at her brother's situation.' His voice was soft and polite enough, but she had no doubt that his words were warning her.

'Of course,' she said.

Knight held Venetia in the full blast of that icy gaze for a moment longer, then he pulled Marianne's hood to shroud her identity and led her from the room.

The door clicked shut, but Venetia was still staring at where they had stood.

He would rather say nothing than offer a lie! Lady Marianne's words seemed to hang in the air like an echo, making her feel as if all the air had been sucked from her lungs as she remembered words that were so similar.

A knock sounded. The face of the stagehand, who had come to fetch her, appeared around the door. 'It's time, Miss Fox.'

'Thank you,' she murmured but she made no move.

'Miss Fox,' the stagehand urged.

She gave a nod and had no choice but to follow him out along the corridor towards the stage.

The seconds were running out. She reached the wings just in time, a heartbeat and then the lights came to life and she was walking out onto the stage as Rosina to the whistles and whispers and murmur of voices all around. So many people filled the auditorium that the theatre seemed to heave at the seams. She heard someone shout Linwood's name and it was all she could do to show no reaction.

She contrived to be Rosina. Only Rosina. Speaking the words written in the script, moving across the stage as Mr Kemble had directed her. But she was not Rosina. She was Venetia, and all she could hear was the beat of her heart and the whisper of the pact she had made with Linwood. Her blood ran cold. *We are sworn to speak the truth or say nothing at all.* She kept on acting, kept on going. But everything was falling into place in her mind. The explanation had been before her the whole time, but she had been too blind to see it. She stopped where she was, midline, stood there silent in the middle of the stage. The enormity of the realisation was such that it made all else trivial in comparison.

She stared around her at the facade of Rosina, at the costume and illusion, and her leading actor, Mr Incledon.

The prompt whispered her missing words from within the hidden box at the front of the stage.

The life of the man she loved was at stake.

The cue came again, so loud this time that the front rows of the audience heard.

Venetia looked out at the huge sea of faces. There were murmurs from them now, a fascinated horror in those expressions. Mr Incledon carried on, delivering the next line of his role as Belville and watching her with mounting anxiety.

But it did not matter. None of it mattered, not the play or the audience or the acting career of Miss Venetia Fox. The only thing that mattered was to know if she was sending an innocent man to his death. And there was one simple way to discover that. *We are sworn to speak the truth or say nothing at all.*

When at last she spoke it was not as Rosina, but as Venetia. 'I must go to him,' she said and walked off stage, leaving Mr Incledon and the entirety of the Theatre Royal gaping in stunned silence.

Chapter Sixteen

From somewhere beyond the prison yard a church bell sounded eight times and Linwood knew that the divine Miss Fox would be on stage now, playing a part while all of London watched. The betrayal felt bitter in his stomach, yet if it were to happen all over again he knew he would do nothing different. It seemed, somehow, that from that first moment upon the balcony of the green room all that followed had been inevitable. As if he ever could have walked away from her. She was the other side of himself. Two people removed from the rest of the world as it played on.

A draught made the candle flames flicker wildly and a commotion sounded outside his cell. Raised male voices, whistling, cheers, shouts, wolf whistles of male appreciation. And then silence. A ripple of foreboding whispered against his ear, followed by the scrape of the key in the lock of his door. The scent of her perfume touched his nose. He raised his eyes and saw Venetia standing there, dressed as Rosina.

The guards stood transfixed by the sight of her and he could not blame them. Venetia Fox was a sight to take any man's breath away. The luminous pallor of her skin contrasted with the cascade of dark satin of her hair and the deep red of the costume she was wearing. The dress was very risqué, the bodice laced tight to hug her waist and allowing the peep of a white chemise beneath. It outlined the hourglass curves of her body, its low neckline barely containing the swell of her pale breasts. In the soft flickering candlelight she was the very epitome of every man's fantasy. He felt his blood heat at the memory of her in his arms, of that silken skin beneath his hands, of their bodies merged as one, of the soft cry of his name upon her lips as she found her climax. It took every ounce of his self-control not to show any reaction.

'Lord Linwood,' she said, but the formality did not hide her slight breathlessness. She stood there, seemingly as calm and controlled as ever, and yet she was not as calm as she pretended. He could see it in her eyes, in the too-rapid rise and fall of her breasts, feel it in the tension that vibrated in the air between them.

'Miss Fox.' His eyes met hers and across the distance of the cell feelings he did not want to name shimmered between them. He shifted his gaze to the guards, pinning them with it. They backed out, closing the door behind them, turning the key, locking Venetia and him alone together in the prison cell.

He made no move.

Nor did she.

'Don't you have an appointment on the stage of the Theatre Royal?'

She shook her head. 'Not any more.'

'Why are you here, Venetia?'

'I have something I need to ask you.'

'And you think I will tell…you, of all people?'

'Yes.' She faced him bravely, defiantly almost, as she walked slowly forwards to stand directly before him and look into his face.

He felt his heart beat three times before she spoke. 'Were you responsible for the fire at my home?'

'That you even need to ask, Venetia,' he murmured, feeling the chill blow all the colder through him. Then he glanced away and gave a soft mirthless laugh, before returning his gaze to hers and stepping closer so that she could see the truth in his eyes. 'No. I am not.'

Their gazes held, locked in this torture together. He could see the tiny pulse that throbbed so fast at the side of that pale throat, the dark dilation of her eyes, the steadfast determination of purpose that filled her.

'Did you kill Rotherham?'

He felt the involuntary tightening of his jaw. 'That is not something I am prepared to discuss.'

'Why not?'

'I have my reasons.'

From somewhere close by something small and furry scurried. Water dripped down the wall in a slow rhythmic steadiness.

'Which are?'

'Again, not open for discussion.'

'You did not do it, did you, Francis?'

He raised an eyebrow. 'The same question as the first, in disguise. Thus, I give you the same answer.'

'Then let me rephrase—I *know* you did not do it.'

'Dangerous talk from the star witness for the prosecution, Venetia.'

She glanced away at that, but not before he had seen the guilt and unhappiness in her eyes. Both were hidden by the time she looked at him again. 'We are bound by an oath of honesty, Francis. We have been all along, in every thrust and parry of our duel.'

'Fishing for truths with truths,' he said.

'Yes,' she agreed softly.

Their eyes held, and all of what had been between them, of what still was, pulsated and heaved—a turmoil of barely fettered emotion rattling at its chains.

'You say nothing over the murder charge because to admit it would be lying.'

'Or maybe I say nothing because to deny it would be the lie.'

'They will hang you, Francis.'

'Most probably.'

'By your silence you invite them to believe you guilty of a crime you did not commit.'

'And why would any sane man do that?' He turned away before she could answer, afraid she might see something of the truth in him.

'It makes no sense, indeed…unless you are protecting someone.'

He froze, feeling the chill ripple right through him like ice freezing across a lake.

'You told me once that Rotherham hurt someone close to you.' Still he did not look at her, even though he knew he should turn and fight a defence. Dread was heavy upon him, making it hard to breath, making it impossible to move. He stood very still, forcing himself to feign normality, exerting a rigid control that would reveal nothing.

'All the more reason for mine to be the hand that executed Rotherham.'

'Or to protect the person who did the deed. I have heard tell that your father and Rotherham were old friends once upon a time, until they had a disagreement of such magnitude that they never spoke again. Old friends can become the worst of enemies. Feuds nursed through the years have a way of escalating. And Rotherham was not a man to let things go and move on with his life. My guess is that whatever was between your father and Rotherham lies at the heart of this.'

She was so close to the truth that he felt his blood run cold. He turned to face her.

'Such imagination, Miss Fox. Worthy of a theatre setting. You should speak to Kemble.' The words were stiff and cold even though a nervous sweat prickled beneath his arms.

They looked at one another across the distance of the small cell, he hoping that she would be thwarted, her appearing not one whit convinced by his words. All of time seemed to stretch to eternity in the discomfort and fear of that moment.

'I will not stand as witness against you, Francis,' she said, and in her voice was a curious mix of both resolve and resignation.

'Planning to lie and tell them I said no such thing?'

She shook her head and gave a small half smile that was filled only with sadness. 'Planning to speak the truth or say nothing at all.'

The words echoed in the ensuing silence, words that were etched across his heart.

His heart skipped a beat at her courage and audacity and depth of comprehension. 'You cannot do that, Venetia.'

'I think you will find that I can, Francis.' Her eyes held his with her characteristic challenge and resilience.

'If you refuse to speak, they will gaol you.'

She gave a tiny shrug of her bare shoulders, as if the threat of gaol meant nothing.

'Have you any idea of what it is like in prison?' Did she not understand that she was risking so much more than her career?

She let her gaze wander pointedly around his cell before returning to his eyes. 'I believe that I do.'

'Venetia, you do not understand. You are the most coveted woman in all of London. This place is full of men, men who have long lusted after you. The guards are not above accepting a bribe to turn a blind eye, or even indulging their own needs. You would not be safe.'

'Safe enough,' she said. 'It would not be my life they would take.'

'Do not try to play the harlot, Venetia, for I know you are none of that.'

For a moment the polished mask of the confident, sophisticated woman dropped away and something raw and vulnerable flashed in her eyes. She glanced away, then back again. 'I made a mistake. I will not compound it by standing as witness against you.' There was a stubbornness to her words and an utter resolve in her eyes. And as he watched, her full luscious lips pressed firm together in determination.

He raked a hand through his hair and glanced away. 'God help us, Venetia,' he murmured, unable to help himself.

'I am sorry, Francis.' Her voice softened. For the first time since she had entered the cell her control wavered. 'I honestly thought you were guilty. I did not mean for any of this to happen. I never thought that we would—' She bit her lip, as if to stopper the words and glanced down. And when she looked up at him again, he could see the emotion in her eyes that she was trying so hard to hide. 'I will do anything to save you.' She turned to walk towards the door.

'Anything, Venetia?' His heart was beating too fast.

She hesitated.

'If you are so intent upon this path, there is another way....'

His words made her turn.

He walked slowly to her, closing the distance until he

was standing directly before her, looking down into her face. He could see the glitter of tears in her eyes, the fast pulse that thrummed in her slender white neck, the rapid rise and fall of her breasts above the neckline of the dress.

The silence rippled all around them.

'A wife cannot be compelled to testify against her husband,' he uttered softly.

It took a moment for it to register just exactly what he was suggesting.

'Marry me,' he said and his voice sounded husky.

Whatever it was that Venetia had expected him to say, it was nothing of that. Her eyes widened. She stared at him, even now not sure that she had not misheard. Over the roar of the silence she could hear only the frantic thud of her own heart. Her stomach was turning a sequence of somersaults, her blood rushing so fast that she felt light-headed and weak-kneed. She reached for the back of the chair, but Linwood's arm was there first, solid, hard, supportive beneath hers. Where his hand held against her waist her skin seemed to scorch.

She looked into his eyes, the eyes of the man that she loved with all her heart, the one man whose wife, were their positions and circumstances different, she would have been overjoyed to become, to bear his children. 'You cannot be in earnest,' she whispered.

'Never more so.'

Her eyes raked his face, seeking the truth and finding it. 'It is not possible,' she said. 'You are heir to an earldom and I am an actress.'

'I know what we both are, Venetia.'

And he was a man in prison accused of murder, and she the woman who had put him there.

In the silence that followed she studied that handsome face, the strong straight line of his nose, the harsh angles of his cheeks and chin. And those dark eyes so filled with passion, eyes that could reach deep inside her to stroke against her soul. It was her girlhood dream, a fantasy long forgotten—to marry a man that she loved: a strong man, a man who loved her. She would have married him a hundred times over. But not like this, never like this.

'You would marry me to save me from prison.' The pain tightened in her chest. 'I do not know if I can let you do that,' she said carefully.

There was only the soft sound of her breath and, over it, the loud thud of her heart.

Something flashed in the darkness of his eyes. 'Marrying you is the only certain way that I might avoid the hangman's noose.'

The breath moved in and out of her lungs. She saw the tiny flicker of tension in the strong line of his jaw, and where his hand still held against her waist she seemed to feel the beat of his heart resonate through her body. A beam of sun stole through the bars of the tiny high window of the cell, striping light against his face and softening the black of his eyes. She was not sure that she believed him. Her mind was telling her one thing and her heart, another.

'You did say "anything", Venetia.'

Their eyes clung together and it did not matter as to the reasoning behind his proposal because he was right.

She nodded, her gaze unable to break away from his. 'I did.'

The intensity between them did not waver.

'Could it be arranged in time?' She knew she should step away, but it was not his hand on her waist that held her there.

'My father is friends with the Archbishop of Canterbury. A priest and a special licence with our names upon it will not present a problem.'

With her name upon it. She closed her eyes and felt her heart sink, as the realisation dawned. *Her name.* It did not matter how far she ran, or what she did to escape it, the truth of who she was had always dogged her, snapping at her heels. Always just a breath away.

His mouth tightened. 'Is the prospect really so despicable to you?'

She realised how her response must look to him—that she dreaded to be his wife. 'You misunderstand. It is nothing of that—only...'

His eyes smouldered and glittered with an intensity so razing that it took her breath away. 'Only...?' There was something very dangerous in the way he said it.

The moment of reckoning had finally come. Because to save him she would have to reveal part of what she had spent a lifetime hiding—the truth of what she was to Rotherham. To the one man over everyone that she could not bear to know. It would change everything between them. She took a deep breath and felt her breasts brush against his chest with the movement, and the slight increase in the pressure of his hand upon her waist.

'There is something I have not told you, Francis—something which will make you reconsider your offer.'

'So many dark secrets, Venetia. Amidst the deception of truths was there ever anything of honesty between us?'

Her gaze was locked in his, his eyes raking hers, but beneath his anger she could see his vulnerability. She reached a hand up and traced her fingers along the beard-stubbled line of his jaw. 'More than you will ever realise,' she whispered as she let her hand drop to her side.

The words did not want to come to her lips, but there could be no more evasion. 'I am not who you think me. I am not who all of London thinks me.' She closed her eyes, let herself experience this closeness with him, aware of even the smallest sensation, the warmth of his breath against her cheeks, the scent of him—so enticing and reassuring at once—the heat of his hand upon her waist, the strength of his arm beneath her own. Her body leaned against his in one final caress. The wonder of each sensation gathered up and stored in her heart. She knew everything would be different once she told him.

'Are any of us really who the world thinks us?' he said softly.

She opened her eyes and looked up into that so-beloved face. The moment stretched, until she forced herself on. 'Fox is the name I took when I came to London, the name I chose for a new life upon the stage.'

He said nothing, just waited.

She swallowed and did not let herself drop her gaze, even though that was what she so longed to do. She felt ashamed, and afraid, like the little girl who had stood before Rotherham all those years before. 'My real name is Venetia Clandon.'

She felt his sudden, utter stillness.

'You asked me once who Robert Clandon was to me. You thought he was my employer.' But the truth would hurt him more than that ever could. 'He is my half-brother.' Her fingers were gripping so tight that they were chilled and bloodless. 'We were both fathered illegitimately by the Duke of Rotherham, albeit on different women.' She looked directly into his eyes. 'I am Rotherham's daughter, Francis.'

The silence roared louder than any condemnation could have.

His face was shadowed and unreadable in the candlelight.

'So you were in this every bit as much as Clandon.'

Something in the way he said it made her shrivel with shame. 'Crusaders on a mission of vengeance.'

'It was nothing of vengeance.'

'Justice, then, for the loss of such a loving father.'

'Rotherham was not loving. He was cold and cruel and calculating in ways you could never imagine. Everything I said of him was true. And, yes, it was about justice. I believed you guilty of his murder, Francis, for pity's sake! And no matter what I thought of the man who was my father, he did his duty by me. He took me in when my mother died, saw that I was raised. In the end, I could not refuse to do my duty by him. I owed him that at least.'

They looked at one another through the silence.

'I should have realised. You have his eyes—pale and silver as moonlight.'

She glanced away, not wishing to own anything of Rotherham's when he was everything that Linwood hated. But Rotherham's blood ran in her veins and there was nothing that she could do about it. Besides, Rotherham's blood was only half the story.

'Although there is little in common between you and Clandon.'

'Robert's looks favour those of his mother. She was Rotherham's housekeeper.'

'How fortunate for you both.' His tone was dead of inflection, as cold and emotionless as he was to the world at large. Neither of them had moved. They were standing so close she could feel the heat of his body scalding hers, feel the struggle of the emotions held so tightly suppressed between them.

There was nothing she could say to make it better. The ghost of Rotherham hung between them, and always would.

'Rotherham openly acknowledged Clandon as his son. So why the big secret over you, Venetia?'

'Rotherham would have acknowledged me. I did not wish him to do so.'

'Were it known you were a duke's daughter, even one born on the wrong side of the blanket, it would have done much to ease your path in life, just as it has done for Clandon.'

What he said was the truth. She was only where she was today because of Rotherham's influence and intervention. But she could not bring herself to tell him the rest of it, not that it mattered—to Linwood the fact that she was Rotherham's daughter was enough. 'It was not about having Rotherham as a father.' It took more than a father to produce a child.

'Then what was it about?'

She gave a shrug as if the answer were of no great consequence, when in truth it was the one thing that had dictated every twist and turn she had taken upon the path of life. It was the spur that had driven her night and day in her determination to flee from it. She turned the conversation away from the danger of that avenue.

'So now you know.'

The tension in the cell stretched so tight that she could barely breathe. She felt sick with the dread of his condemnation, of the situation to which she had brought them both.

'I do,' he said in a hard voice. 'And it need not influence our plans.'

She gaped at him in disbelief. 'You wish to marry me, even knowing that I am the bastard of the man you hated so much? A man who hurt someone close to you so badly that you are willing to hang to protect them?' The blunt vulgar truth resonated in all its shocking audacity between them.

'I will send word of the day.' His expression was closed, hiding what he was feeling, but the look in his eyes was dark and angry.

To marry the man that she loved while knowing how he must hate her...to endure his contempt for the rest of her life... Prison seemed almost preferable. She glanced away, feeling her chest ache where her heart lay bruised and bleeding. But this was not about her. This was about saving Linwood from the noose she had tied around his neck.

'Be ready, Venetia.'

She nodded. Finally, he released her from his gaze. She had betrayed an innocent man, in more ways than one. A great wave of guilt flooded through her. She should have listened to her heart, she thought. Her heart had always known. She turned quickly away, knocking on the door of the cell to summon the turnkeys, before she weakened and betrayed herself by starting to weep.

When the door swung open she did not look back at him. Just walked out of the cell, out of the prison, leaving behind the man that she loved, the man she would marry, the man she had condemned.

Chapter Seventeen

Contrary to her expectation Venetia did not hear from Linwood the next day, or the one after that or even the next again. The days passed and the calendar crept closer to the date of the trial, so close that she feared he had changed his mind and could not bring himself to marry her after all, or that something had gone terribly wrong. She wanted to go to the prison again, to see him, to know what was happening, anything other than this turmoil of imaginings and doubts and fears. But her pride would not let her and she resigned herself to her original plan of refusing to speak as a witness at his trial. She did not know if she felt better or worse at the prospect of prison, only that she was the sole barrier that stood between Linwood and the hangman's noose, and even then she was not certain that by refusing to speak she could undo what she had set in motion. And all her dreams and all her waking hours were locked within that nightmare.

The letter finally arrived two days before the trial. The familiar hand that had penned her direction, so strong and bold, made her heart skip a beat. She slipped the letter into her pocket before Alice's watchful eyes and did not trust herself to open it until she was alone in her bedchamber.

Her hands were shaking as she finally broke the seal and unfolded the thick-laid paper embossed with his crest.

His words were scant, the message brief: *Tomorrow at the eleventh hour.* It was signed *L.*

The relief was immediate and overwhelming...and transient. Tomorrow. Her stomach clenched tight at the prospect of what that day would bring.

A knock sounded before the door opened.

'Venetia?' Alice stood there, her face creased in concern.

'You had better sit down, Alice. There are some things that I have to tell you.'

The next morning Venetia and Alice sat together in Razeby's unmarked carriage as it carried them towards Newgate. Venetia had not slept at all since Linwood's letter. Not for one minute of that long dark night. And yet this morning, on the way to her wedding, she felt strangely calm. She was wearing a sober plain afternoon dress of dark forest-green beneath a dark cloak and her hair was pinned up in a classical and tidy style. She wore only a pair of single, white drop-pearl earrings and not one other piece of jewellery. Hardly an outfit for a wedding, but she had no mind to tip off anyone who might be watching of what was about to take place. She dared risk nothing that might jeopardise the ceremony.

Alice glanced across at Razeby and bit at her lip before leaning close to Venetia and saying in a low, hesitant voice, 'It's not too late to change your mind, Venetia.'

Razeby must have heard Alice trying to persuade her against marrying his friend, but he made no comment. His usual smiling demeanour was gone. He looked almost as cold and serious as Linwood himself. There could be no doubting the gravity of Linwood's position.

Venetia swallowed and carefully smoothed a wrinkle in her beige kid-leather gloves, such a small foolish detail over which to fuss given the magnitude of that in which they were enmeshed. The danger and desperation, the bald fact that Linwood's life was at stake. She did not let herself think of what would happen if they failed in this venture… or, indeed, what, if they succeeded; just kept her thoughts still and her mind focused on doing what she knew she must. Even now she was playing the role of Miss Fox, even now pretending that she was cool and unaffected by what was happening. Even when both Alice and Razeby knew the truth—of her name and her feelings.

'You know that I am not going to change my mind.' They had been through the argument a hundred times since yesterday.

She heard again through her head Alice's questions. *What if you've got this all wrong, Venetia? All the evidence supports his guilt. What if it's right and he really is the man that shot a bullet into your father's head?*

And her own answers, adamant and determined in their faith. *He did not do it, Alice.* It was against all logic, against all evidence to the contrary, but she felt the truth of it in the marrow of her bones and every beat of her heart.

And even were she wrong, it made no difference. She could not hang him.

Linwood was alone in the cell when they arrived. He had shaved the stubble from his face and his clothes were clean and as well presented as if his valet had dressed him. Just one glance at him and it was as if she had forgotten how devastatingly handsome he was, how very much he affected her…and how very much she loved him. She felt her heart miss a beat, felt the slight catch in her breath at the sight of him.

'Miss Fox,' he said coolly as if they weren't just about to marry, then diverted his glance momentarily to Alice. 'Miss Sweetly.' He nodded at his friend. 'Razeby.' And then his eyes met hers again and she glimpsed the passion and intensity and emotion smouldering in their dark depths. He could hide what he was from the world, but not from her. The awareness of him tingled through every inch of her being. They were connected on some underlying intrinsic level, attuned, bound. What they were about to do was about saving him, nothing more. How could it be anything else after all that had happened, and all that she was? But beneath it were all the complexities of betrayal and deception…and of love and longing. There always had been.

The cell door opened and his father, the Earl of Misbourne, entered the cell and by his side was a tall thin man, dressed in the robes of a priest, a small battered black-leather book clutched in his hands. The sight of the priest slammed home to her the reality of what she was about to do.

The priest was a man older than Misbourne and he looked distinctly nervous, which was not surprising given how the authorities were liable to interpret the reason for the marriage. Venetia wondered if he had been coerced into being here. One look at the expression on Misbourne's face and she knew that there were not many men who would argue with the earl.

The priest's long bony fingers opened the book at a page marked by a thin red strip of ribbon. His eyes met hers, and she was not sure what it was she saw in them—curiosity, disapproval, pity? She refused to look away, to be cowed or ashamed in any way, just met his gaze with all of Miss Fox's brazen confidence. It was the priest's gaze that faltered, pretending to find his place on the page. She angled her head high and walked to stand by Linwood's left side, but she did not look at him again, nor he at her.

'Proceed,' Linwood commanded the priest.

The priest began to speak. Words that would bind them together in law and in the eyes of God. Words that could not be undone. Words that would save Linwood from the unspeakable fate to which she had condemned him.

She gave her responses, as calmly, as unemotionally as Linwood himself, acting a part to hide the storm of emotions within her. Only when Linwood took her left hand within his and slipped his ring onto her finger did she betray herself a little. His hand was warm against the ice of her own, his touch light, but possessive as it closed over the tremble that beset her fingers. She did not dare look up into his face, lest the sight of those dark eyes break the fragile threads of her control.

The priest's voice sounded again, speaking words which she did not hear. All she was aware of was the touch of Linwood's fingers against her chin, turning her face to his, of the dark intensity in his eyes as he lowered his mouth to hers, of the heat and passion and promise in the meeting of their lips. He kissed her as if they were alone in the prison cell, as if the priest, his father, Alice and Razeby were not standing so closely by, watching. He kissed her as if she were not Rotherham's daughter, as if she had not betrayed him. And, God help her, she responded to him as if she were the wanton the world thought her. Only when he broke the kiss did she step away, opening up a distance between them.

'It is done,' the priest said.

'Thank God,' said Misbourne and she saw the way the hard expression dropped away and the relief and fear that lay beneath it.

'Congratulations, old boy.' Razeby said the words

lightly as he shook his friend's hand, but the look that passed between the two men betrayed the seriousness of the situation.

Alice put her arms around Venetia and dropped a peck of a kiss to her cheek, but she could not bring herself to offer congratulations.

No one wished them happy. No one thought there could ever be any chance of that. And, absurd though it was, that small ridiculous omission made Venetia want to cry.

'Let's get you home,' Alice said and slipped her arm through Venetia's.

Venetia did not let herself look at Linwood. She feared that if she looked at him she really would weep. She fastened her cloak around her shoulders and began to follow Alice across the cell, as the tread of the priest's steps fell in behind them.

'Venetia.' Linwood's voice stopped her in her tracks.

She felt the shiver run all the way down her spine. Felt her stomach flip-flop, because she knew even before she turned what he was going to say. She closed her eyes, tried to gather herself, but it was no good. Her pulse kicked to a gallop. Her heart thumped hard as a hammer in her chest as she faced him.

'If the marriage is not consummated, it can be annulled.'

'You are surely not expecting her to…' Alice's voice died away in horror and indignation. 'Not in this place.'

'They will use any objection they can to invalidate this marriage,' said Misbourne.

The silence was loud within the cell.

She could feel the pressure of Alice's fingers against her forearm. 'You don't have to do this, Venetia.'

'Linwood is right. And…I want to do this properly.' Yet the thought of what must come after the ceremony, obvious though it was, had not occurred to her. Despite a lifetime in the *demi-monde* and being proclaimed England's most beddable woman. Despite the blood that flowed in her veins. She smiled wryly at the irony.

She looked past the pity on Alice's face and gestured to where Razeby was standing in silence. 'Razeby will see you home, Alice.'

'It would be my pleasure,' said the marquis. His eyes met Venetia's fleetingly and she saw something of understanding and respect. There was very much more to Razeby beneath his usual image.

She watched them all leave. And even when the door had closed behind them she did not turn round to Linwood.

He made not one sound, but it seemed to Venetia that she could feel his every breath in her own lungs, feel the thrum of his blood through her own veins, feel the beat of his heart in her own chest.

The door clanged shut and the jangle and scrape of the key turning in the lock was loud in the silence.

'We cannot wait until nightfall, Venetia.' His words were unhurried, cold, clinical, yet she could hear the faint undertone of something else. 'News of our marriage will spread quickly. It would be expedient to have closed the loophole before any man of law can arrive.' As if it were some legal process to be completed rather than an intimate act of lovemaking between two people.

'I understand.' She could not bring herself to meet his gaze. Her fingers were calm and methodical as they moved to unfasten the pearl buttons that ran in a line down the back of her bodice. Those she struggled to reach, Linwood dealt with, before stepping away again. She peeled the dress from her shoulders and, with the help of a little shrug, it slid down her body to land in a heap around her ankles. The single petticoat, and thin silken shift beneath, clung to the voluptuous curves of her body.

She made no sign of having heard the harsh intake of his breath. Her fingers plucked at the ties, allowing both to slither down in the wake of her dress. She stepped free of the clothing pooled around her feet and, reaching up, plucked the pins from her hair, so that the tight pinned coils unwound, to spill long and free and beckoning, over her shoulders. The fullness of her breasts nosed through the long curling strands of hair, the pale flesh so stark in contrast to the ebony of her hair, the rose-pink tips already defined and taut.

He could not help his eyes from tracing every line of that hourglass body, the roundness of her breasts, following in to the slender waist and soft womanly belly, and out to the curve of her hips. And despite everything of their situation, despite that he was a man used to wielding a control of iron over his feelings and desires, and the fact that the turnkeys were undoubtedly listening at the door, his body's reaction was as uncontrolled and immediate as if he were still in his salad days.

The grille within the door slid open suddenly and the face of a turnkey leered in.

Venetia must have heard the opening of the grille, but she did not look round, just stood there, with her head held high, naked save for her white silken shoes and stockings.

However, Linwood moved swiftly to block the lecherous little man's view before he had a chance to see what every man in London had wanted all these years, producing a wad of notes from his pocket, to dangle before the guard's face.

'To ensure that the grille remains closed for the duration of this day and the night that will follow.'

The turnkey's greedy little eyes fixed on the roll of banknotes.

'The same sum to follow in the morning when you have upheld our deal,' Linwood said coldly.

The turnkey licked his narrow lips at the temptation, but he still hesitated, his gaze flitting beyond Linwood's shoulder in a fruitless attempt to catch even the smallest glimpse of Venetia.

Linwood leaned his face closer to the grille and smiled a smile that held all the deadly promise that was in his heart.

The turnkey blanched in response.

Linwood lowered his voice and looked the man in the eye. 'The lady is my wife. And I am charged with the murder of a duke, no less. Yet I will be set free. I am sure that you understand how I will deal with any other man who looks upon her naked form. Do you think the law will prevent me?'

The little man swallowed nervously. 'I'll ensure that does not happen, my lord. Many congratulations on your nuptials.'

'I am glad we understand each other.' Linwood held the money to the grille, and a grubby hand relieved him of it.

'Much obliged, m'lord.' The cover snapped shut against the grille.

He turned to the sight that the man had been so desperate to see—the rear view of Venetia. The daylight kissed her body, marking its glory and its nakedness as all the more shocking. She had not moved, just stood there as if she were carved of the same perfect white marble as Venus herself, seemingly proud and cool and untouched by the man's lechery or anything that was unfolding around her. He did not let himself acknowledge a single one of the emotions that were crowding in his chest. He had married her, and now he would lie with her, to save her and himself. He did not let his mind think any further than that.

He walked round to stand before her. 'We will not be interrupted again.'

She gave a single regal nod, but still her eyes would not meet his.

He peeled off his coat and threw it to land on the table he used both for dining and letter writing, then loosened the knot in his cravat and, pulling the wrapped linen free, let it flutter to the ground. His waistcoat followed before he unfastened the button of his shirt collar, shrugging the fine white linen off over his head and discarding it. He sat down on the chair to divest himself of his boots and stockings. And then stood to drop his breeches and drawers. When he came to her once more he was naked.

Her focus remained upon some distant spot in the corner of the cell, but as he stood there and waited she slowly moved her gaze to meet his.

Her eyes really were like Rotherham's, the pale blue silver such a stark contrast with the darkness of their expanding pupils, but what was in them was nothing of what he had seen in the duke's.

Whatever blood flowed in her veins, whatever the truth of Venetia's heart, the substance beneath the smoke and mirrors of their game was real and reciprocal. She was as powerless to turn away from him as he was to turn from her.

It was just sex, just lust, he told himself, and knew that he lied. He did not want to analyse what he felt for the woman standing before him, but he knew it involved his heart. She had breached his defences in a way that no one else ever had. She had beaten him at his own game when she thought him guilty. And was determined to save him now that she thought him not. She was Rotherham's daughter. And she was his wife.

He felt the threat of emotion tighten in his chest and

thrust the weakness away with the practised hand of a master. He said not a single word, just let his gaze drop to take in the rapid rise and fall of her breasts, the fine feminine line of her jaw and glistening temptation of her lips. And whatever the complexity of anger and hurt, desire and connection, surging through him he knew that right now, when the prospect of his own mortality and the truth of all that he had done, pressed so close, he needed her.

He could hear the sound of his breath coming too rapid and feel the hard thud of his heart. The quietness of the cell seemed to hum with the tension of all that was barely held in check between them. Raw guttural desire, lust…love. He snarled at the thought of the last of those, as if to deny it.

She wetted her lips, those lips that had tortured his soul with their truths and deceptions, and it was like the touch of a match to dry tinder. The illusion of self-control shattered as all that was between them ignited. He reached across the distance between them and pulled her into his arms.

She came without resistance, her mouth meeting his with a passion that matched that which burned in his soul. His hand wound itself in her hair and he took her with nothing of tenderness, angling her face to allow him access to the tender skin of her neck. She gasped at his onslaught and he felt her fingers digging into the nakedness of his back as she clutched him to her all the harder.

Their mouths were hard and hungry in their reunion, their bodies heated and slick and urgent.

One hand caressed her breast, his fingers greedy upon its bullet-nosed tip, while the other slid against her hip, cupping her buttock, lifting her against the thrusting rigidity of his arousal.

He felt the scrape of her nails against his own buttock, felt the way her hand sought his heated manhood.

He lifted her up and she wrapped her legs around him as if she would take the length of him into herself as they stood there. He carried her to the bed and, laying her down upon it, covered her body with his own, desperate to sheath himself within her, desperate to ease this torture that was twisting through his blood, desperate to relieve the tightening ache in his chest.

The scent of her filled his nose, the softness of her skin as silk against his. She filled his every sense, she was everything he had ever wanted, everything that he ever needed—the woman who filled the void in his soul, the only woman that he had ever loved…the woman who thought he had tried to kill her. He forced the thought away and nudged his knee to splay her legs wider, ready to thrust within.

She gasped, and even as her hips rose to meet him he felt the sudden tremor of tension that ran from her fingertips to her ankles that were hooked around his calves. He stilled, staring down into her eyes while their breaths rasped and panted in unison. *She had been a virgin until he had taken her.*

He felt the way her hands pressed the tighter at his hips, urging him on. 'Francis!' she whispered and the shimmering silver of her eyes had shrunk to be replaced with the full blackness of desire.

He reached his hand down to the place between her legs and, stroking his fingers there, found her wet and slick for him. He massaged her, teasing against the sensitive bud that would bring her her pleasure, until she groaned her need aloud and arched her back.

'Please…' she gasped as her teeth nipped at his neck.

'Please…' he pleaded against her ear, before moving his mouth to hers again. Her teeth grazed his chin, his lips, before she kissed him and it was a kiss that mirrored both the desperation and the torture in his soul.

He slid his fingers into her and watched the heat flare all the hotter in her eyes. And when he replaced his fingers with himself he waited, letting her grow used to the girth of him, watching her, and all that was between them, this thing that was so much more than desire and lust, shimmered and throbbed and roared its strength.

'Francis...' Their eyes clung together as he began to move within her, slowly at first, and then faster and deeper and stronger as she rose to meet each thrust, until she sighed her relief and he spilled his seed within her.

He kissed the breath from her mouth with a gentleness that belied the fierceness of their lovemaking. And in his eyes, his dark soulful eyes, she saw not anger or condemnation, only tenderness and hurt...and something that looked a lot like love.

I love you, she whispered in her mind, and kissed him with all that was in her heart. She clung to him as if she could capture this most precious of moments for all eternity. *I love you,* as she drifted back down to earth in the strong protection of his arms. But the words were silent on her lips, and as the light and the magic and the moment faded she could not speak them.

He rolled off her and lay on his side. He spoke not one word, but his eyes held hers for a moment and she saw in them the echo of all that had just been before he turned away and climbed from the bed. He did not look at her again, just dressed himself quickly, smoothly, efficiently, the expression on his face closed, serious, as coldly handsome as the first night she had seen him. And the chilling silence of the cell cooled the wonder and the warmth and togetherness from her soul, leaving her feeling raw and empty and alone.

She swallowed down the lump that was sticking like a rock in her throat, too proud to show anything of her hurt. She rose and donned her clothes, affecting an unhurried and calm demeanour, ever the consummate actress, as if she were not weeping inside. The silence between them was louder than any words.

She kept her back to him as she fastened the pearl buttons of the dark green dress in which she had been married. Those buttons she could not reach she just left, but when she would have let the heavy hank of hair drop to disguise the gaping green silk, Linwood's hand caught it, making her breath catch at his sudden silent proximity. There was a smallest of hesitation before she felt the brush of his fingers against the exposed skin of the nape of her neck. Her heart was thudding hard enough to escape her chest, but he stepped away when it was done.

'We need to talk about tomorrow,' he said, his voice betraying as little emotion as his face.

She gave a brief nod. 'We do.' They sat down on opposite sides of the little table. And like two strangers, rather than lovers, they began a cool and dispassionate discussion of what would take place at the trial. And in her line of vision, over Linwood's shoulder, Venetia could see the bed and the rumpled sheets and covers still warm from the heat and passion of their lovemaking.

Chapter Eighteen

Within the cell afternoon faded to evening and evening to night.

'Do you wish me to leave?' Her hair still hung loose and long over her shoulders. She was almost as cool and self-possessed as the divine Miss Fox had been.

He knew he should send her home. She was his wife and no one could now doubt that the marriage had been well and truly consummated, not with the colour that touched her cheeks and the tousle of her hair and the beautiful wanton air of a woman well loved that clung all around her.

He shook his head. He did not want to say the words, did not want to admit the weakness, and yet he did not want to be without her, not tonight of all nights. He swallowed. 'Stay,' he said quietly, 'if you will.'

She nodded and he felt the wash of relief spread through him.

His soul was filled with regrets and hurt and confusion. Shadows of the past and disillusions and betrayal. What did a man say to a woman under such circumstances, when she was his wife, when she was the woman that he loved?

'Venetia…' What words could he speak when heavy upon him was the knowledge that the morning would weigh his life in the balance and who knew better than Linwood that the best-laid plans could go so awry, just when you thought them done and dusted? The darkness hovered so close. He raked a hand through his hair.

She came into his arms as if she understood. Without a single word she pressed her mouth to his. And everything of his torment faded away. They loved with passion, with need and with tenderness. Loved through the darkness of that night. So that for those few hours they could forget the shadows of the past and the threat of future, and lose themselves in each other.

They had loved, and loved again, before the dawn came and it was time for her to leave, and travel home.

They did not speak, only moved in silence to dress and ready themselves for the day and all that it would bring.

He fastened her buttons.

She tied his cravat.

The whole of the prison slept. All was silent. All was still.

'Francis, I...' Her hand lingered, light as a breath, against the lapel of his jacket, her gaze was fixed as if she could see through the layers, the superfine and linen, the flesh and bone, to his heart. So many unspoken words whispered in the silence between them. Her eyes rose slowly to meet his, so beautiful and beguiling, and even now, even poised on the brink of losing everything, he thought he would not have done anything differently between him and Venetia.

She leaned so close that he thought she meant to kiss him; instead, she laid her cheek against his and let it rest there. It was such a small gesture, but it touched him in a way he had not expected. He could feel the warmth of her breath and the slight tremble in it. 'I love you, Francis,' she whispered, and then she stepped so quickly away that he could not catch her and banged upon the grille, pulling the dark hood of her cloak up to cover her hair as the door opened.

'Venetia…!'

As she walked away through the doorway she glanced back over her shoulder and he saw the shimmer of tears in her eyes. But it was too late.

The door closed between them.

Venetia sat in court later that day, her face a mask of sublime control and confidence, while beneath the soft black leather of her kid gloves her knuckles shone white with the strain. With every fibre in her body, every ounce of her willpower, she prayed that it would all go to plan, that there would be nothing to allow the conviction of an innocent man.

'M'lord, with regard to the witness for the prosecution.' The barrister, in his black-and-white robes and the neat wig upon his head, addressed the judge presiding over Linwood's fate upon his high bench. A hush fell over the public gallery within the courtroom. Each and every gaze turned to the woman who they thought ready to take the stand and send her lover to the scaffold. They stared with macabre and fascinated expectation. Within the small family group of the Earl of Misbourne, sitting there on those public benches, the pale blond hair of Linwood's sister caught her eye. The two women exchanged a glance before Venetia turned her gaze to remain on Linwood alone.

'Miss Fox refuses to take the stand and she cannot be compelled…given that she is no longer Miss Fox, but Lady Linwood.'

There was an audible gasp across the courtroom followed by the buzz of exclaiming voices.

'The defendant and the witness for the prosecution are man and wife,' the barrister added, in case anyone was in doubt.

'Bleedin' hell, he's only gone and married her!' someone shouted from the gallery.

'Order!' bellowed the judge, his elderly face stained ruddy. 'I will have order in this courtroom.' His gaze shifted to Venetia and lingered there for a moment with beady accusation before returning to the prosecution.

The gallery quieted to hear what he would say.

'So now you are without Miss Fox, have you any evidence at all that Lord Linwood started the fire at the Duke of Rotherham's London town house, or that he is in any way linked with His Grace's murder?'

Her stomach squeezed in a tight knot of nerves. Her mouth was so dry that the sides of her throat stuck together and made it difficult to swallow. Beneath her gloves those demurely crossed hands gripped so tight that Linwood's heavy signet ring upon her finger bruised the skin.

'No, m'lord,' the barrister for the prosecution finally said.

Thank God. Her eyes shifted to Robert, looking at him for the first time since she had entered the courtroom. His expression was sullen and angry. He sneered and gave a small shake of his head as if he could not believe the audacity of her and what she had done. All the sympathy was with the murdered duke's son. All the antipathy with Linwood. She wondered what would happen if they knew that she was the murdered duke's daughter.

She turned her attention to the judge as, at last, the moment for which they had waited arrived.

'In light of the evidence presented before me, or lack thereof...' the judge's gaze flickered to Venetia's and lingered for a moment '...with regard to the accusations brought against him, I have no choice but to direct the jury to find the defendant...'

And despite everything Venetia held her breath along with the rest of the courtroom.

The seconds seemed to stretch. Linwood's gaze was focused on some distant point. His face wore its usual closed expression—handsome, cold, impassive, as if his life did not hang in the balance. And still the judge paused, stretching the agony until she did not know how much longer she could bear it.

'Not guilty.'

Her eyes closed as the breath she had been holding escaped with a sigh. The relief surging through her was so strong that she thought she might faint.

The courtroom exploded in a flurry of voices and activity. Venetia's gaze met Linwood's across the room and in that tiny moment before the bodies moved to obscure him something more than relief and success passed between them.

The formalities of the procedure were concluded in a blur, and then Razeby was by her side, guiding her away from the clamour of newspapermen.

The clock ticked loud and slow from its place on the mantelpiece in Linwood's drawing room. Misbourne and his wife, and Marianne and Rafe Knight, all of them knowing that she was Rotherham's daughter and yet saying not a word about it, had finally departed, their carriages cutting a defiant and triumphant swath through the crowd of pressman filling the road outside. Linwood dismissed his manservant, the same manservant she had faced so brazenly and boldly on the night she had come here to ruin the man who was now her husband. And only now, for the first time since the trial, were they alone.

Linwood stood by the edge of the window, watching the reporters in the street below as the light faded to dusk.

She sat in one of the armchairs by the fire.

The silence stretched between them and Venetia did not rush to fill it. Now that it was all over, exhaustion and uncertainty had replaced the strain and fear and dread. She rubbed her fingers against the knots of tightness in her forehead.

Linwood turned away from the window and came to stand before her. He watched her for a moment, with an expression she could not fathom. Then, reaching his hand down to hers, he drew her up so that they were standing with their bodies flush together. The fading light accentuated every harsh handsome plane and angle of his face, and revealed the dark smudges that sat beneath his eyes and a fatigue she had not seen in him before. And she felt her heart squeeze at the knowledge that he was not so unaffected by the day's proceedings as he pretended.

'It is finally over,' she said and let her forehead rest against his shoulder.

His lips brushed her hair. 'No, Venetia,' he whispered and tilted her face up to his. 'It is only just beginning.' And there was a warmth and tenderness in his eyes that lit a hope in her heart. 'What you said to me as you left the prison cell...'

Her heart lay exposed before him, ready to be crushed. 'It was the truth, Francis. With you it has always been the truth, no matter what else you might think.'

'You love me.'

'Yes, I love you.'

His thumb caressed her lips as if he sought to capture the words, his eyes studied hers. 'I love you, too, Venetia.'

Her breath trembled. Her heart blossomed. 'I know.'

He kissed her and, sweeping her up into his arms, he

carried her through to his bedchamber, and with her port-manteau lying there unpacked, he laid her on his bed and made love to her.

Lord Murder walks free. Linwood secures freedom and the Divine Miss Fox with six-figure sum and lure of title. The headlines were scathing.

'You could not stop them going to print?' Razeby nodded towards the newspapers spread across Linwood's desk when he called the next morning.

'We do not own all of the newspapers in London.' Linwood topped up both their coffee cups.

'Only most,' smiled Razeby.

'It means the scandal can be contained to a certain extent.'

'That is indeed fortunate.' Razeby's gaze moved from the headlines. 'Has Miss Fo—' Razeby caught himself. 'Has Lady Linwood seen them?'

Linwood nodded.

'That is not so fortunate.'

'Perhaps, but Venetia understands how the press works and forewarned is forearmed.'

Razeby glanced down at his coffee cup. 'Perhaps the two of you should get away. Go to the country and lie low for a few months until the worst of it blows over. I have a hunting lodge in Scotland that you are welcome to use.'

'Thank you, Razeby, but you know I cannot do that.'

'No, I suppose not.' Razeby's expression was grim.

'We mean to face down the scandal.'

Razeby gave a nod and sipped at his coffee. 'For what it is worth, Linwood, there are a lot of people who think Rotherham got his just deserts.' Razeby's eyes met his, communicating the message at which his words only hinted.

Linwood was very careful not to give even the slightest reaction, but he felt the shadows flit across his soul.

The soft rustle of silk sounded. Linwood glanced up to see Venetia standing in the doorway that led to the bedchamber. He wondered how much she had overheard.

'Lady Linwood,' Razeby murmured and set down his coffee cup. Both men rose to their feet, but only Razeby bowed. 'Forgive me if the hour of my call is too early. I did not intend to disturb you.'

'Your visit is nothing of disturbance, Razeby, you are very welcome here,' she said smoothly, as dignified and self-assured as any duchess, but with an underlying edge of coolness.

'You are very gracious, but I will take my leave of you both. Lady Linwood…Linwood.' Razeby made his bow. He looked again at Linwood. 'If you change your mind about the hunting lodge…' He clapped a hand against Linwood's shoulder.

Venetia came fully into the room and sat down in the chair that Razeby had vacated.

There was a small silence before she said, 'I heard what he said to you of Rotherham.'

He waited.

'He thinks you guilty.'

'He does.'

'Yet he is your friend.'

Linwood's gaze flickered away before returning to hers. 'Venetia, all of London thinks me the man who got away with a duke's murder. They will always do so.'

'Not if they were to find the real murderer.'

Tension flickered in his jaw. Darkness flashed in his eyes. His gaze moved to the distance, his expression was pensive.

'But that is not what you want, is it?' she said softly.

His eyes moved to hers again, his gaze searching hers as if he could look within and see her very soul. 'No,' he finally admitted. 'It is not.'

The admission hung between them.

'Why must you ever protect him?'

'It is not him I protect.'

'Then who?'

He shook his head. 'It is not my secret to tell, Venetia. I swore an oath of secrecy and I honour my oaths… all my oaths.'

And in the silence the marriage vows he had sworn seemed to whisper between them, along with the words of another vow. *We are sworn to speak the truth or nothing at all.*

'I know. It is what betrayed your innocence to me.'

He smiled and there was both sadness and cynicism in that smile. 'Despite all of the evidence to the contrary.'

'Yes.'

He reached across and brushed his lips against her forehead. 'Thank you, Venetia.'

She smiled.

'Even with my father's and my own influence upon the newspapers… You know this is not going to be easy.'

'Nothing good ever is,' she whispered.

They shared another smile. And then his lips found hers and he kissed her properly.

But through the days that passed, no matter how much Linwood tried to hide it, Venetia knew that he was worrying over something. She could see it brooding in his eyes when he thought she was not looking. In the small hours of too many nights she woke and sensed him lying awake beside her in the darkness. Sleep seemed loath to visit him and when it did it brought nothing of rest, only dreams that haunted him all the more. And she knew that all of it centred around Rotherham's murder. Her husband had not killed Rotherham, but he knew who had. And whatever dark secret lay at the heart of the mystery, it was important enough that Linwood would have given his life to protect it, just as he was prepared to bear the unjust label of the murderer who had evaded justice.

She was worried for him, worried over the terribleness of the secret—and what it would mean for them both. She could not kiss the worry from his eyes, as many times as she tried, and she had no right to object to his keeping the secret, not when she was still keeping one of her own.

A feeling of such tenderness and overwhelming love for him welled up in her. This man who had endured so much because of her and to whom her heart was tied. He loved her, in spite of the fact she was Rotherham's daughter. And she could not bring herself to tell him the other half of it, for fear that she would lose that love.

One night she awoke to find the bed beside her empty, the sheets cold. She climbed from the bed and, pulling a long black shawl around her shoulders, went to find him.

He was standing by the side of the window in the drawing room, staring out into the night. The room was in darkness, the light of the moon kissing the nakedness of his body silver.

'Francis,' she whispered his name, feeling the chill of his skin as she slipped her arm around his waist and kissed his shoulder blade and the top of his arm before moving to stand by his side and share his view.

'Venetia.' His hand slid to rest upon her hip and pull her closer. 'I did not mean to wake you.'

'You did not.'

They stood together and looked out at the clear night sky. The moon was a sickle blade, silver and slender, and sharp enough to see the tiny shadows that spotted it. And the myriad of stars that scattered across the darkness of the heavens were brighter than any diamonds. Her eyes found the familiar shape amongst them, that meant so much to them both.

'Pegasus,' she whispered.

'Yes.' He kissed the side of her brow.

And they stood in silver silence and traced its constellation.

'You are worried.'

'A little.'

'Over Rotherham.'

He nodded.

'They cannot hang you, even if they do think you guilty.'

'That is what concerns me, Venetia.'

'Francis?' Her eyes leapt to his in sudden fear.

'Do not worry. I have no wish to dance upon a gibbet. But will it stop them seeking another neck to place within that noose?'

'Everyone believes in the guise of your guilt. How can it be seen as justice if they start looking for another?'

'I hope you are right, Venetia.'

'And I wish I was wrong.'

He stroked his fingers against her cheek. 'If you knew what that would mean, you would not wish it.' And there was something so sad and dark in his voice that it made her shiver.

His lips pressed where his fingers had touched. 'You are shivering with the cold. Let us go back to bed, Venetia. Tomorrow we have my parents to face and the first full scrutiny of public glare.'

Through the darkness his hand found hers and interlaced their fingers.

* * *

The clock's ticking was loud within the Earl of Misbourne's drawing room and the chink of Lady Misbourne's fine bone-china cup even louder as she set it down upon the saucer. Linwood's mother had not looked at Venetia once since she had come into the room.

'Perhaps your…wife…would care for more tea,' she addressed Francis, her face almost pained at the word *wife*.

Venetia looked as unperturbed as ever. She set her cup down in its saucer with careful refinement. 'More tea would be delightful, Lady Misbourne.'

His mother made no move to pour the tea. She did not even glance at Venetia. Her mouth was as pinched as if she had been sucking on a lemon, her expression stubborn and hostile.

The moment of awkwardness grew.

Venetia reached out and lifted the teapot. 'Would anyone else care for more tea?'

Misbourne cleared his throat and murmured a decline.

'Thank you, but no,' Linwood said and felt as proud of his wife as he was ashamed of his mother's pettiness.

'In that case…' She calmly topped up her own cup alone and set the pot down.

Lady Misbourne's face was aghast. She glared at Venetia. 'How dare you play hostess, madam?'

'Very easily, when you are too rude to do so, Mother,' said Linwood.

'Rude?' Lady Misbourne gasped and stared as if he had just slapped her. 'I will tell you what is rude—bringing that woman into my home and expecting me to wait upon her!'

'Lest you forget, *that woman* is my wife. And if you cannot treat Venetia accordingly then we will leave right now.'

Lady Misbourne's face began to crumple and she clutched a wisp of lace handkerchief to her eyes.

'Have a care how you speak to your mother, Francis,' Misbourne chided. 'She is of a sensitive disposition and this is not easy for her.'

'It is not easy for any of us,' he replied. 'You should remember that were it not for Venetia I would be swinging upon a scaffold.'

Misbourne scowled and got to his feet. 'Hell's teeth, boy! She is the one who placed the noose around your neck in the first place! Were it not for her, you would have got away with it scot-free. She has manoeuvred you to her advantage. The apple has not fallen far from the tree. After all that Rotherham did to this family, we end up with his bastard lightskirt daughter as part of it. How he must be laughing at us from beyond the grave!'

Linwood knocked his cup over as he got to his feet and squared up to his father. 'You go too far, sir!' he said in a deathly quiet tone.

Venetia rose and laid her hand against his arm to stay the tense ready-to-strike muscles beneath.

His father backed away. 'Maybe. But you are my son, my heir. I might have gone along with and organised your marriage to her to save your life, but you cannot expect me to like anything of the situation.'

'The situation is not how you imagine.' Linwood's gaze held that of his father. 'Not with Venetia and me...nor any of the rest of it.' It was as close as he could come to telling him.

And maybe Misbourne understood something of what he was saying, for he put his head in his hands and sighed a sigh of resignation and sadness. 'Why does it have to be her?'

It was Venetia who answered, her expression strong and angry as she did so. She looked beautiful and incensed. 'You are asking the wrong question, sir.'

Misbourne's brow creased. He turned to stare at Venetia.

'You talk of him getting away with it!' She shook her head. 'Your son, who was so determined to take the blame and go to the gallows, and yet could not admit the murder. Did you ever even ask him if he was gui—?'

'Enough, Venetia,' Linwood stopped her, but her unfinished word, *guilty*, echoed unspoken in the air.

'Is it, Francis?' She turned to him, a fierceness flashing in her eyes. 'I hope so.'

His father's gaze leapt to his, and Linwood saw the shock and the sudden pallor beneath the grizzled grey of his beard, and, for the first time, doubt.

'Francis?' his father whispered.

'You never asked me,' he said. 'Not once. Such faith in your knowledge of me.'

'But…?' His mother stopped fretting with her handkerchief and got to her feet before his father. 'What is he saying, George?'

But his father was still staring at him with an expression of frozen horror. Misbourne's face was ashen, his lips pulled tight and colourless. Linwood met his father's gaze, looked directly into those black eyes that were so like his own, and lowered his guard to let his father see the truth.

'My God…' his father whispered as he finally understood.

'George?' His mother sounded frightened.

'I will leave you to explain, sir.' Linwood bowed. 'If you will excuse us, my wife and I must ready ourselves for this evening.' With Venetia's hand upon his arm they turned and walked away.

Chapter Nineteen

A few hours later Venetia stood before him in the hallway of their own apartment, waiting for him to slip the dark-velvet evening cloak around her shoulders. The evening dress she was wearing was the same deep dark red she had worn on a night on a balcony that seemed a lifetime ago, the silk of the skirt sweeping down to caress the curves he knew lay beneath. Her hair was the same dark-satin lustre, pinned and coiled, with an arrangement of cascading tendrils and curls that teased enticingly around her neck. She looked even more beautiful than she had done on that night that had sealed both their fates, because now when he looked at her he saw not the sensual sophisticated actress, but the truth of the woman beneath.

From his pocket he produced a black leather box and handed it to her.

The breath escaped her in a small gasp as she opened the lid. Inside the necklace of rubies glowed as deep and dark and translucent as the dress she wore and the surrounding diamonds glittered brighter than the stars in a midnight sky.

'The Linwood rubies,' he explained. 'My mother sent them round. As my wife, they are yours by right. It is her attempt at an apology, and a statement of support before all London when you are seen wearing them tonight.'

'They are beautiful,' she whispered.

'Not as beautiful as you,' he said as he fastened the stones around her neck.

They stood in silence in the candlelit hallway, their eyes clinging together, both of them knowing what they were going out to face in the theatre that night.

'Are you ready, Venetia?'

'With you by my side, I will always be ready.' She placed her hand upon his arm and together they walked out to their town coach.

The reaction at the theatre was as Linwood had anticipated. There were stares and gaping jaws. There was the buzz of gossiping lips and the too-loud whispered words he could not fail to hear. *Murderer. Harlot.* Those who had been lifelong neighbours of his parents, the woman who was his godmother, men who had called themselves his friends, turned away, giving both him and Venetia the cut direct. He felt the slow fuse of his temper ignite, not for himself, but for his wife. The *ton* was cruel and petty and blind to its own hypocrisy. He felt the pressure of Venetia's fingers against his arm and looked down to meet her eyes. The woman that he saw there was stronger, calmer, more confident than Venetia Fox had ever been. She smiled at him and, despite everything, he smiled back.

'We would not wish to disappoint them now, would we?' she murmured and, lifting her lips to his, brushed them with a kiss.

The ladies surrounding them gasped in horror, the men sighed in longing.

'You are incorrigible, Lady Linwood,' he whispered in her ear.

'As are you, Lord Linwood.' Her smile deepened.

And his heart skipped a beat.

He followed her into their private box, ready to face the world.

Venetia stood by the window of their day room the next afternoon and watched the dark figure of her husband ride away to his meeting at his club. She watched until he had disappeared from sight. The sun was shining, but the air held the damp chill of fast-approaching winter. She pulled her shawl a little tighter around her shoulders and went to write her letter to Madame Boisseron.

It was only twenty minutes later that the knocker sounded against the door and the butler appeared. 'Lady Marianne, Mrs Knight to see you, my lady. Are you at home?'

She nodded. 'Please show her in.'

And then Linwood's sister was before her, a look of uncertainty upon her face. 'Lady Linwood...Venetia... I was just passing and I wondered if you and Francis might like to come to dinner one evening next week.'

'That is very kind, Lady Marianne.'

'Just Marianne, please. Are we not sisters now?' Lady Marianne smiled shyly.

'We are.' Venetia returned the smile. 'Thank you, Marianne. I know how hard it must be for you to come here.'

'Not hard at all. I am only sorry that I did not come before.'

'Well, you are here now and that is what matters. Please sit down. Will you join me for some tea?'

Marianne smiled again and relaxed a little. 'I would like that,' she said and took the chair opposite Venetia's. Her eyes flitted to the writing block on the desk and the half-written page that lay there. 'I have disturbed your letter writing.'

'My hand is glad of the rest,' said Venetia.

They spoke of small inconsequential things, anything that was safe, and far removed from Rotherham and the trial, and Venetia's past. Until Marianne set her empty tea cup down upon the tray and rose to leave.

'Thank you for saving my brother's life, Venetia.' She paused. 'I was right that day in the ladies' withdrawing room. You do love him.'

'I love him more than words can say,' she admitted.

There was a silence.

Marianne fidgeted with the seam of her glove and made no move to leave, giving the unmistakable impression that there was something more she wanted to say but was not sure how to say it. She worried at her lip before finally raising her gaze to Venetia's and asking, 'Has he told you why?'

The clock ticked upon the mantel. A lump of coal cracked and hissed within the fire.

'It is not his secret to tell,' she replied.

'No,' said Marianne softly. 'It is mine.'

And Venetia remembered Linwood's explanation for his hatred of Rotherham. *He hurt someone close to me very badly.*

'Rotherham,' she said slowly and felt her stomach tighten with a dreadful foreboding.

'He was your father, Venetia, but he was also a monster.'

'He hurt you.' She felt sick at the thought.

Marianne was silent for a moment. 'He raped me.'

The shock and horror rendered Venetia speechless before she managed to recover herself. 'I am so sorry, Marianne.' And she understood in that moment Misbourne's angry words and what it must have cost Linwood, and them all, to have Rotherham's daughter in their family. 'I had no idea…'

'We covered it up very well. I would have been ruined otherwise.'

'Even though it was nothing of your fault.'

'We both know the unfairness of society when it comes to condemning women, Venetia.'

'Yes.'

The two women's eyes held.

'Rotherham fled to the Continent before my father and brother could reach him. They swore they would kill him if he ever returned. We never thought he would dare… but he did.' Her voice tightened on those last words. The dark eyes so like Linwood's closed and she took one deep slow breath, and then another. When she opened them again she was in control of herself once more. 'Francis is a good man.'

'And a man who keeps his oaths,' Venetia added in a quiet voice.

'I wanted to tell you, because I knew that he could not. You do understand, don't you, Venetia?'

Venetia nodded. 'I think I am beginning to.'

'Then I am glad that I came here today.'

'I am glad, too,' said Venetia, but she could not smile and she did not know whether she was being honest.

She watched Marianne's carriage draw away and when she turned to face the little room the autumn sunshine had faded from the room and in its place was a cold grey light.

Venetia could not rid herself of the thought of what Rotherham had done to Marianne. The knowledge sickened her to the pit of her stomach. She felt chilled to the bone, no matter how close to the fire she stood. She wondered what Robert would do to any man that raped her.

And the ties that bound Linwood to his sister were closer than the ones that bound Robert to Venetia.

Yet Venetia could not help remembering the hurt in his eyes at his father's assumption of his guilt and the expression, too, on her husband's face when she defended his innocence—the gratitude, the love and something more, something that touched the very core of her heart and soul. She respected the fact that he had kept Marianne's secret. He was a man of his word, an honourable man, the man that she loved. As he loved her. And yet she could not dispel the uneasiness that gnawed at her soul. Over a family bound so tight through the darkness of the past, and whom were so utterly convinced of his guilt.

There was an agitation in her, a disquiet that nothing could ease—not tea, or letter writing or staring endlessly out of the window. She could not settle.

She paced, anxious for her husband's return, but the hour of the clock crept later and Linwood did not come. Darkness spread across the sky and the rain began to tap against the window panes and the wind began to howl, stirring the curtains hanging by the window's sides.

She sat down at Linwood's desk and stared straight ahead, thinking of all that Marianne had told her, thinking of the darkness that had brought her and Linwood together. So much had happened in such a short space of time. What had been weeks seemed like years. And she remembered the last time she had sat at this desk alone in the night. The night she had come to search for the evidence that would prove his guilt.

She closed her eyes, remembering the terrible conflict of emotions in her breast, both wanting to find the pistol and book, and dreading it, too. And the moment when he had displayed the contents of his safe. The painting still hung there, the horse parading so proudly before its stable. She wondered if the theatre programme and the hand-kerchief were still locked in the safe behind, or if he had discarded them when he discovered that she had betrayed him. She turned her gaze away to the bookcase, unwilling to dwell on that thought, or the painting that had provoked it.

What had he thought when he learned that Rotherham was her father? Only in the light of Marianne's revelation did Venetia appreciate just how difficult that must have been for Linwood. She thought of the cold gaunt man who had been Rotherham and of her mother who had loved him. And she felt the usual shame and anger. He really had been a monster. She pushed the memories away and saw the books that lined the shelves, all the same books that had been there that night. The books on stargazing, the one she knew held the diagram of Pegasus sitting snug beside the book on the daily lives of wolves in Britain. And on the shelf below—a second copy of the very same book on wolves in Britain.

Dread tiptoed down her spine, dipping a hollow in her stomach and turning her blood cold. She wondered why she had not noticed it before. *Wolf.* The word seemed to leap out from the title, making her think of the silver wolf's-head, with its two emerald eyes, at the top of her husband's walking cane.

She took the copy from the lower shelf and laid it on top of the desk. There was a horrible gaping feeling inside of her. She did not want to look inside the book, but she knew that she must. Her fingers were trembling as they touched the dark blue leather cover and opened it.

Her heart did not beat. Life ceased to be. Everything she had believed crumbled to dust. There was no printed frontispiece, no monogram upon the interior of the cover that claimed the book as Rotherham's or Linwood's, only a thin neat handwriting that she recognised too well...beneath each dated entry of a journal.

It felt as if she had just been punched in the stomach. She could do nothing more than stare, reeling by the shock of it. She could not move, just stood frozen in disbelief, while all the world outside moved on around her. It could not be true. But she knew very well that it was.

'Oh, God, help me!' she whispered. 'Oh, God!' She clutched her arm around her stomach while the nausea roiled and expanded. She felt sick, sicker than she had ever done in her life. 'Please no!' she prayed, but nothing changed the fact that it was Rotherham's journal lying there upon the desk.

Her lungs felt small and hard, and there was a terrible cold tightness in her chest as if a band of iron had been fastened around it and was tightening more second by second. And where her heart had been was a pain of such searing intensity that it made her gasp aloud.

She did not know how she made it back round to perch upon the desk chair. She sat in the gathering darkness, numb with shock and pain. For she knew there was only one place from which Linwood could have taken the journal. And she knew what that meant—Robert had been right.

She felt like her heart had been gouged from her chest and she did not really understand why, because she could understand why Linwood had done it, she could even forgive him...for the murder. What she did not think she could forgive him was the betrayal. It was the betrayal that hurt so much. Her own stupid naivety, defiant and ignorant in the face of everyone else's assertions. And she cringed when she thought of what she had said to his father. At her own gullible determination to defend him.

Linwood had not lied to her. He had never claimed to be

innocent. So why did she feel this way, like her every belief of the man that she had married, the man that she loved, had been turned to dust and blown away in the wind? She had thought the game of deception through truth over, that there was only him and her. But Linwood had been playing all along, even after he had won.

She could not cry a single tear. Inside her was a terrible blackness and an anger that seethed and a bleakness that stretched eternal. She could do nothing other than sit there and wait, while outside the wind howled and the rain beat in a rhythmic incessant torrent.

Chapter Twenty

It was later than Linwood had anticipated by the time the meeting of the Order of the Wolf finished. He did not go for a drink with the others, but came straight home. He knew as soon as he opened the door of the drawing room that something was wrong.

It took a moment for him to see her sitting there in the darkness. The fire had almost burned itself out. The room was chilled and dark.

'Venetia?'

He picked a candle from its holder and lit it from the glowing embers on the hearth, then used it to light the others in the candelabrum.

Taking it with him, he moved towards her. 'I did not think you would still be up. The meeting went on longer than I expected.'

'Did it?' she said and there was a deadness in her tone that made his blood run cold.

'What has happened?' he asked, coming to stand before her.

'Marianne came to see me today.'

'Ah,' he said softly.

'She told me what Rotherham did to her.'

'Then you understand why I could not tell you.'

'I understand that.'

'I am relieved to hear it.'

'But not why you lied to me.'

'I have never lied to you, Venetia.'

'Have you not?'

'No.'

'What will you swear that on, Francis?'

'Whatever you wish.'

'My life? Or Rotherham's, perhaps?'

'What is this about, Venetia?'

Her eyes held his for a moment and then moved pointedly to the desk.

His scalp prickled as he followed the direction of her gaze. There, on the top of his desk, lay the journal he had taken from Rotherham's study on the night of his murder. 'I see.'

'So do I. At last. Rotherham's journal. Did it amuse you to make me believe you innocent? Were you laughing at my naivety? And your parents, too? And I am the one supposed to be trained in acting!'

'It is not as you think. I can explain the presence of the journal.'

'As you can explain the murder of Rotherham? Or are you going to keep on deceiving me with your clever game?'

His lips pressed firm. 'The game between us was over a long time ago, Venetia. And even through it, I have never deceived you.'

'No, perhaps not, if one wants to be pedantic about it. How very clever you have been—such careful choice of words, such cunning tactics.'

'For once in my life I used nothing of cunning.'

'No? Swearing an oath to me to speak the truth or nothing at all. Then staying silent rather than make a defence.

I would call that cunning.' She laughed, but it was a bitter sound. 'No wonder you never could deny it, not even to me when we were alone. And I, fool that I was, thought it was because you were protecting someone.' She gave an angry laugh again but this time he saw tears in her eyes. 'And you were—just not in the way that I thought. You killed Rotherham to protect Marianne.'

'Venetia—'

'And do you know the worst thing of all, Francis?' She faced him in defiance of the tears in her eyes. 'Had you been honest with me, had I known that you killed him, I do not think it would have made any difference.' The tears spilled to run down her cheeks. She swiped them away with angry fast movements. 'You have made an utter fool of me.'

'You are wrong, Venetia.' He came to her, but when he went to take her in his arms she fought against him and tried to turn away. He stopped her with a gentle grip, forcing her to look at him, knowing that she had to hear the truth.

'I did not kill Rotherham. I give you my oath on that.'

The words echoed loud in the silence. Outside the rain battered in great swaths against the window and the panes rattled and the curtains swayed in the onslaught of the wind, making the flames of the candles flicker wildly and casting his face in dangerous shadows.

She was breathing so hard and fast that every in-breath grazed her breasts against his chest.

'You have his journal.'

'I do. But I did not kill him.'

A heartbeat and then another and the agony in her eyes tore at him.

'I can tell you of it, all of what happened that night, now that I am not bound by Marianne's secret.'

She looked into his eyes a moment longer, then she gave a nod.

'Tell me,' she said.

Linwood walked to stand by the window and stared out at the dark fury of the night. 'You were right. It was all about protecting Marianne. She told you what he did to her?'

'Yes,' she whispered. 'I can understand why you wanted to kill him.'

'Believe me I did. My father, too. And we would have done three years ago, but he ran, fled to the Continent.'

'And you burned his house as a warning to him not to return.'

He shook his head. 'I burned his house to destroy his journals. He had documented the details of his interest in Marianne through the years, what he had done to her and his past association with my father. If anyone had read them…I could not risk what that would do to my sister.'

'But Rotherham did not stay in Italy. He came back to London earlier this year.'

'For Marianne. He was obsessed with her.'

Venetia shuddered at the thought. 'She is younger than me, his daughter.'

'It was of no account. He was a man who took what he wanted. And he wanted Marianne, even after she was married. You have met Rafe Knight, Marianne's husband.'

She nodded. 'He is a man one would not wish to cross.'

'Indeed.' Linwood remembered just what it was like to cross Rafe Knight. 'Knight would have killed Rotherham had Marianne not stayed his hand.' He did not see the darkness of the street outside, but the sun setting against Hounslow Heath on a day not so very long ago. 'Rotherham was allowed to escape with his life on the proviso that he again left the country. But he was defiant. He stayed, even attended the same social occasions as Marianne. It was as if he were intent on taunting her, on taunting us all.'

'I can only imagine what that must have been like.' She slid her hand to cover his.

There was a silence.

'I went to the house he was renting that night, to warn him that he had a day to leave London. But when I got there...' Linwood closed his eyes remembering the scene. 'He was already dead.' Rotherham slumped over his desk and the great pool of dark blood that glistened and dripped in the candlelight. He could smell the metallic tang of it even now. 'Someone had beaten me to it, but only just. He was still warm.'

'You thought it was your father who had shot him.'

'My father's arm is weak.' She remembered the way Misbourne's arm had hung stiffly by his side. 'He cannot fire a pistol,' he said. 'It had to have been Knight. He loves Marianne, you see.' He paused, turning round to face her. 'So I found the journal and I left. The weeks that followed were a torment. I was glad that Rotherham was dead, but I was angry, too.'

'Because you knew that there would be an investigation. And you feared that Marianne's name would be uncovered.'

He nodded. 'And because part of me wanted to have done the deed myself.'

'And then I came asking questions,' she said softly.

'And then you came asking questions.'

They looked at one another.

'You did not offer a defence because you could not risk them digging deeper and finding Knight.'

'If they hanged Knight, it would destroy Marianne. And she has suffered enough.'

'It must have been a heavy burden to carry alone.'

'I am glad that I can finally tell you, Venetia.'

The silence was loud and so filled with emotion that she thought it would burst. The tears were rolling down her cheeks freely now. She made no move to wipe them away. He opened his arms and she went into them and pressed her cheek against his heart and wept with relief, and wept for his pain and all that he had endured. She wept and outside the rain and wind raged as surely as the emotion in her heart.

He held her until there were no more tears to shed, until her eyes were dry and gritty. He held her until the storm, both inside and out, subsided and there was only the comforting beat of his heart. She turned her lips to where her cheek had rested, to the fine white lawn of his shirt, wet through from her tears. She could feel the beat of his heart beneath her lips. She kissed him there, his heart, kissed the pulse point in his neck, kissed his chin, kissed his mouth, with all the love that was in her heart. Their mouths slid together, clung with such sweet tenderness. And then she stared into his eyes, so dark and soulful, as her hands stroked against the sleek wetness of his hair.

'I love you, Francis,' she said and loosened his cravat, unwinding it, letting it slip away to the floor. She unfastened his collar and kissed the shadowed hollow of his throat. Her hands swept over the breadth of his shoulders and down the lapels of his coat, feeling the dampness of the rain in the wool and the warmth of the man beneath.

'You will catch a chill.' She peeled the coat from him and let it fall to land with a soft thud on the rug below. The waistcoat followed. She tugged the shirt from his breeches.

He slipped it effortlessly over his head and she saw it no more.

She laid her fingers against his heart and felt its strong steady beat. She kissed it again before sliding her hands over the smooth skin of his chest, over his back, and down lower to the ribbed muscle of his belly.

She felt the way he trembled, heard the way he caught his breath as her fingers made light work of the button on his breeches, opening the fall to brush her hand against the length of him that strained so hard against the linen of his drawers.

He made a soft gasping sound and caught hold of her wrist, moving it gently behind her back while he drew her hard against him, her breasts flat against his chest. He kissed her and unfastened the buttons of her dress, sliding it from her before removing the rest of his own clothing, until they stood naked in the candlelight.

'I would bear the darkness and the pain and the burden a hundred times over because it led me to you. I love you, Venetia. Completely. Utterly. That is the final truth.'

She felt her heart weep with love for him as he took her in his arms and loved her.

The next morning all traces of the storm had passed. The winter sky was clear and blue, and a cool white sunlight lit the morning. He felt as if a great burden had been lifted from his shoulders, even though there was still the worry that the authorities' questions would lead them to Knight. And no matter what had happened in the past, no matter what the future held, the fact that Venetia loved him made everything all right. He understood now what it was that Knight felt for Marianne. If it went anything near what he felt for Venetia, he marvelled that his brother-in-law had not killed Rotherham sooner. If any man hurt Venetia, he knew what he would do.

The sunlight made her skin glisten so pale and perfect. Her cheeks were still pink-tinged from their lovemaking. She was his heart, his life. She looked up from her coffee cup and caught him watching her, and she smiled. It was a smile that echoed the joy he felt in his heart. She reached across the table and took her hand in his, her fingers so white beside his own olive skin. She still wore his large ring upon her slender wedding finger.

They stopped by the bookcase and the morning sunlight shone upon the open pages of Rotherham's journal where she had left it lying.

'To think that it was here all along. I did not notice that there were two books with the same title.' She smiled a little sadly and closed it over. 'In plain view,' she said softly, 'just as I knew it would be.'

It took a moment for her words to register, and when they did his heart began to thud. 'But you came here looking for the missing pistol…not the journal.'

'I came seeking both.'

'You knew that the journal was missing?' He stared at her and could not disguise the urgency and shock from his voice.

'Not that it was a journal, but yes, I knew you had taken a book.' She smiled and drew him a puzzled look.

'By what means, Venetia?' He tried to keep his voice casual, but every nerve in his body was alert, every muscle poised and tense.

'Robert told me. His witness saw you carrying the book as you left.'

'Clandon!' The word was like a curse upon his tongue. The scales dropped from his eyes. He reeled with the shock and audacity of the realisation. 'I have been a damnable fool!' he murmured and pressed a hand to his forehead.

'What do you mean?'

'It was Clandon who shot Rotherham, not Knight.' He winced at how mistaken his own foolhardy assumptions had been.

'Robert? That is absurd!'

'The only way Clandon could have known I had the journal was if he was there in the room that night.'

'But the witness—'

'I was wearing a greatcoat. The journal was well hidden within it before I left the study.'

'Maybe my brother saw the book was missing.'

'I left no space to betray it. Besides, Clandon did not even know of the book's existence before he watched me take it.'

'You cannot know that.'

'But I can, Venetia.' His eyes held hers.

'The other book in your bookcase—the one of the same title,' she said softly.

He drew it out, offered it to her. '*My* journal.'

'I do not understand.'

'Rotherham was a member of a particular club, a very secret club—the Order of the Wolf. I am a member, too.'

Her finger traced along the gilt lettering on the spine, lingering over the words Wolf. 'Your wolf's-head walking cane…'

'The wolf is our symbol. Every member is obliged to keep a secret daily journal. And every member hides it in the same way.'

'The same book,' she whispered.

'In a colour to match his library. No name must be written. Only the volume number on the front cover identifies the owner. We are forbidden to speak of the existence of the club or any aspect of it to any man. You know the manner of man Rotherham was, Venetia, everything to the letter, everything so precise.'

'Yes.'

'He would never have told Clandon.'

She closed her eyes. 'I cannot believe it. Robert would

not do such a thing. Rotherham was good to him. He acknowledged him as his son, introduced him to Society, gave him a generous allowance. He even paid off his gambling debts. My brother is far from perfect, but murder... There has to be some other explanation.' She glanced at the journal—Rotherham's journal. 'Have you read it?'

'I could not stomach to read much.' He gritted his teeth. 'He makes much mention of his thoughts on my sister. '

She paled at his words. 'There may be some clue written within the days preceding his death.'

Linwood gave a nod. 'You are right.'

'I will read it, Francis.'

Linwood met her gaze, grateful that she cared enough to offer such a thing. 'I would not subject you to that,' he said quietly.

'Even if I need to do so? Marianne is your sister. But Robert is my brother. I need to know the truth.'

He nodded, understanding that she was right. 'We will read it together.'

Her insides felt chilled, her stomach swimming with nausea as they sat together on the sofa and read the words Rotherham had written. No matter that Linwood had warned her, no matter the number of men and their appetites she had been exposed to in the past, it was different when the man in question was her father. But she knew that, however hard this was for her, it must be harder still for Linwood.

They read together in silence, starting at the day of the murder and working backwards in time. They did not have to read far to realise the truth. A matter of days only.

Venetia closed her eyes and sighed.

Linwood shut the book.

They read no more.

'You do not have to see him, Venetia. I can do this alone.'

'We do this together. I have to see him. I have to give him the chance to explain.'

'Together,' he said and curled his fingers around hers, and in his grip she found the strength she needed.

'You free our father's murderer and now you have the audacity to come to my door and level such an accusation at me?' Robert's eyes narrowed as they shifted from her to Linwood and back again. He shook his head with such convincing incredulity that, beyond all reason, she felt a flicker of hope that, in some way, both the journal and Linwood were wrong. She wanted to believe Robert, and, unfair though it was, she wanted it to be Knight who had killed Rotherham, even though she had read the journal and in her heart she knew the truth.

'My own sister!' said Robert with contempt.

'My own brother,' she replied softly. 'I know the truth, Robert.'

'You know nothing other than what Linwood has put in your head. He is not content with walking free from his crime, but must seek to go further and turn you against me.'

'I trusted you, Robert.' She shook her head.

'I forced the confession of the fire from his lips, did I? And still you take his word over mine. All for the sake of a title and respectability. Why will you not see what is before your very eyes, Venetia?'

'I do.' From beneath her cloak she withdrew Rotherham's journal and held it close. She saw Robert's eyes drop to it. 'It is the book that you sent me to look for. The one that Linwood took from Rotherham's study that night.' She paused. 'You did not know it was Rotherham's journal, did you? Only that it could be used to incriminate Linwood.'

Her brother's Adam's apple bobbed.

'Rotherham wrote of you in it.'

He paled.

'I knew you liked your pleasures, Robert, but I had not realised just how much your gambling and drinking and… other excesses…had run out of control these past years. And neither had Rotherham. When he returned from Italy to find you living a life of indolent debauchery, deep in River Tick and with your creditors threatening foreclosure, he was more than a little angry.'

'As if he were some paragon of virtue,' Robert muttered.

'He thought you were trading on his name. Bringing it into disrepute.'

'I did nothing more than he had spent a lifetime doing.'

'You were indiscreet.'

'We all make mistakes from time to time.'

'Rotherham paid off your debts…as you expected.'

'And I am supposed to have killed him for that, am I?'

'No. You killed him because he intended to change his will.' She waited for him to deny it, wished so much to hear those words. But the silence was deafening and she could see the truth written all over his face, see it in the weakness of his jaw and the anger and self-pity in his eyes.

Robert glanced away. And when he looked at her again his eyes were like blue marble—cold and hard and filled with loathing.

'He was going to cut me out completely. His own son. And leave it all to you. He wanted to teach me a lesson, the vindictive old bastard.'

'So you killed him.'

'It was an accident.' He glanced away, a faraway look in his eyes, his brow pinched, his mouth tight and twisted as if he were remembering that night. 'We argued. He said that rot must be dealt with or else it would spread. He said it was for my own good. That it would be the making of me. *The making of me?* Our argument became heated. For God's sake, Venetia, he was throwing me out of my own house!' His eyes met hers. 'The pistol was there newly cleaned and loaded and mounted on the wall, so I took it down and threatened him. And do you know what he did? He laughed at me. Said I would not have the guts. So I showed him that I did.'

She felt sick to hear the words. Robert had always been spoiled and indulged, but she had not thought him capable of murder. 'Why Linwood?'

'Wrong place, wrong time,' Robert gave a shrug. 'I was going to make it look like the old man had shot himself, but then I heard someone coming. There was not time to leave so I hid. And there was Linwood, who I have never liked. Let us face it, he would not exactly win any prizes in the popularity stakes. Everyone knows both he and his father are touched with something of the night.'

'You would have let him hang!'

'I would have been doing the world a favour. He is not a good man, Venetia. Anyone will tell you that. And he did burn our father's house, although that little gem was an unexpected bonus. I was keeping the pistol so carefully only to discover that I did not need to plant it after all.' He glanced at Linwood. 'She is quite something, isn't she? What red-blooded man could resist?

'I do not understand.' Venetia looked at Linwood. 'What does he mean?'

'Your part in this was never really to glean information. As far as Clandon knew, there was no confession to be had. It was always his intention to publically establish you as my mistress.'

'Bravo, Linwood.' Robert gave a mocking applause.

'No,' she whispered and stared at him. 'Why would

you do such a thing when you knew how I felt about such arrangements?'

'I needed a credible witness. And who better than his mistress? The woman who shared his bed. But then you had to go and spoil it all.'

'It was you behind the fire at my house?'

'I never meant for you to be there when they did it. You were supposed to have left for the theatre.'

'You made me believe it was Linwood!'

'You were softening towards him. And I could not have that now, could I? I needed something to make you see how very dangerous he was.'

'You bastard!' she cried.

'No more bastard than you, dear sister. Me the son of a housekeeper, you the daughter of a cheap bawdy-house whore.'

She gasped as his words echoed in the silence, frozen and afraid to look round at Linwood.

'Ah,' said Robert softly. 'You had not told him that little detail, had you? He knows the ducal sire, but not the mare that was tupped.'

Her mouth was drier than a desert. The shame made her want to curl up inside, both at the truth of what she was and for having Linwood learn it in such a crude, cruel way.

'You are as mistaken in this, Clandon, as everything else. Venetia has told me all. It is of no consequence.' Linwood's voice was cold as the rush of gratitude she felt to him was warm. He moved to stand between her and Clandon, shielding her from her brother.

'Well, then, you will understand that it is her—how shall we say?—Achilles heel. She would do anything rather than have that particular little dirty secret revealed...even go to the police and tell them of her lover's confession.' Clandon smirked.

She felt the last vestige of blood drain from her face and yet still she stood there and endured.

'Bad enough that your wife is an actress and illegitimate, oh, and let us not forget to mention the daughter of the man it is believed you murdered. Just think of how much worse the scandal will be were they to discover that Rotherham begot her on a trip to a bawdy house. You and your father do not own all of the newspapers, Linwood.'

Linwood moved so fast she could do nothing to react. One minute he was standing there; the next he had slammed Robert hard against a wall and held him there by the throat. 'I do not think you are going to be talking to anyone, Clandon.'

'My lips are sealed on the matter. As long as we help each other out.' The words rasped, strained and hoarse, from her brother's mouth. 'I am sure we can reach some amicable understanding.'

'Like hell we will,' said Linwood softly.

Robert's eyes slid to Venetia. 'Think of the shame of it. Your darkest secret exposed to all the world. All that you worked so hard all these years to hide. Convince your husband to stay quiet on my involvement and I will not publish.'

'You will not publish, Clandon. I will see to that.' Linwood's promise was as dark and deadly as his face. 'I will not let you hurt her.' She saw Linwood's grip tighten around her brother's throat.

'Francis!' She gripped her hand to his arm. 'Please stop.'

Linwood's eyes met hers. And it was not condemnation she saw in them, but understanding. He stayed as he was for a moment longer, then finally released his hand from Clandon's neck.

Robert gasped his relief and rubbed his fingers against the bruises that were already starting to form. 'Linwood is free,' he said. 'They cannot retry him. I am not asking much, Venetia.'

'Only for him to remain damned in the eyes of the world.' She held her head up and looked her brother in the eye. 'Publish and be damned, Robert. I will stand witness against you myself.'

While Robert gaped in disbelief, she rang the bell to summon the footman.

Two hours later and Venetia sat staring into the flames that flickered on the hearth of their own drawing room. Her husband stood by the fireplace, but she could not bring herself to meet his eyes as in a low faltering voice she told him the final piece of the truth.

'My mother was a whore in a bawdy house Rotherham frequented. He took her to his bed and called her his mistress...until eventually he tired of her and sent her back to the bawdy house. She died when she was only nine and twenty years old, aged beyond her years. Prostitution does not make for an easy life, but she had no other choice. She was poor and alone, unskilled, uneducated and with a child born out of wedlock. There was nowhere else she could go, nothing else she could do.'

'It is why you run your refuge house in Whitechapel, why you seek to help those women who wish to escape prostitution. And why you never gave yourself to any man before me.' He understood at last.

She nodded. 'I swore I would not make the same mistakes as my mother. I hated Rotherham for what he had done. But, much as I loved my mother, I hated that she had let Rotherham do it. I thought she was weak. Because she loved him, you see, despite everything. She always told me a woman could not choose who she fell in love with and I did not believe her, not then.' She paused. 'Not until I met you.' She met his gaze. 'I am sorry, Francis. I should have told you myself, a long time ago. Before we were married. Before it was too late. But I was too ashamed.'

He took her hand in his and raised her to her feet, staring into her eyes all the while. 'You have nothing to be ashamed of. I love you, Venetia. Nothing changes that.' He stroked a stray tendril of hair from her face. 'But I know how painful and private this part of your past is for you. We do not have to do this with Robert. No one need know of your mother.'

But she shook her head. 'People think you did it, Francis, that you are the viscount that got away with murdering a duke. They think we struck a deal, that you bought me off with marriage.'

'It does not matter what they think. We know the truth.'

'It does matter. I saw what it did to you to have even your closest friends and family believe so readily in your guilt.'

'They had good reason. Clandon is right, I am a villain, Venetia.'

'No, Francis. You are a good man and an honourable one.'

'You have not asked me what I would have done had Rotherham not left London when I threatened.'

'Would you have killed him? she asked softly.

'I cannot say that I would not.'

'And you cannot know that you would. What matters, Francis, is that you did *not* kill him. Everything that you have done was to protect your family. The world needs to know you are an honourable man. And that is why I will not back down from this.'

Their eyes held.

'Even if they hang him?' he asked.

She nodded, but she could not stop the tears that welled

in her eyes or their escape to roll down her cheeks. She glanced down.

He tilted her chin and raised her face to look into his. 'What if they were to transport him instead?'

'It would be a mercy.'

'Then we will ask for mercy, Venetia...from those who hold influence.' She followed his gaze to his silver wolf's-head walking cane, that leaned against the wall by the side of the fire, and saw the glitter of the two emerald eyes.

The trial had not been easy for Venetia. Robert spilled his guts on her mother, but it was not as bad as Venetia expected. Indeed, there was a curious sense of liberation in having the secret exposed. She had nothing more to hide. Linwood loved her, all of what she was, and all else paled in comparison to that. Robert was found guilty of the murder of his father and sentenced to transportation to Australia, never to set foot in England again.

A week after the sentencing, Venetia stood in the early morning light at the drawing-room window of their home in St James's Place. She wrapped her dressing gown more tightly to cover her nakedness and stared out at the first flurry of snow that fell like tufts of soft cotton to lie on the street below. Winter had come. Soon it would be Christmas. And she thought how much her life had changed in the turning of one season. All of her core beliefs of the past, of herself and the future challenged and reformed. From celebrated scandalous actress to viscountess. Success and power, fame and fortune, did not make for true happiness. That came from the heart, from loving another, wholly, completely, and knowing that they loved you. Her heart felt expansive and warm and brimful with love for the man who lay sleeping in the next room.

A soft noise sounded and Linwood, still naked and

warm from their bed, came up behind her, slipping his arms around her waist and brushing a kiss against her hair.

'I thought you were still sleeping,' she said.

'Not without you,' he murmured. He glanced out at the snow scene and then his beloved dark eyes moved to hers. 'Have you things on your mind, Venetia?' The words echoed those that had passed between them on a theatre balcony a lifetime ago.

'Only good things. And all of which you know.' She smiled. 'I am glad that your name is finally cleared.'

'Thanks to you.' He whispered against her ear. 'I love you, Venetia.'

'I love you, too, Francis.'

Out of secrets and a game of dark deceit had come a love that was brilliant and glaring in its honesty, a love that would stretch to all eternity.

He smiled and nuzzled her neck. 'Come back to bed, my love.'

'Yes.' She smiled and, slipping her hand into his, let him lead her to their bedchamber.

They had the rest of their lives to live in love and in happiness. And as if to mirror the wonder that was in both their hearts, outside, the snow, so pure and white and radiant, fell in silent joy to render the London streets beautiful.

* * * * *